THE ENUMERATIONS

BY MÁIRE FISHER

THE ENUMERATIONS

BY MÁIRE FISHER

For further information, write info@catalystpress.org
You can find out more at catalystpress.org.
In North America, this book is distributed by
Consortium Book Sales & Distribution, a division of Ingram.
Phone: 612/746-2600
cbsdinfo@ingramcontent.com
www.cbsd.com

In South Africa, Namibia, and Botswana,
this book is distributed by Protea Distribution.
For information, email orders@proteadistribution.co.za

Originally published in 2018 by Umuzi,
an imprint of Penguin Random House South Africa (Pty) Ltd.
Library of Congress Control Number: 2024942019

For Hannah and Colleen,
with love from Noah and Kate

There are very few monsters
who warrant the fear we have of them.
—ANDRÉ GIDE, *AUTUMN LEAVES*

I wait, looking for somewhere to call home. I listen;
my ears are keen.

I hear voices, so many voices, but not one of them is right.

I listen for a certain pitch. A tone, if you will. A feeling.

Patience, I tell myself, give it time. And so I float, in the deep.

*Nothingness, I think you'd call it, but it is more than that. It
echoes with all the sounds of the world, all the connections
being made. Feelings calling, feelings answered. But me? No
luck. I have no voice, no body to call my own.*

I wait in the echo-filled emptiness.

I know that soon you will arrive, ready to be found.

*I am yours, and you will be mine. If you weren't here,
neither would I be. I'm the creature of your mind. I grow in you
and with you. I grow for you.*

*I almost have hold of you. You're almost mine. I hear your
voice, then you fade away. Yet something remains.*

*I'm close. Close to each beat of your heart, each breath, each
word. Once I am in, your every thought can become mine. I can
direct what you do, how you do it, why.*

All I need is a chink. A small sliver of space.

And here it is, and in I shall slip.

I

30 January 2013 / 08:32

Noah Groome is strung out. He can't concentrate, can't think straight. He's overslept this morning, for the 13th time in a row, and now he's running late. 13 times his alarm has failed to wake him, 13 times he has had to leave his room without checking that all is where it should be, as it should be. 13 dog-nights, yipped into shreds.

Everything is off-kilter, out of balance; the scales are tipping, and Noah doesn't have time, can't find time, to set it all to rights.

He's hurrying now, head bent, to get to class.

Move it.

A hissing from the Dark. A blur of shadow gathers as Noah tries to get things right.

He stops. Takes a minute he can't afford to breathe in...2 3 4 5 and out...2 3 4 5.

He needs more time, to call on the 5s to restore order, but there's none to spare. He's *so* late, but he'll slip into the back row as quietly as he can. That's what he always does, that's where he always sits.

Noah is tall. Taller than most of the boys in his class, but he does his best to be unseen. It doesn't work, though. He's the one who:

1. cannot open a door unless he pushes on the handle 5 times (down-up-down-up-down).
2. taps his fingers (1 2 3 4 5) and beats out 5 with his feet.
3. counts under his breath, and sometimes louder tha that.
4. takes his pen out of his pocket and puts it back in (and out-in-out) before he can start writing.
5. keeps 5 pebbles in his pocket to run through his fingers like worry beads.

And that's just the start of the 5s.

It's hard for them not to notice him. He can't move without counting under his breath, can't pass a corner without tapping it quickly 5 times. He's that boy who slips along corridors, a lanky shadow, head down, counting the steps between classrooms. He tries to stay below the radar. He offends no one, but he can't make himself invisible.

Today, Kyle Blake is also late, as are three of his friends, but not because they've been counting the tiles in the boys' washroom, not because they can only step carefully in sets of 5. The smell of nicotine is strong on them and Noah's nostrils flare; his lip pulls back.

"Hey, what's with you, Nuh-nuh-nuh-nuh-Noah?" Kyle is almost as tall as Noah, with the pale, etiolated look of a weed that has shot up in the dark. His chin and cheeks are dotted with acne and his blond hair flops over his forehead and falls into his eyes. He jabs Noah in the chest.

All Noah wants is to get to class and not be too late for English, not hear Mrs. Simpson ask, Late again, Noah?, but Kyle has chosen this moment to have some fun with him. He steps away, but Kyle is in his path, weaving from side to side as Noah tries to get past him.

"What's the problem, Nuh-nuh-nuh-Noah?" Kyle's friends laugh as he taps Noah on his left arm and then on his right. Noah feels the Dark stir.

You don't have time for this.

"Hey, Nuh-Noah?" Kyle's hand moves up to Noah's face, taps him on the cheek—

Noah wants to get away, that's all he wants, that's what he tells Dr. Lovelock, six afternoons later: I wanted to get to class, that's why I pushed him.

It's not much of a shove, but Noah keeps his body fighting fit, exercising daily, morning and night (when nothing interrupts his routine, when he has time to make sure everything's as it should be, before he opens the door—down-up-down-up-down—to face a new day).

Kyle goes sprawling and the three boys behind him snigger. Then Kyle is up and leaping onto Noah, grabbing at him, his breath hot and foul in Noah's face.

There's no time for this.

That's when Noah twists Kyle's arm up and back.

The sound is a dull pop in the quiet corridor. Kyle wavers, his arm at a weird angle. There's a split second between that and his mouth

2

opening with a howl.

Now look what you've done.

Noah steps back, feeling it again: Kyle's arm in his hand, the way his elbow just gave, the sudden yell.

"What's all this racket?"

It's Mr. van Blerk, his classroom door open, looking at Kyle, taking in his oddly dangling arm. "My God, what's happened?"

And then Kyle is jabbing the air with his good hand, pointing. "Groome," he pants. "That bastard's broken my arm."

Kate had to get out of the house, away from the phone that would ring and tell her what was going to happen next and when and where. *They'll be in touch*, that's what Mr. Reynolds said when she was called in to the school to meet the accusing stares of Kyle's parents, Leonie and Buddy Blake. "We'll be in touch soon, Mrs. Groome. The sooner we can get things sorted, the better for all concerned."

The better for whom? Kate thought as she saw the smug satisfaction on Leonie's face. The better for Leonie, for Buddy Blake, without a doubt. Buddy, one of those men whose nicknames follow them from school and into the golf club and the bar after work. Better for Kyle Blake. And, of course, the better for the school. God forbid that even a whiff of scandal taint those exclusive halls.

But what about the Groomes?

"Perhaps you should keep Noah at home for a few days. Not a formal suspension, mind you. We wouldn't want that on his record, would we?"

"No, no, of course. Of course not," Kate said, picking up her bag, stumbling to the door. Avoiding Leonie's stare. Not looking at Buddy's face. Wishing Dominic had been able to leave work and come with her.

She's sitting outside a café now, watching the gentle swell of the sea, the holiday makers dipping into the waves and out of the heat. She should move out of the scorching sun, but she can't summon the energy. Her coffee has gone cold, her hands are bunched tight in her lap. Relax, she tells herself. Breathe. Think. Mr. Reynolds has set the ball rolling and Kate doesn't know how to stop it.

She and Dominic need to talk. "Let me get more details, Kate, find out what they plan to do next and then we'll work things out." That's what he promised her last night.

Kate wishes now that she'd been quicker. Sharper. Replies churning in her head, the put-downs you never think of until it's too late. But what about *your* son, Leonie? Buddy? I hear Kyle and his friends torment my son endlessly.

"Not just Noah, Mom," Noah's sister, Maddie said the night before, eyes blazing, her small frame bristling with frustration. "They pick on other kids too."

So yes, "What about the bullies in your school, Mr. Reynolds?" *That's* what she should have asked.

Too late now. The Blakes are out for blood. They've reported Noah to the police and are even threatening to press charges. Nothing Kate can say about how this is the first time Noah has been involved in an altercation like this is going to make any difference. She feels it in every worrying memory of Noah mumbling under his breath and tapping his fingers. There are the notes sent home from school— "Noah's constant tardiness disrupts the class;" "Noah's behavior is a distraction"—and all the visits they have already made, to the school counselor, to one therapist after another, the meds they've prescribed, their inability to get to the root of Noah's anxiety, his behavior.

His medical records will probably be examined for proof of an ongoing "condition." For proof of the fact that Noah has a "problem."

Kate imagines Leonie Blake nodding sanctimoniously. What she wouldn't give to have Leonie sitting opposite her right now. Or maybe not. One assault against the Blake family is enough.

"Kate?" The voice is familiar, friendly.

Kate looks up. It's Monica Ryan, another wife, another school mother.

"Are you okay?"

Kate wonders if she should ask the same. Monica's hair is uncombed, her pink sweatshirt stained. But before she has time to notice anything further, Monica has sat down.

"You don't mind if I join you, do you?"

Kate can't say no; that she'd rather be left alone, away from the silence of the house, away from the phone waiting to ring to deliver the next installment of bad news.

Monica catches the waitress's eye. "Another one for you, Kate?"

All Kate can do is nod, unknot her fingers and lay her hands on the table. Unlike Monica's, they aren't shaking. In fact, everything about Monica looks shaky, gray-skinned and tired. She leans closer and Kate catches a tell-tale whiff. She wonders how much Monica drank the night before, whether she started the day with vodka in her coffee. Or cane. Cane's not supposed to leave a smell, and there isn't one, just a slight sourness.

"I'm so sorry, Kate," Monica's saying now, and Kate looks up and meets her gaze.

"You're sorry?"

She knows what Monica's talking about, what they're all talking about.

"Someone was saying the Blakes want to take it further."

"Further?" Kate looks at her blankly.

"Lily said they were talking about it yesterday. All the mothers in the—"

"The carpool?" Kate's voice is resigned.

"Are you okay, Kate?" Monica is concerned. "When Juliet had to go away, it was hard, especially for Lily. She worships her sister. And now it looks like she's going back there. Back to Greenhills."

Kate isn't listening as Monica talks about Juliet and Lily. She's latched onto two ominous words: Go away. Then she remembers that Monica's daughter had been in some sort of clinic, and more than once.

She knows she should be asking about Juliet, but all she can manage is, "Go away?"

"Eleven o'clock."

That's what Mr. Reynolds says over the phone. "The Blakes have agreed to a mediated process, Mr. Groome. It's a method that has proven very successful in the past, and it protects our students from unnecessary publicity."

"Protects his fancy school more like it," Kate says when Dominic puts down the phone. "How did that smarmy little shit ever get to be Principal? All he wants is to settle things with the minimum fuss."

Dominic is at the window, looking out over his garden. Everything's under control there, growing to demand, season after season, only his indigenous plants allowed to run wild, and even they are limited to one corner.

Just like he controls his garden, he controls his work environment, regulates his diet, maintains a routine exercise regime. Everything in his life runs like clockwork, or at least it would if it weren't for this situation. The moment he heard what Noah had done, Dominic knew they stood no chance. Kyle Blake is the wounded party. Noah is the aggressor, the one who wounded.

"The best thing to do is listen," Dominic says now. "I'm sure we'll come to a sensible agreement."

"*Sensible?*" Kate looks at her husband as if she'd like to shake him. "Where's the sense in a bully being given more power than he already has? They want revenge, Dom. I saw it in her eyes. Buddy wouldn't even look at me. They want to crucify our son. It's as simple as that."

Maddie is Noah's younger sister, but she often feels that it's her job to protect him. He's such an easy target for people like Kyle Blake. Noah would never hurt anyone, not on purpose, she's convinced of that. Part of her would have loved to have been there, to see Kyle go flying, see the shock on his face, hear his friends laughing at *him* for a change. If only that was all that had happened. Then people like him would know better than to mess with her brother. But now, with his arm, and the Blakes, and Mr. Reynolds not even trying to get to the bottom of things, it's looking really bad for Noah.

Maddie wishes she could *do* something. Get a petition going, chain herself to Mr. Reynolds's door, like Emily Pankhurst and the suffragettes they've been learning about. Refuse to move until Kyle admits his part, accepts that his arm wouldn't have been broken if he hadn't been such a jerk.

Justice for Noah. That sounds like a good cause to fight for.

She won't though. Her parents have enough to deal with, without her adding more to worry about.

What Maddie has learned, right from when she was very little, is that she's the "easy child," the designated good child who never gives her parents any problems.

Maddie knows the script that's been written for her. She's never going to be a rebellious teenager; she's never going to kick up a fuss. She's the one Kate and Dominic rely on to be normal, to be happy. Maddie's job is to dance through life, to sing when there's a gray cloud of misery hanging over the house.

"Maddie was born that way," her mom says. "She was born smiling."

She's the uncomplicated one. Even if Mom doesn't say it in so many words, Maddie knows it's her job to stay that way.

"You can't just throw money at a problem and expect it to vanish."

Even so, Juliet's father has decided to fling thousands of rands at Greenhills' residential program.

Full-time resident, Juliet tells herself as she packs. That's me now, in it for the duration, thanks to him. Her father hasn't spoken to her since that afternoon, the clincher that sealed her fate. She knows she'll have to talk about it to Ellen, the therapist, finally tell her everything. But for now, it's all she can do to stuff some clothes and her folders into a suitcase. She can't take her camera with her, or even her cell phone for quick shots. That's going to be hard. As for the "occasional furniture" she is allowed—desk lamp, a rug—she can't be bothered. The only personal item she chooses is the framed photo she took of her sister a few months before.

"Just what sort of example are you setting for Lily?" her father had raged when Juliet was suspended because of the sort-of thing with

Mr. Wright, one of the math teachers. That he'd kept his job, while Juliet had been asked to leave, had further angered her father and given her mother an additional reason to head to her secret stash for a surreptitious swig and flinch when her husband banged his palms on the dining table and made the cutlery jump.

Mom had sent Lily to her room so she couldn't hear what was being said. But the walls weren't quite thick enough, which was why she asked her sister what the word "nympho" meant.

Not *exactly* her father's words, Juliet remembers. She throws the last of her clothes into her case. "A fucking nympho!" That's what he'd yelled after spending over an hour in Mr. Reynolds's office, where nothing her father had said or offered made him change his mind.

Her mother hadn't said a word; Juliet knew all she wanted was to get home as quickly as possible to get to a drink. Her father harangued, cajoled and harangued again. Sitting there in quiet contempt, Juliet knew he was never going to accept the principal's decision with good grace. But if he would just shut up, they could all get out of there.

Eventually, Mr. Reynolds had held up a hand. "I'm sorry, Mr. Ryan. There is nothing further to be said. Mr. Wright's behavior has been exemplary, and he reported the situation immediately." To this he'd added, "I also have it on good authority that this is not the first time Juliet has...erm...exhibited this sort of behavior. And nor, I believe, is it the first time she has received 'help.' Perhaps you should consider getting to the bottom of this problem once and for all. Mr. Wright said it was almost as if Juliet *wanted* to be caught."

With that, Juliet was damned. She stared at her father until he looked away, silenced at last.

Not for long though. In the car, all the way home, he laid into Juliet's mother. This was all her fault. She'd always been too soft on her daughters.

Naturally, it could never be Bart the Great's fault, Juliet muses. Even though, when it comes to setting examples, he's far from perfect. He's leaving his family to play house with a girl fresh out of university, a bright rising star at Goodson, Stander & Groome. Something, Juliet thinks, as she grips the handle of her bright blue shell case, she'll enjoy saying in one of her sessions at Greenhills. "My dad's shacking up with a twenty-two-year-old girl and it looks like she's going to be my second mom. And *I'm* the one with the problem?"

⏀

A mad dash, that's what Mum used to say.

Come on, Gabe, let's make a mad dash! Then they're running across the sand and into the sea. A mad dash and Dad's laughing and Mum's tummy is as round as the beach ball he blew up when they got to the beach. The water is cool around Gabriel's ankles and then his tummy and then Mum is holding him and his legs are around her and the sea is rocking them and everything is calm.

Gabriel loves being with Mum and Dad and watching how Dad makes Mum laugh, her head tipping right back, her eyes closed tight against the sun. He loves waiting on his towel, making sure not to kick sand near the picnic basket, "Otherwise we really will have *sand*-wiches, Gabe," Dad always says, and that makes Gabriel laugh and he throws his head back just like Mum does and squeezes his happy eyes shut against the sun.

Dad's telling him all about a man called the Earl of Sandwich who used to love gambling. He gambled all day and all night says Dad, and suddenly Mum's not smiling any more. She's listening very hard, and so is Gabriel, because Dad is a font of information. He says it's useless, but Gabriel disagrees; Dad has much more information in his head than any of his friends' dads and that's probably because they don't study the *Encyclopaedia Britannica*, like Dad does, and they don't know that the "a" and the "e" squash together like that because it's Latin for "British Encyclopaedia."

Dad and Gabriel look at the pages together. They've got the complete set, because Dad bought them cheap off a man who was selling them in the pub. Shame, Martha, he was really down on his luck and I was pretty flush.

Sometimes Dad's pretty flush, and sometimes he's also down on his luck, but he always says, Don't worry, Martha, our ship's coming over the horizon.

So Dad knows all about John Montagu, the 4th Earl of Sandwich, and how the sandwich was named after him when he spent twenty-four hours gambling and only eating bits of meat between two slices of bread.

6 February 2013 / 11:00

Noah follows his parents as they walk into the small room and sit down opposite Leonie Blake. He looks around at the 8 straight-backed chairs with blue padded seats arranged in a circle. It's very informal; no table with a place at the top and 1 at the bottom, just a ring of seats: 1 for Mr. Reynolds, 1 for the mediator, 3 for the Blakes, 3 for the Groomes. No particular order, Noah sees. The mediator should be at 1 end of the table, Mr. Reynolds at the other. Noah and his parents should be on 1 side, the Blakes on the other. Circles don't work in a difficult situation. You need sides.

Mrs. Blake's mouth is a mean line between her thin cheeks. She's dressed for battle: khaki trousers and a boxy jacket open to reveal a plain, black T-shirt. Her short, manicured nails are painted a dark, dark red. Her feet are firmly on the ground, her arms are stiff in her lap. She looks straight ahead, refusing to meet anyone's eye.

The door opens again, and in comes Mr. Reynolds, followed by Kyle and Mr. Blake. Kyle's father is a complete contrast to his well-groomed wife. His collar is undone, his shirt is untucked and his tie looks as if it's been thrown on at the last minute.

Mrs. Blake turns her head and looks at her son. "Here, darling." She pats the seat next to her.

Kyle moves forward slowly, one arm strapped to his body in a sling. He lowers himself gingerly into the chair and winces as he makes contact with the arm rest.

"Shame, sweetheart. Is it still very sore?"

Kyle grunts.

Mr. Blake sits on the other side of his son and there they are: 3 Blakes facing 3 Groomes. Mr. Reynolds takes a seat and they all stare at the empty chair, waiting for the mediator to appear.

Dominic glances at his watch and stifles a small sigh.

"Oh, I'm so sorry, Dominic." Mrs. Blake's voice is as sharp as the creases pressed into her trousers. "Are we keeping you?"

"No, not at all, Leonie. I was led to believe this meeting would start at 11." He smiles at her.

Now Mr. Reynolds is the one looking at his watch. "It's not like her to be late," he says and Noah feels a flutter of relief. This mediator, the woman who's going to determine his future, likes to keep to her timetable. Something unexpected must have delayed her.

There's the sound of running in the corridor. The pace slows, then stops outside the door. A moment of silence and it opens. A small woman stands just inside the doorway, still trying to catch her breath. Her eyes sweep the room, flicking from camp to camp. The chairs might be in a circle, but there's no doubt as to who is with whom.

"Ah, Miss Moloi." Mr. Reynolds jumps to his feet. "Good, good." He ushers her to her seat.

Noah slips his hand into his pocket and counts his pebbles, 1 2 3 4 5. His thoughts turn to David, who walked out onto the battlefield to face Goliath, with 5 smooth stones in his shepherd's pouch. Noah tries to let his thoughts wander, tries take his mind off the folder in the mediator's hand, the clipboard she has balanced on her knees, the pen she's just clicked open.

"Good afternoon. My name is Linda Moloi." She directs a bright smile at all of them.

Noah sees Goliath swaying where he stands. And then, like a huge tree that the lumberjacks have been sawing away at, down he crashes.

"I'm so sorry I'm late. The traffic was impossible." Noah's mother smiles at her, his father nods. In Noah's mind, the battle between David and Goliath plays out again, keeping Miss Moloi's voice at a hum as she goes around the circle, asking their names, checking that everyone is comfortable, whether they need anything to drink, or to use the bathroom. "I'll start with a brief rundown of how the process works," she says, "and then you'll all get a chance to speak."

Noah's side of the story is pretty obvious; Kyle's arm says it all.

Kyle's mother is on the edge of her seat now, leaning into Miss

Moloi's words, waiting for the first available opportunity to dive in.

Noah's focused on his 5s, his stones are keeping him still. So far, no need to tap, or time his breathing. Not yet. If he can just keep side-tracking, he'll get through this.

Mom told him the tale of David and Goliath over and over when he was small. At tidy-up time, Noah would put everything away. He'd march his animals into their wooden ark, 2x2x2, then park his cars in their Duplo garages, one color at a time—blue into the blue garage, red into red, black into black, green into green and yellow into yellow. Then it was "Hop into bed, Noah!" And there was Mom, ready with a story from *Fairy Tales from Around the World* or *Bible Stories for Children*. David and Goliath was always his favorite.

But that was so long ago. A bedroom, a mother and a son from another life, another family.

"I'd like to ask you to try not interrupt each other."

Noah briefly tunes back in to his surroundings.

"Let's make the process a respectful one," Miss Moloi says. "Give everyone a fair chance to talk and be heard. I can assure you, you'll each have an opportunity to share—"

"Noah's behavior was un-ac-*cept*able." Mrs. Blake can't contain herself any longer. She turns to her husband and he nods.

"*Un*acceptable," he says, his voice an obedient echo.

Mr. and Mrs. Blake feed into each other, deliberately touching Kyle as they speak.

"Noah needs to take responsibility for his actions."

"There must be consequences."

Kyle is leaning back in his chair, his face blank. He glances at Noah and raises an eyebrow. Miss Moloi notices the interaction and, as she catches Kyle's eye, he adjusts his position and winces audibly.

"Do you see?" Mrs. Blake is glaring at the Groomes. "*Now* do you see?"

The mediator raises a hand, but Mrs. Blake won't be stopped that easily. "A gunshot," she says. "That's what Kyle's friends told me. That when *your* son broke *my* son's arm it sounded like a gun going off."

The mediator tries to regain control. "Mrs. Blake, let's try to get all sides of the story. I'd like to hear from everyone."

But Kyle's mother won't be silenced. "How many sides can there be?" she demands. "He *dislocated* my son's elbow." Her voice is shrill. "Do you realize how complicated an injury like this is? And it's his matric year. This is the last thing he needs." She turns imploring eyes on Mr. Reynolds.

Mr. Blake opens his mouth to say something in the small space his wife allows, but the mediator is quicker than him. "It would be good to resolve this as soon as possible," she says.

Mr. Reynolds nods eagerly.

"Perhaps we should hear from Kyle and Noah," Miss Moloi says.

Noah's been preparing for this, listening to his sister saying, "You have to *tell* them, Noah. You have to let them know what Kyle and his friends are like." He licks his lips, lets his hands rest firm on his thighs. He can do this. He can tell the mediator what Maddie's already told his parents: "It wasn't his fault. Why should Noah have to pay when he was just defending himself, standing up to that bully?"

Noah sits silently, Kyle straightens, flinches, and begins. "Well," he says, "I was running to get to English. My friends and I were a bit... uh...late." He smiles deprecatingly. "And I bumped into Noah here, said sorry, but I don't think he heard me. You see, the thing is, Noah doesn't really hear when you talk to him. It's like he can't. He's too busy talking to himself...So anyway," Kyle continues, "I bump into him and then he just pushes me. Like hard. Really hard."

Leonie Blake draws breath and rests her hand on her son's shoulder and Kyle smiles bravely. He looks directly at Noah. "So yes, he pushes me and I fall down and all my friends are laughing." He looks at the Groomes, says apologetically, "Sorry Mrs. Groome, Mr. Groome. I mean, he shoved me for no reason, so what was I supposed to do?"

He stops, shakes his head and his blond hair flops onto his forehead. "I retaliated. I shouldn't have, I know." He bites his lip. "I thought I could stand up to Noah and look what happened. Who knows what he might do if someone else gets in his way and—"

"*That's* what we need to worry about." Mrs. Blake jabs in Noah's direction. "The next time, and then the time after that."

"I'm sorry," says Kyle. "I know I should have walked away."

Mrs. Blake nods virtuously.

"The thing is, Leonie," says Noah's mother, her voice almost conciliatory, "I've heard that this isn't the first time Kyle has 'bumped' into Noah. Or called him names—"

"I knew it!" Mrs. Blake's voice is triumphant. "What did I tell you? I knew she'd try to make it all about Kyle and not her son. I'm not the only one, you know."

"The only one?" Noah's father's voice is quiet.

"A lot of the other parents feel the way I do. About your son. About him being at the same school as our children." Her voice softens and she leans forward. "Don't you see, Kate? Dominic? Noah needs *professional* help."

Noah's mother is ready to speak, but it's his father who answers. "So what is it you want, Leonie? What exactly do you want us to do?"

Mrs. Blake is about to answer, but Miss Moloi quickly steps in. "Perhaps Noah would like tell his side of the story? I'd like to hear what he has to say."

Noah opens his mouth, closes it again.

Don't even try, Noah.

Noah's right hand flies to his face. His mother looks at him pleadingly. But he can't help it. His lips, 5 taps, and then both hands are there, holding back the words. His feet have started tapping, 5 times to the left, 5 times to the right.

There's nothing you can say, Noah. Nothing can make this better. The moment the barking started, that was it.

Audrey and Dave Parfitt are the Groomes' next-door neighbors. They were there when Dominic and Kate moved in, but their interactions have barely moved beyond quiet "Good mornings" from David and strings of polite complaints from Audrey—if she manages to buttonhole Kate at the fence that separates their properties. Both Audrey and Dave have now retired; Audrey from her job as a PA to a local attorney, Dave from the town planning department. But it still took Kate entirely by surprise when Audrey announced one day that they were going to get a dog. "Now that we're both going to be at home all day, we can finally have a pet," she said.

And so, Dave gave Audrey a puppy for Christmas. "Only he can't join us immediately, my dear," Audrey called out to Kate on Boxing Day. "They don't like to take them away from their mothers too early, you know. They need the best possible start in life. We're picking him up on the ninth of January and we're calling him Tigger! Oh, Kate, I'm so excited, I can hardly contain myself."

Kate nodded and smiled, edging her way back towards the house.

"Maybe the puppy will be good for her," Maddie said. "Maybe she'll keep her nose out of our business."

The Groomes are all agreed that they can do without Audrey's never-ending phone calls, her "Yoo-hoo Kate, Kate, could I have a quick word with you?" Always about trivial matters: the noise the children make when they're playing outside; the way their trees shed leaves all over Audrey's lawn; how their automatic garage door clangs when it closes; why Kate never brings their bins in immediately after the garbage has been collected. The complaints are endless.

Each time, Kate cuts her short with another, "I'm so sorry, Audrey."

But no apology was issued from Audrey when Tigger finally arrived, with one of those shrill, incessant barks that punctured Noah's head like an arrow.

Every morning, usually around 2 a.m., Noah was woken by Tigger as he bounced from one end of the fence to the other, *raff-raff-raffing* his way up and down, yelping at imagined shapes, chasing his tail with wild excitement. Every morning, Noah tried to block out the noise, but he couldn't.

By the time Tigger had been in residence for 8 nights, Noah had had to adjust his timetable considerably.

When Tigger started his yapping, Noah had to get out of bed and watch the dog tear up and down, up and down. 4 times in 1 minute. It usually took 12 or 13 minutes (2x5+2/3) for the puppy to do his thing. Fine for Tigger, but not for Noah. Falling asleep had always been stressful, ages spent watching the clock, calculating how many valuable minutes he was losing every night, and now he was losing minutes more.

For the first few nights, Spit and Spot had woken up too. They'd ambled down to the fence, greeted the little dog with a sniff, then returned to the comfort of their baskets. From then on, it was only Noah who woke up, and stayed awake.

"She's besotted with that dog." That's what Noah's mom said, and it was more than obvious. Mrs. Parfitt would stand at the front door, her voice as shrill and yappy as her new pet's.

"Tiggie," she'd yip from just inside her front door in the early hours. "Here, Tiggie-Tig!"

Tigger would pause, prick up his ears, cock a leg and mark his territory.

Noah dreams of running, balancing, measuring. If he wakes up during the night, he cannot go back to bed until he's completed all his chores, done them perfectly. Sleep is Noah's enemy. He can't manage without it, but he hates the way it steals his hours, cuts them out of his day.

And now, with Tigger, it's even more of a problem.

Don't think you can drift off again. Find a way to earn more hours.

So Noah watched carefully through the window as Tigger yapped along the fence. He kept a record of the times the noise started, when it stopped, and how long it took Mrs. Parfitt's voice to pierce the night calm (2 minutes on average). He noted how many times Tigger ran up and down and whether the dog lifted his leg against the fence (✓), or squatted next to it (✓✓).

Every morning, on the way to school, there was Mrs. Parfitt, at the fence, pooper-scooper in her gloved hand, cleaning up after her precious pup, with Tigger jumping around her.

"Full of beans and full of bounce, he is," Mrs. Parfitt would say fondly as Noah trudged to the car behind his sister.

"This can't go on," Kate said on the morning of the thirteenth day. "What are we going to do about it? You have to speak to her, she'll listen to you, Dom. I've had enough and Noah's exhausted."

She had, in fact, already tried the week before. "Audrey," she'd said gently, "could I talk to you about Tigger? About his barking?"

Mrs. Parfitt was washing Tigger's "spot" on the fence. She looked at Kate incredulously. "His barking? What on earth do you mean, Kate?"

"Well, it's just that he's waking Noah," Kate said. "Every night, with his barking. When you let him out, perhaps you could try—"

"But Kate, dear, we have to train him. Every night, dear, every night." Audrey scooped Tigger up, held him close. Two pairs of brown eyes bored into Kate's.

Her voice wavered, but she carried on: "Yes, but you see, Noah—"

"Well, I don't know what you expect, dear. He's a *dog*. You can't expect him not to bark. There is absolutely *nothing* I can do about that."

Before Kate had a chance to reply, Audrey turned on her heel and trotted into her house, closing the door firmly behind her.

"He's a rat of a dog," Noah's mother said. "I can't do it again, Dom, I just can't. You have to talk to her."

So on that 13th morning, his father walked up to the fence to talk to their neighbors about Tigger. Noah watched her soften as he approached.

"Audrey," he said. "Audrey, we seem to have a bit of a problem here with Tigger's night-time barking."

She was holding Tigger, but her arms loosened and her puppy slid to the ground with a yowl. Noah's father looked down at the small creature.

"I'm sure we can come up with a reasonable solution? Especially now that the little fellow's a bit older?"

"Well, yes, yes," she gushed.

"Perhaps," said Noah's father, "you could let him out into the back garden instead of the front?"

"The back garden? Of course. Why didn't I think of that?" Audrey was fiddling with her hair, smiling. "What a good idea, Dominic."

He left her blushing at the fence and walked over to the car. "So much fuss over one little dog," he muttered. What he meant, really, was so much fuss over Noah.

"I tried to suggest that to her a week ago," Noah's mother said. "Silly cow."

"Anyway, let's see if the back garden works. She's promised to try it the next time she lets him out at night."

But there wasn't a next time. That morning, after 13 sleepless nights, Noah broke Kyle Blake's arm and everything changed.

8 February 2013 / 10:35

"It was just to stop him hitting me. I didn't mean to hurt him."

"He was clearly provoked," says Dr. Lovelock, the psychiatrist Miss Moloi "strongly recommended." A tall, gaunt man with narrow shoulders, he looks as if he's been folded into his chair.

Kyle Blake's parents refuse to consider that Kyle is in any way to blame. They want to see Noah in a proper facility. If he stays with a program, gets the treatment he needs, they will drop all charges.

"Well, Mrs. Groome." The psychiatrist passes a sheaf of brochures to Kate. "Let's have a look at these."

Noah's fingers slide across his pebbles as Dr. Lovelock talks and his mother listens and nods her head. Dr. Lovelock looks over the top of his spectacles. Does he even need them, Noah wonders. He peers over them at Noah and his mother and examines the paperwork on his desk.

The words "residential" and "program" snap Noah back into the present, back into the gloomy room where Dr. Lovelock tells them what has to be done.

"According to the terms of this agreement, you have to choose a suitable residential program, and I will have to approve it."

Noah's fingers move faster and faster as his mother nods, his pebbles clicking quietly. He tries not to look at the brochures, tries not to count the number of glossy options. His mother's studying them now, her face intent and unhappy. He should speak up; maybe it's not too late to set things right. His breathing speeds up, puffs out in short bursts, more than 6 inhalations and exhalations per minute; that's not good.

Slow and controlled, Noah. You know how to do it.

His mother's on her feet now, looking earnestly at the psychiatrist, thanking him and saying, "We'll try it, Dr. Lovelock, anything that helps Noah."

We? Noah wants to yell, Who's your "we"? But the words won't come.

"I'd recommend Greenhills," Dr. Lovelock says, his voice treacly as he guides her out of his rooms.

The words on the tip of Noah's tongue pour down his throat, along with their commas and question marks and apostrophes. They taste terrible, yet are strangely easy to swallow. He's eating words, chewing punctuation, but it doesn't help. Noah's world is tilting and he's losing control.

It's 5 steps to the door, and then another 5, and the psychiatrist's at Noah's side, and he's saying, "Trust me, Noah, this is for the best. You'll see."

His mother nods again when Dr. Lovelock reminds her about Greenhills. "They offer a three-month residential stay. I can get in touch with Ellen Turner, if you wish. She's an excellent therapist. If you like the place, she'll see all of you before he checks in. Given Noah's situation at school and his high levels of anxiety, this isn't the worst thing. It will be a blessing in the long run."

Dr. Lovelock's ready with a prescription too. "Better up his meds for now, too. Just temporarily."

His mother's holding up a glossy pamphlet—all pristine white buildings with red tiled roofs, tall chimneys and neat lawns.

"It all looks very nice—"

"It is," says Dr. Lovelock. "Just right for Noah. And it will definitely satisfy the conditions stipulated, provided he's willing to work with the program."

Noah stares at the floor. He's busy slicing words into sets of 5, seeing them hang—perfect in the air—before they slowly melt away.

Finally, it's time to leave. 5 steps to the middle of the waiting room, 5 to the door, 5 to the lift.

Greenhills.

Green-hills.

It should be two separate words. Green and Hills—5 letters for Green. 5 letters for Hills.

That's something at least.

His thoughts are looping, he can't make them stop. He should try—now would be an excellent time to start working on the problems that landed him here—but he's scared. It's too big a risk to take. He can't expose his family to danger.

Everything lucid and rational tells him that his precautions and safety measures do nothing, mean nothing, but the moment Noah allows himself that thought, a heavy shadow descends, woken by him.

Green has 5 letters; hills has 5 letters.

Noah's hanging on.

3x5 steps from the lift to the door that swings into the street, 6x5 more and there's the car. He's tapping his forehead now and then his nose, cheeks, mouth.

His mother watches him, but this time she doesn't tell him to try not to count, try to think of something else.

The shadow is growing, dark and menacing, but it's okay because Noah's at the car: 5 taps on the handle, 5 pats on the seat and Noah's left foot is 5ing and his right is too.

5 fingers pressed against his thigh on one side, 5 on the other.

They want to take him away from his parents and Maddie, but if he's not there, who's going to keep them safe?

At the age of twenty-one, Kate found herself engaged to a man fifteen years her senior. His name was Dominic Groome and he was the most fascinating man she had ever met. Handsome—incredibly handsome, her friends said, clustering around her, exclaiming at the ring on her finger, a large solitaire diamond.

They made a striking couple. He was tall, green-eyed, dark-haired, she almost as tall with blonde hair and deep brown eyes. But it wasn't his looks alone that had initially attracted Kate—had first made her want to cross the room and stand near him, get a better look.

What drew her to Dominic was the serious look on his face, as if he was standing alone in the room, that the dozen or so women who were all looking at him, gorging themselves on his beauty, didn't exist, and neither did their husbands in their dark suits and quiet ties with their over-loud talk of mergers and markets.

When one of the women said something to him, he looked at her and smiled, a courteous smile that softened the sharp planes of his cheeks and lit up his green eyes. The woman said something else, touched his arm lightly, and Kate felt jealousy surge hot and strong.

"Who are all these people?" she asked her date, a young man whose hopes included impressing his bosses with his beautiful companion and then plying her with enough alcohol to get her into bed later that evening.

"Let me introduce you," he said, and started her on a round of the room, taking her further and further away from the tall, quiet man. She met husbands and wives: Jeremy, Leonie, Bart, Isolde, Buddy, Delia, Monica. No names she wanted to remember, certainly no one she wanted to talk to. Kate remembers the women sizing her up and one man holding her fingers too long in a hot hand.

And then her date was propelling her towards the center of the room. "This is one of the big guys," he whispered in her ear. "And the youngest partner in the company." He couldn't have sounded more awe-struck if he'd tried.

"Dominic Groome," her date said, "I'd like you to meet Kate Cilliers."

Kate offered him her hand, hoping he'd hold on to it forever.

A brief smile was all she got, a light handshake and a polite greeting. Soon after that, the evening was over for Kate, and for her date too. He was drunk and angered by her insistence on calling a taxi. He was equally insistent that he was fine to drive; his place was just around the corner.

"It's only five minutes away." He grabbed her hand. "Come on, Kate. It's really close."

"No." She turned away and came face to face with a man in a white shirt and navy tie.

Dominic's voice was quiet as he removed the keys from her date's hand. "I'll ask security to park your car," he said. "You can collect your keys from them in the morning."

The drunk young man, abashed now, mumbled a thank you and began to weave his way home.

"I hope he'll be all right," Kate said, although she really couldn't care less.

"He'll be fine." Dominic said. "Now, my car's right here. Can I give you a lift?"

This is the part of their story that Kate will always remember clearly.

"Yes," she said. "Yes, please." Gone was the cautionary voice telling her she didn't even know him, because she did, of course she did. She'd known him all her life. All he'd needed was to appear, and there he was—her boyfriend to be, her fiancé, her husband and the father of her two children, Noah and Maddie. Her family.

According to the brochure Dr. Lovelock gave her mother, the Tranquillity Trust administers several private facilities, or "Houses," as it prefers to call them. Each one offers a "specific type of treatment" and has a gentle name.

Greenhills.

NoH-where, Maddie thinks.

That's her name for Greenhills. She watches her mother fill in the admissions form. Name of Home it says on the first line and thereafter NoH.

When her brother walks into the adolescent unit at Greenhills, which according to the brochure *supports young people with a range of issues using appropriate techniques in a safe and caring environment*, that's where he'll be. In a NoH-where place filled with NoH-bodies.

The only thing she can do right now is to make things as smooth as possible for him. Take him through the Greenhills brochure, suggest what he might like to take with him to make his room more "home-like." That's what the Greenhills information booklet says: *A few small personal items.* She gives her mother a shopping list of bits and pieces she thinks Noah might need. His own teaspoons, a plate for his biscuits, a ream of paper for creating new timetables. He won't have his laptop, or a printer, like he has at home, so an extra stash of pencils, a couple of erasers, and some colored pens.

Ever-practical, Maddie has found a cardboard cylinder for the charts that cover his walls, those that detail the minutiae of his daily routine, his homework schedule, his exercise regime, not to mention the ever-expanding Family Tree diagram filled with name after name from their mother's side of the family, all the way back to when the first Cilliers wrote in their Family Bible—the book that Noah pores over whenever they visit Ouma and Oupa.

Their dad's side is completely blank—no matter how often Noah asks, his father stonewalls him with the same exasperated reply: "There's nothing *to* tell, Noah. How many more times do I have to tell you?"

"C'mon. Let's roll them up," Maddie says, but Noah doesn't reply. Her brother's reached the point where he can hardly talk, despite Dr. Lovelock's adjustments to his medication. Maddie's seen him anxious before, but never like this. He's sitting at his desk, both hands drumming out fives. She carries a stool over to the wall near the window, to the first printout. Small boxes, annotated by Noah's neat hand. She pulls carefully at the bottom right-hand corner. The Prestik parts from the wall. Nothing tears.

"I'll do the bottom corners, Noe," Maddie says, "but you'll have to help me with the top ones. I'm too short. Right?"

Her brother nods and hauls himself to his feet.

2011

"Families, religions and traditions."

"This is going to a fun project," Miss Khan said, in that chirpy voice that never faltered, not even when the whole class groaned and Kyle Blake sniggered behind his hand. She ignored him and the laughter that rippled along the back row.

Noah glanced down at page 60 in his Life Orientation book. There was a picture of a family eating a meal, and alongside it a list of questions about mealtimes in the home, but that wasn't what Miss Khan was talking about. She was writing on the whiteboard, red letters stark against white.

Family Tree

"It's so important," Miss Khan said, "to know who we are and where we come from." She scribbled a few sentences on the board.

How well do you know your family history?

Knowing about your family can help you understand who you are.

And underneath that, their two-week project.

Researching my family.

"Go as far back as you can. As far back as your grandparents, if that's possible. Ask them where they came from, where their parents came from. Maybe they'll even be able to tell you about *their* grandparents. Collect every bit of detail—it's all useful. Find out where they were born and how many brothers and sisters they had. Did they all stay in one place or settle somewhere else. What jobs did they do? When did they get married? How many children did they have? See what stories they have to tell you about how things were when they were young, and how much things have changed since then." Miss Khan smiled at them cheerily, unaware of the turmoil brewing in one of her student's minds.

"Then I want you to write a short paragraph saying what was easy and what was difficult to find out."

More groans from the class, but Noah had stopped listening. His tree was taking shape in his mind. Laden with fruit, but only on one side. The thin shoot on the other side was completely bare.

Part of the reason why Charles Darwin wrote *The Origin of the Species* was to demonstrate that certain conditions are necessary for evolution or change to happen. Now, thanks to Miss Khan, Noah needed to establish how he had evolved.

He already knew part of his mother's family story. Their surname was Cilliers, Huguenots who'd fled to the Netherlands to escape religious persecution. They'd formed part of the first group of emigrants to sail from there, arriving in South Africa in the late 1600s and settling on land in Franschhoek—the French Corner. All he needed were the names and dates of their descendants, all recorded in their Family Bible.

In as much time as it took to eat a sandwich, Noah came to understand his position on the Cilliers' family tree. But he is only half-explained. As is Maddie, for that matter.

When he looks at himself in the mirror he sees how green his eyes are. His hair is dark, almost black, but nowhere near as curly as Maddie's. As far as he knows, she's also the only one in the family with dimples, a genetic trait that must have come from somewhere.

The branches on his mother's side are like vines, heavy with grapes, but what about his father's, which bear so little? Just two fruits there, Noah and Maddie, and he doesn't know how they were formed.

At home, Dominic's desk is clear of papers and the walls of his study are lined with shelves carrying an assortment of books. "The library," he and Kate called it when they first moved into the house, but over the years, as Dominic brought home more and more work, it became his space alone. His children know not to disturb him when he's working and to knock before opening the door.

It's where he is now, legs outstretched, gazing out over his garden, thinking about his son.

Noah, who will not move until he's counted the right number of things the right number of times. Who will stay rooted to the spot for no discernible reason and have to touch his lips and his cheeks five times before he can move again. Who, once he's moving, has to count his steps, stop at each corner, tap the wall five times.

It's been over a year since Noah has eaten with them. He finds it impossible to be at a table where things aren't placed exactly as they should be. So now he eats alone, after they've all finished, with Kate flapping around him. "All right, Noah?" she asks, over and over. If she's lucky, she'll get a nod in response.

When it's time to leave for school, Noah will be doing one of two things: standing next to the car, tapping his foot anxiously and looking at his watch, waiting for Maddie to get there, or making them late because he's still in his room, counting—

Counting God-knows-what.

Some days, Kate will come to the front door and shrug helplessly. "Just go," she'll call. Those are the days when Noah hasn't been able to count his way out of his room. He'll be standing frozen, because something, somehow, hasn't tallied in his mind. Or otherwise he'll be circling, his eyes darting from object to object, counting fives aloud, repeating them over and over as he almost spins. On days like that there's no point saying they'll wait for him. It can take hours before he's worked himself free of whatever mistake he's made that forbids him to move before he's corrected it.

"Have a good day, darling," Kate will call to Maddie. "Bye, Dom," and he'll see that she's frantic to get back inside, see what help she can offer her distressed son. Kate's so caught up in all of this, he barely recognizes her. She's far from the sunny, spirited woman she was before...

Before Noah. Dominic despises himself for thinking of it this way, and he would never say it aloud, but it's what he thinks when he looks at his son.

In the days when they'd all sat down to meals together, Noah would enter the dining room and do a quick three-sixty. It had taken Dominic every ounce of restraint not to yell, What does it matter? What does it matter if the chairs are pushed in or pulled out, or the knives are this close or that close to the plates and the water jug's in the center of the table? And why, for God's sake, is it such an issue if we have spinach, even though your mother said we'd be having peas?

When he sees his son walking to the car, head bent, he knows he's doing that wretched counting. When he's putting out the garbage, filling the dogs' water bowls, walking to a chair in the living room to watch the news, he counts every step. So yes, even Dominic, the father who finds it impossible to buy in to the need for ongoing therapy—for all the good it does, Kate—knows that his son counts in fives. It's a bit damn hard not to. He also knows he can't simply tell him to snap out of it or beg him to stop.

And at this point, four therapists down, it's not because Dominic is worried about hurting Noah's feelings. No, the reason is mean; spiteful even, you might say—Kate certainly would. Dominic cannot interrupt his son when he is counting because if he does, the counting will start from scratch. If Noah's thrown even slightly off balance, he'll begin all over again, leaving Maddie and Dominic waiting for him at the car—or leaving without him.

So Dominic never interrupts his son, and if eating alone is easier for Noah, that's fine with him.

Does he love him?

Does Dominic love his son?

He does. Of course he does. But truth be told—truth absolute, deep, dark and shameful—Dominic couldn't be more relieved that Noah is going to Greenhills.

A man arrives and bangs on the door and Mum jumps up from her chair. Gabriel races out of the sitting room. It's going to be Dad! He knows it. He just knows it. But when he opens it, he sees it's a short round man with a smiley face and twinkly eyes. Is your mother home, son? he asks. His voice is fat and jolly, the sort Father Christmas might have if Gabriel ever heard him speak. But this Father Christmas hasn't arrived with a bag full of presents for children who have been nice. He may have a list, and he may be checking it twice, but that's only because he needs to be sure he hasn't missed anything.

You'd be surprised, he says in his Santa voice. You'd be surprised, Mrs. Felix, what people try to get away with. But my eyes are all-seeing, so no funny stuff please, no squirrelling away.

So no, no presents for Harry and Gabriel, even though they've been so good for Mum. Instead, Father Christmas is taking items away, packing them into a large van. Where's he taking everything, Gabriel wonders. Will he wait for Christmas Eve, hitch his reindeers to his sleigh and sweep across the skies, looking for a family who needs them more than they do?

How that can be possible, though, Gabriel isn't sure. Because now there is hardly anything in the house and Mum's on her knees, she's staring at the wall where the TV cabinet used to be and crying, I don't know what to do. Where can we go? What am I supposed to do? And then she's screaming and yelling and calling his father's name. What am I to do, Joe? How are we going to survive?

There's a stuttering cough outside, the sort Mum's car makes when she's trying to start it, and she runs to the window. My car, she's screaming. I need my car, you bastards. She crumples over again. She lies on the floor for what seems like hours. Gabriel wonders if she'll ever get up.

Much later, Gabriel hears her voice. That's it, Joe. We'll have to go to him. There's nothing else I can do.

She's talking to Dad, but there's no answer because he isn't there.

There's more, much more, that Noah can and can't do, will and won't do; trying to make a full list is something Dominic just doesn't have the energy for.

In the early days, when Kate heard about "Obsessive Compulsive Disorder," she sent links to Dominic. He read numerous articles, learned that OCD "presents in a number of ways." Noah might be compulsive about cleanliness, for example, washing his hands and body parts in a ritual way. Dominic watched his son's hand twisting the tap one, two, three, four, five times before opening it fully. After that, Noah would check his watch, wash briskly, check his watch again and record the time.

End of story.

Counting and balancing, timing and re-timing, tapping out five when things become ultra-stressful, those are Noah's main things. Counting, checking, balancing. The irony isn't lost on Dominic. That's pretty much how he operates—checking and balancing, weighing future risks against the current climate, seeing how robust the economy is, what it will tolerate.

In the masses of material Kate forwarded, Dominic learned how OCD reveals itself, the numerous other ways his son's condition might have manifested.

There are the Counters, who add and subtract and weigh and measure and line things up and need to make sure that every minute in a day is accounted for.

The Washer-Cleaners, who are petrified of contamination.

The Prayers, who fear the destruction that will rain down if they deviate from various sets of self-manufactured observances and strictures.

The Destroyers, who can't take a step for fear of the death or destruction they will cause to others.

The Sexually Obsessed, whose thoughts sicken and shame them.

The Scrupulous, who are anxious of failing, ethically, morally or religiously.

The OCD Hoarders, who can't throw anything away, not even empty cans or egg boxes.

"For people with OCD, seemingly small things become far more important than interpersonal relationships." The more he reads, the more Dominic realizes that fear is the determining factor, the common denominator. Fear, uncontrollable and irrational, controlling and dominating. Fear that if everything isn't just so, the consequences will be catastrophic.

Noah's life is almost completely governed by rules and regulations that Dominic cannot even begin to understand. In the beginning, he tried. Now, though, the frustration that rises in him as he waits for his son to get to the car, to quit arranging the utensils on the kitchen counter, to stop looking at his watch every time the car stops at a traffic light, is almost insurmountable. Yet he knows that telling Noah to shut his mouth so he doesn't have to listen to him counting under his breath, have to hear the f-f-fuh that precedes the word "five" before it exits his son's mouth, would only make things worse for everyone.

"We have to try and understand," Kate says. "It's so tough for him, Dom."

One day Kate tells him she won't be sending him any more links. One of the therapists Noah is seeing—his third, or his second, Dominic isn't sure—tells Kate to stop. "A little knowledge is a dangerous thing, Mrs. Groome," she is told.

"Basically he's saying, 'Leave it to the experts, Mrs. Groome.'" Kate's face is flushed. "In other words, don't you worry your silly little head about it!"

Dominic doesn't respond. He's relieved. Hopefully it means there'll be fewer after-dinner conversations about whether Noah is manifesting a symptom that Kate has read about in some online journal. All he has to do now is pay the latest bills and wonder if the money he sends off for every session is doing any good whatsoever. For as far as he can see, Noah is getting worse. Not that he shares this with Kate. He won't do anything to exacerbate the anxiety that is affecting his wife.

All he says is, "Well, Kate, he might have a point. Perhaps we just need to focus on being his parents." His response is deliberately mild.

Even so, she still looks hurt, but Dominic's used to that. When it comes to Noah, Kate's like a long-wave radio station and Dominic can never quite pick up on her frequency.

2011

"Maybe there's *something* we can learn, Dom?"

Noah paused outside the dining-room door.

"Noah may be on to something. If we did some research, found other members of your family, we might come across information that would help. With Noah, I mean."

"I've told you, Kate, this isn't up for discussion."

"But, Dom..." His mother wasn't giving up. "Remember that article I sent you? The one that says OCD's linked to all sorts of factors. Family history, even."

Noah could have told her that. Though there was nothing conclusive to prove that OCD could be heritable—not yet—couldn't his Dad see? Who *he* was, who *he* came from, made Noah who *he* was.

Since the first therapist mentioned those words: "obsessive" and "compulsive," Noah had been reading too. Not that everything was fully founded or researched, but still worth thinking about.

First, there were 5 key words he'd identified:

1. *Obsession* and everything linked to it.
   - Intrusive, recurring, unwanted, uncontrollable, urges, thoughts, anxiety, distress. (✓)
   - All the things to worry about: germs, illness, death; fear of awful things happening, fear of doing something wrong, desperation if things aren't just right. Fear of hurting others...(✓)

2. *Compulsion* and everything linked to it.
   - Everything you have to do (in the strictest, meanest, most domineering way) to purge the worry, prevent "catastrophe." (✓)

3. *Checking* and rechecking; excessive repetition in order to get things absolutely right, starting over if they aren't. Ordering and arranging. Relying on important words or numbers. (✓) (The more his list of "must-dos' grew, the more time it stole from his day, but he *couldn't* stop.)

4. *Triggers.* People who've experienced bullying (✓), abuse or neglect might develop OCD. Sometimes it starts after an important incident, a bereavement or a traumatic event (✓✓).

5. *Personality.* People who develop OCD often tend to be:
   - neat (✓)
   - meticulous (✓)
   - methodical (✓)
   - concerned about high personal standards (✓)
   - anxious, often with a very strong sense of responsibility for themselves

and others (✓,✓ and ✓)

And then there was the stuff he couldn't talk about. His mother filled his previous therapists in on what had happened, but Noah hadn't been able to say a word. The Dark wouldn't let him, it forced him to keep it secret.

And you know why, don't you? Don't give anything away. You'd do well to remember that.

"Kate. It's a dead end. I've tried." Noah heard a chair scraping back and ducked into the sitting room.

"Dom. Darling. Where are you going?"

"For a run."

When his mother saw him a few minutes later, she tried to smile. "Noah. Everything all right?"

No, he wanted to say, it's not. He wanted to tell her how sorry he was. If Noah was doing a balancing act, trying to keep his family safe, his mother was too. Noah and his "condition"; his father's silence and anger; his little sister who just wanted to be an ordinary kid. His mother was doing everything she could just to keep the family whole.

If Noah could find out more about his father and *his* ancestors, he'd learn why he looked the way he did, or if there were other Groomes who'd had Maddie's curls and dimples. Even more, though, if he could establish *why* he was, as well as *what* he was, that might help his family. Dogged persistence was the only way forward. And if anyone was an expert at that, it was Noah.

Noah couldn't say any of this to his mother, he didn't want to let on that he knew what she and his father had discussed. What he could do, though, was walk up to her and pat her on the shoulder. 5 quick pats.

Noah's mother often talks about "before."

"He wasn't like this before," he'd heard her say to therapist 2 at their initial consultation. "Before" is part of Noah's history. It goes into the notes when Kate goes in alone to talk about Noah and what he's like to live with and how he's changed and why.

"If you could just talk about it, darling," she urged before each session, but Noah's tapping fingers ensured his lips stayed sealed.

2011

"Right then, we're onto the Gs and Hs." Mrs. Simpson ran her pen down the class register as she picked the debate teams for the following week. "That means Janice Garrett, Zoe Glynn and Noah Groome, you'll be Team One. Nicholas Guthrie, Lungelo Hadebe, Peter Harper, Team Two."

Noah wasn't much good at debating—he was too concerned with making sure all data was delivered accurately, preferably from at least 3 credible sources. Not easy to deliver reams of information in the short time each speaker was allowed, especially when his team members were as concerned with inflaming passion and arousing indignation as they were with hitting the opposition with the facts. But hard facts were what Noah was good at. Give him a topic and he would research it until the last trail had run cold.

"Look," said Zoe Glynn at recess, when they met to discuss the topic, "why don't you second, Noah. Stick to the facts, dazzle them with graphics. I'll open and Janice can conclude."

"Keep your side of things short and sweet," Janice added. "But don't forget we'll be relying on you, Noah. If they come up with info that's inaccurate, let us know. Pass us a note or something."

"And you can help us with our prep," Zoe said. "Research as much as you can. Relevant stuff that they won't be able to argue against."

Noah nodded. That he *could* do. He'd get onto it at once, email them everything they needed. They could bring emotion, he'd provide the shocking, incontrovertible truth.

Gun Control or Gun Rights?

That was the topic Mrs. Simpson had given them for the debate, and Zoe, Janice and Noah were arguing for Gun Control.

He set to work the moment he got home. Typing in key words, following leads from site to site, trying hard to concentrate on facts and figures as he clicked from stories of children killing other children with firearms found in the home, to suicides that might have been prevented if guns hadn't been available, to gang-related shootings and active shooters out on a killing spree.

He watched clips from *Bowling for Columbine*, saw footage of Dylan Klebold and Eric Harris, found a list of the weapons they'd carried in duffel bags to kill their school mates: a pipe bomb that failed to go off; a 12-gauge pump-action shotgun; a 9-mm Carbine; a 9-mm semi-automatic handgun; and a 12-gauge, double-barreled, sawn-off shotgun.

He saw Michael Moore opening a bank account and being given a free hunting rifle; he watched the two planes crashing into the World Trade Center to the accompaniment of "What a Wonderful World."

He read articles that tried to explain the behavior of recent shooters: theories ranging from narcissistic arrogance, to being bullied at school, to listening to alternative music, to religious mania, to schizophrenia. Irrespective of the circumstances and regardless of the justifications, Noah established one common denominator in the American shootings: most of the perpetrators had opened fire using legally obtained weapons.

Noah also found the stats for gun-related deaths and murders in South Africa. The Firearms Control Act 60 of 2000 was meant to regulate the ownership of guns by civilians, but there were still plenty of unlicensed weapons in circulation, many of them responsible for daily shootings and deaths.

The statistics were staggering. He watched YouTube clips of distraught mothers, fathers, teachers and friends calling for a halt to gun-related violence. It was shattering and, as he read on and watched more and more footage, mind-numbing.

He scrolled through multitudinous comments on gun sites where gun owners bemoaned the influence of "libtards" who wanted to control them, violate their Second Amendment rights. He documented the weapons used in active shootings, showing how semi-automatic rifles outnumbered the use of other types of firearms. He compiled a list of suicides, accidental fatalities, homicides and justifiable homicides per capita per country, with a promise to Janice and Zoe that he'd construct graphs to push the point home.

There wasn't time to collate everything, but after a couple of days he felt ready to send them his material. He listed the reasons proponents of gun rights gave for wanting to be allowed to buy guns, then countered each of those with arguments from people who demanded increased gun control. Janice and Zoe would have no shortage of ammunition—Noah winced at his inadvertent use of the word, remembered Michael Moore walking into Walmart and buying bullets over the counter.

He sent it all off midweek, leaving Janice and Zoe plenty of time to shape it into an impassioned argument for Monday's debate. In the meantime he'd get to work on the graphics, let deep red blocks on bar charts illustrate the points they would be making.

Janice replied almost immediately: *Thanks Noah! This research is gold. Wouldn't it be great if we could get rid of all the guns in the world?* ☺

Zoe's email followed shortly.

Noah closed his laptop, leaned back in his chair and stretched his arms over his head. He couldn't imagine how Team 2 could find anything to dispute the hard evidence his team would present. His data spoke for itself.

And then, that Friday, 22 July 2011, in Norway, Anders Behring Breivik carried out 2 lone-wolf terrorist attacks. The first, a car bomb explosion in Oslo, killed 8 people and injured over 200. The second, an attack on the island of Utøya in Tyrifjorden, Buskerud, where the Workers' Youth League of the Norwegian Labour Party had organized a summer camp. Wearing a fake police uniform, Breivik picked off young people with cool precision, killing 68, injuring more than 110. A 69th victim died 2 days after the massacre.

Noah sat in front of the TV, watching the news footage over and over again, flashing back to scenes from his research: mounds of flowers at the sites of mass shootings, accidental deaths, homicides, suicides...more funerals than he could bear to contemplate. And now there were going to be so many more.

Noah wondered if Mrs. Simpson would cancel the debate. He hoped so. In the wake of such a brutal massacre, who needed even more evidence shoved down their throats? Breivik's actions had taken Noah's facts and turned them into the faces of grieving parents, classmates and teachers. This wasn't something edited by Michael Moore to drive home a point, valid though that might be. This was raw, uncensored footage, and Noah found it devastating to watch.

The forces of the universe seemed to have gone berserk, off-course, rampaging wildly out of control. Noah felt the scales tipping. And then, 4 days later, all sense of balance was blown away.

⊕

26 JULY 2011 / 19:22

They were waiting inside the gate as Noah and Kate pulled into the driveway. Three men, concealed in the shadows. They stepped forward and took shape when Kate opened her car door. She tried to close it, but she was too slow.

They wanted her ATM card, her PIN and her iPhone. Oh, and her car, of course.

When the police officer came to take Kate's statement, he said, as if it would be of some comfort, "Audis are very popular these days."

"Thank you, Constable." Dominic ushered him out of the house as quickly as possible, away from his wife, his children.

⊕

14 FEBRUARY 2013 / 15:56

Before Noah can start his program at Greenhills, the Groomes have to meet Ellen Turner.

Dominic leaves work early and Kate sends a note excusing Maddie from gymnastics. Noah, naturally, just needs to be able to get in the car. Kate watches her son push the front door handle down (up-down-up-down), sees him counting his way to the driveway. He's counting out loud again, has been ever since the Greenhills decision was made.

Greenhills. Kate doesn't allow herself to think ahead to the next trip they'll make, when they'll be leaving Noah there for three months.

Three months! She forces herself to concentrate on how the next couple of hours will pan out.

"Fancy," Maddie says, as they pull up to a pair of imposing wrought-iron gates.

It's easy to imagine it in its halcyon days, a large and gracious home. Yes, that's the way to see it, Kate tells herself. Noah is taking up residence in a beautiful old Victorian house. He'll be here for a few weeks and then he'll come home and they can put all of this behind them.

There's a guardhouse at the gates, a stone building with a large glass window and two doors, one outside the gates and one inside. A man approaches the car, carrying a clipboard. Nothing unusual in that, Kate thinks. Just like any gated community.

Dominic, giving their details, tells him who they've come to meet. "Ms. Turner," he says. The man speaks into a walkie-talkie that crackles back at him.

"She's expecting you," he says. "Drive through to the main parking lot and then turn to your left. You'll see a smaller building. Our adolescent wing." He glances inside the car and Kate wonders if he can tell which of her children is going to be making Greenhills their home for the next three months.

"When you leave, after you've signed out, I'll lift the boom. Make sure you drive over this square." He points to a yellow square with an X inside it. "The weight of your car will activate the gates." He pushes a button and the gate facing them swings open. There are two booms, paired end to end, and the guard raises the one on their side to let them in.

"Don't forget," he calls, "the yellow square with the X on it."

Dominic waves in acknowledgement and the Groomes enter the grounds of Greenhills.

16:01

Ms. Turner is waiting for them at reception. "Thanks, Sally Anne," she says to the woman sitting behind the counter. "I'll see the Groomes to my office. Could you ask Mr. Bill to meet us there in half an hour?"

She leads them up a long staircase, along a corridor and down a short flight of stairs.

"Bit of a rabbit warren, I'm afraid," she says with a laugh. "I'm still finding my way around here."

"You're new?" Noah's father asks.

"New to Greenhills? Yes. This is my third week here."

Ms. Turner smiles at Noah. "We can learn our way around together, Noah," she tells him.

He doesn't reply.

Ms. Turner's room is large and bright with deep sash windows that look over the front lawns. To the left of the door is her desk, pushed against the wall, her swivel chair facing a black and white poster of two men walking a railroad track. Tucked in alongside the poster are the same sort of framed certificates that Noah's seen hanging in his previous therapists' rooms.

Further in is an easy chair, upholstered in a botanical print, a scattering of delicately drawn sugarbirds and proteas on a cream background. Ms. Turner's chair, Noah reckons; it's within easy reach of the desk. A comfortable 2-seater couch covered in warm sunyellow corduroy faces her seat, flanked on either side by wicker chairs, their cushions made up in the same floral material.

The botanical theme carries into the rest of her room: framed prints of bold orange Clivias, delicate pink belladonna lilies, pincushion proteas and wild irises touched with yellow and mauve. Noah recognizes most of them from his father's indigenous garden.

"Sit," she says, "please, sit."

Noah's parents take the couch, Maddie and Noah the single chairs.

"This won't take long," says Ms. Turner. "Just a quick intro as to what Noah and I will be doing while he's here."

Noah listens intently as Ms. Turner talks about appointments and routines and how his days at Greenhills will be organized.

"It's all here," she says.

He looks down at the sheet of paper she hands him. His day, sectioned into neat blocks. Meals, 3 a day, of course, plus morning and afternoon tea. Exercise, "group," open-door time, room time, activities like art and pottery and "free time," with accompanying suggestions about walking and going to the meditation circle.

"Mr. Bill will explain it in full detail, Noah. You'll be one of his group. If you have any problems, you can go directly to him, or come to me, of course."

All the while Noah's family sits quietly.

"Do you have any questions?" Ms. Turner asks.

His mother laughs. "So many, I don't know where to start."

"It is all a bit overwhelming at first," Ms. Turner says, "but you'll be surprised at how quickly Noah settles in."

Noah wants to laugh out loud at that, but he can't. He's trying not to tap, trying to keep his body still. His right hand is in his pocket, his fingers run over and over the 5 small stones. Slow breaths, deep breaths. In. Out...2 3 4 5.

A new timetable, Noah? A room to organize? Steps from here to there to Godknowswhere? There will be no settling in. Let this Turner woman know.

Noah's left hand is at his ears, his fingers stroking 5s as unobtrusively as possible.

Ms. Turner goes on. "And, of course, we'll have family counselling sessions as well. Give everyone space to talk. I'll want to meet with your family as a group, Noah, and there'll be a few sessions with just you, Mr. and Mrs. Groome."

Even though she knows the answer—"Don't worry, sweetheart, we'll see you two weeks after you check in for visiting time'—his mother still asks when they'll be allowed to visit.

"Not for the first two weeks, Mrs. Groome."

"Yes, yes, of course..." Her voice fades and she looks down at her lap.

Ms. Turner leans forward and looks at them more seriously. "I've looked at Noah's file," she says, "and I know a program like this isn't what you'd have chosen. He has had therapy, after all."

Noah nods slightly.

"Yes," his mother says. "It's all there, in his folder."

Hours spent holding in words and thoughts, all 4 therapists having settled on the same diagnosis: OCD, without a shadow of a doubt. And all 4 have suggested medication to calm the anxiety that eats at Noah if any part of his day is thrown off balance.

"Everything is fine, so long as Noah's routine isn't disrupted," his mother tells Ms. Turner. "That's why we all try to—"

Ms. Turner raises a polite hand. "But it's not really, is it?" she says. "It's nowhere near 'fine,' especially for Noah."

No one says a word.

His father's jaw is working furiously. Maddie's looking at him, clearly worried.

Noah's mother sighs. "No," she says. "Nothing's fine."

"Chances are that outpatient counselling would eventually have been successful," Ms. Turner says carefully. She glances at the file. "However, the best thing about an intensive residential program like this is that Noah can concentrate, we can all work together, and move more speedily."

She leans forward and smiles. "OCD *is* treatable," she says. "And it's more common than you think. I'm not promising miracles, no one can do that, but I *am* saying there's hope. Noah can learn to manage and minimize its effects. We'll be using a form of therapy called CBT. You've probably heard of it."

Kate nods. "Cognitive Behavioral Therapy," she says. "One of his therapists mentioned it."

Ms. Turner smiles. "Unfortunately, not all therapists are fully trained in CBT," she says. "But it is one of my specialties. Noah and I will be using a combination of CBT and something called Exposure and Response Prevention, or ERP. It sounds complicated, but we'll take it one step at a time. Basically, I'm hoping that Noah will be able to identify thoughts that distress him and tackle them head on."

She looks kindly at Noah, trying to reassure him. She's not terribly successful. If anything, the thought of sitting here, session after session, makes his fingers move faster over his pebbles, heightens his urge to let his feet tap.

"Dr. Lovelock wants him to stay on the increased dose of medication, and then, when he's settled in, we'll start slowly lowering it until we find a happy medium." Ms. Turner's still talking. "The process itself is all about Noah learning to face his fears, using controlled, measured exposure. We'll introduce situations that trigger his obsessions, and then work on strategies to prevent his usual coping mechanisms. For example, we're all aware of Noah's need to count." She looks at the Groomes as if she's talking about the weather.

"Yes, but we don't...That's to say...We never talk about Noah's counting." His mother's tripping over her words.

We certainly don't. And nor should this Turner woman. Stop her.

Ms. Turner leans back in her chair. "We will though," she says. "Bit by bit. Hopefully, we'll get to the point where he can look beyond his rituals and compulsions to their underlying cause." Once again, she smiles at them.

"The more we do, and the more Noah learns to react differently, the more his compulsions should decrease and his obsessions feel less powerful. I've got plenty of material you can look at if you'd like."

"Would that be acceptable?" Noah's mother looks uncertain. "One of his other therapists didn't encourage me to do too much research. 'A little knowledge is a dangerous thing' is what he said."

"I disagree," says Ms. Turner. "The more you research, the more you'll understand. Please, read, and then come to me with any questions. Any time. There will be challenges," she continues. "I'm not saying the circumstances that brought Noah here were ideal. Not in the least. But now that he's at Greenhills, this could be a golden opportunity to break his OCD cycle as effectively as possible. Give Noah some head space to call his own."

Your own? What exactly is she getting at?

Noah begins to 5. Left foot, right. Cheeks, twice on his lips.

His father notices and frowns. His mother and sister pretend they haven't seen.

Ms. Turner has noticed. Of course she has. "It's nearly time for Mr. Bill to show you around," she says easily. "There's quite a bit to see, and a lot to take in. Just one last thing, Noah." She says his name firmly and he raises his head. "How well you do here greatly depends on you. All I ask is that you try to be as open with me as you can."

Noah's feet tap faster.

"I'll be asking you to keep a list of all the things you feel compelled to do, what time of day you have to do them. Things like that. We'll work together."

Together? The only together is you and me.

"That's it," Ms. Turner says pleasantly, "for now."

Noah's mother reaches for her husband's hand and gives it a squeeze, but he doesn't squeeze back.

"We have a pretty full schedule here," Ms. Turner says. "Noah's going to be doing some hard work. Speaking of which..." She reaches for a sheaf of papers on her desk and hands them to Noah. "I'd like you to fill in some of these, Noah."

"5 Things About Me" is printed at the top of each sheet with the numbers 1 to 5 below.

"These are very useful," Ms. Turner tells him. "Especially when you're in group. It gives you something to say, helps the others to get to know you better. If you bring them to our one-on-one sessions, they'll give us some starting points."

Noah looks at her blankly, then reads the words again. "5 Things About Me."

At least it's 5. It could be worse. It could have been 4, or 6.

Left foot, right. Cheeks, lips.

A soft knock at the door breaks the silence.

"That'll be Mr. Bill," says Ms. Turner. "See you soon, Noah." She touches him lightly on the shoulder then turns to shake his father's hand, then Maddie's and finally his mother's. "It'll be fine," she says to them. "You'll see."

His mom doesn't smile; she barely even nods.

The door opens and in steps a tall, broad-shouldered man with close-cropped hair.

"This is Mr. Bulelane Mabatle, Noah," Ms. Turner says.

"Call me Mr. Bill." The tall man shakes Noah's hand.

"Noah's mother and father, Mr. and Mrs. Groome," says Ms. Turner. "And Maddie, of course."

Once the introductions are done, Mr. Bill ushers the Groomes out and leads them up another short flight of stairs. It opens onto a quiet corridor flanked by white doors on either side.

"They're all in group now." Mr. Bill smiles broadly. "That's why it's so peaceful." He opens one of the doors. "This will be your room, Noah."

A skinny rectangle; wide enough for the single bed and nightstand, long enough for a desk with a swivel chair, a kettle on a narrow shelf with 2 sockets. Next to that, a small sink with a drainer. There's a cupboard built into the wall, the doors open to show 4 empty shelves and 1 small hanging space. At the far end of the room, angled to look out over the lawn, is a deep-blue easy chair. Noah can bring a cushion for it from home if he wants to, says Mr. Bill.

"And here," Mr. Bill steps out into the corridor and points to a door further down the corridor, "is the boys' bathroom. And," he points at a payphone further down the passage, "the phone. No cell phones, laptops or cameras while you're here, I'm afraid, but you can make and receive calls after you've been here two weeks. You'll get a phone card then. But it's a privilege, the same as watching TV or using allocated Internet time on the computers in the Rec Room. Break the rules in any way, and they can be revoked."

They follow him to the dining room, the Visitors' Lounge and past a closed door where there's a murmur of voices. "Group," says Mr. Bill. "You'll be joining in there soon, Noah."

Group. Where Noah will have to tell them 5 things about himself.

15 FEBRUARY 2013 / 17:48

"Noah?"

Noah looks at his watch. He doesn't have much time to spare, but then she says his name again. He turns in the doorway. His mother is at the window, her back to him.

"Yes?"

"I'm so sorry."

Looking at his watch is a reflex action and Noah can't help doing it now, glad she can't see him. He doesn't want to be rude, doesn't want his mom to think he can't make time for her.

You can't. You've got plenty to get through before supper.

"It's my fault."

"No, Mom, really."

"It is. If only I'd listened to Maddie when she told me they were bullying you. Those boys. Kyle Blake."

"No, it wouldn't have made any difference. Seriously."

"But, Noah, if I'd listened, we could have gone to Mr. Reynolds, told him about Kyle. At least then we'd be on record."

"Mom..." Noah pauses. He's going to have to use words now, so many of them, but his mother still hasn't turned around. "Mom. Don't. Please. I didn't want you to. I should have stood up to him earlier."

Stood up to him? How, exactly, when you can hardly make it through your bedroom door on a bad day?

And at the same time she's saying, "Oh, Noah. I'd never expect you to do that."

Great. Even Noah's mother doesn't think he has what it takes.

The man's skin is white as plaster of Paris, as white as a plaster cast, and he's leaning on a walking stick. It's a wooden walking stick with a cruel head, a dragon with long teeth and a pink tongue and red eyes and when he leaves it in the corner the dragon looks at Gabriel, ready to breathe fire. Ready to burn the flesh from his face and leave his bones exposed and gleaming and white.

The dragonstick is pitiless. It catches him behind his legs if he isn't moving fast enough, flicks up to nip at his cheek if he is insolent.

Impertinent. The old man does not like impertinence. And when he's in the mood for sport, the dragonstick sneaks out and tangles itself around Gabriel's ankles and makes him fall to his knees, and grovel there while he tries to hold back his tears. The cruel stick supports a cruel man and Gabriel can't understand how he came to be in their life, but there's nothing they can do about it, Mum says.

Gabriel wonders what happened to Dad, the laughing man who was here one day and gone the next. One time he asked Mum when the old man was in the room and she looked fearfully at Gabriel and told him to be quiet, there's a good boy.

He learns quickly to be quiet. He learns not to ask, never to want to know how or why when he sees the bruises on her cheeks or at the top of her arms, and once, when her skirt rides high on her thigh, like a dark purple band. It's safer that way. For him, for Mum, and for Harry.

He doesn't like it here. It's not his home. It's the place they moved to when Dad left, and now they are here with the man who tells him to call him Grandfather. But Gabriel doesn't want to. If he's Gabriel's grandfather, that makes him Dad's father, and Gabriel doesn't like him joined to Dad like that in his head. He's old and white-haired and white-skinned and Gabriel doesn't call him anything, which makes him mad, and when he's mad with Gabriel he gets mad with Mum.

Gabriel can't understand how they came to be here. One day he's at home with Dad and Mum. Mum's crying and asking why and Dad's saying, I'm sorry, Martha, so sorry. I didn't mean, and Mum has her head in her hands and she's saying, But that's just it, Joe, you never mean, and you're always saying sorry. What are we supposed to do now? Where are we supposed to go?

Harriet is crying and crying and Dad says, Hadn't you better feed her?

Feed her? Mum says. With what, Joe? There's no food in the house, no money.

And then, Bam! Bam! Bam! at the door, and Dad's looking over his shoulder, looking scared.

Gabriel is scared too. Dad, his laughing, happy Dad, isn't laughing any more. He's looking at Mum and his eyes are wide and he's plucking at the sleeve of his shirt, fingers busy and quick.

Gabriel looks at Dad's fingers and watches them moving up and down like he's playing a guitar. It's easier to look at Dad's fingers because he doesn't want to look at Dad's face. He doesn't want to see Dad's scared, wide-eyed face staring at Mum like he's asking for something.

She's staring back at him saying, Go. Just go. I'll talk to them.

Dad's saying, I'm sorry Marty, as soon as I'm sorted I'll—

Mum's not letting him talk, she's just saying, Go, go.

Then Dad bends down to Gabriel, down, down, down, until he's kneeling on the floor. He holds Gabriel tight and says, Look after your Mum for me, Gabe. Look after Harry. Can you do that? Be a big boy and do that for me?

Gabriel blinks and blinks and Dad says, Please son, don't cry.

Gabriel can't talk. He nods and watches as Dad stands up and gives Mum a quick hug. Then the back door opens and closes quietly, so quietly Gabriel can only hear the softest click, and then there's more knocking at the front door, loud bang-bang-banging and Mum's saying, Coming, I'm coming.

Harry's crying. Mum scoops her up and goes slowly to the door. Gabriel follows. Mum opens the door and there are three men standing on the step. Three big men in dark suits, white shirts and black ties and shiny shoes. They're pushing past Mum and saying, Where is he? Where is he, Martha?

I don't know, Mum's saying. He didn't come home. One of the men grabs her arm and shakes her and still Mum's saying, Sorry, sorry, I don't know where he is.

Gabriel pulls on the man's arm, pulls and pulls and tries to make him let Mum go because he promised Dad.

He'd promised he'd look after Mum and Harry but he isn't doing a good job of it, not at all. Because now the other man's come into the room, and he's saying, Nothing. He's gone. Now both of them are grabbing Mum and pushing her between them and Mum's trying to hold on to Harry, hold her close. I don't know. I don't know where he is, she's shouting.

Harry's screaming and the other man, the third one, grabs Harry and says, Martha. Martha-Martha-Martha. Tell us what we want to know. He's looking at Harry, and at Mum, and suddenly his hand shoots out. He's got Gabriel by the neck and his fingers are like claws, and he's talking to Mum, very softly. Just tell us where he is, Martha. That is all we need to know. And then we'll all be happy.

Mum's eyes are shaking and spit's coming out of her mouth and she's speaking very fast, saying, Please, please. They're just kids, it's not their fault.

Gabriel remembers what Dad said, just before he left. Look after your mum, Gabe. Look after your little sister. Can you do that? He can, yes he can, because now he feels himself unfreezing and he knows what Dad meant.

Gabriel starts yelling. He isn't here, my dad isn't here. Leave my mum alone. Leave my sister alone.

The big man bends down, down, just like Dad did earlier. He's still holding Harry and Harry isn't crying any more. The room is quiet and the big man is saying, What's your name, kid?

Gabriel tells him, and then he says, Leave my mum alone. My dad's gone. He's gone. He went through the back door, and Mum says, Gabriel, and her voice is a sad whisper.

But Gabriel can hardly hear her because the big man's saying, Through the back door, hey? When was that, Gabriel?

When he saw your car. My dad left when he saw your car. He went through the back door.

Gabriel knows he's done the right thing, because the big man lets go of his neck and puts Harry down, gently, very softly, on the couch and says, He won't have got far. Get out there.

The two other men run out of the room. Their hands are at their belts and Gabriel sees their guns, big and black. Mum's looking at him. Her eyes are wide and her mouth's tight shut and her whole body is shaking from top to toe. Slowly, slowly, her eyes move to the window and slowly, slowly they shift back and she looks at the ground.

You do know we'll get him, Martha, the big man says. He can't get away from us.

Mum's sobbing and Harry starts crying again. The man walks out of the room and Mum looks at Gabriel and she's saying, Oh, Gabe, what have you done?

Gabriel knows what he's done. He's looked after Mum and Harry, just like Dad told him to.

26 JULY 2011 / 19:26

All 3 of them, dressed in black, hands in black gloves, no skin showing, only their eyes. Dark pools in the slit of one balaclava, a glint of silver in another.

If Noah rushed the 3 of them, his mother could run, shout for help and hope a neighbor hears. Maybe Mrs. Parfitt would say to her husband, "David, did you hear that, David?" But even if she did, Noah couldn't see David stepping out into possible danger. Maybe they'd phone the police, though, report noise on the street.

Neighborhood watch! They patrol every evening. If they shouted, yelled loud enough—

Thoughts clicking in and out of place so fast. First thing—run at them. Maybe even take both of them out. They weren't armed, not as far as Noah could see. He was bigger than any of them. Taller. Probably fitter too. If he could just—

No time to think, take them off guard, wait for 1 of them to turn—

And now!

And now—

A gun in a hand, the butt of it swinging up and crunching against his cheek, the shock of pain and his mother screaming, "Noah, Noah!" The gun pointing at her now, 1 of them talking in a low voice.

"Shut up."

The gun moved from his mother and levelled at Noah.

"Not a word..." a low, calm voice said. The gun swung back to Noah's mother. "...not a sound. Don't move unless we tell you to."

His mother nodded and nodded, and didn't say a word.

The men were behind them now, prodding them up the driveway, in front of the car.

"Sit."

His mother sank to the ground.

"You too. Back to back."

Noah hesitated and his mother whispered, "Please, Noah. Please."

"Yes, *pleath*, Noah."

A giggle as 1 of them lisped and the sound was somehow worse than anything so far. He fastened cable ties around their wrists and ankles, silenced their mouths with foul-tasting gags, used a length of nylon rope to tie them together.

On Sunday afternoon, Kate's son moves in to Greenhills. They've all come, all helped to carry his bags, his rug, the box filled with his blue mugs. (Kate buys him mugs whenever she sees the right ones, plain, regular, always a similar shape, and always a shade of blue: baby blue, periwinkle, royal blue, teal, navy blue. Noah arranges them on a spectrum from light to dark. Kate has learned to be prepared. She has a small stock of them and if one breaks she replaces it with another of a similar color.) Two packets of biscuits are tucked in next to the mugs, his wall charts are stowed safely in their cardboard cylinder. Everything he'll need for his stay in Greenhills. And now they're standing in his narrow room, not sure what to say or do next.

Noah's eyes are darting from wall to wall, to his desk, to his cupboard. Maddie offered to help him put up his Family Tree, but his reply was straightforward: "No, thanks, Mads. It's fine." Everything's fine, everything's okay. He doesn't want them to stay, they don't know how to leave. What words do you use when you're saying goodbye to your son, leaving him somewhere like Greenhills?

Dominic is the first to move. He doesn't look at Noah, just makes an inane comment about how they'd better go soon if they don't want to get caught up in traffic. Kate wants to brain him.

Maddie asks Noah where he'll put his mugs, is there enough space in the cupboard for his clothes, whether he likes his desk. She's dawdling, spinning out the last few minutes with her brother. Kate would do the same, ignore Dominic's mumbles, if it weren't for the fact that she knows Noah needs them to leave. His hands are restless; Kate knows what's going to happen next. She watches as he lifts them to his lips and starts tapping five after frantic five.

Still, Kate can't find the words to say goodbye. She doesn't have to though, because Mr. Bill appears.

"All good, Noah?" he says. "Ready to start unpacking?" Noah nods, and nods again, and Mr. Bill pushes the door open a little wider, a gentle invitation for them to go.

"Bye, Noah." Maddie loops her arms around him. "We'll see you soon, it's not too long." And she's off, speeding away from his room.

Kate touches his arm. "Bye, darling." That's all she can manage. She steps past Mr. Bill, says a hurried thank you, and squeezes past Dominic. She hears him say goodbye and then their son closes the door.

⊕

17 FEBRUARY 2013 / 18:02

Noah's room is hot. The temperature's been rising ever since morning, the beginning of another Cape Town heatwave. He opens the window, but it's even warmer outside. He won't be needing his duvet. He walks back to the bed, rolls it up neatly and tries to put it on the top shelf of his cupboard, but it doesn't fit properly.

He's still alone in his room. The bell will ring for supper at 6 p.m. That's what Mr. Bill told him and that's what Noah is waiting for now.

Noah's room is clean and tidy. The charts on his wall look strange. There are odd gaps. These he will fill, once he learns all the new routines here. But for now he's done all he can. There's nothing left but to wait for the suppertime bell. Then he will make his way to the dining room. But Noah doesn't remember where the dining room is. Follow the crowd, Mr. Bill said. They'll all be going that way.

Noah doesn't like the sound of that. He likes to walk by himself. How else can he time his journey to the dining room? That in itself looks like a problem he is not going to solve easily. And when he gets there—

A shrill noise interrupts this last thought. Noah glances at his clock, which is accurate to the last second. 18:03:42. The supper bell is late. Noah sighs. Is this how it's going to be here? His schedule thrown out by minutes and seconds that will need to be—

And then he hears it. The rumble of feet outside his door, a swell of voices. He has to open his door now, step out into the corridor and follow the herd to the dining room.

Noah wishes he were at home. No surprises there, no confusion outside his bedroom door. No one telling him to make his way to the dining room and find a seat.

Where is he supposed to sit when he gets there? Will there be separate chairs? Will he have to squash himself between people he doesn't know? Noah thinks hard. The dining room. Yes, definitely benches, not chairs. And now, when he gets there, he'll be one of the last to arrive.

He steps out into the corridor. There's only one person there now, a girl with a bright yellow flag of hair. She turns to look at him. "Hey, Noah?"

Noah stops, but only for a second.

"Juliet Ryan," she says. "We're at the same school? I'm in Grade 11."

"Oh, right."

"You don't know who I am?"

Not only does he not recognize her, he can't afford the time for introductions.

Keep moving, Noah. You don't have time for this.

"You're not just being polite?" she asks.

He shakes his head, his feet itching to move.

She laughs. "You must be the only person who doesn't know about the Notorious Juliet Ryan. That's amazing."

Not that amazing, Noah wants to say. He doesn't really notice many people at school. Making it through each day there without losing track is enough of a mission.

He looks at his watch and starts to walk. He'd count his steps if he could, but the girl's still there, still talking.

"My father works for the same firm as yours," she says, "GSG. Goodson, Stander & Groome. Right?"

Noah nods and quickens his pace, but that doesn't stop her. She just skips to keep up.

"My father's Bart Ryan. Middle management, that's him. My mom's Monica. Bart and Monica, good ole Mom and Dad, and their shitty marriage and their mess of a daughter. No doubt Ellen's going to want to know all about them. Ellen Turner. Are you seeing her too?"

Another nod.

"I can't believe we've landed up here together."

She's talking and talking, this girl called Juliet. There's no stopping her. Her words are gushing out, like someone turned on a tap and forgot about it.

⏱

17 FEBRUARY 2013 / 18:07

At home, Noah thinks, as he walks into the dining room, everything would be as it should. His mom, dad and sister would all have eaten. A single place would remain, set specially for him. There would be plenty of space to sit. He could spend a minute or so arranging the table so that his knife, his fork, his glass, the water jug, the serving spoons, the dishes with his food in them were all perfectly aligned. He could stand back from the table and see that all was as it should be before pulling out his chair, sliding into it, and starting to eat.

Here, at Greenhills, it is all wrong. All completely and utterly wrong. His mother hasn't cooked this meal. He does not know what is on the menu.

He stands in the doorway and does a quick check. How many steps from here to the long table where people are eating? Ms. Turner mentioned "group" quite a few times. Is this Noah's group and will he be able to sit in the same place every time? He needs to get his note-book out now and write these questions down. He'll need to update his timetable, remind himself to get to meals a few minutes early, before everyone else arrives.

There's no time today, though. The same girl, Juliet, is nudging him in the back. "Grab a tray, Noah."

So that's the next thing. A stack of trays at one end of a large table. A range of food to choose from. Ham, chicken, salad, coleslaw, cheese, watermelon, yoghurt.

Noah places a plate on his tray and slides 2 circles of ham off a platter, uses the salad servers to take 2 leaves of lettuce, 5 baby toma-toes. Next he helps himself to some coleslaw and a wedge of cheese. Finally, a ¼ slice of watermelon.

Now for the hard part. Juliet's ahead of him. She's making her way to the table, putting down her tray, squeezing herself between 2 boys.

There's 1 space left now. Noah has to perch on the end of the bench next to a large boy who takes up more space than any of the others. He's taller than Noah, sandy haired and freckled, with sloped shoulders and a non-existent neck. He's talking to the girl sitting next to him, long dark hair framing a pale face. Her name is Sadie, Noah learns, and his is Morné.

A boy called Wandile looks up and nods when Noah arrives. Another, a jittery boy grabs Noah's hand and pumps it up and down. "Simon," he says, "please call me Si." Next to please-call-me-Si is a girl in a long-sleeved sweatshirt called Vuyokazi. She's picking at her food—they all are.

These are people Noah is going to spend hours with—he'll see them in group, whatever that is, at mealtimes, and during those yawningly blank spaces on his timetable labelled "unstructured time."

He'll need to examine them more closely, to see if they have preferred seats and if he'll be able to move away from Morné, who takes up too much room. But Noah can't consider details like these now. He's busy aligning his knife and fork on his tray, repositioning a tomato that has rolled too close to the coleslaw, moving the 1/4 circle of watermelon so that it sits in the center of his side plate.

They're all looking at him as he does this, but Noah can't afford to worry about that. If he doesn't set up his place properly, he'll begin to tap. If he begins to tap, he'll need to count, and there's so much to count in this room. He needs to pour himself some water and place his glass directly to the right of his knife. Then he'll take 1 slice of bread from the basket in the middle of the table, butter it and cut it into 5 equal strips.

Tomorrow he'll study the others. For now, he'll be doing well if he makes it to the end of suppertime, the 18:00–19:00 slot on his timetable.

There's not much talk going on, which suits Noah just fine. The heat has slowed everyone down. The ice cubes in the water jug have melted, leaving the water cooled, but not cold. Butter slides from the knife and falls in a soft splat next to the bread on Noah's plate. Now, all he wants is the watermelon, garnet with a green tortoiseshell rind. He picks it up and sinks his teeth into the center. But even the watermelon has succumbed to the temperature and juicy mush fills his mouth.

Juliet looks around the table and grins. "So, who has what?" she asks. "I'm guessing a couple of eating disorders, a dash of depression and/or anxiety, definitely an obsessive compulsive or two, perhaps—"

Shut her out. Don't waste time on her.

There are days when Gabriel cannot remember how long they have been at the old man's house. How many cold nights he has spent huddled on his bed waiting to hear the scuffle-scuffle-tap of the old man's progress down the passage and the click that says his door has closed for the night and it's unlikely they will see him or hear him again until the following morning.

Then the gray light of morning comes and Gabriel's hopping up and down to keep warm and Mum's in the kitchen making breakfast, and Gabriel sees her face and how empty it is. She picks Harry up and hushes her quiet, she brushes back Gabriel's hair and says, Have a lovely day at school, but she doesn't ever call him Gaby Baby and she hardly says anything to Harry but Hush hush hush, as if all she wants is a silent child, a no-noise baby who won't disturb the house.

Can't you keep that child quiet? Gabriel hears the old man say, and his voice is like heavy stones crushing Mum flat and Mum doesn't have a voice big and strong enough to answer him back.

Sometimes Gabriel goes to his little sister and picks her up and rocks her gently until her face breaks into smiles and she laughs and reaches up to pull his hair. Then the old man says, That's just the job for a sissy-boy, looking after babies.

Gabriel doesn't say a word, or even lift his head to look at him, he just lets Harry grab his finger and take it to her mouth and gnaw and gnaw and he feels her hard gums, the small nubs of her teeth pressing down on his finger as she drools and grins.

It's after supper and the light in Noah's new room feels different. Less sunny glare, more warm glow. It touches on the fabric of his easy chair and lets it shine deep blue. It glances off his sisal rug, slate gray, the one he was encouraged to bring to make his room feel more like home. The only problem is, the rug doesn't belong here. Nor do his wall charts, not even the clothes in his cupboard. They should all be at home. That's where they belong, and so does he. Nothing is going to make him feel "settled."

Here, all he can see are lawns, stretching on and on beyond his window, dotted with white benches. He knows what those are for, he's seen mothers and fathers sitting on them with their sons and daughters.

How much talking goes on, though? Is that where he'll have to sit? With his parents and Maddie? Will Ms. Turner observe him from her rooms, watching to see if he is talking? Or "interacting," as she calls it. That's one of the reasons he's here. To learn how to interact with people, to fit them into his life. Not an easy task, not when Noah already has so much to squeeze into the blocks of his day. How much time does she want him to spend doing this interacting? How many people is he supposed to talk to on a daily basis, and for how long? And who will these people be?

Noah is compiling a list for Ms. Turner, for when he sees her at 09:00 on Monday. That's tomorrow, and Noah has hardly had a chance to work anything out. He needs to think about getting to breakfast on time. He needs to allow time to get from one place to another, count his steps as he does, note them down. He's expected to make his way around Greenhills without any guidance about how to adjust to this new world.

"Settling in," says Ms. Turner. But how is he supposed to settle in to a place he doesn't understand when he hardly has time to breathe, let alone plan? "Mr. Bill will tell you everything you need to know, Noah," she told him.

But Mr. Bill isn't here now, is he, Ms. Turner?

Noah makes a decision. He walks to the cupboard and takes out his washbag and his towel (both from the 2nd shelf down, for now). He removes a pair of loose cotton pajama pants (navy) and a pale blue T-shirt from the shelf above. He takes his blue terry cloth robe off the back of his door. It said in the Greenhills brochure that he should bring one and his mom bought it for him specially. He keeps one hand free to open the door (down-up-down-up-down) and then it's 2 steps across the passage and 3 along and he's standing in front of the door that says "Boys' Bathroom" with a picture of a tub with bubbles in blue. When Noah opens the door, there's a row of shower cubicles with blue plastic curtains. There's a row of toilet cubicles and some sinks below a large mirror. Gleaming white tiles and fluorescent strip lighting. No bathtubs.

He hangs his robe, pajama pants, T-shirt and towel on a hook outside the shower. The right order for when he gets out. Then he unzips his washbag, takes out shampoo and liquid soap, and puts them on the small shelf inside the shower. He pulls the handle of the water mixer forward, strips quickly, hangs his clothes on the next hook along, then steps in. Tomorrow he will take off his clothes in his room, loop the towel around his waist and wear his robe. That's probably why they put it on the list.

The water temperature's almost right. He adjusts it towards "Hot" and takes note of the position of the handle.

Noah starts the timer on his waterproof watch.

1. Wet and lather hair: 1 minute.
2. Soap body: 1 minute.
3. Rinse off: 1 minute.

And then—his routine is so messed already—he uses 1 minute extra to stand under the jet of water, feel it needle his shoulders, draining the tension that has been building all day.

4. Towel dry and dress: 3 minutes.
5. Brush teeth: 3 minutes
   Upper teeth: 1½ minutes
   Lower teeth: 1½ minutes

Once he's finished, he'll go back to his room and recalculate bathroom time. Only, on his chart, he will call it "Shower Time."

1 day down at Greenhills. Tomorrow it will all begin properly with Week 1, Day 1. And then there will be 11 weeks and 6 days to go.

II

Noah pulls himself out of his dream. He was running free, no need to count his steps, or his breath, or stop and count again when he made a mistake. He often dreams of running, or balancing, suspended high above a city street, moving nimbly on a wire that dips and sways with the weight of his body but never lets him fall. Below him there are shadows threshing, a wild yowling, but he floats above it, step after perfect step. Nothing fogs his brain or slows his speech or dulls his responses.

His fingers move to his pulse, beats waiting to be counted for 1 minute exactly. As that minute ticks away, his breathing relaxes and his heart slows and the running no longer pushes his body on.

Step by slowly measured step he starts his day, 1st allowing his eyes to open, then checking each corner of his new room. 1 2 3 4 and—a quick glance to the center—5. He sits up slowly, letting the sound of running fall away. He swings his legs to the side of his bed; 1 leg, 2.

Next he forces his body to stand and begin its slow walk around the room. Step by step, he examines his space. If he can count in batches of 5, so much the better. The main thing, the most important thing, is that he counts every object, every article, and that everything is where it should be.

But it's all newly positioned here. If he makes a mistake he will have to begin again, move more deliberately. This is his punishment for carelessness. Starting over, more slowly, more carefully, against the relentless tick of the clock. The slower he goes, the louder it grows, chastizing, hectoring, but if he hurries, he will make a mistake. And then he will have to start again.

A vicious circle. But that's life, Noah. That's life.

His eyes sweep the room one last time. Everything is in its right place (for now), which is just as well because today is Monday, his first proper day at Greenhills and Noah has to speak to Ms. Turner. He thinks of the sheet he filled out last night. "5 Things About Me." It sits on his desk and he picks it up, folds it into 4 and slips it inside his notebook. He doesn't like the way the twice doubled-over sheet distorts the spine. He will have to devise a new system for storing the lists. This is something he can talk to Ms. Turner about.

He still hasn't worked out the distance between her room and his— *Hurry along, Noah. You can't be late.*

"It really is the best place for him. It's what Noah needs."

Maddie's mom sounds like she's trying to convince herself, like she wants someone to pat her on the back and say, There, there, Kate, you did the right thing. Maybe she's waiting for Maddie's dad to get up from his chair, walk over, put his arms around her and say, Don't worry, darling. He's going to be much happier there.

But he doesn't.

He's sitting at the table, his egg in front of him in its porcelain eggcup. The spoon's on the saucer next to it and there's toast in the basket and fruit juice in his glass. Her mom asks if he wants a cup of coffee, but he's staring out the window. He doesn't bring his gaze back to the table to where what's left of his family is sitting. Her mom pours herself a cup of coffee and sips it in silence. She traces a pattern on the wooden grain of the table.

Down the passage, the door to Noah's room is wide open, the bare patches where all his wall charts used to be on full display. No need to knock five times to gain admission, or check the clock to see that it's the right time of day to speak to him. No need to perch on the very end of his bed so as not to wrinkle his duvet.

Just because Maddie hopes that Greenhills might be what Noah needs doesn't mean that she's not going to miss their daily ritual. It's not as if they said much when they were together. Her brother would be at his laptop. He'd swing around in his chair and smile and she'd smile back. No need to talk. Noah never had much news, and nothing in her day touched him. Or interested him, really.

Even so, it was a good place to be, sitting in silence with her brother. Calm silence, not the sort that sits between her parents now, cold and angry and solid.

Maddie pushes back her chair. She bends down and hitches her school bag over her shoulder. "Ready, Dad?"

"What's that? Oh, yes."

"Dom, you haven't eaten your toast, or your egg," her mom says.

Maddie feels a quick stab of sympathy. Her mother poured so much time into Noah. How is she going to readjust, change her patterns, now that he's not here, stressing about getting everything done properly and on time? Waiting to be called to eat—but only after the rest of them have left the room.

Maddie hated not having her brother there at mealtimes, but her dad was more relaxed, not having to watch Noah counting peas, or positioning his glass so that it was exactly in line with the top of his knife.

There's the sound of a car starting and Maddie runs to the door. "Bye, Mom." She stops and looks back, but her mother doesn't even look up.

Kate listens as the car moves down the driveway. She should get up, clear away the breakfast dishes, pour the juice Dominic hasn't drunk down the sink, mash up his egg and toast for Spit and Spot. She hopes he'll find time to eat, sometime during the morning—

Dominic could have eaten his damn egg. Kate picks it up and cradles it, stone cold in her hand. He could have eaten his egg *and* his toast *and* drunk his freshly squeezed orange juice *and* his freshly ground coffee with its hot milk warmed in the microwave seconds before he arrived at the table. And then—Kate's hand tightens around the egg—he could have asked Maddie how she was, he could have asked Kate if she'd managed to sleep. He could have broken the silence surrounding Noah and where he was.

Kate's dressed for her day: blue jeans and a short-sleeved white blouse, low-heeled pumps, makeup expertly applied. She should climb behind the wheel of her car and go to her local Woolies. But she's tired. She didn't sleep well and her makeup doesn't hide the shadows under her eyes. She doesn't feel like being a housewife today. She doesn't want to think about planning a week's worth of meals or choosing a dress for the next office party or making a dental appointment for Maddie. What she really wants to do is talk about leaving Noah at Greenhills and how he looked in his new room.

Kate wants to walk outside and stand on her front lawn and bawl at the sun. She wants the world to hear her scream.

Maddie sits in the car with her school bag on her lap. The moment her dad stops she'll catapult out. She fiddles with the catch of her seatbelt. Two more blocks and they'll be there and she can join the throng of students streaming in through the gates. Without Noah. It feels so strange not to have him at her side.

"Sticks and stones," her mom had said when Maddie first told her about the teasing, how they called out after him: "Nuh-nuh-No-aaah-hh!"

Sticks and stones. Their words were sticks and they were stones and they broke her brother into little pieces and all Maddie wanted was to smack the grins off the girls' faces and bite the boys' hands.

Smack and bite Noah too. Anything to make him fight back. He was so passive, taking their crap, day after day, until the moment he lashed out.

She shoots a quick glance at her dad. He's staring ahead, and she wishes he'd say, "Don't worry, Mads, it'll all come right in the end." But the only sound in the car is the voice on the radio, warning them about a pile-up on the M3.

DAY 1 / 09:08

"Small steps, Noah." Ms. Turner's voice is calm. "Small steps, one day at a time."

Keep those defenses up. You're good at that, building high walls to keep danger out. She is a threat. Don't let her in.

"Small steps," Noah repeats and it's permissible that 2 single-syllable words slip out, because inside his mouth he's eating the other 8. Small steps, small steps, small steps, small steps.

He nods. Steps are what he does.

1. Steps.
2. Counting.
3. Adding.
4. Dividing.
5. Balancing.

And wobbling, trying not to let the walls come tumbling down, trying to keep the Dark from sidling in.

"Fear doesn't come from the outside, Noah. The enemy is inside you."

She's right. He's heard this before. His fears are irrational, a monster isn't waiting to tear his family apart; he can't ward off evil; he doesn't hold the power to keep his family safe. But "rational" and "OCD" do not belong in the same sentence.

And don't forget, Noah. What if...?

The moment those words creep in, Noah's breath quickens. What if he *does* hold the power?

He marshals his thoughts, forces them to make sense. No. He can't ward off evil; he doesn't hold the power to keep his family safe.

His mind sets out to sabotage him, each and every day. He knows this, even through the thick fog in his brain, when his dulled fingers are too tired to tap and he's sitting, slowed and silent, staring at Ms. Turner's mouth and wishing he could arrange her words into sets of 5.

He can't control his thoughts. No one can. But the problem is, if he doesn't keep it all in order, in neat boxes, categorized and subcategorized, there's no telling what might happen, who might get hurt.

He's screwed. Damned if he does, damned if he doesn't, stuck in Greenhills, caught in a thick soup of new rules and new systems.

No matter how often he tells himself otherwise, every day he is away from home the barricades he built there get weaker.

Weaker than you can possibly know.

Noah's thoughts are shadowed; his 5s are hovering, but he can't reach them.

"Now that you're here and the stress of moving is done with, I'll talk to Dr. Lovelock about your medication, see when he thinks we should start to reduce it," Ms. Turner is saying.

He looks at the clock on the wall. Only 10 more minutes, 600 seconds (5x12x10), and he can leave, head back to his new room and lie on his bed and tell his muggy brain that all is okay. Soon the fog will clear and Noah can concentrate on what he has to do to get out and get home. The Dark lifts a fraction. Ms. Turner's going to speak to Dr. Lovelock. A good sign. And she's finished virtually on time.

Noah stands to leave, but Ms. Turner isn't finished.

"Before you go," she says. Noah tenses. All he had to get through was 6 more seconds, but she's saved a bombshell for the very end, just as he was feeling calmer. Not better, but definitely calmer. And now she's running over time.

This Turner woman? She has no clue, does she?

Noah might as well give up. He's never going to keep things in order if people like her are set on disrupting his schedule. He wants to glance at the clock on the wall, look at the time on his watch, but he doesn't. He can't give too much away. She's learned enough already.

Her words are breaking through. "I'll be seeing you every other day, Noah..." and he wonders why she's wasting time, telling him what he already knows, "...and of course there'll be plenty of group sessions where we are hoping you'll share."

Share?

Noah struggles to get her words in order. Maybe then they'll make sense. "The best place to start," Ms. Turner says, "is with your "5 Things" sheets. Have you filled one in yet?"

He has, but there's no way he's getting into that now, not with precious seconds ticking away, stolen from the next block on his timetable. Noah can't even remember where he's supposed to be next, but he's not going to stop and look at his notebook. So, no. No discussion about that, or anything else she might light on to make him later than he already is.

He shakes his head. "Sorry."

"No need." Ms. Turner's standing, finally. "It's easier to work with what you're happy to share. Fill one in for group, just in case. It might help, especially in the first few sessions, until you're more relaxed."

Share?

The Dark is gathering. If Noah opens his mouth, he will breathe it in.

Share?

"Okay," Noah mumbles and "okay" again, when Ms. Turner says, "Just give it a go, Noah."

That is the very last thing you will do.

It's 20 steps down the corridor, 65 to the foyer where Sally-Anne sits, plump and perfumed behind the counter, waving a white hand. "Hi Noah, how are you today?"

But he can't answer. He's too busy turning words into alphabet soup, sprinkling it with lost commas and full stops and apostrophes. Shadows push past his stepping, past his tapping fingers and his touching-tapping walk.

They'll always be here.

Those are the words Noah isn't able to swallow as he lies on his bed and thinks about Ms. Turner and her office and the circle of chairs he saw in the Rec Room ready for group.

"5 Things About Me" says the heading on the sheets, and there even 5 has lost the power to console and protect. Nothing can stop the Dark from spreading.

Things cannot continue like this. You have to find a way to resist.

26 JULY 2011 / 19:31

"We're taking the car," said the smallest of the three men. His voice was calm and carried in the dark. "Don't make any noise. If you do, we'll come back. Take everything you have, start with your children. Understand?"

Kate nodded furiously.

"Good."

The tallest man smiled, his teeth a white slash against his mask, his eyes crystal gray in the dark. He moved around to where Kate and Noah were sitting on the ground. "Not a fokken sound." His breath was stale and meaty, his eyes burning points of light. White teeth, tongue pink against red lips. He jerked his head and the last man stepped forward.

"Eathy now, eathy," he lisped, as he crouched down next to Kate.

He was missing a front tooth. Identification, she thought.

He looked her over from top to toe, his eyes dark and slow. A sweet scent moved around him, covering another rising rank and sour. "You lucky it was uth," he said and the words whistled as his tongue caught on the gap.

They're sitting at the dining-room table and the old man's waving a greasy finger in the air. He's not happy about something, but then, he never is. He doesn't want them in his house. I told you when you left, he's saying to Mum, you and that waste-of-breath son of mine. I told you, I never wanted to see you again. I said if you went, you needn't bother coming back. So why did you?

Mum's head is bowed. She never answers the old man, not unless he demands that she speaks. She reaches inside the sleeve of her jersey and pulls out a handkerchief. Gabriel knows what she's going to do next. She's going to dab at the corner of her mouth, touch the hanky to her swollen lip. The old man watches her. He doesn't smile, but Gabriel knows he is smiling inside.

So why did you come back? His voice is louder now, and Mum's going to have to answer. It's a question he taunts her with regularly and her answer is always the same. We had to. We had nowhere else to go.

After supper, Gabriel goes into the bathroom to brush his teeth. There's a mirror above the sink, mottled with brown spots behind the silver. If he climbs onto the edge of the bath, he can see his head and his shoulders and part of his chest.

Gabriel lifts his arms, and flexes. If he was big, with muscles like Dad's, he could stop anyone with one mighty blow. Even the old man with his strong white teeth and his strong body. Old people are supposed to be weak. Not this one.

DAY 1 / 12:33

Journal's a timetabled slot, after lunch.

Noah takes his pen out of his pocket (in-out-in-out). It's muggy, and his hand is sweaty. He'd like to stretch out on his bed, try to doze, but then he'd have to journal later, and he can't afford any delays.

He stares at the white wall, wipes his hands on the towel he's put on the corner of the desk, folds it and picks up his pen (down-up-down-up).

He doesn't know what to write.

Of course you do.

There's stuff he can't tell anyone, about the Dark, how it looms when he tries to explain his 5s.

Maybe that's where he should start. The things he can't say, instead of all the things he should.

He can't tell anyone

1. What the Dark tells him.
2. How he has to obey it.
3. How it's never the same.
4. How he tries to push it away.
5. About the fear that filled him on the night it arrived.

There you go, Ms. Turner. 5 things about Noah that he can't share with anyone. He caps his pen, puts it back in (out-in-out-in) his pocket. There's still another 10 minutes to go, but that's all for today.

DAY 1 / 13:08

"Hey, Noah."

It's the girl from yesterday. Juliet Ryan.

Noah checks the time. 13:08. 7 minutes more and he'll have to stop and put on the kettle, make tea in his powder-blue Monday mug.

"Do you mind if I..."

She's not really asking, though. She's sliding down the frame of his open door, coming to rest on the floor.

"Open Door Time" it says on the timetable above Noah's desk. According to the information booklet, that's one of the times "residents are encouraged to socialize, spend time getting to know each other."

Now she's propping her feet against the other side. No shoes, Noah notices. Short denim shorts and a skimpy black vest top.

"So, how long are you in for?"

She makes it sound like a prison sentence. Noah checks the calendar on his wall. Another 83 days, he could tell her. He could even give the exact number of hours and minutes, but he stays silent.

Juliet looks up at him from under her fringe and blinks slowly, 1, 2, 3 times.

"I'm here for the duration," she says, "the full three months." She blinks again, 3 times more, and Noah wonders if she's counting.

She's still talking, telling him that her parents are always relieved when they can shunt her off to Greenhills. "My third time," she says. "But this is the longest. Not that my mom notices much. She's pretty much out of it from the time she wakes up until she goes back to bed."

Another blink, and now Juliet is running her tongue back and forth over her upper lip. She leans forward and her top slides off one shoulder to reveal the strap of the sort of bra Maddie wears for gym. She looks over at Noah quickly, but he's looking at his mugs, wondering how he's going to solve the tea-time dilemma.

"My dad couldn't care whether I'm there or not," Juliet continues. "We're one big disappointment to him, my mom, my sister and me."

Too much information, Noah.

She's telling him all this stuff and Noah's not sure why. Plus there's the blinking and lip-licking. Maybe it's some sort of nervous twitch, like when call-me-Si jumps if someone says his name.

He doesn't have time to listen though. He needs to put the kettle on right now. If she stays here much longer...

He stares at his mugs, willing his fingers to keep still.

Juliet's still talking, about her sister now. Lily.

"She's three years younger than me. Just started senior school."

Her voice slows and she looks at Noah, her blue eyes misty. "I wish I was back home," she says. "Keeping an eye on her."

Noah sees Maddie, standing near him, warning people off with her glare. Juliet is a big sister. She looks after Lily, her little sister. With him, it's different. Maddie stands guard over Noah. Something to think about, maybe even tell Ms. Turner, but he seriously doesn't have time to think about it now. If she doesn't leave, he's going to have to have his tea and biscuits while she watches. He can't see any way around it.

Tell her to leave. It's as simple as that.

It's not simple, though. Noah can't be that rude. He'll have to choose the lesser of the two evils. Make tea for just himself, and then maybe she'll take the hint and leave. She doesn't seem to be very good at that though. Taking hints. When people don't answer, it means they don't want to talk, but she's not reading the situation very well.

He gets up, switches on the kettle that Greenhills provides.

"Ooh, tea. Lovely," says Juliet.

Noah shakes his head.

"Oh. Right." Her voice is understanding. "Never mind, dude. I get it. It's not like I haven't met my fair share of OCDs. Seven mugs. Seven days of the week. All color-coded. Light blue all the way through to navy. Right?"

Indigo, Noah wants to say, but he just nods and opens the tin where he keeps the teabags.

"But the water, that's not a problem? I mean you don't measure it or anything?"

He shakes his head again.

"Cool. Give me a sec."

She's gone and Noah feels his shoulders relax.

But not for long.

She's back at his door in seconds. "Crisis averted," she says, handing him a mug with a teabag in it. "Black for me, please. And not too strong."

There's nothing for it. He takes her mug and fills it with boiling water, extracts her teabag quickly.

"Perfect," Juliet says.

A quick dash of milk and Noah's tea is ready. He looks at the biscuits but Juliet's there before him. "Help yourself, Noah. I only like biscuits if I have coffee."

His faces mirrors alarm and she laughs. "Don't worry. I'll bring my own tomorrow."

Tomorrow? She's coming back here again?

Juliet settles back down on the floor and sips. She looks at Noah over the rim of her mug and blinks, more of a flutter, really, a quick movement of her eyelids. "Greenhills isn't too bad, actually. Not as far as places like this go." She blinks again and shifts slightly so that her vest gapes.

Noah doesn't have time for any more of her. It's 13:48. If she doesn't leave soon, he's going to run short of time. He still has to wash his mug, tidy his tea shelf, sort out his desk, check the number of steps to the Rec Room and get there before everyone else does so that he can assess the seating situation.

That's something he can ask this Juliet girl. He clears his throat and she looks up at him, without any fluttering.

"The Rec Room?"

"Yes?"

"The seating?"

Juliet's puzzled for a while and then she smiles. "Oh. Sorry dude. You can't choose where to sit. It's pretty much whoever's last in winds up next to the therapist. Who, as of a short while ago, is our new arrival, Ms. Ellen Turner.

"Actually, we'd better get a move on. I'll see you there." Juliet slurps the last of her tea and leaps to her feet.

Finally. Noah stands too.

"See you there, Noah Groome." She leans into his room and places her mug on his desk. "I'll grab this on my way back, okay?"

Before he can say, "No, not okay, definitely not," she's gone, sauntering down the corridor, leaving her unwashed mug behind her.

13:53. There's time to rinse them quickly in the small sink next to his shelf. He'll place hers next to the kettle, in the front of his mugs.

Noah pushes his chair into his desk, straightens his desk organizer and puts his notebook into his top pocket. He checks the clock again. 13:56. He has 4 minutes to count the steps to the Rec Room and find a seat.

1. Rec—where group meets.
2. Rec—sounds like "wreck."
3. Rec—short for re-creation, where they want to make you over.
4. Recuperate—where they want to you to recover.
5. Recreation—where you play.

Good thing he hasn't been asked to factor relaxation into his new timetable. He couldn't handle that. It'll be bad enough having to head to the Rec Room every day for group. Bad enough having to pick up his mat and walk there for Exercise. Noah couldn't handle much more Rec.

DAY 1 / 14:04

Noah's sitting next to Ms. Turner in one of the chairs that has been pulled to the middle of the Rec Room. The chairs are quite close together, and Noah shifts in his seat. What if things get tense? What if he feels the need to count? He can't guarantee he'll be able to keep the numbers in his head and off his lips. And if they're on his lips, he'll have to tap to keep them there. The thought gets his feet going; small quivers, unnoticeable, unless someone like Ms. Turner's on the lookout for them. He needs to distract himself, calm down before slight fidgets become full-on tapping.

He looks around. 4 males and 4 females. There's Noah (1Male) with Vuyokazi next to him (1Female) and then Morné (2M). Sadie's next to Morné (2F) and Wandile is next (3M), followed by Si (4M). Juliet (3F), sits between Si and Ms. Turner (4F).

The circle could be better organized. Male, female, male, female, male, female, male, female would be good. That would be perfect. Or, for that matter, split it: 4 males on one side, 4 females on the other.

The ceiling fan turns in slow circles, barely cooling the heavy air.

Noah's brain is almost too dulled to think, but he has to. If he could just get a seating plan worked out. Not that he'd expect anyone to follow it, but it would be good to get an idea of how the circle *could* be arranged, even if it's never likely to happen.

You should be working on more important matters.

Noah's hand slips into his pocket, barely moving as he checks his pebbles, once and then a second time. So yes, boys/males/men on one side of the circle, girls/females/women on the other. 180 degrees precisely for both males and females. An organized circle in a large rectangular room.

If they came to group and sat in a logical fashion, then he could turn his attention to the chairs. Ms. Turner told him he'd be welcome in the "circle," but the chairs are a jumble: some are closer to others, some are completely out of alignment.

Noah sighs.

"Noah?" Ms. Turner says.

All heads swivel to look at him and Noah realizes it's because he's made a noise that could count as a contribution. Ms. Turner's obviously eager to make use of it.

He looks down and shakes his head.

"Whenever you're ready, Noah."

Which will be never. Let the woman know.

You aren't supposed to be here, the old man tells Mum over and over, but if he has to put up with her and her little buggers, then they can earn their keep. He fires the woman who has worked for him for years. Gabriel hears her weeping, pleading for the sake of her children, but she's out the door. I want your room cleared, the old man tells her. I want you out the door by this afternoon. Mum can do the cleaning, the old man says, and the cooking and the ironing and this little bugger, the dragonstick prods his back, this little bugger here can help you.

Gabriel has to clean the grate in the kitchen, sweep out the miserable heap of ashes that falls from the small pile of wood the old man allows them to burn in the evening. Outside the sky is gray, the sun a pale disc straining through the clouds. It's raining and everything is damp, everything is cold. Mum drapes a clothes horse with washing and places it near the grudging fire, but nothing dries.

Gabriel has other chores. He has to sweep the kitchen floor, wash the dishes after supper. He has to weed the garden, dig his hands right into the cold ground, the soil compacting under his nails. The old man has shown him how to ease the weeds loose so there's no chance of them shooting up ever again.

Nothing comes free here, you understand, the old man says as Gabriel kneels on the ground. The dragonstick points and points again. That's a weed, he says, and jabs the offending plant, and that one. Make sure you get them all. No point in weeding if one of the little buggers is left behind to spread.

Gabriel also has to feed the hens. They wander the garden, roost in trees, watch him as he arrives with a pail of greens, carrot tops, vegetable peels. Their eyes are beads, their beaks are small and pointed. Gabriel stands in the rain, water running into his eyes, mixing with tears as the hens gather around him. Come rain or shine the hens must be fed, come rain or shine Gabriel has to feed them and collect their eggs. He throws the peels, scatters them as fast as he can, but he's never fast enough to avoid the sharp pecking beaks. Sharp enough to cut through his thick, gray school socks and draw blood.

The hens don't like Gabriel. They don't like the way he creeps into their coops, slides his hands into the damp straw. They don't like it when he steals their eggs and puts them into the plastic bucket the old man has given him.

The rain falls and falls on the tin roof of the old man's house. Sometimes it falls so hard that it's hard to hear Mum when she talks. Her voice is quieter by the day, her eyes darker. There's a small shake to her hands and she walks softly, as if she's afraid to make any more noise than necessary. She hushes Harriet when she cries, whispers to Gabriel when he comes home from school. Now she calls him her Little Man when she smooths his hair back from his forehead, when she leans over his bed and says, Sweet dreams, my Little Man.

Gabriel lies in bed and listens to the rain on the tin roof. The sky is gray when he goes to sleep, the moon can't shine through. It's gray when he wakes up in the morning. Gabriel lies in his bed and listens to the drip-plop-drop of the rain falling into the bucket in the corner of the room. Everything is wet, everything is damp and cold. There are three small, deep holes on the outside of his hand from where the hens have pecked it. He sucks them and draws a little blood.

DAY 3 / 18:07

Noah has already re-packed his small cupboard 3 times. He doesn't have to wear school uniform here, but he's brought his white shirts to make dressing easier. He doesn't know if there's a laundry or if he'll have to do his own washing. So, 10 white shirts hanging. 3 pairs of jeans, each on their own hanger, and all the space taken up.

Shelves next.

5   T-shirts (navy blue, spares until the laundry
     question is addressed)
5   T-shirts (light blue, ref navy blue ones, above)
10 pairs of underpants (5 pale blue, 5 navy)
5   pairs of cotton pajama pants (navy)
5   pairs of shorts (navy)
10 pairs of socks (5 pale blue, 5 navy)
2   pairs of trainers (navy)
1   pair of flipflops (navy blue soles with light blue thongs)
1   pair of slippers (navy blue, sheepskin-lined, stowed at
     the back of the cupboard, too warm for the rising heat).

All of the above would be fine—just enough shelf space—if it weren't for the duvet. He's folded it in ½, and in ½ again, but it still takes up a whole shelf and soon escapes over the edge, so closing the door properly is almost impossible. He takes it out (again) and spreads it over his bed. That looks neater. Hopefully he'll be asleep when he kicks it off during the night and he won't be obliged to get out of bed to fold it neatly and find somewhere to pack it away until the morning. He can't be held responsible for what happens in his sleep.

You're always responsible, Noah. Asleep, awake. You have your duties.

Sorting and resorting, shelving and re-shelving, sitting back to make sure that each pile (of, for example, T-shirts) is as close as possible in height to the pile next to it, that the navy blue on one shelf aligns perfectly with the navy blue above and/or below, that heels of his shoes line up with the bottom edge of the shelving...

When his room is as close as he can get to perfect, for now, he sits at his desk and carries out a check. His wallcharts are squashed together. He doesn't like that, but there's nowhere else to put them.

Nothing is working the way it should. You'll have to start again.

He can't though. He needs to work on his new timetable, see where he can shave off seconds, save minutes. He turns to his desk, to the sheet of paper he has broken down into small squares. At home he'd be able to use his laptop, get it all set out on an Excel spreadsheet. Here, he has to make do with a pencil, ruler, and handwritten notes. More time than he wants to spend, but he can't skimp on this task. It's too important.

At least everything has a place now, so that's something, even if it's not 100 per cent perfect. His bag's fully unpacked...

Noah gets up, goes to his cupboard, reaches to the back, behind his 2 pairs of trainers and his slippers. There's the bag his clothes came in. He unzips it, takes the duvet off the bed, folds it, folds again, squashes it in on itself. Then he reaches for the bag and jams the duvet inside. It puffs out a bit, and he can't quite close the zip, but at least he can push it under his bed, next to his rolled up exercise mat, and out of the way.

Now he can close his cupboard door, and he's gained an extra shelf, which may be a good thing. Who knows when he might need it, given the unpredictability of life at Greenhills?

Gabriel walks past Mr. George Fat's house and hears him cursing in the garden, ferrchrissake, about something. Mrs. Cleans-Her-Windows gives him a big wave and a smile, but Gabriel doesn't stop to listen or to wave back. He's been kept late after school, held in to hear that he and three other children in his class have been chosen to enter a Junior Primary Math Olympiad, and, because Gabriel is usually the quickest to get to the answer, he's been made the chief worker-outer, while another child, one louder and more confident than Gabriel, will deliver the team's answers. So, I'll need you four to stay on after school, learn to work together as a team, the teacher says. But Gabriel can't tell him, No, I can't do that, I have to get home quickly every day to check that Harry and Mum have been safe without me there to look after them.

Gabriel hurries down the muddy path that leads to the front door. The old man comes out of one of the outhouses, dragonstick in hand. Gabriel walks fast, but the old man moves faster. You're late, he says, and Gabriel freezes on the path. Mr. George Fat's head pops up from behind the hedge. Fucksake Gladys, where's my spanner, and he looks over at Gabriel and the old man. The old man pushes Gabriel, but not too hard. Inside, he says. Get inside. He raises a hand in greeting to Mr. George Fat and closes the front door.

Gabriel takes a note to school. It says he cannot participate in the Math Olympiad.

DAY 6 / 12:34

The rings under Noah's eyes are purple, nearly black, his eyes bright in his pale face. It's supposed to be Journal Time, but first Noah has to make sure everything is as it should be. He is standing in the center of his room, four paces in from the door, two in from the wall. And then he turns:

1. Corner.
2. Corner.
3. Corner.
4. Corner...
5. ...and back to the center.

Once more to be sure, and once more again.

Noah does the last two rounds slowly. So far, so good.

For now.

Time to open his journal, pick up his pen (put it down, up-down-up) and write. He has to, otherwise the block that says Journal on his timetable will grow larger and glow whiter and fill him with guilt. A timetable is a sacred thing, even here in Greenhills. Noah has to be able to account for time wasted, minutes left floating and unused.

It's all a challenge here, Noah. You're not up to this. You're safer at home.

That's so true. But for now, Noah has to find something to write. No one will read what he says in his journal, so he can say how tired he is, how his newly balanced meds make him feel scratchy inside, like his skin doesn't fit, how, when he reaches out, he wonders if his hand will land on something solid, or sink right through it.

Home is a strange space without Noah. And now, a week before they visit him for the first time, Kate and Dominic have a meeting with Ms. Turner. "Not too a long session," she says over the phone. "Just to get you up to speed about Noah and how he's doing. It's a good idea for us to have a chat."

Chat. Such an inoffensive word, but for Kate it's loaded.

Ms. Turner has a pleasant face. She is not threatening. Yet Kate finds her so. All that learning, all those ideas bundled into that pretty head, living behind those pretty brown eyes, waiting to be spoken by that wide, generous mouth. All her degrees and qualifications framed and sitting behind glass. Any moment now, she's going to open her mouth and further shatter Kate's world.

The blame will all be on her. She's the one who brought up the children while Dominic worked morning, noon and large parts of the night. To provide for the family, he said, but Kate knew better. What better place than work when you don't want to be at home? What better excuse than the need to provide for your family when you don't want to spend any decent length of time with them? Breakfast-and-sometimes-supper Dad. And over the weekend, when he isn't running or holed up in his study, two-hours-on-a-Saturday and sometimes two-on-a-Sunday Dad.

So the children have always been Kate's responsibility. That's all she's had to do, and without messing it up. The words were never spoken, but they might as well have been, because that's what Kate knows she's done. All she had to do was look after her house and her children and she couldn't even get that right.

Now she's sitting on the comfortable couch, staring at prints, probably from the Kirstenbosch Botanical Gardens, and words are coming out of Ms. Turner's mouth. "OCD never quite goes away," she's saying. "It's a chronic condition that can definitely be managed with the right treatment, but there is always a chance that it might reappear, perhaps in a different form. That's why it's so important that we make the best possible use of this time and teach Noah how to recognize his warning signs and symptoms. It might be necessary for him to return to therapy from time to time."

Dominic tenses. His neck stiffens, his spine straightens. He's ready to go into battle, but Kate can't allow that, not when she has worked so hard, pleaded with Dominic, begged him to come with her to Ms. Turner's rooms for this last session of her day, one that allows him to stay at work as long as possible, one that doesn't interrupt his morning or the early afternoon.

Kate does what she always does. She lays a hand on Dominic's forearm. He looks down blankly, as if some strange, tentacled sea creature has made its way to shore. She keeps it there until his arm relaxes and his shoulders drop. Ms. Turner's voice filters back through.

"I know it's difficult," she's saying, with a smile.

Kate tries to smile back, but she can't.

"And this might seem even more difficult," Ms. Turner's saying, "especially with all that's happened lately, but I have a small exercise for all of you to try."

Dominic tenses up again.

"Sometimes," Ms. Turner says, "it's helpful to remember the good times. The times when you laughed together, as a family, as a couple. Good times with Noah."

The front door of the house is open as Gabriel walks up the path, but there's no light inside. The old man won't let Mum switch on the lights until it's so dark she's tripping over things and falling in the gloom and then he laughs and tells her to stop being so bloody stupid, and turn the lights on, woman.

It's still winter and Gabriel can hear the hens clucking. They're all huddled together, keeping warm, and Gabriel wishes he could do that, crawl into Mum's bed and get warm, because the blanket on his bed is thin and it's getting colder every night.

Maybe the hens are huddled together and clucking softly under their breath because they're also scared of the man, that he might come tap-dragging along the drive and into the yard and whack them all with his stick, whack and whop until feathers fly and they'll never lay another egg in their lives.

There weren't any eggs this morning. Don't ask me, Mum says. She doesn't have a clue. She's still learning, she says, it's different out here in the country. It's not really the country—there are houses close to them, neighbors across the road and everything. But there are no street lights, and at night the darkness is black and deep. Back home there were street lights, outside the house where they all lived with Dad, when Mum's tummy was getting bigger and bigger and Dad used to go up behind her and wrap his arms around her and say, well what d'you think, Gabe, boy or girl, and his hands were big and making circles on Mum's tummy, and Gabriel's toes would curl with happiness because he was going to have a little brother, or a sister. Not so much to play with, Mum says when she tells him, not at first. But I know you'll be a good boy, Gabe, you'll help Mum and Dad look after the baby, won't you?

Back home, eggs arrived in cardboard boxes and when they were empty, Mum let him use them as hills for his plastic soldiers to crawl behind and wait to ambush the enemy on the ridge.

Here, Gabriel has to put his hand into the straw and feel for the eggs—and sometimes they're still warm. Freshly laid, Mum says.

The path up to the house is muddy and Gabriel tries to step on the dry patches because the mud gets thick and sticky on his shoes and it's hard to make them shine the way the old man likes them to. Mum is in the kitchen and when Gabriel walks in she turns her head away. Hello my Little Man.

All he can see is the back of her head and how her hair doesn't shine because there's hardly any light in the kitchen. Gabriel can't see her face, but he knows there's probably a new bruise there.

26 JULY 2011 / 19:34

His mother was crying, Noah could tell by the way her back shuddered against his, but she didn't make a sound. GapTooth still crouched near her, too near. He reached out a dirty hand and stroked her cheek. She flinched and pressed hard into her son's back. He stood then, quickly, and nudged her with his boot. Then he kicked the gap between them, his boot ramming into their backs.

Noah struggled to stay upright. He couldn't fight. He couldn't leave the men bloody and bruised, begging for mercy, whimpering, but he could lean back in with all his might, keep his mother from falling over.

"Enough!" A voice whipped the dark and GapTooth paused, then turned away slowly. Noah watched him walk to a bag in the driveway, take out a set of number plates. Noah strained to see the numbers, but they were hidden in the dark.

"Keys?" said the quiet voice.

"Right here, Boss."

BossMan was small, trim, an almost invisible stripe in the dark. He beeped the remote and the Audi's headlights turned on, blinding Noah and his mother.

Maddie's mom tells her about Ms. Turner's suggestion about the good times.

"She said you should try it too, Mads. And she'll ask Noah to do the same."

"That's such a cool idea, Mom," Maddie says.

Sometimes, when her parents talk about her brother and where he is, it's as if everything about him is difficult and complicated, but it wasn't always.

Maddie remembers sitting in the garden with Noah, making mud pies, hers lumpy and misshapen, Noah's set neatly in rows. She was only four years old, and that's what Noah said to her, "Don't worry, Maddie, you're only little. When you're as old as me, your pies will be much better."

Maddie remembers the mud on her fingers, how it became darker and shinier as Noah added water. He knew just how much, as well. The mud couldn't be too sloppy, nor could it be too dry. When it was just right, Noah dipped his hand in and scooped up a little, rolled it into a ball, then reached behind him for the twig lying ready. A quick flattening and the mud pie lay there, perfectly formed, the same size as the one next to it.

Maddie's brother may not talk much, but he's always there to listen. He's kind and generous. And he was the best mud-pie maker in the world.

Juliet's mother smiles at her from the photo that used to sit on top of the piano. She's young, carefree, her face a wide smile that says, Isn't life wonderful? Or at least that's what Juliet imagines her saying. Or maybe she's saying, Let's have a ball, party the night away. Get me another drink. And another drink and another and another.

It's black and white, but she knows that when her mother was young her hair shone white-gold and her eyes were the same cloudy blue as her daughter's. Her skin was fresh and her cheeks full. She's laughing, her head thrown back on her long neck. There are no wrinkles, no bags under her eyes, no ashen unsteadiness, no fingernails rimmed with dirt because she hasn't had the energy to get up and out of bed and into the shower.

The girl in the photo is a million miles from the woman who calls, "Jules, Jules, could you come here, sweetheart?" The woman who says, "Juliet, darling, the shopping," and smiles weakly when Juliet says, "Sure, Mom," and reaches inside her mother's bag for the keys. The girl in the photo is only a few years older than Juliet is now.

Juliet is fifteen. Too young to drive, too young to shop for a week's worth of groceries, too young to sign for the delivery at the door when the local bottle store drops off a different kind of supplies. There's no sign of her father in the photo on the top of the piano. Juliet wonders whether that laughing young woman even had a clue that she was about to become one part of a couple.

The old man doesn't always use his dragonstick. Some days he walks straight and tall and swings his long arms and draws breath into his lungs and puts his shoulders back. Those are the days when he talks about what life was like when he was young, how his father made him work hard for every penny he paid him, dammit. How there was no such thing as running to parents for help, asking, begging, crying like a baby, always needing a little more. Just this once, please, Father.

I warned him, didn't I?

He waits until Mum nods her head, and then he goes on.

When I say last time, I mean last time. You'd better remember that, boy. Enough is ebloodynough, that's what I said to him. I'm not pouring more good money after bad. And look at me now, wasting more of my hard-earned savings on his little buggers.

And now he's pushing his chair away from the table, walking out of the room, leaving the dragonstick behind him.

Some days he's bent, his hand gripping the dragonhead, knuckles white with effort. He snarls more, snaps more. Gabriel looks forward to those days, feeling a small spurt of happiness when he sees that even a man as hard and strong as this one is can feel pain.

Some days, Gabriel thinks, he simply likes the fear he sees in Gabriel's eyes when the stick hisses close to his leg, likes to see him wince as it nicks the skin of his calf, catches him between his ankles. That's the only time Gabriel ever hears him laughing.

And some nights, the old man tap-drags his way to their room. He cracks the stick across the headboard of Mum's bed, or whacks it into her pillow and Mum startles out of bed to scrub a floor that's already clean, to wipe down picture frames that have gathered dust that only his old-man eyes can see.

Gabriel has learned to keep his eyes closed as the old man shouts, Out of bed, woman. He lies quiet in the dark, waiting for Mum to come back. He waits for her to lean over his bed and say, It's all right, I'm all right. You go back to sleep now.

Some nights Gabriel hears the old man tap-dragging after Mum, hears his voice cracking out more orders, more instructions to Do it right, otherwise we'll just have to go back to square one.

Some nights he leaves the dragonstick behind him, and Gabriel stares into the dragon's eyes. They burn red in the night, but nothing can burn as fiercely as the hatred raging inside Gabriel as he listens to the sound of his mother trying so hard to do it all right.

"He's so OCD, it drives me mad."

Kate hears the words from across the room, and her buttocks clench. It's hard enough coming to these evenings, doing the obligatory-smile-and-ask-polite-questions to people who seldom bother to ask you anything in return.

Monica Ryan is on her sixth Scotch and soon she'll start slurring and Bart Ryan won't stand anywhere near her the whole evening. Not until it's time to gather her up and pour her into the car. In any case, he has other concerns.

Leonie Blake's always ready with a snide comment about another woman's hair, or dress, or weight, or makeup.

Trudi Meyers prefaces every comment with "But Andrew says," as if only her husband's thoughts and opinions carry any weight.

Delia Magnusson has to run every day, burning off calories before she can eat them, smoothing her hands over the black knit dress that rests on the jut of her hip bones.

It's Delia who made the OCD comment. Her gaze flicks over to where Kate is standing, and the eyes of the women she is talking to follow. They've got Kate in their sights and their daggers are razor-sharp.

Delia is winding her way across the room now, her arms extended stick-like for a hug, her cheek turned for a mwah-mwah. "Kate. How are you?"

Kate's face stretches in a smile. "Fine," she says. "And you, Delia?"

"Oh, you know me." Delia's eyes are picky, assessing the price of Kate's dress, her shoes, the diamond bracelet on her wrist.

Yes I do, Kate wants to answer. I know you only too well. You're here for the kill. Because Delia knows, all these smiling women know, that Noah beat up a kid at school, used his "superior strength" to dislocate his elbow.

Delia's eyes have stopped darting. They've settled on Kate's face and she's coming in for the kill.

And here it comes.

Delia glances over to where Trudi and Isolde and Leonie Blake are standing in a little cluster. "How *is* Noah, Kate?"

Kate smiles. "He's fine, thank you, Delia."

"He is? Oh, that's good. Only I heard, correct me if I'm wrong, but I heard he's joined the residential program at Greenhills." Delia's got the knife in now and she's twisting. The others edge closer, keen to catch every word. "You know, the one Monica and Bart's daughter's gone back into."

Everyone knows about Juliet and that this stint in Greenhills is her third. Kate recalls standing silently on the outskirts of a group like this, watching Monica fumble through explanations, Juliet's whereabouts, her expected date of discharge, whether the treatment had worked. How she had clumsily ducked the truth about what was wrong with her daughter, which only led to more speculation once her back was turned and the assembled women could stab at her safely.

"Can *anything* be done to help her?" Delia had asked then. Kate had caught Monica's eye but looked away quickly. That's the way the pack works. You might not be in the inner circle, sharpening tooth and claw with the rest of them, but you don't want to be exiled to the frosty wastes either.

This time it's Kate's turn to be interrogated.

Monica looks sickened by the whole thing, and Kate feels a flash of gratitude. It would be so easy for Monica to look quietly satisfied, but she doesn't. It seems she's the only person who isn't out to get Kate, to pull her down a peg or two, teach her that *no one* is inviolate, no one is safe from a sniping attack. Kate wants to reach out to her and say, Don't worry. I'll get through this, somehow.

Only now, Monica's looking panicked. Her hand is flying to her mouth, and she's spewing. There's vomit all over Trudi's Jimmy Choos but Delia has suffered the worst—it's splattered across the front of her dress. The horde pulls back and away in disgust as Monica mumbles, "Sorry, sorry, sorry."

The bottoms of Leonie Blake's narrow-legged red trousers are dotted with small yellow specks and Kate finds herself wondering if there were egg mayo sandwiches on the buffet table. Surely nothing so pedestrian? Maybe deviled eggs. Chewed and regurgitated like yellow and white confetti.

"Monica. Don't worry." Kate has her by the elbow. "Let's go clean you up."

Bart storms up, his face furious.

Kate puts up a hand to stop him. "Don't," she says. "Don't make this worse."

She steers Monica to the restroom, to the pretty pastels and perfumed air. Delia's gang is already clustered there, talking excitedly, giggling.

"Sorry ladies," Kate says. "Give us a few moments."

"Well—" says Leonie, but Kate freezes her out mid-sentence.

"Do you need to use the loo, Leonie?"

"No, but we—"

"Seriously, Leonie?"

Kate stands silently, holding Monica's arm, willing her to stay upright until the door swings shut behind them. Then she guides her to a chair. Monica slumps forward, her head bent towards her knees.

Kate grabs another chair and wedges it under the door handle. "That'll do for a while," she says.

"Thanks." Monica's voice is thick, tired. "I shouldn't have come, but Bart..."

There's an indignant hum outside the door now.

Monica's staring at herself in the mirror, slowly tucking her lackluster hair behind her ears. "God," she says. "Look at me, Kate." She runs her tongue over her teeth and grimaces. Kate hands her a glass of water.

"I used to get so jealous." Monica sways back in her chair.

"Monica, listen. You have to stand up now. Can you do that?"

"I...I'm not sure. I don't want to go out there. Bart. He's going to kill me."

"You have to. Now listen. We're going to walk straight past everyone. You and me. Dominic will take us home."

"Oh God, Kate. I don't know if I can."

Kate takes one of the rose-embroidered hand towels and drenches it under the tap, wrings it out.

Monica gets to her feet. She stands for a moment then steps forward to join Kate at the sink.

The handle of the door jerks up and down and there's an angry voice. "Monica. Monica, get yourself out here."

Kate grips her hand. "Ignore him."

Monica dabs at her face and then at her dress. Kate opens her evening bag and passes her a wet wipe, a comb and lipstick.

"Thanks, Kate. You're so organized."

Another impatient rattle. This time it's Leonie. "For God's sake, Kate. Enough is enough."

Kate slips her arm through Monica's, feels her draw a deep breath. "Ready?"

"Thanks, Kate," Monica says. "Really, thank you." She looks a little better now, even if the smell of vomit is still hanging over them.

Kate pushes the chair aside and opens the door.

Bart's on the other side, steaming.

Kate smiles at him. "Have you seen Dominic, Bart? I'm going to ask him to take me and Monica home."

"Nonsense!" Bart blusters. "Nonsense."

"Thank you, Kate." Monica turns to Bart. "Stay, Bart." Her eyes scan the small crowd and settle on a lithe young brunette, svelte in a black sheath dress. "I don't want to spoil your evening."

He splutters again, but her back is turned. "Shall we go, Kate?"

Dominic's there now, his face concerned. "Kate? Monica?"

"Hello, darling," Kate says. "Monica and I would like to leave."

"That's fine." Dominic rises to the occasion easily, shepherding the women ahead of him.

"Thank you," Monica says again.

"Don't worry about it, Mon." Kate speaks firmly and clearly. "After all, we Greenhills moms have to stick together."

The small group parts ahead of them and Kate, Monica and Dominic walk out of the hotel, into the warmth of the summer evening.

DAY 7 / 12:42

It's Sunday. On his timetable, it says that, apart from lunch and visiting hours, Saturdays and Sundays at Greenhills are "unstructured." Noah can catch up on chores like cleaning his room or doing his laundry. He can do some of the schoolwork his teachers have sent him. He could do some gardening with Mr. Bill or "socialize with other residents."

Give that a miss for now. Remember what the Turner woman said? Small steps.

That's right. So, for now, Noah will keep to the timetable he's followed for the last 6 days. There's no group, or exercises or handcrafts, but journal time is after lunch and that's what he'll do now, write about his family search, how it started and with it, the need to know, to balance both sides, create stepping stones that would lead him to *who* he is, *why* he is.

Ms. Turner will know about the Family Tree; it's come up in sessions with other therapists so it will be in his file. What she won't know is how much time he's spent on it, how far back his research has taken him. Or not, in the case of his father.

He can tell Ms. Turner, he can even add it to a "5 Things' list. But there are some things he can't share. He's not allowed the words.

His family knows *when* it started, and how. They've seen the rules become more and more complicated, lived with the changes that had to be made. But they don't understand *why* and Noah can never risk trying to explain.

They listened and tried their best to make things easier, to create a space where he was less agitated, less worried.

They watched as he started, stopped, and began again. They could see what was happening, but he was forbidden to share the details, to let them know how he felt.

1. That he had to listen to the commands filling his head, telling him how to count, what to balance, what order to do things in.
2. That he tried and tried to get everything right.
3. That each time he made the smallest mistake, he had to go back to the very beginning.
4. That his heart beat faster as he tried to slow down.
5. That his anxiety grew every second he wasn't holding them all safe.

Even now, as he writes, Noah feels his breathing quicken. He pushes his heels hard into the carpet.

It was no one's fault that he didn't improve; they couldn't do much, because of the rules. He tried, at first, but when he did the Dark descended, full of threat and fear and horror.

So far, Greenhills isn't helping. Every time he makes space to think, to restore order, something changes. Usually it's small, but it's enough to throw everything out. A couple of minutes here, a couple there.

Noah knows what they're doing, and why, but—

They don't understand the dangers like you do.

That's true. And he can't explain any of it.

26 JULY 2011 / 19:36

His mom's fingers reached and Noah's scrabbled back. They couldn't speak. They couldn't see each other, but their hands were locked tight: 10 fingers grasping 10, telling them they were both still fine, both still hanging in there.

"Hurry up. Fucking neighborhood watch'll be round soon. We've got three minutes."

BossMan's eyes darted orange. He stripped off his gloves and flexed his fingers. His hands were small, and barely lighter than the black of his jacket. He clicked a remote on Kate's keyring and the gates opened.

GrayEyes sat in the passenger seat and the door on his side clunked shut. GapTooth packed screwdrivers and number plates into the duffle bag, picked it up, got into the back of the car.

As the engine purred into life, BossMan stared at them, trussed up on the driveway. He checked the rear-view mirror, placed a warning finger on his lips, and then they were gone, the gates sliding closed behind them.

All was dark and all was shadow as Noah and his mother waited to be rescued.

There is a catch, lodged under her sternum, just below her heart. Kate feels it when she breathes in, when the air sighs out of her. At night, as she lies on her back, her hand moves to this strange ache, and she massages it gently. It's just a stitch, she tells herself, an odd sort of stitch, but no matter what she does, it won't go away. It's there when she is walking, showering, driving; it stops her if she turns her head too quickly.

Kate considers going to the physical therapist, to melt the pain out of her body, but this deep hurt is what connects her to Noah.

She stares out of the window to where Spit and Spot lie panting in the shade. Whenever they hear the gate, or the sound of tires on gravel, they look up, ready to bound up to Maddie, expecting Noah to be there to pat them with his large hands and say, "Hey girl, hey boy." Do they feel the same ache, Kate wonders, as they look for Noah and cannot find him? Is it like hers, deep-seated, unmoving, as hard and rough as a rock in her chest.

Dominic's out in the garden again. He could at least have stayed at the table for a while. But when he saw her face, that expression, the one that says, Please Dom, can we talk, he got up and said he needed to see how his new azaleas were doing. He's been nursing them along, keeping the mulch around their shallow roots moist, worried that they'll dry out in the summer heat.

It's not like he hasn't tried to listen when Kate says they need to talk.

But it's the same worries and questions over and over. When he looks at her and says, "Pardon?" and her face takes on that look, Dominic feels something close to rage growing inside him. What does she want him to say? To do? It's not as if talking is going to solve any problems.

The best is to hand Noah over to the experts, they've had success with his sort of disorder, said Ms. Wet-behind-the-ears, almost-young-enough-to-be-his-daughter Turner.

Isn't that enough? He can't delve like Kate does, deep into Noah's life, into their treatment of him, deeper and deeper and deeper. What he actually wants to say is, Kate, enough. We've found him the type of help he needs. It's down to him, not us, now.

Hard and cruel, he knows. But true. He's grateful that his son is no longer in the house, cordoned off behind his self-imposed rules and routines.

Dominic remembers the session they had with Ms. Turner, Kate's gratitude, the way she hung on the therapist's every word. He feels again the spurt of resentment at the suggestion about the "good times" exercise, the way Kate smiled so readily at the idea. Why couldn't she tell the truth? Why couldn't she just say, "Sorry Ms. T, no can do." No, instead she'd nodded her head, beamed and said, "Isn't that a good idea, Dom?"

He had gathered all his love for her into his answer. But even then, his response was grudging. "We'll try."

Dominic ought to rinse his hands at the garden tap, go inside, hug his wife close and say, "Don't worry darling, he'll be fine." But he can't.

If he breaks his silence about this, he might say terrible things. He might say, "I hope they manage to sort him out, Kate. I hope he comes home and all of this weirdness is over."

Maddie's bedroom is her refuge. Her parents respect her privacy—Noah has trained them well in this respect. A closed door is a closed door, if you want to come in, you need to knock.

Not that she has any secrets. If they walked in on her, they'd find her doing her homework or on Facebook with her friends. Or lying on her bed crying silently, like she's doing now, as she remembers waving her brother goodbye. She's filled with too much sadness to keep inside. So she lies on her bed and closes her eyes and lets the tears trickle down the side of her face and onto her pillow. If her mom sees her crying, she'll be filled with concern, worried. She'll try to reassure Maddie, tell her that everything will be all right, that she mustn't worry, that Noah will be fine. They'll all be fine...although it's clear to Maddie that they won't.

Soon she'll have to get up, wash her face, check that her eyes aren't too red. Then she'll find a smile for her parents, a reassurance that their daughter is still okay.

WEEK 2: DAY 8 / 13:16

"They say it's a three-month program, but it's not really."

Noah swivels towards her. "It's not? What do you mean?" He's using his own words, letting his thoughts show. He doesn't have a choice. What Juliet is saying is truly important, and he needs her to carry on.

Juliet shakes her blonde mane. "Don't you get it, Noah? Do the work, and by work I mean the things *they* want you to do, and they'll let you go home. Refuse and they'll say perhaps you need more time."

Noah considers the number of times he's sat mute and closed in Ms. Turner's office. Not so much refusing to talk as not being able to release the information that sets his scales teetering, sees his walls tumbling.

"You've got to do the work if you want to get out of here, Noah."

Mum's telling Gabriel why she chose his name. He never tires of the story, hearing how her voice softens and fills with love as she speaks.

It's a strong name, she tells him. Filled with happiness, joy, and light. The light of heaven, Gabe. As she speaks, Gabriel feels his heart swelling with love. I looked at you, she says, and suddenly my life was filled with meaning.

The kitchen's dark now and she gets to her feet and moves to the switch on the wall. The room flares into light, and there he is, sitting on a chair in the corner, smiling his special smile. The one he keeps just for them, the one that means trouble is coming. How does he manage to move so silently, so quickly? How does he sniff them out so that they can never have time alone? Gabriel's fists clench and the old man catches the movement.

You don't like me, do you? Little boy filled with the light of heaven, you don't much like me.

If Gabriel's name is filled with light, the old man swells with ferocious menace. He looks at Gabriel and smiles again. His teeth are strong; Gabriel has watched him eat, how he attacks his food, picks up a chop and tears off the flesh. He's seen his strong jaws chomping. Everything about him is rugged and hard. His bruising hands, his taut forearms, his still-straight shoulders, the long legs that stride. Gabriel has seen him out in the yard at the back of the house, swinging an axe to split logs. He's old, but he's tough.

Gabriel counts in his mind all the days they've been here. They arrived just before winter, when night came early and the house was cold. Now it's even colder and most nights Gabriel falls asleep shivering. He's been at his new school for nearly a full term and soon it will be time for the long holidays. He won't be able to escape the house. He'll have to be here, day in and day out. He'll have to listen as the man tears into Mum with harsh words, he'll have to leave the room when he is told to and hear the soft-hard sound of fist on flesh. And then, later, he will have to watch as she pretends there is nothing wrong.

Hate swells inside Gabriel, swelling until he feels he will burst. There's a river of hate running through Gabriel, running through the house, lapping at Gabriel's ankles. Lapping at the old man. Gabriel wants to see him drown. He wants to see him flailing, thrashing and scrabbling for shore, the river too strong for him, rushing him along in its current, the old man powerless, unable to swim against it, against the roaring hate that flows through Gabriel.

DAY 9 / 09:21

"May I ask you a few questions, Noah?"

Noah has to be careful around Ms. Turner. She is not to be trusted —all her questions, her desire to have him "open up." "All you need to do is talk, Noah," she tells him.

She is trickery, pure and simple. Do not let your guard down.

He sits mute. Nothing is going to make him open his mouth.

Nothing except Juliet's words.

Careful, now.

Juliet saying—

Careful! Are you even listening?

The Dark hammers in his brain as he recalls her message: Do what *they* want you to do, and they'll let you go home.

That's all Noah wants—to go home.

So...he smiles. He feels it reaching his mouth, makes sure his eyes smile too. He puts all he has into it and then he says, "Yes." His voice is weak, false, but that's another of the things Juliet filled him in on. "Fake it 'til you make it, Noah. It's such a cliché, but they love clichés around here."

Ms. Turner's talking. "Do you like your room, Noah? Are you happy with where everything is?"

"My Family Tree. That was the most important thing." He's following Juliet's advice and telling Ms. Turner he's slowly getting used to seeing his charts up on the wall in his new room.

She nods but doesn't say anything. His other therapists did the same, their way of showing they wanted him to talk some more. The sooner he can open up to Ms. Turner, the quicker he'll get out, so the next words come in a rush.

"The charts, they had to be taken off the wall in my room at home extremely carefully. Some of them had been up there for a long time and the paper was brittle. Maddie and I removed them together.

"Mom was happy about that. She gave Maddie a hug and said, 'Thanks, Mads. I'm so proud of you.' She was proud of me too, for coping with everything so well, all the changes. But she didn't hug me."

"Did you want her to, Noah?"

It's fine to tell Ms. Turner about the Family Tree and his room, but he's not going to tell her how his mom occasionally gives him a quick pat on his back or arm. She thinks he doesn't like being hugged, but he does. It's just, well, there's never time to relax. When he tries, everything grows cold and clammy, and that tongue starts whispering in his ear.

I'll always be here to keep you alert. Never forget that, Noah.

The tension between Maddie's parents pulls tighter every day. It feels like there isn't enough air to breathe when she's in the room with the two of them.

It's a relief when she walks through the school doors and can drop her cheerful mask.

She can make her way to the library and sit there quietly waiting for the first bell to ring. She doesn't have to worry about anyone, especially not Noah. It's good to know that her brother is safe at Greenhills. She doesn't have to look out for him, protect him from the bullies who are drawn to him like a magnet.

That doesn't stop her missing him, though, even the way he organizes her life, the timetables he works out for her, which she tries so hard to stick to for his sake. "Get the studying in first, Mads, that's important. The rest you have to prioritize."

Maddie wishes she could make him do the same. Prioritize, Noah. Stop letting the demands of precision and regulation and the correct order of things control you, leaving you drained, incapable of moving until every task on your list has been perfectly executed.

Greenhills is good for Noah, she knows that, despite all the drama that's taken him away. But still. Maddie hates seeing his room empty, hates him not being there, waiting for her to knock.

DAY 10 / 08:24

Noah looks at his clock.

Time to move, get down to the Rec Room for morning exercises.

He doesn't like this part of the day. It takes up too much time. At home he had his own program, worked out to gain maximum advantage from each set of squats and push-ups, curls and crunches. But this is Greenhills and he has to waste time on Mr. Peterson and his easy, undemanding routines.

"Lift your arms up...up, u-u-u-p, and stretch."

Noah lifts his arms high.

"And...down," Mr. Peterson says, "and u-u-u-p...stretch...and down."

Mr. Peterson needs to up his game. Work each part of the body in the correct order, that's what he should be doing. Functional mobility, HIIT, group muscle exercises (upper and lower body on alternate days) with stretches at the end. That would be better for everyone and then Noah could do some cardio on his own.

"Now then," Mr. Peterson says, "bend. Try to touch your toes."

Morné's next to Noah, bending slowly. There's a small barp, and soon the room is filled with the smell of fresh fart.

Do you have to stand so close to him?

He does. He has to stay in the same place, keep as close to a regular pattern as he can. Counteract the effect of people like Mr. Peterson, who hasn't followed a structured workout in the last 9 days.

"And right leg up, up, u-u-u-p...and stretch...and point your toes... point and point and...Noah, keep that leg up—"

"Keep to a routine," Noah wants to say, but he can't, because if he's going to lift his leg, he's going to do it properly, keep it straight, toes pointed.

"And down," says Mr. Peterson, and Noah's leg floats to the mat.

"And left leg u-u-u-p, u-u-u-p...and stretch. Feel those toes pointing to the wall."

Noah tolerates morning exercise because he must, but now, palms flat on the floor, left leg extended behind as him as high as it can go, he hates them. There's no point in asking Mr. Peterson for a copy of his exercise plan, he'll simply laugh and clap him on the back and say, "Let me worry about that, Noah," just like he's done for the last week.

And now he's telling them to "Breathe in...and out. And in...and out."

Finally, it's time to head back and make adjustments to his personal daily workout. But then Mr. Peterson sneaks in 20 totally unnecessary starfish jumps.

At the door, he has a word of encouragement and praise for each of them as they pass. "Looking good there, champ." He claps Noah on the shoulder.

Noah doesn't like Mr. Peterson's familiarity, he certainly doesn't like his disorganized approach, but he knows not to let it show. All he says in return is, "Yes. Thank you."

⊕

DAY 10 / 13:16

Nothing in Greenhills is reliable. Ms. Turner never sticks to the same format for group, Noah never knows what's going to be on the menu, and just as he thinks he's got his timetable organized, he finds himself having to change it, meet new challenges. Like the one he's working on now. Or rather, he would be if Juliet weren't sitting there again, same place, same time, for the 10th day in a row. The only constant at Greenhills, and the one he could seriously do without.

She's in her usual spot, leaning back against the doorframe, feet propped up opposite. And she's talking. She's been talking non-stop for—he checks again—16 minutes and 40 seconds. And he can't tell her to. Stop, that is. Stop and leave. It's the open-door policy and he hates it.

"So are you cool with being here? Good ole Greenhills, Refuge of the Troubled Teen."

She's always talking like this, as if every noun and verb should be capitalized. Noah's getting used to it. Just like she's obviously getting used to him not answering. Their only real communication is when Noah asks her if she wants tea or coffee. Then she pauses momentarily, passes him her mug, and rattles on, about her mother, her father, her sister, the others in their group, Ellen. Juliet never calls her Ms. Turner. "Small rebellions, Noah. They keep me going." Noah's happy with the more formal approach Greenhills encourages. It allows a degree of distance between him and the therapist.

Juliet's going on about Ms. Turner now, wondering if she has a boyfriend, or girlfriend for that matter. "Or maybe she lives alone. Or has a cat." She's never short on conversation; whatever comes into her head is grist for endless grinding.

Today of all days, Noah could do without her being here.

Stuck to the wall is the list of things he has to do. The regular Greenhills activities fit neatly into their blocks, but 3 words— "Unstructured' and "Open Door'—stare out at him. Ms. Turner wants him to show her how he plans to use his free time. How much time he'll spend studying, how much on personal projects. But she's also thrown him a curveball. She's set him a challenge.

"What I want you to do, Noah," she'd said, "is leave at least one space a day completely blank."

"Blank?" Noah thought she was joking, but no such luck.

"What I mean is "free," Noah. Let's say thirty minutes. Give it a go."

Sessions with Ms. Turner always leave him tapping, but this last one was particularly bad. And now Noah's leaning forward, staring at the timetable he's copied out, yet again, massaging his temples, trying to isolate 30 whole minutes. 30 minutes when he won't know exactly what is going to happen next. Worse, 30 minutes he has to find by shaving precious time from the rest of his day. Time she expects him to simply siphon off into an empty space.

He's already cut 1 minute each off showering and drying, 30 seconds off brushing his teeth, and combing his hair. That's 3 minutes. Where is he supposed to find the other 27?

And, here as always, is Juliet, making things harder, wasting his time. At least she's stopped leaning forward, revealing whatever she's wearing under her top. She only did that for 3 days. She's also stopped the slow blinking thing, and licking her lips. If only she'd stop talking, too. 23 minutes she's been here now. And 32 seconds.

And then it dawns on him. That's more than 20 minutes. That's most of the time Ms. Turner asked him to keep open. If Juliet sticks to this pattern, she will solve his latest challenge! He won't have to steal time from any of his routines. Open door is from 13:00 to 14:00. All Noah has to do is wait for her to arrive.

He looks down at his timetable again. He goes to the block labelled 13:00–13:30 and writes the word Ms. Turner challenged him with. FREE. Who knows, if Juliet stays even longer, or arrives earlier, he'll be able to pencil in even more.

"Why are you smiling?" Juliet asks.

Noah touches the corner of his mouth. There it is, a small smile.

"No reason." He puts his pencil into the circular tube at the back of his desk organizer, places his eraser in the small tray at the front, side by side with the block of yellow Post-its.

The heat catches Dominic's garden in its suffocating grip.

It's a typical Cape Town summer, relieved only by an occasional sprinkle of rain. Puffy clouds rush over the mountain, then slowly evaporate. The sun is merciless and his garden is wilting.

Spit and Spot lie in the shade, then amble indoors and into the kitchen, their long tongues lapping at cool water.

Woody stems crack under his secateurs as Dominic prunes and deadheads, cuts back brittle bark, waiting for his summer garden to bloom bright.

Gabriel finds a large photograph album with a mottled cover. The album is heavy and Gabriel slides it off the bottom shelf and onto the floor. The pages are black and the photographs are slotted into small white triangles of cardboard. There are names under the photos, written in watery white, but Gabriel doesn't recognize any of the people until he gets to one of a little boy wearing long shorts and sturdy shoes. A cloth cap casts a shadow over the top of his face, hiding his eyes. The boy's hands make fists at his sides and his mouth looks like Gabriel feels when he's afraid he's going to cry and show the old man how unhappy he is.

"Edward."

The name has been written beneath the photograph.

Gabriel remembers Dad's other laugh, the loud and not really happy one. Good old Edward, Good old Dad, and Mum saying, But surely he could help us, Joe?

Is this him? Good old Dad? Gabriel can't imagine the old man being a little boy. He turns the next page. Maybe he'll see him again. But there's nothing on the next page or the next. Just near the back, though, there's a bigger photograph. A woman with a soft white face and two chins. She's dressed in a black dress with a white lace collar. Standing next to her is a man with dark hair, his eyes gleaming silver. In front of them are three children, a boy and two girls. Mama, Papa, Edward, Lucy, Abigail, the same writing says. Gabriel bends closer to the photograph. The boy is older here, but his body is still tense, his jaw a hard, angry angle. He stares out as if he would like to rip the camera out of the photographer's hands.

The man with the silver eyes is grasping a cane. It's thin, whippy looking. His large hands cover most of the head but they don't hide its lolling tongue, its fearsome teeth.

Gabriel has learned the word "heirloom." He heard it the first day they moved into this house. No running around mind, the old man's voice, crusty and cross. Don't want you breaking the family china now, do we?

Old plates with blue patterns, silver knives and forks, crystal glasses and bowls. Gabriel has to be careful of them all. They're family heirlooms, Mum says. All of this belongs to your grandfather and his father before him and back and back. One day it will be yours, Gabriel.

Gabriel looks back down at the cane. He doesn't want any heirlooms, thank you. He doesn't want anything that belongs to the old man he refuses to call Grandfather.

There's the sound of footsteps in the passage, thudding on the wooden floor. Gabriel quickly closes the album and slides it back onto the bottom shelf. He'll be in trouble if the old man catches him scrabbling around in his past.

⊕

DAY II / 21:52

It's a 3-month program. Or, to be precise, 12 weeks. 84 steamy, sticky days and for the first 13 days there's no visiting. But in 3 days' time Noah's family will be here to see him.

14.30-16.30. He'll be ready. His meds are working better now, the anxiety's subsiding. He'll be waiting to welcome his mom, his father, his little sister, ward them, build safety around them.

⊕

Dominic's still out in the garden; Kate can hear the hard crunch of the shears from here. He needs to stop now. He won't have time for a shower, but he does need to change his shirt.

"Maddie, it's time to go!" she calls out.

Maddie will be ready. She's been talking about this visit non-stop, meeting Noah in his room, not the Visitors' Lounge where they'd all had tea on the day they'd dropped him off.

"It'll be so good to see him there," she's said, over and over again. "I bet it feels like home to him now."

Kate thinks back to that first day, in his room. How he'd sat upright in the blue armchair and stared out of the window, willing them to leave his strange new space. That was how it had felt, anyway. She'd asked him questions like, "Do you want your rug here, darling?" and "Should I get Dad to hang another corkboard for you?" But she was met with a wall of silence. Not even Maddie could get through to him. Kate had felt a surge of anger so sharp, so violent, that she'd wanted to shake her son and say, "It's not only you. Look at your sister. Can't you see how hard this is for her? Look at *me*. What sort of mother would ever want this? Why should we only feel sorry for you? What about us?" The hurt goes everywhere.

And Dominic? Kate doesn't want to think about how hard it was for him. That's because she's angry with him too.

She opens the window and calls, "Dominic, we need to leave." She doesn't care if Audrey Parfitt is having a nap or that "Sunday afternoons are sacrosanct, so could you please ask the children to keep the noise down, Kate?"

She leans out again, calls even louder. "Dominic!"

If he doesn't get a move on, they'll be late and their son will be pacing up and down, counting steps and watching the seconds tick by on his huge wall clock.

The shears are heavy and Dominic's shoulders ache from holding them above his head to chop away at the bougainvillea. He could have done this yesterday, so why choose to start such a large job less than two hours before visiting time?

He lifts his arm and sniffs. He should shower, get clean and ready to walk in and pat his son on the shoulder and find something to talk about, anything other than the "Condition" squatting dark and depressing in the middle of their lives.

He lowers the shears to the ground. As he turns from the wall his hand snags on a hanging branch. *Shit.* A dark red line scores the back of his wrist. Betadine. He'll have to smear some on, or his hand will get infected. Bougainvillea thorns do that. They carry poison in their curved tips.

"Dominic!"

This is third time she's called him—only now it's a yell, and he glances quickly over to Audrey Parfitt's house. "Nap time, Kate," he says, under his breath. "Careful now." Make too much noise and Audrey will be on the phone. Polite little Audrey with her neat little feet and perfectly pressed clothes, and, of course, her perfectly behaved, perfectly domesticated husband. Even Tigger is being trained to remain silent on a Sunday afternoon after lunch.

Still, he needs to get a move on. They can't be late. Maddie's said this time and again. "It's our first proper visit. He's going to be waiting and I promised him. I promised we'd be on time," her voice louder and more high-pitched than usual. Maddie Sunshine, their happy child who never stresses, never worries.

She even put a reminder on the fridge, pinned there by two magnets:

Noah

Visiting Hours!!!!

Sunday 2.30–4.30 p.m.

Some phrases trigger an instant reaction that twists your gut and tightens your sphincter. "We need to talk," for example—his wife's current favorite, and one of his worst. And now Dominic has another one to add to his list of discomfiting expressions: "Visiting Hours." When he'll need to find something to talk about, for two long and exhausting hours.

Dominic has resorted to making lists of potential topics. In his head at first, and then on paper.

Maddie's school work
The price of petrol
The food at Greenhills
What we had for supper
The state of the nation
The state of the planet
Running
Running away
Another life
Another wife
Another job

And then, of course, fool that he was, he'd left that one on his desk and Kate had come across it and come to him, stony-faced.

He'd laughed it off. "Just me being stupid, Kate. Of course I don't want another wife. Of course I love you, darling." And he does. He just wishes Noah's condition had never entered their lives, carrying poison in its tip.

"Condition." Another word that sends a spasm through him. And, if he's perfectly honest, aversion. The moment he hears the word it fills the room and roots him to the spot.

Worse still, "Noah's Condition." A nightmarish glob that grows larger and darker and more shadowy each time he looks at it. Soon it will fill their house and whump over the walls and into Audrey's garden and under her door and it will smother her, and Docile Domestic David too.

"Dominic!"

Time to get going, otherwise they'll be late and his son will be in a state, a frothing panic, and all two hours of visiting time will be spent trying to calm him down.

He pauses. Perhaps that wouldn't be the worst thing in the world. Settling Noah may be exhausting, but it *is* time consuming. If it takes the best part of an hour, or more, so much the better. Less time to fill, less time to have to "chat."

Dominic is not good at this sort of problem-solving. Give him a column of figures and tell him to make sense of them and he will. Ask him to work out probabilities and possibilities and forecast the future and he can do that too. As long as he has the numbers, he can make them do all sorts of things. His predictions are good. He's one of the best financial analysts in the country. Dominic more than keeps the firm's ship afloat. His skills have helped him become a senior partner, raking in a salary many of his subordinates can only dream about. A good thing too. His son's medical bills are high, and this spell at Greenhills will cost a pretty penny. But there's plenty of money to keep Noah in comfort, in a clinic that offers private rooms; heaven forbid he should ever have to share space with anyone.

Dominic is able to pay for every little thing his family needs. Even for a gardener, for God's sake. But if they had a gardener, where would Dominic escape to when he needs to block out the noise from all the people who demand bits of him, when he needs an excuse to walk out on his wife the moment she says, "We have to talk"?

It's afternoon at Greenhills and the oak trees are doing their job, spreading shade over the white benches where mothers and fathers sit and twist their fingers, looking anxiously towards the double glass doors. What will they be like today? Will they be tense, or excited, manic or deeply sad? Will they sit down and talk or will they hover, stand at a distance, stay silent? These are the questions running through their heads.

There are other trees on another lawn, to the side of the low hedge that borders the driveway. The picture is reversed here. Husbands sit waiting for their wives, children wait for their parents, wives for their husbands, but the watchful expressions are the same on both sides of the hedge. What will visiting hours bring this time?

Nothing is certain at Greenhills on a Sunday afternoon between the hours of 2.30 and 4.30 p.m.

Two hours of hope at the thought that someone is, might be, doing better. Two hours spent trying to find something to say. Anything to fill the gaps left by people who can't speak, no matter how often they have been encouraged to "share."

A breeze drifts across the lawns at Greenhills, cooling faces made moist by the heat. The leaves rustle, sending light whispers through the hedge.

DAY 14 / 14:12

Noah's sitting in the Visitors' Lounge, even though Ms. Turner said he should meet his family in his room. "Entertain them there," she'd said, "maybe make them a cup of tea."

There is a problem with her plan.

His mugs.

He has 1 for each day of the week. He remembers his mother asking if he'd still need that many, his father saying, "For God's sake, Kate. They're just mugs. If he wants them, pack them."

Ms. Turner wants Noah to make his family tea. This means he will have to use 4 mugs. But he doesn't have 4 *Sunday* mugs. And his biscuits? What about them? He does a quick sum. Morning and afternoon, Monday to Saturday, and then tea on Sunday in the Visitors' Lounge. They provide biscuits here on Sundays. The ones in Noah's room are for him: 12 biscuits, 2 a day. Sundays are not a problem. Or haven't been until now.

Mugs and biscuits. What to do?

Ms. Turner's spent time talking about his logistical problems, how to reduce the worries that surround them. "Think it through, Noah. Step by step, and then ask yourself, what's the worst that can happen?"

But you have *thought this through.*

Noah has found a solution that suits everyone. And that's what he'll tell Ms. Turner on Monday.

They can sit and talk, *here* in the Visitors' Lounge. His father can get up and stretch his legs in the garden and not have to talk to him, his mother can look at all the other kids and their parents and share smiles with them and Maddie...Maddie can just be Maddie, and keep them going for the 120 minutes they have to be together.

There's a clinking and clanking along the corridor; it's Amber pushing a tea trolley laden with cups. And 4 plates of biscuits. Enough for everyone. Enough for 2 each, even. The Visitors' Lounge is the place to be. Definitely.

But now Mr. Bill is at his shoulder, touching him. Noah doesn't usually like that, but Mr. Bill's touch is light.

"Come along, Noah," he's saying. "Ms. Turner says you're all meeting in your room today."

Noah steps away from him. "I can't. That's why I'm here, in the Visitors'—"

"Such a nice man." That's what his mother said after they'd had a look round Greenhills. "And he seems to have a knack with Noah." She must be right, because he lets Mr. Bill steer him out of the Visitors' Lounge. Amber smiles at them, and Noah's so surprised to be walking past her that he forgets to count the steps to his door. All he wants is to pull away from Mr. Bill and start again, but he's holding him, just above his elbow.

"Don't worry, Noah. Settle down inside and your family will be here to see you soon. You can show them what you've done with your room."

Noah nods, once, twice, quickly, because he has to get his hand to the door before Mr. Bill does. Down-up-down-up-down with the handle and...open.

There it is. His room, the clock approaching 14:30. He has 7 minutes and 25 seconds to deal with the biscuit/mug problem. He needs to go back to his calculations. Mr. Bill has to leave.

"Thank you," Noah says politely, but Mr. Bill has followed him in. He sits in the chair at Noah's desk, examines the contents of his desk organizer.

Noah needs Mr. Bill to go, to stop messing with his things. The organizer is at an obtuse angle to the edge of his desk, at least 220°. Mr. Bill is up on his feet now and Noah's chair is sitting at a drunken angle. The clock says 14:27. Noah only has 3 minutes left. They'll be here on the dot of 14.30.

"Bye Noah—later, buddy."

He likes it when Mr. Bill calls him buddy, but there's no time for that now.

"Bye, bye, bye."

Noah closes the door and dashes to the desk, pushes the chair right in, as far as it will go, and straightens his desk organizer.

84 seconds to go and you still haven't dealt with the mug problem.

Finally they're at Greenhills. How quiet Maddie's parents are. They've not said a word the entire journey. The air in the car is so thick she can almost taste it.

They drive through the gates at Greenhills, and when they park and get out, they're met by the smell of hot tar. Above that, the scent of grass is sweet in the air; the lawns at Greenhills have just been cut.

Up the wide shallow steps at the entrance, pushing open the doors, breathing in. "A home from home," that's what the NoH brochure says, but Maddie and Noah's home doesn't smell like this.

"Come-on-come-on-come-on-come-*on*." Maddie's galloping down the corridor, heading for the door with the number 8 and under that, on a small card tucked into a neat brass frame, "Noah Groome."

She's racing ahead of her parents, checking her watch, making sure she's not late. "Two-thirty on the dot, Noe," that's what she promised. Almost there, ready to knock five times—rat-tat, rat-tat-tat. She can't have Noah opening the door at two-thirty and seeing no one there. She skids to a stop outside his room and looks at her watch. 2:29:46. She counts down the last few seconds and then raises her hand. Not a second too soon, not a second late. Just as she's finished her Noah knock, he opens the door.

He smiles down at her, that open, wide smile that Maddie loves, and says, "On the dot, Mads. Thanks."

She smiles and moves closer and he allows her to brush his arm.

Kate and Dominic watch their daughter dash ahead. "The sunshine of my life," Dominic used to sing to her when she was small. When did he stop singing, Kate asks herself now. Noah's condition has blanked out the sunshine, the house has become cheerless, smothered in gloom. At least, that's how it feels to her, the failed mother.

And to Dominic too, probably. A man who can't even greet his son, let alone meet his eyes.

When she catches up with Maddie, Noah is still at the door, holding onto the handle like a life raft. He steps back to allow her in. Dominic is still a few meters away. Jesus, Dominic, get in here now. Kate wants to snap out the words, lasso them around his legs and drag him into the room. Snap, like the way he spoke to her two weeks ago. "For God's sake, Kate. They're just mugs." Well, Dominic, this is *just* a room. And this is *just* your son, holding the door open and waiting for you to look at him.

Noah's father slips past him with a mumbled hello and Noah closes the door. Then he leans against it and takes a deep breath.

"I have something important—it's important," he says.

"Yes, darling?"

His mom and his sister look at him, but his father's already on his way over to the window.

He clears his throat and says clearly, "There will be no tea today, and no biscuits either."

There. He had to say that. He had no other choice. In the Visitors' Lounge, they could have had tea. And 1 biscuit. 2 biscuits even. But not here. Not in his room.

Tell that woman. Tell her to think these things through before she gets in her car and drives home on a Friday afternoon.

Kate stands and looks at the door to her son's room. How she wishes she could open it, walk back in, tell Noah she understands his worries about fitting them into his space, sorting out tea and biscuits, having her and Maddie perch on the end of his bed, creasing his sheet.

She wishes she could tell him how sad she is that he couldn't walk out with them to say goodbye, how the moment it was half past four he had leapt to his feet, ushered them out of his room and immediately closed the door.

She watches Dominic striding away, Maddie trailing behind him, casting worried looks over her shoulder.

Kate presses her ear to the door, aching as she hears the scurrying sounds of her son setting his space to rights, erasing any signs that his mother and father and little sister have been there.

The old man is dead. Gabriel's sure of that. The fire has crackled and spat its way into his room, crunched its way through his muscles, burnt his bushy white hair to ashes. It's melted the rough skin of his hands and scorched his horny heels. He's dead now, Gabriel thinks, as he watches the people from Acacia Avenue spilling out of their houses. He's dead and it's not his mother's fault, and nor is it Gabriel's, but who is going to believe him?

Who is going to believe him when he says he smelled the smoke before he saw the fire? That when he woke up his room was hazy and his eyes stung as he opened them. That the smoke wormed its way into his lungs and made him cough. That he followed the smoke down the passage to the kitchen, seeing his feet and hands disappear as the smoke grew thicker. That his mother was standing at the blazing grate, the fire snaking its way around her, and that he saw how it wanted to slither up her legs and feed on her loose-hanging nightgown.

Gabriel. Mum turns to him with a glowing smile. Come, over here darling. It's so much warmer now.

Gabriel's small, and he's quick, and he darts over the snaking flames to his mother's side.

Her voice is bright and happy. I was so cold, Gabe.

I know Mum, I know. Well done, good job.

Gabriel tries to pull her away from the fire, he looks at the kitchen door, standing wide open. All he has to do is edge her towards it, move her away from the roaring grate and the trail of fire.

His mother's hair is sweat-soaked, her face is pink and shiny hot. The fire has reached the curtains now, the dingy red gingham flaring into a terrible brightness. Gabriel hears the window panes crack and then fall out of their frames.

Harry.

He looks around.

Where's Harry, Mum?

Harry? His mother looks at him blankly. Harry's fast asleep. She'll be nice and toasty warm now, Gabe. She was so cold, and so was I.

Gabriel grabs her hand. Mum! He shakes her arm, then shakes it harder, digging his nails into her skin. Mum! I have to get Harry. You have to wait for me outside.

This time his sister's name connects and her eyes widen.

Harry! Mum turns away, panicked.

Okay, Mum, Gabriel soothes. It's okay. You go outside and I'll get Harry.

The path to the door is still clear. His mother nods. I will Gabriel. I will. She edges her way to the door. You get Harriet, darling, and we can all go and sit outside.

Good idea, Mum. Gabriel tugs at her gently and she moves away from the fireplace, away from the fire hurrying along the floor, making its way to the room his mother shares with Harry and Gabe.

Gabriel takes two dishcloths from the sink and holds them under the tap. He drapes one over his head, ties one around his face, over his nose. He's able to breathe better, the air acrid but cooler.

"Terrible-terrible-terrible," Dominic mutters all the way down the steps and into the car and down the road. He stops this refrain every now and again and the silence gathers and then he starts over, under his breath, his lips making the word, moving silently around it, until suddenly it bursts out and the silence is filled with it again. Terrible-terrible-terrible. He sounds just like Noah, with his under-breath droning.

Normally, Maddie's mom's the one to calm him down when he gets into a state, when he starts on about what's happening to taxpayers' money and how the government should be booted out once and for all and how they should just up sticks and go and live on a desert island. Her mom will listen for a bit and then pat his arm or give him a hug and asks if he wants a beer, and should she do roast chicken or mince for supper. Small meaningless questions that pull him down from his irritable high.

But this is different, this mumbling, and her mom is sitting tight-lipped and her knuckles are white. Her left hand's pushing against her door as if she'd like to fling it open, roll out into the road and run.

Her parents are changing into escape artists right in front of Maddie's eyes.

"How could you?" Her mom finally forces the words out when they pull into their driveway. "The whole time we were there, you didn't say one word to him. How could you?"

"Look, Kate," her father's voice is wheedling, filled with apology, "Look—"

"No, *you* look. He's your *son*, Dominic."

"But you know how I hate hospitals, closed-in spaces."

"Oh, please, Dominic. Grow up. How do you think he's coping? Did that thought ever enter your selfish, childish mind?"

Her father isn't childish or selfish. Maddie knows that, and so does her mom, but Noah being at Greenhills has changed the way they talk to each other.

The moment Maddie's dad stops in the driveway, her mom leaps out and runs to the front door. She fumbles her key into the lock and slams that too. Maddie edges along the back seat, closer to the back of her father's head. She wants to smooth his hair, say, "Don't worry, Dad. It'll be fine," but something stops her. She opens the passenger door and slides out quietly. Her dad stays put. He doesn't come into the house until much later, when Maddie's finishing her homework and her mom's calling her for supper.

All he needs is a moment, to get back to being who he is: Dominic Groome, loving husband and father of two, currently residing at 21 Sunbird Drive and a partner in one of the most prestigious investment firms in South Africa. It's going to take him all week to find the parts of him that went flying when they visited Noah and put them back into place, rebuild his carefully constructed self. And then, just as he manages to slot the last piece back where it belongs, it will be time to visit his son again, and it'll be back to square one.

Tonight, though, he just needs to be calm, calm enough to go to his wife and tell her he's sorry, and that of *course* he should have spoken to his son. Agree with her when she says his behavior over the last few weeks has been impossible. And no, of course it's not Noah's fault that he's where he is, and that he doesn't know what comes over him or why he's acting like this.

It's not Kate's fault that he is who he is and it's not Maddie's and it's not Noah's. The son whom he can no longer touch. Not now. Not where he is now. It's his fault. How can a man who was once a boy who was abandoned by his mother and father be anything other than a failure? As a father, a cesspool rather than a gene pool, as a husband, a complete let-down? Dominic's blood is blighted, he's sure of it, and he's passed on his terrible genes and his terrible self to his son.

She should go out and talk to him. Knock on the driver's window, knock and knock until he's forced to turn the ignition and open the window and look at her. Even if he doesn't answer, the very least he can do is meet her eyes.

She doesn't understand any of this. What's happened to her? If she looks back over the months, she sees a life that belonged to another woman. Not her. Not Kate Groome, née Cilliers.

It started to crumble the day she opened Noah's bedroom door and found him bug-eyed and frozen in the center of his gray sisal rug.

"What is it? What is it, Noah?" she'd asked, but he couldn't answer.

It took her a long time to get him to move. "Breathe deeply, Noah, there you go." And she heard him: "in...two, three, four, *five* and out two, three, four, *five* and in...and out two, three, four, *five*..." with a small emphasis on the five.

"I can't—" He stopped. "I can't. I don't know what to do, Mom."

The look he gave her that first time was so piteous that Kate's heart nearly broke in two. Each time after that was harder, each time the crack in her heart deepened.

No, Kate thinks now, nothing's the way it's meant to be. Her son shouldn't be in an institution. Oh, there are other, kinder, nicer words for where he is, but let's get down to basics, shall we, and admit the truth, go for the blunt description.

To add insult to injury—Kate is feeling the injury now, the gasping wound that her life has become—her husband should not be sitting outside in the car, acting like a shell-shock victim, as if he should be in a room that looks like Noah's.

Kate glances at the clock. It's gone half past six, she hasn't started supper and their daughter has school tomorrow.

Should she rustle up something simple like bacon and eggs? Maybe they should get fish and chips—one of Noah's favorites—or pizza, although they've all pretty much gone off that. There's no point asking

Dominic. Her husband isn't talking and her son isn't here to eat fish and chips.

Kate bends over the kitchen sink. Dominic is right. This is terrible, and has been for a very long time.

26 JULY 2011 / 19:39

No cars passed. No headlights beamed up their drive.

What time was it? Kate couldn't tell. The sky was cloudy, no moon, no stars, nothing to indicate how long they'd been there. Dominic would be home soon, though, with Maddie. "Pizzas for supper, I'll collect them," he'd said. That way they get them home quicker, hotter, no need to wait for the delivery guy to bring them, only just warm and starting to get soggy.

Once Dominic and Maddie got home, everything would be better. Once they'd untied them and removed the rags from their mouths and the plastic ties at their wrists, once they could get back inside where everything would be as it should.

Kate tried to speak, choking through the gag. "Ar-ou-ll-righ-No-ah?"

"Mm-ine." His reply was indecipherable but reassuring. *I'm fine.*

Lucky, that was the word in her mind. They were so lucky. Apart from that one blow to his face, they hadn't hurt Noah.

Alive, that was another word. They were both alive. Kate leaned back onto her son's shoulders.

They were alive.

They were lucky.

But she was so cold. Her jacket was in the car, on the back seat.

She started to shake. If it weren't for the gag, her teeth would be chattering. The small movements became larger; a shuddering she couldn't stop.

"M-om, don wo-yy." Noah's hands tightened on hers.

She could hardly make sense of the words, but the sound of his muffled voice helped.

Breathe, she told herself. Breathe.

Alive. Lucky.

$$\oplus$$

The floor is boiling under his bare feet, but Gabriel has to run over it, as fast as he can. Fakirs walk on fire, Dad told him once. His dad was full of useful snippets of information. They move really quickly, Gabe, but don't ask me about the bed of nails thing, haven't a clue how they do that.

The door to Mum's room is open. Gabriel looks back down the dark passage and the flames are behind him, their bright teeth nipping at his heels.

He bends over Harry's crib. His sister's eyes are closed, her cheeks flushed. He places a hand on her chest, feels it rise and fall. Then he plucks her from her cot. Harry wakes with a whimper and Gabriel's saying, Sorry, sorry, Harry. Shhh-shhh, as he covers her face with the damp cloth. He looks behind him. The fire is charging the doorway now; he can't go back down the passage.

The bedroom window is shut tight against the bitter cold. Gabriel's about to push down on the metal catch, but fierce heat is radiating from it and he snatches his hand away.

He looks around. Harry's heavy in his arms, and she's crying now, a low rasping. She shouldn't cry, she shouldn't breathe in more than she has to. She could die from the smoke, it's not just the fire that kills. Dad told him that, too, along with all sorts of other things. Useful information, Gabe, he'd say. Who knows, one of these days it might save your life, and then he'd grin and the wrinkles would squeeze up around his eyes.

Only Dad isn't here now and Gabriel thinks that's because he probably didn't have the right information to save his own life. That's what he's picked up from what the old man has said and why Gabriel's mother can't answer him when she asks her about his dad.

Good-for-nothing piece of shit, the old man says when he talks about his son, but Dad wouldn't be good for nothing now, he'd know exactly what to do.

Noah looks at his watch. 10 more seconds and then it will be time.

Down-up-down-up-down. He opens the door to Ms. Turner's office and there she is, sitting in her comfortable chair, ready with her big wide smile.

"Noah, how was the weekend?"

He can't talk about that yet, he's still checking. Everything seems fine. Nothing has changed since Friday. Nothing that is, except Ms. Turner. She's standing up and pointing to the sofa sitting vacant next to Noah.

"I thought we could sit together today."

He's been practicing what Juliet told him to do, to keep his face deadpan, not to let dismay or frustration or anger show, but really, does she realize what she's asking him to do? Share *his* space with *her*. The space he's become used to in the sessions where she sits in her armchair and he looks over at her.

"I don't—" But she's already there, sitting, patting the cushion next to her.

Anger sparks inside him.

Why doesn't she let you finish a sentence? She's always interrupting, telling you what to think, what to do. It's too much.

Noah has his list in his pocket. He's managed to write 5 things about himself. It's not detailed and it doesn't tell Ms. Turner anything she doesn't already know, but it's a list. He'll even take it to group, because even though Ms. Turner isn't forcing him, he knows that having filled in the sheet will help his case, and that's what he needs.

They have to say Noah is better so he can get out of there.

Kate used to love driving early on a weekend morning, when the roads opened wide, almost deserted. Shifting gears, feeling the car leap forward with a growl. "My rally driver" Dominic called her, and he wasn't wrong. She imagined herself testing her vehicle over difficult terrain, coaxing the best from it, seeing what the massive engine was capable of.

Now the road feels small and tight. Her car is neat and zippy. She can leave it in the underground parking lot and know that it's as safe as any other mid-range car. She misses her Audi, misses the freedom of being behind the wheel and in control. She's surrendered all that to a car that offers less in the way of temptation.

Kate can't remember the last time she laughed. A proper deep laugh—one that came from her belly and wouldn't stop.

The last time she cried? That's a different matter entirely. Kate remembers that and the time before and the time before that. She'll be shopping for groceries and see spears of asparagus and reach for them because Noah loves asparagus, or grapes, or baby tomatoes (arranged on his plate in neat groups of five—food he can count), and then the tears come. She's used to them now, blinks them back fast, always carries tissues with her. But there are times when a blink or a quick dab doesn't work and she abandons her trolley and hurries out of the supermarket. She's learned to leave her car in the deep recesses of the parking lot so she can lean her head against the steering wheel and let the tears rain down.

Kate no longer questions the reasons for their situation. She's given up on that. There are no answers to the riddle and muddle that is her son. Now all she can do is listen to Ms. Turner as she urges her to trust the process. Kate's handed it all over. Let Ms. Turner find a way to understand Noah.

DAY 16 / 12:43

Noah's trying to remember a good time for his journal, like Ms. Turner suggested. Use the time to remember bits and pieces of his life, she said, get used to writing about them, and maybe later, when he's more at ease, he can share some of them in group.

When he was little, some of his best times were lying in bed with his head against Mom's shoulder, watching her turn the pages in his story-books, but only after he had looked carefully at every picture and made sure everything was where it was supposed to be: the red cloak of the little girl who traipses (his mom's voice went all funny when she said that word) down the path into the woods, carrying a basket full of goodies to her long-in-the-tooth gran, the flowers with the round, white petals in the grass next to the bridge, the clippety-clippety-clop of the hooves of the goats as they trip-trip-tropped over it. The huff and the puff and the blow-your-house-down of the wolf and his hot anger as—plop!—he fell into the pot. This was the wolf who wanted to eat the three little piggies, but they used their clever pig brains to make a plan. So, two wolves. One for the pigs and one for the juicy little girl. And then there were the children—Hansel and Gretel, who left a path of crumbs all the way to a witch's house and she invited them for a lovely cup of tea and a slice of gingerbread. There was an apple in the stories, bright red and begging to be bitten into, one small bite, and a young girl lies sleeping forever. There was fi-fi-fo-fum, I smell the blood of an English man, only his mom always said "the blood of a South African."

There were goodies and baddies in *The Children's Treasure Chest of Stories* and they all came alive when his mom gave them special voices, and cuddled him close when things got a bit hair-raising. "Don't worry Noah," she always said, "it all comes right in the end."

And it always did, no matter how wicked the witch, how scary the fi-fi-fo-fuming giant, how bloodthirsty the wolf with the shaggy coat, how sickly green and nasty the troll sitting on a pile of smelly bones under the bridge waiting for the clip-clip-clop and the trip-trip-trop of the Three Billy Goats Gruff.

Somehow, in all sorts of ways, good got the better of evil.

But Noah's not 5 any more. Now he's in a world where everything is dark, everything is dangerous, and safety is never guaranteed.

Every day he checks his lists, ticks the boxes and follows the path, breadcrumb by breadcrumb. And every day the Dark spreads, deepening, blocking out all light.

Vuyo travels with a cushion, which she positions carefully before she sits down to eat or join group. Once she's seated, she reaches into her pocket and pulls out a notebook. It contains column after column of neat figures—just like Noah's, Juliet thinks, only hers records the steps she's tried to take, the time spent sneaking in exercise, all weighed against how many calories she's consumed. She's not allowed to come to morning exercises, but Juliet's seen her lying on her bed, scissoring her legs, cycling in the air. She lifts herself onto the balls of her feet, then relaxes as she waits in line for food, circles her feet under the table while she slices her food into minute mouse-sized pieces. Like Noah, she takes her notebook wherever she goes. She writes in it before meals, and after, stares at the figures written there after her twice-daily weigh-ins.

Vuyo's eyes are drooping, but she sits up straight when Ms. Turner asks if anyone else would like to share.

"Me, I suppose." Her voice is light and breathy. "More weigh-ins. More phone calls from my mother, wanting to know if 'IT' has arrived yet, because, don't you know, the most important thing in her life is whether her daughter will be able to give her grandchildren." Her hands twist as she speaks; their knuckles deceptively large, their skin dry and flaking. "'Not yet,' I tell her. She's not worried about the school work I'm missing, how I don't stand a chance of getting into medicine if my grades aren't right up there. No. It's the babies I might not ever have that are giving her sleepless nights. That's what she said on the phone. I'm giving her sleepless nights."

She shivers and huddles deeper into her denim jacket. It's lined with sheepskin and Juliet feels sweaty just looking at her.

"But hey," Vuyo grins, her teeth large in her stretched mouth, "it's not like I can do much studying anyway. I try, but I'm not remembering much. I used to be able to scan a page and memorize it all. Who knew? Anorexia, the scourge of the photographic memory. Seems food is useful for something after all."

She shifts in her seat and Juliet wonders what it must be like, having bones so close to your skin that it hurts to sit on them.

Vuyo's pen slips from her fingers and Noah bends to retrieve it. She takes it from him, her grip loose.

"I'm writing a lot in my journal." Now her voice carries an angry edge. "I have to, there's nowhere else to talk. I'm so worried about my forum friends. I didn't get a chance to say goodbye to them. They're going to wonder where I am, how I'm doing. And I can't let them know because I don't have any Internet privileges."

Even if you did, you'd be blocked from those sites, Juliet wants to say, but Vuyo's pinched face stops her. Juliet's heard of them, the pro-ana and pro-mia websites, the bloggers and vloggers who post regularly about their progress, the tens of thousands of anorexics and bulimics who belong to them.

Anyway, Vuyo wouldn't have been able to say goodbye to them, when she arrived at Greenhills. She was in a wheelchair, too weak to walk, at risk of being intubated unless she started to eat, started to slowly but steadily put on weight. And she must be. Juliet's heard her weeping after weigh-in, betrayed by the upward-creeping needle on the scale.

26 JULY 2011 / 19:39

"I'm ravenous."

"I'm not surprised."

Dominic has collected Maddie from gym, a late practice. His daughter's been on the go since seven that morning and it's well after her normal supper time.

"Did you remember your lunchbox?"

"Yes," Maddie said. "Good old Mom."

Kate's school lunches were the envy of Maddie's friends, designed to keep a small engine called Maddie running at optimal speed. But the fuel had run low now and the smell of pizza from the back seat was making Maddie's stomach rumble.

"Have a slice, Mads."

"Thanks, Dad."

Maddy's pizza was in the top box. Veggie Deluxe, all the toppings. Maddie leaned back, snagged a napkin, and pulled a slice free. She took a huge bite, then settled back happily.

"Better?" Dominic glanced over at her.

"Mmmm."

Dominic indicated, then slowed, ready to turn left. He beeped the remote and the gates opened. There was something—

"Dad! Stop!" Maddie fumbled with her seatbelt.

"Maddie! Wait!" Dominic didn't know what had happened, all he knew was that his daughter had to stay in the car. "Don't move."

Dominic got out and closed his door as quietly as he could. He stood still, eyes straining in the darkness. Then he heard muffled noises coming from a strange mass on the driveway. Suddenly it dawned on him.

"Kate? Noah?"

Kate was shaking, screaming through the ball of cloth in her mouth.

Noah was silent, his head hanging.

Dominic ran to them, knelt, his fingers fumbling with the tight knot at the back of Kate's head. It was impossible to loosen.

Scissors, he needed scissors

He looked at the house and then at his wife.

"Kate, are they gone?"

Kate's chest was heaving. She swallowed, looked at her husband and nodded.

Dominic turned to signal to Maddie but before he knew it, she was out of the car and at his side, keening. "Mom, Mom. Noah."

"Maddie, Mom and Noah aren't hurt. Do you understand? They aren't hurt."

Kate and Noah nodded.

"Maddie." Dominic said, until his daughter tore her eyes away from them. "I need you to stay right here. Will you do that?"

Maddie started scrabbling at the knots in the plastic rope and Dominic put his hand over hers. "Easy Maddie. Easy. I'm going into the house to get some scissors."

"No, Dad! What if—"

Dominic's voice was soothing. "They're gone, Maddie. Let's stay calm and help Mom and Noah."

2012

At the beginning of his Grade 11 year, Noah told Maddie and his mom about the exams that year and the following one and what they all meant.

"I need to do well in these if I want to get provisional acceptance into Engineering," he said. "They look at your Grade 11 results, then your mock exams in Grade 12. And obviously how you do in your finals. But they've made lots of decisions by then. Places have been allocated. So the sooner I get a head start, the better."

And from then on, it seemed like Noah did nothing but study. Closeted away behind his bedroom door, nose in his books. At first, all he stuck up above his desk was a study timetable, with colored blocks identifying specific subjects. Advanced Program English and Math, Physical Science, English, Afrikaans, Engineering, Information Technology.

He'd appear at supper pale-faced, his hair spiky, his eyes tired, and slump into his chair.

Kate began to worry. "I know these exams are important, darling," she said one evening, "but you look exhausted. Are you sure you're not overdoing it?" She placed a casserole dish on the table carefully, as if the oven gloves holding it had turned to tissue.

He nodded, looking so tired Maddie wanted to get a pillow and let him put his head down on the table and sleep until the circles under his eyes faded and her brother looked like he did before.

Noah leaned forward and repositioned the spoon that had been knocked out of place when their mom put the dish down. "One, two, three, four, five." The numbers were scarcely a murmur. He ran his fingers through his hair, then patted the spoons as if they'd done a good job.

But Maddie had heard him, and after that they were everywhere, as if by naming them softly he'd allowed the numbers out of his head and into theirs. She heard her brother counting his steps under his breath as they walked to the car in the morning. More and more, she noticed him taking a notebook out of his pocket, jotting things down. What time they left the house, when they arrived at the school, the number of steps it took to get to the school doors.

He started writing lists and doing sums, plotting his day as soon as he woke up. Each time Maddie went into his room, the wall above his desk held more and more detail: charts, lists, timetables broken down into an ever-growing number of differently colored squares, all constantly adjusted and readjusted. Asterisks followed by small notes at first, and then ones that grew longer and longer, until he had virtually written an essay on each action of his day. A purple block recorded exactly how many seconds it took him to brush his teeth, whether the food he had eaten affected the time, the degree to which this impacted on the time he had in his day, so that tooth brushing after spaghetti and meat sauce cost him one minute twenty-three seconds more than vegetable soup, but one minute and forty-nine seconds less than lamb chops (flossing = extra seconds).

His activities crept off the main chart and onto separate sheets of paper. Dressing (a bright yellow block), broken down into the separate parts of his school uniform, including shoes, changing out of school uniform and into cotton pajama pants (in summer) or tracksuit pants and sweatshirt (in winter). School tie—never undone. Where to place clothing for maximum efficiency.

Meals (a pale green block), whittling down the time spent at the table, bolting his food so that he could get back to his room to study.

But he wasn't studying. Instead, he was breaking his week down into days and hours and minutes and seconds, counting one thing off against another, rushing out of the schoolyard and mumbling his way into the car, counting faster and faster and louder and louder. And then he was home and pushing the gate open and running up the path and Spit and Spot were racing to meet him, but he only had time to give them each a cursory pat on the head. Maddie wondered when that too would find a place on his walls, when he'd stop fondling their ears and saying, "Hello boy, hello girl." Just like he'd stopped saying, "Hi, Mads!" to her in the morning. Now, he was too busy looking at his watch, tapping his foot and telling her they had fifty-seven (or forty-two, or twenty-six) seconds to make up.

The tapping. That was another thing. He tapped his left foot in sets of five and then it was both feet and soon it was both hands and both feet. Then he started tapping his face, his upper arms, his thighs as well. At school, she saw him running his hand along the walls, stopping at each corner to tap five times. Sometimes, he'd turn back, walk the passage again, tap at the corner and then move on.

If he actually made it to class—and sometimes he didn't now—he'd fret his way through lessons, checking his watch against the classroom clock and the bell. He'd tell teachers if they went over the period, again right down to the second, complain at the office that the bell wasn't ringing on time. Maddie wasn't there to see that, but she heard about it often enough. His classmates laughing about Nuh-nuh-Noah Groome and how weird he'd become. Because of her need to defend him, protect him, and because of the fights she got into as a result, people started avoiding her too. Only her very best friends stuck by her; for the rest she was Nuh-nuh-Noah's sister.

Mad Maddie and Nuh-nuh-Noah, the crazy dude who counted every step he took, every word he spoke, every minute of his day.

When Maddie told her mom about it all, Kate sighed and told her not to worry. "It will come right once the exams are over, you'll see."

But it didn't. It didn't come right at all. Because A+ student Noah Groome barely scraped through his Grade 11 exams.

DAY 17 / 12:38

Whenever Noah thinks about the way things spiralled out of control in Grade 11 he has to fight to keep his body still.

What happened before that? Why not take a quick look at those memories?

Noah's not going to stop writing, he's not going to be forced to go back to where it all started. Not now. He'll get to the end of Journal

Time, keep writing, no matter how sharply words dig into him.

He has to trust Ms. Turner when she says that what he writes in this journal is private; she won't read it, no one will.

"Things are going to be confusing for a while, Noah. I'm going to be asking you to shift habits, try different patterns, be a bit looser. It's going to be tough. But you'll have your journal, and you can write in it whenever you want to. Sometimes the clutter in our heads makes more sense if we can put it down on paper. Get it all out and into order."

She smiled and he knew she'd used that last word deliberately—sort of like a carrot to get him writing. But he didn't mind. She knew that he knew, so it wasn't like she was trying to trick him.

He'd like to write how he feels about visiting hours. But instead of words about his family and how his father hardly looks at him these days, he finds himself remembering more about the beginning of the timetabling, when he moved from being neat, orderly and sort-of quirky and became a freak ruled by time.

Noah stops. Listens.

Not a word, not a sound, nothing gloomy and forbidding gathering.

An added bonus. Writing keeps the Dark out, quietens the voice that's always telling him what to do. If it means that he'll get some peace, he's good with that.

26 JULY 2011 / 19:43

Very gently, Maddie's dad slid a scissor blade between Kate's right cheek and the cloth holding the gag in place. He did the same for Noah, flinching as he saw his son's black eye. He cut through the plastic ties at their wrists and ankles and snipped into the plastic washing line. The moment they were both free and stumbling to their feet, her dad gathered his wife into his arms.

"Kate, are you all right? Did they—"

"No, they didn't." She sobbed, huge sobs. "No, no, nothing like that."

"I'm sorry Mom, sorry Dad."

"Noah? What on earth—"

126

"I should have stopped them."

"Darling." Maddie's mom held her son tight, rocking him back and forth. "They had guns, Noah."

"Guns?" Maddie's voice was shaky. She'd heard all this before—from friends who'd had friends who'd been hijacked; from Miss Godwin, a teacher at school who was held up at gunpoint outside her home just the week before; from the news every night and sometimes in the mornings in her dad's car. "They had *guns*?" Maddie burst into tears.

Every day, people are held up, their cars stolen, their lives stolen. The stats are on the news and in the newspapers, and now crime is here, in their driveway.

The Groomes have become part of a national statistic.

Day 18 / 14:17

"When-I-was-little, I had stomach aches when I had to do something in-front-of-other people." Simon's reading from his "5 Things" list, the words coming out in spurts. "Just thinking about it made-me-sick, my heart would beat-really-quickly and I couldn't breathe. If Mom said people were-were coming-to-our-house, I'd feel a headache, a weird sort of pressure-in-my-head and I'd get dizzy, room spinning like it-would-never-stop. All I wanted was to stay-in-my-room, never-come-out. I still want to do that." Simon smiles wryly and for a moment he looks his age, not ten years older.

""That's not an option, Simon. It's-simply-not-an option." That's what Mom says. And Gran—" he stops. "Gran says, 'Get-that-boy-to-a-doctor-Ingrid-my-bet-is-constipation.'"

"You're kidding, right?" Juliet's voice is amazed.

"No." Another small deprecating smile. He clears his throat again and looks at his list. "Okay. Last-thing. My body still reacts the-same-way, only now I-can-add depression and panic attacks-to-the-list."

He looks over to Ms. Turner. "Is-that, is-that enough? You said to try reading out five-things about how-my-body-feels. And why."

"It's not a freaking test, man," Morné says. Sadie sniggers.

Simon sits further back and folds his list into ever-tighter squares.

Ms. Turner leans forward and manages to catch his eye. "You might want to file that, Simon," she says. "Put the date on it. It's the first thing you've read out in group. Thank you." She gives him a huge smile and he ducks his head, his cheeks flaming.

"Right then. Does anyone else want to say something?"

Noah's hand is in his pocket, pebbles slipping through his fingers. It's time.

Oh no, it's not. It is absolutely not *time.*

But if he doesn't start now, he never will. He takes a deep breath, raises his hand. He's got his lists. He's not using the sheets any more, he's writing them out in the back of his current notebook.

And now he's ready to share, but he's going to be careful. He won't give anything away. It's taken him a while to decide what to say; he's going to have to adjust his timetable to make up for minutes lost (43, to be precise), but it's been worth it. He's making an effort, following Juliet's advice, and so Ms. Turner will see that he's prepared to try. On top of that, he's volunteered to speak.

"Noah?" She sounds surprised, but she wasn't in his room, feeling sick, heart hammering, when Juliet told him about The Work. It's got capitals now. "Do The Work if you want to get out of here on time."

He doesn't *want* to get out of here. He *has* to.

He flicks to the back of his notebook and clears his throat.

"Interesting facts."

Noah reads his heading and then he pauses.

"1. The English language has 5 vowel sounds."

Everyone looks at Ms. Turner.

"That's not—" Sadie's objecting, but Ms. Turner holds up a hand. "Let's not worry too much about that. Let Noah finish."

She nods at him and he clears his throat.

"2. 5 lines hold music in place, ref. also pentatonic scale."

Ms. Turner smiles and nods again, so he continues.

"3. Olympians are linked by 5 circles, each representing a continent of the world."

Sadie's nudging Morné, but he ignores her.

"4. A pentagon has 5 sides."

He throws more information in without saying anything signifi-cant—just facts. "The Castle of Good Hope in Cape Town is a star fort, containing a pentagon inside its outer walls." Don't you see, he wants to add, 5 inside 5, but he doesn't, just like he doesn't tell them any more than he has to about...

"5. Pentamerous symmetry. This is seen in echinoderms
    like sea urchins and starfish. Radial symmetry divides
    their bodies into 5 equal parts."

He tells them that if starfish lose one limb they can grow another. He doesn't elaborate on how long that takes, or that he wishes he had that ability.

He closes his eyes, feels the comfort of the pebbles in his pocket.

"Thank you, Noah. I'm so glad you've shared one of your lists. Have you written others?"

Of course you have, and she knows it. Very devious.

Ms. Turner's not trying to be sneaky, however. "Encouraging" is a better word. "When you're ready to share again, we'd all love to hear. Right?" She looks around the small circle—well, not quite a circle, but Noah's not going there now—and everyone nods. Juliet smiles and gives him a thumbs up; Simon looks relieved that the spotlight's off him.

Greenhills sends every parent written reports, and Noah's pretty sure Dr. Lovelock gets them too. "Noah has shown a marked willing-ness to participate in group sessions." That's what he wants Ms. Turner to write in his next one. And he hopes she'll have more words of praise to add. For today, though, he's done enough. Now he just has to con-centrate on keeping his fingers still, at least until the end of group.

"It's not fair," Sadie whines. Morné nods in agreement. "He didn't say things about *him*, Ms. Turner. What's the point, if he doesn't do things properly?"

If she only knew. You have told them an enormous amount. This Sadie is not good at picking up clues.

That's right. Behind every fact Noah has recited to the group, there's much more. Looking up words. Weighing one word against another. Balancing the strength carried in, say, pentacle...

He stops on that thought.

Quite right. Never give away more than you have to.

Juliet wonders about Morné. What brought him to Greenhills? If Juliet's world is held in delicate balance, what is Morné's like? What expectations and disappointments have shaped him into a boy so mountainous and round? Morné doesn't let much slip in group. He settles himself on a chair, always next to Sadie, where he's quick with mumbled asides that make her laugh. What a pair.

Vuyokazi's regular seat is on Morné's other side. What's it like for the two of them to sit so close to each other? They could give each other tips. How to binge; how to purge. Does Morné count calories? Juliet's never seen him do it, but he's quick and clever. Maybe he keeps track in his head.

Morné's never on time for exercises. He slouches in late, shuffles to the back of the Rec Room, mutters under his breath as he sweats his way through the class.

He's clever, though. He talks in group, contributes, but never in a way that says anything about him. He'll bring up topics that get them all talking: the quality of food, why they have to have lights out at ten, isn't there something more interesting to do in art therapy, whether it's possible to get a doctor's note to be excused from exercises. After a good fifteen minutes spent discussing his "issues," he's off the hook for a couple of sessions.

The thing is, in other groups this might have worked, but Ellen's pretty switched on. Juliet knows exactly what he's doing, deflecting like crazy so he doesn't have to talk about himself. Will he be able to keep it up, though? Something has to crack soon, or someone.

Gabriel looks at the bed, at the thin blanket wrinkled across it, the flimsy pillow. He's searching with his eyes, every nook, every cranny, every corner. And then he sees it, hiding in the dark, tucked into the corner near his mother's bed, its sharp teeth bared, its glassy eyes staring. The long flick of its body leans against the wall. Gabriel thinks of Mum standing in the kitchen, her legs, naked from the knee down, the reddish-purple stripes he's grown used to seeing. There's a smudge of blood on the crumpled sheet and a grin on the dragon's carved face.

Gabriel puts Harry down against the wall near the window and she screams and coughs and screams, pulling hot air into her tiny lungs. Gabriel's a Fakir now, springing across burning planks. He leaps over to the bed and grabs the cane by its spitting head and jumps back to the window with its large grimy pane. He swings that dragonstick back and over his shoulder the way Dad showed him when Gabriel got a set of miniature golf clubs for his seventh birthday and Dad told him how to stand and lift the golf club back and over his shoulder and keep his legs slightly apart.

Gabriel still has time, still has a moment or two before the fire runs at him. It's at the bed now, grabbing the worn blanket and tossing it flaming into the air before settling down to the serious work of destroying the mattress. *Useful information can save your life*, Gabriel remembers, like how to stand and how to swing. He steadies himself on his feet and then brings the cane and its club-like head forward and gives the glass a mighty thwack, as mighty as a nine-year-old boy can muster, and it breaks wide open.

What Gabriel's Dad forgot to tell him, what Gabriel doesn't know, is how hungry fire is for air, how it leaps forward to gulp it into its growling stomach. As the freezing air enters the room, the flames behind him jump closer. No time to spare now. The flames have gathered strength, they're seeking something juicier, something altogether more appetizing than a musty foam mattress. Gabriel's lungs are burning. Harry has stopped crying.

Gabriel strips off the old jersey he wears over his pajamas and wraps it around his hand. He bashes at the shards of glass that are left, swipes at them with the dragon's head and then with the tip of the cane.

He grabs Harry and leans over the windowsill. It's not far, but he can't climb out carrying his sister. He leans out as far as he dares and lets her fall, hears her mewling cry as she lands. Then Gabriel scrambles over, the jagged teeth of glass scraping his skin, the dragon smoking on the floor behind him, the glass beads of its eyes glowing.

Gabriel gathers Harry into his arms and runs around the side of the house. Mum is standing at the kitchen door, holding a metal can. He recognizes it at once. It's the petrol container the old man uses to start the ancient lawnmower he keeps in the garden shed.

We must remember this, my Little Man, Mum tells him. It really is the best way to get a good blaze going.

When Kate and Dominic got married, they decided to buy a house. Dom's apartment was adequate, but it didn't feel like home. It was utilitarian, designed for one person; a lock up and go, somewhere to return after a long day's work. Kate's flat, all she could afford on her salary, added new meaning to the word "small," and she shared it with a friend. Too small to swing a mouse, never mind a cat. Dominic filled the lounge, he could hardly find space to get out of bed in the morning.

They wanted a house with more than one bedroom, two bathrooms, a garden, maybe even a pool. They were an estate agent's dream. Plenty of money to spend, no set idea of where they wanted to live, but the more the agent showed them houses in the narrow streets of the southern suburbs, the more Kate realized she wanted space to breathe. They might have to commute into the city, but that was a small price to pay for the chance to feel the sea air, have a view of the mountain, walk on the beach, swim in the mornings, run up mountain paths.

And so they began a new search, one that took them along the M3 and over Ou Kaapse Weg, to Muizenberg, Harbiton, Simonstown and beyond.

They found the house just outside Harbiton, along a gentle road up the mountain, and then up a long drive. The house was simple, a broad, deep stoep that looked out over the bay, a pool just in front of it, large airy bedrooms, an open-plan sitting room, kitchen and dining room.

"The rooms breathe," Kate said.

That was true, it felt as though the air blowing down from the mountains flowed through the rooms.

The house was single-storey, with high ceilings and shuttered windows. The walls were a garish medley of colors, but Kate saw past them to a cool off-white, to jeweled rugs and squishy sofas, to a large bed with a cream quilt.

"Shall I show you around?" the agent asked and Kate nodded.

Dominic didn't move. He stood looking out over the bay to the smudged silhouette of the Hottentots Holland Mountains.

Kate followed the agent from room to room, mentally stripping each of its furniture, picturing herself and Dom sitting on the stoep, having breakfast.

It didn't take long to get the house sorted out. Dominic mobilized a team of builders and painters, plumbers and tilers, and before you could say, "The House that Dom Built," everything was ready.

The day they came back from their honeymoon, Kate and Dominic drove along Main Road, and just past Harbiton. At Sunbird Drive they turned right and along to number 21. Mr. and Mrs. Groome—ready to start life in their new home.

Dominic stopped at the door (newly installed, its woodwork gleaming) and took two keys from his pocket. "One for you," he pressed it into Kate's hand, "and one for me."

Before they opened it, he turned her gently so that they were both looking out over the bay. It was a late winter afternoon and as they stood there, the air chilly on their cheeks, a light flicked on across the water and then another and another. Soon a chain of brightness rimmed the bay, glinting orange in the gathering dusk.

Gabriel looks over his mother's shoulder to where the kitchen is a leaping square of orange and gold.

He takes the can out of her hands. It's light, no liquid sloshing. But still, it's evidence. If he throws it into the flames they will find it and then the old man will know how the fire started and there will only be two people for him to point his bony finger at.

He shifts Harry into his mother's arms and then he's off, cannister in hand, sprinting across the garden, the grass frosty and sharp-tipped under his bare feet. The lane is lined with houses, all on large plots, just like the old man's, all with outhouses and stables and country-living kind of buildings.

Somewhere there he'll find a place to tuck the can away, hide it in the clutter of a garden shed.

Only as he reaches the verge, ready to head for the house at the end of the lane, does a thought stop him, dead in his tracks.

The old man.

Gabriel has saved his mother and he's saved Harry, but he didn't once think of saving the old man.

In the distance he hears the wail of the sirens and across the road he sees Mr. Fat and Mrs. Thin coming out and Mr. Fat's looking down the road to where the lights are flashing.

Gabriel melts into the darkness, he steps as soft as a shadow, breathing lightly, trying his hardest not to cough.

He's carrying the can in his scraped hands and he'll hide it, in the clutter of someone's garden shed.

DAY 19 / 04:13

Running feet on a cinder track. Noah shifts, his legs quivering under his sheet. He's doing laps and each time he crosses the 400-meter mark the stopwatch clicks and his speed is recorded on the brightly lit board. He pushes himself on, further and faster and longer. He stops, eases the stitch in his side, gasping, pulling air into his aching lungs. And then the clock clicks, the numbers grow and he sets off again, try-ing to keep up the pace.

Tick-tock, Noah. Tick-tock. You cannot afford to lose a second.

He will never tell Ms. Turner about this clock. If he does, she will keep prodding, trying to find out what it means. She will want to find out where these thoughts come from, as if mapping the inside of Noah's head will lead her to knowledge and understanding.

Really, he's being kind to her. He wants to save her the fuss of trying to comprehend the workings of his mind. There's nothing here for you, he wants to tell her, but that won't work, because her ears will prick up and her eyes will focus on him, her gaze will narrow and pin him down.

"Nothing? What do you mean, when you say 'nothing,' Noah? What does nothing mean to you?" That's what she'll ask.

He's tired. Beating the clock is exhausting and the last thing he needs is Ms. Turner taking him through each of those laps, trying to make sense of a meaningless dream. Noah sets no store by his dreams, so why should Ms. Turner?

Honestly? There's an area of your life that you don't obsess over?

Noah has no choice but to speak to Ms. Turner, answer her questions. But if she starts with more dream questions, she'll want to talk about his running dreams. She'll ask: "Are you running away from something, Noah? Do you like the feeling of running?" He wishes he had never told her about his dream of freedom. That's what she's calling it now and all because one day she asked him about his dreams, and he told her that running felt like freedom. The word was on his lips and off his tongue before he could swallow it down. He'd only said that to keep her quiet, give her something to think about, instead of talk-talk-talking. Noah is all about time, and Ms. Turner is all about talk.

It's Saturday afternoon and Ms. Turner has asked the Groomes to come to her rooms for a quick family meeting.

"Every week, a small victory." That's what she's saying now, to Maddie and her mom and dad.

Noah's there too, but he might as well not be. His attention is fixed on the array of pens on Ms. Turner's desk, and Maddie knows he's itching to get up and straighten them. Set the world straight and keep it balanced, that's all Noah wants to do.

Maddie's heart goes out to him. Don't worry, Noe, she wants to tell him. Not that her words would have any impact, the reassurances that rush to her lips whenever things get tough for her brother.

Now he's looking from the certificates hanging on the wall, to the potted plants on the windowsill, to the books on the shelf in the corner of the office, flicking from the top shelf to the bottom. Ms. Turner's probably slotted them back in different places since the last time Noah was in her office.

Keep your books in order for him, Maddie wants to say, line your pens up properly. That way my brother won't be eaten up by the need to reorganize and reposition, he won't be wondering how his therapist can even think about setting his mind to rights when she can't even keep her own environment neat and orderly.

There's silence in the room. Noah's mouth is moving soundlessly. He touches his fingers to his lips five times and Maddie hears their father's sigh of exasperation.

And then Ms. Turner tells them why she has called this family meeting, the day before their regularly scheduled Sunday afternoon visit, and what she wants them to do the moment they leave her office. No time to prepare, or think things through, or work anything out. She has a "family task," that's what she calls it, and she wants the Groomes to work on it immediately.

When Maddie sees Noah she thinks of boxes. There's her brother, and there's his life on his walls, neatly contained in the small squares of his spreadsheets. Color-coded, contained, and the moment one becomes too small to hold data pertinent to a certain activity or regulation, a subsection is added. And then another, and, if needs be, another. That's her brother. Boxed within a prison of rules that make sense to him but confuse everyone else. Its gates are a thick mesh of minutes and seconds, steps, and walls waiting to be tapped. His five fingers rattle out distress calls, but there's nothing she, or her mom or dad, can do to help him. The prison he built has such thick walls and gates so securely locked that unauthorized entry is impossible. Only Noah has the power to dismantle it, block by heavy block. Their job is to let him do it, in his own time and in his own way...Or that's what Ms. Turner says.

So, no more waiting as he completes his self-imposed chores, no humoring his need to eat alone, or keeping his door closed. Once Noah comes home, his routine will have to change to meet theirs. It will be hard work.

But that's all in the future. Right now, their task is to persuade him to leave his room and join them outside.

Ms. Turner wants them to walk with Noah into the garden, sit there with him there for at least ten minutes. "It's not going to be easy," she warns them, "but persevere. At least get him as far as the main door. I want Noah to meet you out there tomorrow, for visiting hours."

Ms. Turner's right. It's not easy at all.

"Shouldn't we just go there straight away?" Maddie says as the door of Ms. Turner's office closes behind them. "Get it over and done with? It'll probably be *much* easier than we think." Her face is hopeful, but Noah's not listening. He's hurrying ahead of them, getting to his room as fast as he can, no tapping at corners, no counting at all. He opens the door and walks to where his calendar and timetable are stuck to the wall.

"It's Saturday," he says. "Look. *Here.*" He jabs a finger at the calendar and then another at a list on the wall:

Saturday Chores
1. Sweep/dust.
2. Change sheets.
3. Laundry.
4. Tidy cupboards and desk.
5. Clean windows.

"*And* I've got more to fit in—catch up on homework, studying."

Noah's speaking fast, a rush of words he has to say. He points to the activities listed at the bottom of his Greenhills timetable. "They *say* it's unstructured, but it's not. It's just more difficult to organize. How am I supposed to fit all that in?" His hands are at his face, fives to his cheeks.

"I don't have *time* for extras. Not today. Ms. Turner's already interrupted my chores. We've spent one hour with her. And now..."

He stops, fingers at his lips now, mumbling through them. "I can't waste time on visitors."

Maddie's mom flinches.

"*Sunday* is visiting day." Her brother's tapping the timetable now. "Here, or downstairs, in the lounge. Not outside on the lawn. And *not* today. Not Saturday."

Their mom's blinking, still dealing with the hurt of being lumped into the "visitor" category. "We can help you, darling," she says. She peers at the list. "Look. It's not that much. We'll help you save time on your chores so you can come out into the garden for a little while. We'll choose a bench and then, tomorrow, you can wait for us there."

Maddie groans. Mom knows better than that. They'll never be able to do each chore according to Noah's specifications. He won't trust them, he'll do it all over and it will take even longer because they might have inadvertently moved something or disturbed the air molecules, or fractured the sound waves—whatever it is that sends her brother off on his twitchy circling, walking the floor, mumbling under his breath, pausing to draw a frantic breath and then continuing.

No, that won't work, and as Mom is suggesting that Noah show her where to find the broom, Maddie interrupts. "Mom, leave it. Noah has to do his chores by himself. Right, Noe?"

Her brother looks at her with a flash of gratitude, and for a second Maddie remembers when Mom treated them both as ordinary kids, when Maddie and Noah took it in turns to incur her wrath, or her blessings. Now she's dithering around him, scared to talk to him, scared to touch him, worried that the slightest wrong move will set him off and he'll become even stranger, more foreign, even less of the son she has consigned to the care of NoH-where.

"Treat him normally," Ms. Turner said in the family meeting. "He's not an invalid. He's your son, your brother. Talk to him, don't tiptoe around him."

Maddie glances at her father, standing alone at the end of the long room. If her mom is helpless as far as dealing with Noah is concerned, her dad is worse. He doesn't know what to say, so he says nothing. He doesn't know what to do, so he does nothing. He doesn't want to be there. And it shows. So that when they get to Noah's room, Dad mutters something and turns to walk back to the end of the room and look out of the window. "Trimmed the hedges, I see," he says to no one in particular, "and weeded those flowerbeds." Meaningless life-lines the garden throws out to contribute something to the conversation. He doesn't see how Noah listens when he speaks, doesn't notice his son taking out his small notebook, flipping to the back of it and jotting something down.

Anyway, on this day, almost four weeks after Noah moves into Greenhills, Maddie isn't bothered about notebooks, or the state of the garden, or even how, from the back, her father looks as if he wants to flatten himself to the glass of the window and melt through it, bound across the lawns and over the tall wrought-iron gates, and down the road, as far away from NoH-where as possible.

Today is all about following Ms. Turner's suggestions and seeing how far they can persuade Noah to go. At least her mom is standing still now. She's staring at the gray rug, at his bed with its hospital cor-ners, the pages and pages of fine web-like diagrams of his Family Tree.

Maddie follows her eyes. So much about his room in Greenhills is familiar and yet everything looks so out of place.

She still can't believe that every Sunday afternoon for the next eight weeks they'll be pointing the car in the direction of NoH-where. She can't think about that now. She has to put herself inside her brother's head, figure out how to get him out of his room and onto the lawn. She remembers Ms. Turner's request. "At least as far as the doors."

Think differently, she tells herself. Think Noah.

She's able to do that at home. Deflect him, divert him. Steer him onto a different path, one he doesn't mind walking.

That's at home, though, where everything is familiar and she can work with his code so that it's not an absolute train smash if they're having spinach for supper, not carrots, even though Mom specifically said it would be carrots and Noah wrote that into his "Menus" chart.

"Take your time." That is Ms. Turner's solution to everything con-nected to Noah. "Don't expect it all to happen overnight. It could take a good few weeks, months even, before Noah changes his patterns.

He's already put a great deal of effort into working out new routines for life at Greenhills. He's going to cling to them like a limpet. They'll be his new lifelines."

"Shouldn't we leave them in place, then?" Maddie's mom had said, so worried by it all. She'd been almost as agitated as Noah, but Ms. Turner had an answer for everything.

"It would be *easier*, but not necessarily better. Noah's created a new set of constants. We need to introduce changes within those constants—some small, some more challenging. For instance, from Monday to Wednesday, Noah can stick rigidly to his timetable, but we might ring a few changes on Thursday and Friday and then on Sunday something slightly different will happen. Or,"—she looks at all of them when she says this—"in this case, Saturday, when you persuade him to go out into the garden."

Slightly different? Maddie wants to laugh out loud, but there's no time for that either. She has to get Noah to take one step towards the door. Away from his chores. Ms. Turner's working on all of them, not just Noah. They also have to change their patterns, their habit of accommodating Noah, making space for the demands of his "quirks."

Quirks. Maddie hates that word.

She joins Noah, looks at the careful categorization of things to do and when to do them.

"Nice work, Noe," she says.

Noah nods. "Thanks, Mads. It's all more or less approximate for now."

Maddie's gazing at the timetable. "What's this?" she asks eventually. Her finger's on the block of activities, resting on the words "Quiet Time."

"That's for everyone," he says. "After supper."

"In your room?"

"Yes. "Time to think," Ms. Turner says. We can write in our journals if we want to."

"You know, Noah," Maddie says, "it's such a waste of time not to be doing something *and* thinking at the same time." She wonders if Ms. Turner would approve of this strategy, multitasking so that each minute is used to the full. But she doesn't care. Ms. Turner has given the family this impossible task; she'll have to live with the methods they use. Especially when—Maddie glances to the window again—her dad's standing immobile and detached and her mom's getting more jittery by the minute.

"I suppose..." Noah's mulling this over and Maddie cuts in.

"Sweeping, Noah. Sweeping and thinking. So maybe...maybe some of your chores?"

Noah checks his chart. "That could work."

"Yes," says Maddie. She glances at the list. "And windows. Dusting, cleaning windows, thinking, sweeping and thinking. Before you know it, Quiet Time will be over, Noah. And then, on a day like today you can use the time that's left over to do other things."

His eyes dart around the room.

"Just for getting to the garden and back. Because here's the thing, bro. Tomorrow Ms. Turner wants us to meet you out there, on the lawn, with the other kids and their parents. And it's going to be really hard if you don't walk it out now. Count the steps, time them. You know. And, if we do it now, it'll save you time in the long run. Otherwise you're going to spend forever wondering about how many steps to take between here and'—she looks beyond her father's stiff shoulders to a white bench—"that big oak tree. The one with the bench under it. That's where we could sit."

DAY 20 / 15:07

Noah's been forced into yet another corner at Greenhills. One where he has to do what he's told, follow the rules so they'll let him out and let him go home.

He and Maddie are perched on a bench, his mother off to the side, exclaiming at "all the freshness, Noah," and "Isn't it so much cooler out here?" and "Isn't this lovely?"

But it's not. It's not cooler at all. The air is muggy, and it isn't lovely, it's awful.

His father's standing with his back to them, looking like he's going to bolt at any second, make his getaway as soon as he can. He shoots his sleeve back as if it's the one action he's been wanting to make all day. "It's after three," he says, his voice false and cheery. "Time to be on our way and let this young fellow get on with his..." He pauses. "His chores."

Young fellow. He's never called Noah that before.

"Come along, Kate, come along, Maddie." His father can't wait to get them out of there.

"Goodbye, darling."

"Bye, Mom."

"Bye, Noe."

"Bye, Maddie."

Maddie leans in and gives Noah a kiss, one that leaves him rubbing his cheek as they walk away.

This young fellow. Is that who you are now?

"But what about Noah?" Kate is shocked. "I thought we were all going to see him together?"

"I can't." Dominic's at the fridge, filling his water bottle. He's in his running shorts and vest, trainers laced tight, short socks just showing.

"I need this exercise, Kate. It's important, if I don't get these hours in—"

"Then what, Dom? What will happen?"

She's turned away from him, talking to the garden outside the window. "You'll lose a second off your time, gain a millimeter round your waist?"

"I'm sorry. It's my routine, you know that."

Of course she knows it. There are times in her husband's week that he holds sacred, and his Sunday-afternoon run is one of them. But surely—?

"Can't you make an exception, Dom, juggle a few things? Just for now, while Noah's there? I promised him, two thirty."

"I can't," he says again.

His week is busy, she's aware of that. His job's important, and his health, and his need for space. But surely not at the expense of seeing his son?

"Besides," he's saying now, "I'll see him at the meeting with Ms. Turner." He touches Kate lightly on the arm. "I've rearranged my diary to fit it in. Isn't that more important? You and Maddie can do this afternoon together."

Do, like their son is a chore who has to be *done*.

"Tell Noah I said hello."

"Fine," says Kate quietly, "and should I send him your love while I'm about it?"

Dominic watches Kate's car disappear down the drive. Sweat is trickling down his chest but there's no point showering.

Inside, he goes into the dressing room and opens his wardrobe. He pulls out a pair of chinos and slips them on over his shorts. Then he takes a golf shirt from the top of a neatly stacked pile. He's told Kate he's going to run the Newlands Forest path, and he will. After.

Dominic grabs the car keys from the hallstand. Twenty minutes' drive, another thirty when he gets there, and then he'll get back in his car and drive to the forest.

His phone rings just as he gets to the car.

"Hi."

—

"Yes, of course I will."

—

"I'm sorry, I couldn't make it last week."

—

"Yes, yes. I know. Don't worry. I'm on my way."

Dominic's in the garden, shears in hand as Kate and Maddie pull into the driveway.

Snipping, thinks Kate. He's always snipping.

"Kate, Maddie," he calls as she slams the car door. "How was Noah?"

Kate doesn't reply, but Maddie does. "He was fine, Dad. I thought he was fine, didn't you, Mom?"

Kate doesn't answer. She smiles at Maddie and then asks her to go and put the kettle on.

Maddie runs inside, into the house, and Kate looks at Dominic, fresh after his shower, his shorts loose and casual, his golf shirt crisp. Her perfect husband.

Her hands are sticky from the heat of the steering wheel and all she wants is to get inside and run them under the tap. The day may be cooling down, but Kate is burning with anger.

She walks up path and opens the front door, leaving her husband to his garden and his incessant pruning.

People tell Kate she is beautiful, but she's not really. She's too tall, her nose is too big, her feet are boats. She's a great clothes horse, but way too scrawny for a bikini. She's nothing like the girls boys used to go for at school: cute, bouncy, just the right height to snuggle under an armpit. When boys kissed Kate—and there weren't too many of those as she grew up, and up—*she* was the one who had to bend a little at the knees.

She grew into her height, learned not to slouch, how to enter a room floating, cool, soignée.

She no longer corrects people who tell her she's beautiful, doesn't say to them, "Unusual, perhaps," the way she used to. She's learned to accept compliments with a smile and a thank you. She's even learned to appreciate the sight of her and Dom reflected in a mirror. A striking couple, a perfect foil for each other.

"You're beautiful," Dominic said, shortly after they met. "Inside and out."

When he said things like this, she wanted to hush him, tell him he didn't know her, not really, and if he did he wouldn't say that. Especially now. Not that she has committed any terrible crime or is hiding some deep, dark secret, but because, truth be told, not only does Kate feel she's not that beautiful on the outside, she thinks her inside is mean-spirited and small. She looks at her friends with their perfect children and she envies them. "Happy Child, Happy Parent Syndrome," she calls it, and when she allows this rancor to happen she feels stunted and twisted and thinks she doesn't deserve children, any children. Surely she should be happy? There are women out there whose barren wombs are crying out for children, and here she is with two, unhappy because one of them—

It's not that she doesn't love Noah, she reassures herself, and it's not that she doesn't want to do everything she can for him. It's more that she doesn't feel like she's a mother to him. Surely, even if a child pulls away, the mother should still reach out, and if the child steps back, the mother should step forward so that there's never a space between them? If, for every step away, there's a step to, the gap will never grow.

Kate has taken false steps, not true ones. Why else is there this forever-growing space between her and her son?

She's good on the surface, to look at, to talk to. Funny even, at times. But that's all she has to offer. Skin-deep, that's as far as her beauty goes.

Not that anyone has caught on. Even when she tells them she's a fraud, they demur.

Now she stands in her kitchen and she feels it again, knows it again. They've just come back from seeing Noah. That's who she should be thinking of. Poor boy, how hard this all is for him.

Instead, she's consumed by rage. At her husband for starters. How dare he leave this all to her? The thought fills her head so completely that there isn't room, even at the corners, for compassion, care, concern—all she should be feeling for her son. She leans against the sink and grips tight to the edge because, if she lets go, she might grab something and hurl it at the wall. Something small and breakable, and once she starts, she won't be able to stop and the kitchen will lie in smithereens.

How dare he? The thought is there again, and the rage. *She* deals with their son on a daily basis. *She* had to organize a place for him to stay. Everything, everything. She has done everything.

And Dominic? Anything he's done has been mean and reluctant.

Take today. Ask him to visit Noah, a small request, and he shrivels into himself. He cannot bear to see his son, let alone stand and talk to him.

WEEK 4: DAY 22 / 13:32

"So, Noah." Juliet's looking at him seriously. "Don't take this the wrong way, okay?"

The wrong way? What does she mean? Why can't people say what they mean exactly as they mean it? If they did that, there'd be no chance of taking anything the "wrong way."

Noah sighs but she doesn't hear him. She's too busy rushing to finish her thought. Her cheeks are flushed and, if it's possible, she's talking even faster than usual—all about Noah and girls.

"Aren't you even interested, Noah? I mean it's cool if you're not. Plenty of guys aren't. Or maybe you're interested in boys?"

He wishes she could see the lists he's made, about how he does notice girls, but that would be giving away too much. More than he's shown Ms. Turner, more than he'll ever speak about in group. Anywhere in fact.

"Noah?"

She's off again.

"Sorry, man. I didn't mean to offend you."

"You didn't."

It's worth using two words to take the worry off her face, but that's all. There aren't enough minutes in his day to think about the "Noah Groome and Girls" thing, let alone explain it all.

20:15

Just because Noah doesn't have time for girls—or friends, really—doesn't mean he doesn't like them. Girls, that is. It's not like he doesn't see them, or notice the way they walk and the way they talk.

Maddie tells him he's one of the best-looking boys in his class, and maybe that's what girls see first. Tall, dark hair, green eyes, clean shaven (very). The boy-next-door, someone to take home to meet their parents. They'd approve, trust him with their daughters.

But then, the girls notice how he's always wearing the same make of shirt, jeans, trainers...If they look closely they'll even see the same make of socks. And there's always a notebook in his top pocket.

Odd.

And that's *before* they see him with his 5s.

Not exactly the catch of the century, Noah.

DAY 23 / 09:12

"So, Noah," says Ms. Turner, "maybe it's time to talk about your family."

Talk? Doesn't she know by now that talking isn't what he does? She wants him to use his words to tell her about his mother, about Maddie—and his father.

She wants you to describe your feelings for your father?

Super-Dad. The disappointing son discusses disappointed Dad.

"SuperDad?" she'll say, one-wording it.

Super-rich, super-successful, super-good-looking, super-loved by his super-beautiful wife...

All he needs is the cape and he can fly around the city—no, forget that—the country, the globe, solving everyone's problems. Nothing's too much for Super-Dad.

Except, maybe, being able to talk to his super-disappointing son.

DAY 24 / 02:43

Sometimes, when he's had a good day and everything's balanced and boxed as it should be, Noah's dreams escape the counting and measuring. Instead, he might dream about Spit and Spot and racing with them, round and round the lawn, his mother watching, Maddie laughing at the top of her voice. Even his father looks up from his pruning and watches as they tear up and down. Noah ends with a mighty leap into the pool. Spit the fearless sails in after him, while Spot stands and barks at the edge.

So some nights it's Spit and Spot, and other nights, like this one, it's about sitting down to eat an ordinary meal with his family, not worrying about what's on the menu and what's landed up on his plate and whether anything's touching and what order he should eat in and how many mouthfuls (approx.) it should take to eat the meal and how many it actually takes. Conversation's flowing freely and he's joining in and the jokes he cracks are quick and funny and his father's grinning and saying, "Good one, Noah." He's asking Noah about his studies and will he have enough time for sports, because he's such a good sportsman and so lucky to have such natural talent.

His mother wants to know if he wants another helping but he's wiping his mouth hurriedly and saying, "No thanks, Mom. That was great."

His sister starts giggling. "Don't you see, Mom? Noah's got to hurry. Noah's got a date!"

He flicks her cheek gently, and smiles at his parents and rushes to shower and change because yes, he does have a date and it's with a special girl.

His mother yells at him not to waste the hot water, and then he's standing in front of the mirror, combing his hair and his clothes look just right. He's cool and easy-going and he likes to joke, but he'd never be mean about girls, especially this one. She's special. Then he's at the front door, lifting Mom's keys from the rack at the door, calling, "You sure I can take the car?"

"Of course. Drive carefully, Noah."

He's driving into the dark. There's no moon, but that's not a problem. The headlights cut the darkness and he travels the quiet road, happy to be out there on his own. Happy to know she's waiting.

It doesn't matter that he never gets to her, never stands waiting for her door to open and show who's behind it.

It's enough that he's on his way and the road is wide and the night is quiet. He knows where he's going and his heart is happy.

But awake, Noah knows that, however much he'd like it, there'll never be a girl like that waiting, a special girl, a girl just for him, Noah

Groome. Awake, the wide road disappears and takes his happiness with it.

2002

"Soon you'll be six," Mom told him one day. "Nearly time for Big School. Won't that be exciting?"

Noah didn't want to be 6. He wanted to stay 5, come home from play school, go to his room, and take out red car, blue car, black car, yellow car, green. He wanted to go through his dinosaur book, picture by picture, and tell himself all about Achelousaurus, Tyrannosaurus Rex and Triceratops, Noah's favorite with its bird beak, three horns and frill around its neck.

That's what he wanted but when his mom said, "Soon you'll be 6," his room faded away and with it, all his 5 lined-up cars.

Noah had to hold on to 5. He could count to 5. There were 5 steps to his door if he stretched his legs wide, to the handle for down-up-down-up-open on 5, then into the passage for 5 steps and 5 more and 5 more and he was at the bathroom door, 5 small steps to the sink, 5 spokes on the tap that he could twist open, closed, open, closed, open 5 times when his mom wasn't there to tell him off for wasting water.

1, 2, 3, 4, 5,

once I caught a fish alive.

6, 7, 8, 9, 10,

then I let it go again.

Noah caught 5. And he never wanted to let it go.

His mom couldn't understand why he didn't play with his ark any more, the one they bought him when Maddie was born. "Noah's Ark, isn't that just perfect?"

No. "Perfect" to Noah was having 5 fingers on each hand, 5 toes on each foot. Noah was happy finding 5s. They kept him safe and sound.

He loved Mom, though, loved to lean against her and listen to her reading to him. He watched her hands with their polished tips. 5 nails on each pretty hand, 5 polished toes on each pretty foot. He saw them one summer's day when she wore sandals and said, "Isn't this weather glorious, Noah?"

That's what she said, but her voice sounded like she was trying to make it cheerful.

He didn't answer. His head was down and he was watching his feet step 1 2 3 4 5, and seeing his mom's 5 pretty toes, flashing their way to the door of the Grade R classroom and all the way inside to the teacher's table where Mom said, "This is Noah. Say hello to Miss Jonas."

Miss Jonas was cuddly and soft, like the baby animals who used to march 2x2x2 into Noah's ark.

He wanted to hold on to his mom's hand, but he couldn't. He couldn't grab for her and he couldn't run after her because his feet with their 5 toes were frozen in place and Mom was saying, "Bye-bye, Noah. You'll have a fine time, sweetie-pie."

He watched her reach the doorway. She turned and waved, and he lifted his 5-fingered hand in a starfish salute, and watched her leave.

"Here's your peg, Noah, see here," said Miss Jonas.

He felt a bit better when he saw his wooden peg was 5th in line on the wall.

He hung up his bag and then walked, 1 2 3 4 5 and 1 2 3 4 5 again, and sat on a cushion in the corner where he could see the whole classroom. He looked from object to object to object, fixing them in his mind like a sailor on the ocean, an explorer with a compass charting a brand-new world. Over and over he looked for his bag, hanging bright blue and new on the hook with its number 5 made of red stars. Each star had 5 points and that made him feel a little better.

His breath came out in a whoosh.

He sat quietly on his cushion, 5 and 5 steps from Miss Jonas's table, 5, 5 and 5 steps from the classroom door, with all the steps in-between-and-outside waiting to be counted.

"I have my work cut out for me." That's what Dad said when he had a difficult job. This new place wasn't going to be easy. Noah had his work cut out for him. Lots to explore and count. No wonder people said school was hard.

Gabriel's mother is on the lawn, clutching a bundle close to her chest, rocking slowly, crooning to the child wrapped in blankets. Shusha-shushashusha shhhhh.

Ma'am? A young man approaches her, shows himself to be a police officer. Ma'am?

Where's my boy? Gabriel hears her call out. Where is my Little Man?

Another child? The policeman's voice is loud, panicked. There's another child! Behind him the house is burning to the ground and the neighbors are gathering. A motley assortment of nightgowns and dressing gowns and sleeping shorts and, in one case, a man with a large towel wrapped around his large middle and his wife snapping for God's sake, George, will you get back inside and put on some clothes! But he doesn't answer her. His eyes are pinned on the flames munching their way steadily from room to room, on the firemen controlling the snaking hoses.

They're too late, George says, and several people near him nod their heads. All around them is bustling action and men and women asking frantically, is there another child? The question snaps George back to attention. God, yes, of course. Gabriel.

Gabriel? Is that his name? Can you describe him, sir?

And George, eager to help, says, of course. He's about this tall. He raises his hands and his towel falls to his feet, revealing him in all his glory.

Sorry, sorry, he mumbles. His wife shoots him a murderous glance. Sorry, sorry. Her husband scuttles off, towel bunched in front of him, his backside wobbling behind.

He's about ten. Tall for his age, and skinny, his wife tells the young policewoman whose face shines in the firelight. Quiet child. Strange, I'd say, but I never really got to know him that well. Keep themselves to themselves, that lot do.

⊕

DAY 25 / 09:08

What Noah likes about Ms. Turner is how she takes who he is and works with it.

So far...Remember, she is not to be trusted.

Ms. Turner's talking about his 5s.

"I've been thinking about how important five is to you, Noah. Perhaps there's a way we can work with that."

She pauses, looks at him carefully, but he keeps his face neutral, doesn't let her see how hard it is to hear her use his number so casually. Be careful, he wants to say to her. It's powerful.

She's tossing it around like it means nothing.

She's still talking and Noah forces himself to listen.

"So, Noah. You know we have five senses?"

This is dangerous. Stop her, right now.

Noah can't, because he has to listen to her. He has to breathe, and he has to tap. He's gathering strength. He's going to have to push back at her, but—

"What I'd like you to do is try a really easy meditation technique. I'm going to hold on to your hands at the beginning. Will that be all right?"

Noah's not sure, but he nods.

"Pull your hands away from me at any time, Noah. I won't hold them unless you want me to."

She's holding them now, and Noah's becoming more agitated. He wants to tap, to feel his fingers moving, but he can't. Instead he calls on his feet and asks them to beat faster and faster. If he could just get to his stones, but her hands are firm on his and he doesn't want to let them go. If he can get through this—

Then what? Are you hoping for some kind of miracle cure?

Noah shakes his head. No miracles, he knows that, but if he does The Work...It doesn't mean he's going to let down all his defenses. It will show he's willing to try.

"Trust me, Noah."

He looks at her and her face is the same as always, kind, open.

"I'm not trying to trick you. I won't ask you to do something unless I think you can. It's all part of a process. If you trust it, it could work really well."

Her voice is quiet. Commanding, almost, but not strong enough or firm enough to fight the Dark.

Trust *her? Think of the consequences.*

Its voice is blacker than a scowl. More frightening than it's ever been.

Listen! Look at me.

A glint in the deep shadow, burning orange, bright and fearful. Ms. Turner's holding his hands, holding him still and talking about 5s.

"Stop, Noah. Let everything slow down."

Her voice is soft. He listens, takes in her words. The swirling in his head slows, quietens.

"Once you're calm, Noah, I want you to do five things. Breathe now. Tell me when you're ready."

He breathes. He breathes. He breathes. He breathes. He breathes. The world stops spinning.

"Ready," he says.

"Close your eyes, Noah."

He closes them.

"Now, listen. Find one sound to concentrate on."

So many sounds. Running feet outside in the corridor. A telephone ringing from another room. Wandile and Simon talking outside on the lawn. And above them all, the rough gwaa-gwaa-gwaa of a hadedah.

"The hadedah," he says.

"Good. Listen to him, Noah."

She's still holding his hands, keeping them—him—in place.

"All good?"

He nods.

"Next, Noah, I want you to taste. Concentrate on the taste in your mouth."

That's easy. Minty toothpaste still fresh after breakfast.

"Run your tongue around your mouth, Noah. Can you taste it?"

Another nod.

"Great."

You are too obedient. This is not the time—

She's talking again. "Breathe in, Noah. Only this time, what do you smell?"

She's close to him and he picks up the scent of her shampoo. Something lemony. Beyond that, the sprig of jasmine on her desk, its faint perfume reaching across the carpet to where they're sitting. Does heat have a smell? He breathes into the warm air and inhales the sharpness of the soap he used to wash his hands after breakfast.

In the end, he settles on the sharp tang of Ms. Turner's hair. It's the strongest, the easiest to identify; it's fresh, not blurred by heat or muggy air.

"You're doing so well, Noah. Are you okay?"

A nod.

"Right. I'm going to let go of your hands now. But keep your eyes closed."

Her hands let go of his.

"Find something to touch, Noah."

He moves his hands to his hair, to the fabric of his white shirt, to his jeans, to the skin on the back of his hand. Back to his hair, washed that morning. He rubs a lock between his fingers, stops to wonder for a moment how many individual hairs he's holding, remembers his mom telling him how she loves him, more than all the hairs on his head, thinks how much he loves her too, and Maddie...and his father.

What is this nonsense, Noah?

His hair is soft, slippery, and if he concentrates, he can block out every noise.

He's still thinking about his family, feeling his hair under his fingers when Ms. Turner says, "Now open your eyes. Slowly. Look around. Let your eyes rest on one object."

His eyelids feel as though they have weights attached to them and it's a strain to open them. The room is filled with sunlight. It shines on Ms. Turner's lemony hair and makes the indigenous flowers glow brightly in their frames. He settles on the graceful beauty of the wild iris.

"Good, Noah. Now, one last thing. I want you to tap."

He swivels to face her. "What?"

"I know." She smiles. "Who'd have thought? But this is why. One tap for what you hear. One tap for what you taste. One tap for what you smell, one for what you see. One final tap for the fingers doing the touching. Do it lightly and quickly."

He looks at her and she's not joking. With unexpected permission, he taps lightly and quickly, ears, mouth, nose and eyes and a final tap of his fingers together.

"Now choose one sense, Noah."

His hand moves up to his hair.

"You're doing so well. So, then, Noah, can you tell yourself exactly where you are? Tell me too, if you can."

"I'm here. In your office." The words are out in a flash.

"That's right. You're here. And the time is now. Right this very moment. Agreed?"

"Yes."

"So, when you get worried, Noah, or anxious, take the time to pause. Ask your five senses to help you. Hear one thing. Taste one thing. Smell one thing, feel one thing, see one thing. Then, choose just one of your senses. It doesn't have to be the same one every time. Concentrate on the very one you have chosen. Let the others fall away. Go from five, to four, to three, to two, to one."

Her voice is soothing, hypnotic and as she speaks his eyes close. Gently, he rubs a few strands between his fingers. The sound of the hadedah fades, he can't taste toothpaste or smell Ms. Turner's hair. He doesn't look at the botanical prints that remind him of his father's garden.

"Tell yourself where you are, Noah."

"I'm here."

"Tell yourself what time it is."

"It's now."

"That's good Noah. Really good. We're almost finished."

Her hand is back again, covering his free one.

"Where are you Noah?"

"I'm Here and Now," he says, and he likes the way capitals form for the words.

"Can you do anything about what happened in the past?"

"No," he says. The Dark blooms.

His hand pulls back, but relaxes slightly as she holds on. "Feel your hair, Noah. Where are you?"

"I'm Here," he says. "And Now."

"That's right. You're in here, and it's now. So tell, me, Noah, if you can, can you do anything about the future?"

It's too much.

He pulls his hand away and uses both to tap the arm of the chair.

"Don't worry," Ms. Turner says.

He looks at her and noise surrounds him, at full volume.

Do not say anything else. *Not a single thing. It's a cruel trick.*

He's shaking, but Ms. Turner looks exactly the same. Same kind smile, same calm face. She's talking, as if nothing has happened.

"We'll do this again, Noah. Practice it together. And once you get the hang of it, you can do it on your own."

He gets to his feet. Three minutes left of their session, but he must get out, away from the place where she's used his 5s.

Used them against *you. Underneath all that sweetness, she is twisted and crooked.*

His getaway isn't quick and easy. It never is when he leaves her office. He's shaking, fear-filled.

She stops him at the door and asks him a question. "May I ask one thing?"

He manages a small nod.

"How did it feel, Noah?"

"What?" His voice is an angry croak. "How did *what* feel?" His hand is on the handle and all he wants is to down-up-down-up-down, but she's asking again. More specifically.

"How did it feel to rest a while? Right here, right now, without letting the past back in. Without"—Don't say it, he's begging in his head, but her voice continues—"worrying about what might be waiting in the future. Think about it, Noah. Until our next meeting."

Down-up-down-up-down and the door's open.

26 JULY 2011 / 20:32

"These ous," the constable had said, as Noah's father showed him to the door, "I tell you, they're one step ahead of the game all the way. Looks like the work of this syndicate that's been hitting the area. Same method. Cars, cash, keys, cell phones's all they want. In and out. Job done. But one of these days they'll slip up—make a mistake. And then, ma'am, we'll get them." He'd glanced at Noah's mother reassuringly. "We'll be on them like a ton of bricks. You'll see."

"When they make a mistake?" his mother said, when his father came back. "They need to get them *now*. He's leaving us alone, vulnerable. They have our keys, they know where we live. They'll know we called the police." Her voice rose hysterically.

Noah's father put his arms around her shoulders. "We had to," he said. "If we don't follow the correct procedures, they'll have won, Kate."

Maddie was upset too. "Can we go to sleep, Mom, Dad? Is it safe?"

"Don't worry, Mads, don't worry." His father is on his phone. "Andrew Meyers. He'll know what to do, Kate. The same thing happened to him a few weeks ago."

A burst of Mr. Meyers's loud voice and then his father's. "Andrew? Hi, it's Dominic. Look, I'm sorry to disturb you in the evening, but we've had a...Kate's car's just been stolen...No, we're all fine. Thanks, Andrew. Yes, yes, in the drive, and they got the house keys too. Hacked the security code at the gate."

Another burst of noise and Noah's father scribbled something down. "No, no, it doesn't matter what they charge. We need this done tonight—otherwise none of us will sleep."

The pizzas sat cooling on the kitchen counter, but their stomachs were too knotted to eat.

The Speed Key van arrived within half an hour. The four men got to work at once, checking the perimeter, fitting a new lock to the front door. They replaced and recoded the gate sensor, all the gate buttons and did the same for the garage. They worked quietly and efficiently and within three hours everything had been completed. Noah's mom asked if they had eaten and they were happy to take the pizzas with them. His father used the new remote, the gate rolled open and the Speed Key team drove out.

The kitchen was filled with silence.

"At least..." Noah's mother began, and his father picked up on her words quickly.

"At least they didn't hurt you, darling."

"And," she tried to follow on, "at least..." and then she was shuddering. "Why us, Dom?"

"Just bad luck, Kate. Men like that respect nothing."

That's what the constable had said too. "No respect for the laws of the land, these ous."

"We can't give in to it," said Noah's father. "We have to try to maintain law and order. If we don't, we're asking for chaos."

That was the thought circling in Noah's head when he went to bed. That and the others that filled his head all through the night: Columbine, Gun Control, a lone wolf and his unspeakable acts of violence... Noah stayed awake, tense, ready to leap to the defense of his family.

He had to maintain order, keep chaos at bay. He'd have to work hard, though, because a shadow was forming at the gate of their newly secured home.

Always there.

Always waiting.

DAY 25 / 12:35

"Think about it, Noah. Give it a few moments' thought until our next meeting."

Of course he thinks about it. How can he not? How can he ignore the lightness and peace that filled him when he said "Here and Now," before she asked him about the past, before she tricked him about the future.

1. He is *not* interested in the here and now (no caps) of Greenhills.

2. All he cares about is what's happening *out there*, which is where he is not.
3. He's not there to protect them.
4. He's *stuck* in the here and the now of Greenhills.
5. His power has been sabotaged.

Kate picks up the envelope. Every two weeks she gets a report, an update to show her how well the staff at Greenhills are managing her difficult son. It's printed on thick creamy paper, beautiful, with an elegant letterhead, but it's not nearly thick enough to absorb the misery of the words typed on it. Ms. Turner writes the reports; she's careful to stress the positives, mentioning Noah's slow but significant progress. Ms. T—that's what Maddie calls her—is nice enough. Competent. And she doesn't talk down to Noah like Dr. Lovelock did.

Kate remembers his report; it was long and complicated, puffed up and puffed out by medical jargon. She can picture him writing it, his thin lips tweezered, his convex chest sunk in on itself, his stork legs jointed sharply at the knee. Does he like any of his patients? Kate wonders. Or is it just the two of them? Her beautiful, imperfect son, product of a bad mother. He'd talked down to Kate, too, as if Noah's problems stemmed from her. As if she didn't feel enough guilt, always wondering if there was anything she should have done differently.

All the way to the moment of conception, that's how far back her guilt goes, and from there through each of the trimesters of her pregnancy. Kate spends hours racking her brains, trying to remember what she drank, if she'd been in the same room as people smoking. Should she have spoken differently to Noah as an infant, as a young child? Had he been overstimulated? Under-stimulated? Had she fed him the right food? What about their occasional forays over to the dark side, to fast-food joints with their grubby play areas?

Today's report is kind, hopeful, encouraging, not unlike Ms. Turner herself. Even so, Kate cannot see a light at the end of this tunnel. There is one, Ms. Turner insists. Just keep going, keep trying; the work will be worthwhile. But Kate needs more than a glimmer of hope. She wants to be blinded by a flash of miraculous light.

It's the second time they've met outside in the grounds and Kate's sitting under their oak, watching Maddie, Noah and Juliet. They're on the lawn and Juliet's chattering away, her hands flying. Maddie laughs and Noah almost smiles.

Kate feels a twinge of jealousy. It isn't up to Juliet to make her son smile. That's her job, her responsibility.

"Mrs. Groome?"

It's Mr. Bill.

"They seem to be getting on well," he says, looking over to her children, and Monica's child.

"Yes." The word sounds tight and mean and Kate forces more out. "It's good to see Noah looking more relaxed."

But is it? Why does Juliet have to be there at all? It should be Kate, Noah and Maddie against the world. No one else. Dominic can stay locked away in his selfish little space.

Kate doesn't let any of this show. She's learning the rules of survival and the first one of these is to smile. Smile when people ask how Noah is doing, smile when Ms. Turner sits across the desk from her and asks how things are going, smile at the red-faced man in the car next to her at the traffic lights, smile at the young woman at the checkout, smile at the man who finally arrived to fix the pool pump... and smile at Mr. Bill.

"May I?"

She gestures to the space beside her on the bench and Mr. Bill settles next to her, burly and buff.

Buff, that's a word her children use, one that conjures images of men toughing it out at the gym, gleaming with sweat, muscles pumped and straining inside their skin. Dominic has the build of a long-distance runner, lean rather than chunky. He's a cool, elegant presence, whereas the man sitting next to her fills every inch of his space, bursting with energy and good cheer.

"Your husband couldn't make it?"

"No, he had to work." Kate wishes that Dominic was with her, watching their son, seeing his eyes move from Maddie to Juliet and then back again as the two girls laugh. He'd see Noah smile as he looks at his little sister, see her leap to her feet.

"It's easy. Look. I'll show you," Maddie says. Two backflips and a somersault and then back to her seat on the lawn, her face beaming. Juliet laughing, Noah saying something Kate can't hear.

"She's a livewire, that one." Mr. Bill's also laughing.

Kate smiles. "She is, and she adores her brother. She misses him so badly." Suddenly, it's all spilling out, how strange it is not to have Noah at home, how she's learning day by day how his routines and rules dominated their lives, hers especially. She doesn't mention Dominic, though, doesn't say that his life hasn't been affected that much, that the more their son's condition intrudes on their lives, the more he withdraws, leaving her to deal with most of it.

Mr. Bill listens intently, focusing on what Kate is telling him. It's easy talking to him, a total contrast to Ms. Turner in her rooms, where every single word she says carries significance, where Kate worries about being unkind about Dominic or betraying her son by saying the wrong thing.

Kate runs out of words. "I'm sorry," she says, "I didn't mean—"

He stops her with a gentle touch on her arm. "Don't be sorry," he says. "It's good to get things out." He looks over at Noah again. "Noah's a good kid. He's managing to get by, day by day."

He's calm, unflurried, and his words reassure Kate more than any of Noah's previous therapists, more than anything Dominic can bring himself to say. More than Ms. Turner, even. She wants to grab his arm, hang on for dear life and say, "Really, Mr. Bill, really and truly?" Instead she turns to him, finds another smile and says, "Thank you, you don't know how much that means to me."

He smiles back, gets to his feet. "Time to start gathering the troops."

And it is. Time to call Maddie, smile at Juliet, walk up to Noah and say goodbye to her son for yet another week. But first, time to say goodbye to Mr. Bill and thank him again.

"Okay, Noah?"

They've just been through his senses and Noah's sweating at the thought of not using his 5s to hold the future safe. He can't say it's been any easier than the last 3 times he's tried this. "It'll come, Noah. We'll keep trying until it does," she says. "It is a good technique. Trust me."

Is she serious?

His eyes flick over to the framed poster of two men, walking railway tracks, looking like they're ready to hop onto a boxcar and hitch a ride to the next town. One older than the other, neither of them young. Sigmund Freud and Carl Jung, Ms. Turner has told him. There's a quote from Jung at the top of the poster; it could have been written as encouragement just for Noah: "In all chaos there is a cosmos, in all disorder a secret order." At the bottom of the poster, equally encouraging, words attributed to Freud: "Out of your vulnerabilities will come your strength."

"So, Noah," Ms. Turner says casually, but he's learning (fast) that she never says anything casual, or without some sort of reason. "Let's talk about your family tree."

He looks away from Sigmund and Carl, her question hanging between them.

"The thing is," she continues, "by now, as part of your therapy, I'd have asked you to work on a family tree, but you've already drawn up an extensive one."

He nods.

"Your mother tells me you started it in Grade 10?"

Another nod.

"And you're still busy with it?"

"Yes."

"So how far back have you managed to go?"

He takes a deep breath. It's harmless talking about this. There's nothing she wouldn't already know from her notes. "Quite far," he says. "Back to when the Huguenots arrived in the Cape."

"That's impressive. Whose side is that on, Noah?"

She knows the answer. Why this pussyfooting?

"Do The Work..." Juliet's words drown out all distraction and he answers, "On my mother's."

"That's a lot of research, Noah. It must have been fascinating." The closer she gets to asking him the hard stuff, the more she uses his name.

"I used our Family Bible. It wasn't too difficult."

"And your father, Noah? How far back did you go with him?"

"Nowhere." He manages 1 word (2 syllables).

"But you'd like to?"

He's back to nodding.

"It's important, isn't it, Noah?"

There she goes again. What did I tell you?

Noah nods.

"Would you like to tell me why?"

Relief floods through him as he realizes he can answer. "It's about balance," he says.

What—?

But Noah has a plan.

"Both sides should balance. It's really important."

He can tell her this; it's nothing she wouldn't have guessed anyway.

So, Noah does The Work, but not all of it. He doesn't tell her how important it is for him to gather clues about why he is the way he is.

"Balance," she's saying now. "Yes. I can see that balance would be vital, Noah."

She looks at her watch. "This has been good."

Noah waits for the zinger, the sting that waits in the tail of every session. But today, there's nothing.

"Thank you, Noah. I appreciate all the hard work you're doing." She smiles and adds, "And your honesty."

You got her, well and good. Excellent!

Noah feels no satisfaction. Tricking Ms. Turner feels mean-spirited.

He worked on his senses with her, and that brought a few moments of real peace, but now it's like the hour was wasted. He didn't do The Work, at least not the way he should have.

Gabriel is still hiding. He's crouched down behind the hedge that borders the house across the road, the one that belongs to Mrs. Thin and Mr. Fat. He doesn't know the surnames of the people who live around them.

Every weekend Gabriel sees Mr. Fat in the driveway of their house, under his car, his feet sticking out. Swear words coming out too, and he says he's tinkering. Tinkering is a happy word, but Mr. Fat doesn't sound happy. He's throwing out words like Fuck this for a lark and Who engineered this piece of crap anyway? and Gladys! And Mrs. Thin is running out and saying Yes George and he says Get me a beer before I moer this fucking piece of shit to pieces and she's saying Language, George, the neighbors, but Mr. Fat just pulls himself back under the car on a funny little pallet with wheels and Mrs. Thin goes back into the house.

So, it's Mr. George Fat and Mrs. Gladys Thin's house, their hedge, where Gabriel is hiding. Across the road, his house is blazing, but Gabriel knows Mum is out of danger, because he's seen her, and he knows Harry's safe because Mum's holding her.

One of the onlookers is yelling. There's someone else, an old man, he cries.

Gabriel raises his head above the hedge, and waits for them to storm the house and bash down the front door and make their way down the burning passage and use their crowbars to force open the door and find the old man and bring him out, but they aren't moving. They're spraying the house with their thick hoses, huge spurts of water lit pale orange in the dark, playing in the dark, water falling with a sizzle and puff of steam on the roof of the house and on its walls, but no one is going inside.

It's too late, he hears someone say. Mrs. Pink Hair from the house on the corner. She's talking to Mr. Rose Grower from the house next door to hers. Her voice sounds excited, and almost happy. Her face glows in the light from the fire from the house where—

Gabriel doesn't want to think about that. He lifts his hands, feels the sting from where the glass cut him, smells the throat-choking smell of petrol, imagines the small flare of a match in Mum's hand, the thin thread of fire, the flames on their way. Voices are calling his name. He ducks back down.

Gabriel, Gabriel, Gabriel.

He curls himself into a small boy-sized ball. Tucks his head between his knees. He is a small boy in shorts and a T-shirt. A small boy who was asleep with his sister. He doesn't know anything. He didn't see anything. He is hiding behind the hedge in Mr. George Fat's garden and all around him he can hear the voices calling.

Dominic is living a lie. He is not the good father everyone believes him to be.

"If I could do it over, I'd never have gone into business." That's his partner, staring into his glass, motioning to the waiter for another, his fifth brandy of the evening, and Dominic knows he'll be driving him home, helping him up the path.

"What about you, Dominic?"

Dominic is silent. And then he says, "I always said I'd own my own company one day. I'd never have to work for a boss. So, I guess I'm pretty far along that track."

He can share this much, and then he can listen as his partner talks about the art classes he's been taking, how good his teacher says he is, how he did it at school and got an A for Matric. He listens and says, "You're doing it now, that's good," but he doesn't say that he never saw himself as a father, can't believe that he has two children to look after. If he did, he'd say he loves them, of course he does, and he always will, but he thought he'd always be alone, a bachelor, until his dying day. That had been his refrain until he met Kate and fell head over heels in love.

And now, now what does he have? A beautiful, unhappy wife. A sad, damaged son and a daughter who loves him far more than he deserves.

Maddie, the daughter who makes the sun shine. Noah, the son who brings the clouds, who grays their days. When his son's out of the house, it's easier, lighter. Without Noah, the days are crisp and bright.

Without Juliet, everything will fall apart.

What will her little sister do without Juliet to keep her secure? What will her mom do without Juliet to keep things going? Thoughts of home float in and surround Juliet. Her father's angry shouting, the silhouette of a full glass at the side of the sink, the shape of the empty bottle in the bin. Lily's worried face, the slurred gray of her mother's voice.

So much Juliet could write in her journal, but nothing she's ready to examine that closely.

The sound of her father's voice won't go away. All that hate, so much disgust. So little love for his wife and daughters.

Juliet picks up her pen. She has to write something in this stupid journal, and she won't be betraying anyone if her topic for this afternoon is *Me and My Dad: The Wonderful World of Juliet Ryan and Bart, her Fabulous Father.*

He doesn't say much, her father. Not to Juliet, anyway. It's different with her mother. He's got plenty to say to her about the state of the house: For God's sake, Monica, can't you keep the maid under control, what exactly are we paying her for? Her mother, quiet, always quiet, then apologizing again and again and again. I'm sorry, Bart. Sorry, Bart. That's her mother's litany when he comes home, her hands shaking because she needs a drink.

Juliet has seen her mom shake. Seen her scurrying, Sorry Bart, sorry, flitting from kitchen to dining room to lounge to stoep. Trying to straighten rooms that never look properly clean and tidy no matter how many times she asks the latest maid to Please do this, and Could you do that?

Bart Ryan.

She can't see how her mother's ever going to escape him. If he had his way, Juliet would be in his power too, pinned down by his hard eyes, reduced to stuttering and mumbling and shuffling and trying, always trying. And then, finally, the desired result. Sorry Dad, sorry Dad, sorry.

Those are words Bart Ryan will never hear his daughter say.

Gabriel is sitting on a wooden bench in a police station and Mum walks past and she doesn't even look at him.

Mum, he says, Mum, where are you going? Where's Harry? but Mum doesn't answer. She walks past him and the policeman shuts the door behind them and leaves Gabriel all alone.

It's hot. The policeman sitting on the bench next to him has big rings of sweat under his arms, staining the deep blue of his uniform. There's sweat on his face too, shining on his forehead. He's there to keep Gabriel company while they talk to his mum. And then they can all go home.

Gabriel wants to lie down on his bed in the corner of Mum's room, next to Harry's cot, and close his eyes and sleep. From there, he can see out of the window, watch the moon rise and light up the roofs of the houses gathered across the street. He can hear the clank and rumble of the garbage truck coming to collect the waste. None of the places in the old man's house are safe, but at least when Gabriel's in his own bed, he can escape into sleep.

Gabriel closes his eyes and an orange glow lights up behind his eyelids. People come and go and talk and there's a man shouting somewhere down a corridor, yelling and saying, It's her fault. Why don't you talk to the bitch, and the policeman on the other side of the counter is laughing at something and the phones are ringing. There's so much noise, but it isn't loud enough to drown out the sound of fire as it sweeps along the path that's been set for it. So fast.

Gabriel never knew it could move so fast. Huge leaping bounds and as it runs it grows. Bright, brighter, looking for somewhere to stop and guzzle.

So, Gabriel. The policeman sitting next to him says his name and Gabriel opens his eyes. Do you want to tell me what happened?

Later, years later, Gabriel knows that the man should never have spoken to him. He should never have kept Gabriel from closing his eyes and falling asleep. He should never have asked the same questions over and over again while Gabriel's mother was in the room with the other policeman, the one who's walking up to them now.

I couldn't get anything from her, Gabriel hears him saying to the sweaty man sitting on a wooden bench next to him. Any luck here?

None, says the other. All you need to do is smell the kid, though.

Gabriel's eyes are closed, but he hears the voices behind the crackle and pop of the fire, behind the running, jumping, munching of the fire, he hears their voices. But he's too tired to open his eyes, too tired to speak and tell them what happened.

Ever since Noah went to Greenhills, Maddie's mom is doing things she'd never have done when he was home. Like reading the newspaper and then abandoning it on the couch. Not folded along its seams and neatly flipped in two and aligned with the edge of the coffee table. Today, for example, it has been left wide open, displaying the contents of pages twelve and thirteen.

Maddie notices it shortly after she gets home from school and looks surprised. Her mom apologizes and goes to tidy it away, but Maddie stops her.

"Don't worry, Mom. It's all right."

That night at supper Maddie says, as she loads food onto her fork, "Have you noticed that now that Noah's gone, we're not so pernickety?"

"*Pernickety*? That's an odd word," her dad says.

"Yes, but it's a good one for how we were with him."

Maddie's mouth is full now and she knows better than to continue talking. Standards might be dropping, but not that far.

27 JULY 2011 / 00:57

Kate moved through the house, from room to room, from window to window, staring out into the dark of the garden. The house was secure, a new key and remote hung from her keyring. Tomorrow, her husband said. Tomorrow he'd look at a new car for her.

"Something small," she said. "That's all I want, Dom. A car no one will go to any effort to steal."

Dominic agreed. There was no guarantee that anything was safe, but he'd do all he could, and more, to keep his family from further harm.

So, a new car for Kate. That was a job for the next day, but just then Dominic had to stop Kate's restless pacing.

"Come, Kate."

She stood in the center of the living room, looking around her. She'd chosen that sofa, long enough to stretch out on, doze off on. She'd chosen that table, that vase. She'd arranged those irises, tall and violet-blue, just that morning. She'd decided on the curtains, more wisp than drape, to allow a better view of sea and mountain.

Now, she wanted curtains that were dark, double-lined, heavy. Ones she could close tight against the outside.

"Darling." Dominic was at her side, a glass of water in one hand, a small white pill in the other. A sleeping tablet. Kate didn't want to take it, but tomorrow there would be lots to sort out. New phones, for starters. She'd have to call the school, update their numbers. Phone Speed Key, praise the quiet efficiency of the men who had come to help them. What else? Check the kids' timetable on the fridge. Did Maddie have another gym practice? She was so keen to make it onto the team, but would she even want to go to school tomorrow? Was there a protocol for situations like this? Did you hunker down inside your house and wish the world away, or head out in the morning with a smile on your face and a breezy hello for Audrey Parfitt, as if nothing had happened?

Only something had, and no doubt Audrey had seen the police car drawing up outside the Groomes' house, the Speed Key van that followed it, the lights that blazed from every room, that were still blazing at one in the morning.

Sleep was essential if Kate was going to get through the next day.

⊕

It's Noah's fifth week at Greenhills and already Maddie's finding it hard to remember life with him at home. They're slipping into a new routine too easily, she thinks, when she remembers how carefully, how meticulously they had to observe the demands of his timetable, to make sure that their days fitted in around his schedule.

Now, he holds a different place in their lives, the one labeled: "Sunday Afternoon, 2.30–4.30 p.m." Two hours a week, that's all.

Maddie misses him so much. At times it feels like all the air has been sucked out of her. Now she understands the power of sorrow.

Then again, when she doesn't have to worry about him, think about what he needs or how he might react to something out of the ordinary, the heaviness lifts and Maddie can fill her lungs and breathe.

⊕

Day 31 / 13:41

"I used to be friends with a mermaid."

Juliet's working hard, trying to get Noah to pay attention, look away from his calculations.

"A what?"

"A mermaid. Jeez, dude. Don't you ever listen to anyone?"

No, he wants to say. Not when he's trying to fill in his time sheets. It's always the same story—ever since he got to Greenhills—trying to balance minutes lost with minutes gained, and on top of all that, figuring out how to fit in the latest task Ms. Turner has set. Last week they walked the lawn together and he managed to cross it 3 times without having to count. Then he caved (and counted and tapped), but the next day they managed it 7 times, and the next a few more, Ms. Turner at his elbow, talking, "about anything and everything, Noah, as long as it keeps you distracted."

Today, though, it's completely different. She wants him to try it on his own. "Ten minutes in the morning, Noah, and ten in the afternoon, out in the grounds. Try walking across the lawn and back again without counting, without following any of the paths."

She's insane, she must be, to ask him that. But no, there's the infuriatingly understanding smile that always follows when she sets another of her stupid tasks. "Think of them like doing a few chores for your mom, Noah. Like emptying the trash, rather than climbing Mount Everest."

Does this Turner woman not understand the meaning of consequences?

It *is* more like climbing Everest, even if she says he can turn back whenever he wants to, that she'll talk him through it, show him how not to count—

"She's always there..." Juliet's saying and Noah drags his attention away from Ms. Turner.

"...or at least she was when I was a little girl. She'd be on the rocks in the far corner of the beach. Sitting, smiling. Waiting for me. You'd think I'd have outgrown her by now, and I suppose I have, I know she's not real. But that doesn't stop me hoping she's still there, waiting for me to arrive."

He's listening. He might as well now. Juliet's non-stop talking, thinking about Ms. Turner—his chain of thought's completely broken. The numbers he had lined up, ready to add, are dancing around in circles.

It's a bit of a problem, this. He finds himself talking to Juliet, using words unnecessarily, wanting to know more about her, about mermaids, holidays Juliet went on as a little girl. So, he listens, promising himself he'll get back to his calculations later.

Later? And when exactly is later *going to be?*

"Every summer, when Mom and Dad took us away, off to the seaside to play Happy Families, I'd go straight to those rocks to find her. She'd always be there, smiling, humming, waving at me."

Juliet's sitting still and her voice is quiet. "One of these days I'll take Lily back there and we can go mermaid-chasing, see if she's there, if she remembers me."

DAY 32 / 06:18

There is no one and nothing. The space around Noah is clear and blue. He's deep in crystal blue, shining and clean. He inhales and fills his lungs and heart with blue, his eyes, his ears, his open mouth. He breathes it in until every vein in his body runs blue.

When he wakes up, he doesn't try for his pulse. He doesn't scan his room.

He breathes in and out. He feels inside himself for blue; it's still there. Cool, calm.

He sits up. He has to start. Let fingers find their way to his pulse, check and check again, but for a moment he sits on the end of his bed, bathed in blue.

There's the clank of Amber's cleaning trolley, the smell of antiseptic following her. Morné's deodorant, sweet in the corridor.

He touches his finger to his pulse. Slow, steady, regular. He can do his check now and then go to his cupboard and take out his Tuesday T-shirt, jeans, a clean pair of blue socks.

A quick check of the clock. He's running to time.

Another quick check.

How could he have missed it?

His organizer has been moved. It's balancing on the edge of his desk. If he moves too suddenly, it will topple to the floor and spill pencils and pens, his eraser, Post-its. And then they will all have to be gathered up and put back exactly where they belong. He will lose minutes. And more minutes, because...

He checks his pulse and it's galloping. His breath is coming out in short bursts, his hands are cold. Where to begin? Where to start? He stands up, creeps across the room. Slowly, slowly, he reaches for it, slides it gently back to the solid, secure space of the desk.

Last night, while he was dreaming, someone was in his room.

Noah had been floating in a sea of blue. Blue above and blue below. Blue of sea, blue of sky. Blue to hold the fishes. Blue to hold the birds. Blue had allowed him to sleep, deep and cool and untroubled. He'd dropped his defenses against the Dark, and in that time, someone came into his room. A prowling shadow had found its way to the desk and slid an object to its very edge.

27 JULY 2011 / 01:49

Noah's room was dark, there was no moon to throw light from the sky. It made sense that home invaders operated on nights like this, evil unseen, slipping shadow-like from deed to deed, leaving despair and chaos, anger and grief in their wake.

"We were lucky," his mother had said as they'd stood huddled together. "They didn't hurt us."

But in a weird way he wished they had. He wished they'd knocked him to the ground as he tried to defend her. He wished he'd had the chance to fight back, throw them down, one by one. Tie *them* back to back, gag *them* so they couldn't scream, their mouths filling with spit and blood as they forced their tongues against cloth, trying to bite free.

On the thirty-second day of Noah's time in Greenhills, Kate phones Dominic in a panic. "What if we're doing the wrong thing, Dom?" She's standing in the hallway, her phone hard to her ear, and she hears him sigh. Not loudly, but it's there, that small, impatient exhalation.

Noah's door is open, his walls are bare. Kate walks into his room and breathes. She can just about catch him on the air.

Dominic's voice is loud, "Kate? Can you hear me?"

She turns, just as she's seen her son doing, looking from corner to corner to corner, her head moving the same way as his.

"Kate?"

Kate can hear him just fine. She hears every word Dominic says, catches every inflection, worries about his ongoing lack of response. When was the last time he answered her properly?

"Kate?"

She's tired of asking, tired of worrying, tired of trying to get Dominic involved. She's alone in this.

The thought enters like a blessing.

She cuts Dominic off. She's not going to tell him she's fine, that she's coping, that it's all for the best. It's not her job any more.

Family photos line the hallway: Noah at two, Maddie dressed as one of the three kings in the school nativity play, her gappy grin beaming at them.

She remembers Dominic's hand on her knee, the way they shook with laughter as Maddie shouted out her line. How nothing distracted her from giving her gift to the new baby: "Myrrhizz mine! And! Bits! Of! Perfume!"

That was a good time.

The phone is silent. Dominic hasn't called back.

She should get busy, she should be grateful she has a daughter and husband to shop for, a house to manage, a meal to cook, a car to drive. She should be counting her blessings, not wondering if she'll ever hear Dominic in a panic, his voice rushed and worried, anxious about Noah and where he is.

Then she thinks about the list for Ms. Turner.

Has Dominic made his? She doubts it. He hasn't mentioned it to her, they hardly discuss anything these days.

Kate has other things to sort out. Noah is still growing and his white shirts aren't tucking in as well as they should. She knows the brand, knows what the next size up will be.

This is something she can do for her son. Go shopping, make sure he always has seven white shirts ready to wear, creases ironed in, just so, pocket deep enough to hold his notebook and pen. Kate picks up her bag and opens the front door. Fifteen steps and she is at the garage. She's counting for her son, measuring her steps in batches of five. Breathing deliberately, in two, three, four, five, out two, three, four, five. She touches the handle of the door five times, opens it and slides behind the wheel. In her bag, her phone rings. The screen glows and her husband's name flashes up at her.

Kate shifts into reverse and backs down the drive. The gate slides open and she eases into the traffic. She'll get Noah's shirts first and then shop for supper.

27 JULY 2011 / 02:15

Dominic started awake and reached for Kate. He ran his hands along her body, felt for her face in the dark.

"What is it?" Kate was groggy with sleep.

"Nothing, Kate. Go back to sleep."

He lay there, his eyes following the shadows as trees moved in the garden.

A man's home is his castle, but what happens when the defenses are breached, when invaders swim the moat and let down the draw-bridge?

2002

Noah's second day of Big School. Mom took him as far as the door of the classroom. He didn't like it when she bent down to kiss him good-bye and he didn't like it when Miss Jonas told him to hurry along and hang up his bag.

His hook was still there, and his stars with their 5 points. That was something.

"At least the sky didn't fall on our heads, hey, Noah?" That's what Mom always said when "things could be worse."

He knew, from his first day, that a bell would ring soon. Miss Jonas called it break time. As soon as it rang he could go to his hook, take down his bag and open his lunchbox. Mom said she'd packed a sur-prise for him for today, but he'd have to wait to find out what it was.

He waited, all the way through painting shapes with potatoes in-stead of paintbrushes and putting lucky beans into cups and taking them out again and doing interesting things with Plasticene. At least Miss Jonas said they were interesting, but all the colors had been squished together and the clay was a browny mess, so all the things he made looked the same.

When the bell rang, everyone got up and started rushing to their bags, but Miss Jonas said, "Children, children, back to your places, please." She said she was teaching them how to behave for when they got to Grade 1. They had to learn how to wait, and how to take turns, and "no pushing or shoving." When they were all quiet they could get up and "walk *quietly*, please" to their bags and take out their lunchboxes.

Inside his lunchbox Noah found 5 little sandwiches cut into small stars, each with 5 points. There was one cheese and one PNB (that's what Mom called peanut butter) and one strawberry jam and two just-butter. For the first time on Noah's second day it felt like things were getting better, and at least that was something.

A girl was sitting next to him, the one from yesterday who said she wasn't scared of big school. She was wearing black shiny shoes and her socks had frills around the tops.

"Swap?" she asked.

Before he could say he didn't know what "swap" meant, she'd put her hand into his lunchbox and took a butter-only sandwich, the one he was saving for last. Then she put a bit of sausage where his butter-only was supposed to be and smiled.

"My feet are sore," she said, but he didn't care. He wanted to kick her shiny black shoes with his new red tekkies, but Mom said you shouldn't hit girls.

So he counted to 5 and wished Miss Jonas would clap her hands and say, "Tidy up children, no crumbs please," but instead she walked over and looked down on him and said, "Come along, Noah, you must eat up." He stared at her, and he hated her, and he hated ShinyShoe girl and her stupid sausage.

When Miss Jonas's hands finally went Clap! Clap! he liked her again because eating was over and he could go to his hook and hang his bag and touch the points of his star.

"Don't worry," Mom said. "Soon you'll make lots of friends."

He wished he could make just *one* friend, but when they all went outside to play on the swings and in the sandpit and on the jungle gym everyone had someone to play with except him. So he sat on a swing and used his feet to push off. His legs were long, so he was able to go higher and higher, and at least that was also something.

Then, Clap! Clap! Miss Jonas went again and it was time to go inside and do stuff and wait for the bell that said soon Mom would be there to collect him.

Ms. Ellen Turner sits back in her chair and looks at them, her expression serious. A little girl playing at being doctor, Dominic thinks sourly, with her black jacket and name tag, her hair pulled back into a stubby ponytail, her short-cropped nails, just the top of her white shirt showing. Dark trousers, too, and plain black pumps with a low heel. All very professional and conservative but none of it helping to make her look a day older than twenty. And she, this near-*child*, this wet-behind-the-ears child, wants to talk to them about guilt.

"What I want to talk about," Dominic says, "is why I'm paying a pile of money to come here and be lectured by a girl young enough to be my daughter."

He knows that Kate wants to creep under the young woman's desk and look up at her beseechingly and say, "I'm so sorry, Ms. Turner, my husband didn't mean—"

But Dominic's tired. He's tired of all the talking and the tiptoeing and the to-and-froing and the endless talk, talk, talk about Noah. He's tired of Kate trying to make out that this is the sort of thing that happens in every family. It isn't, and he knows it, and Kate knows it, and Little Ms. Therapist with her serious face and her kindly concern knows it. Just like she knows that Kate is crawling with guilt, that it keeps her awake at night, and her guilt is trying to invade him too, send him from their bed to sit at his computer, clicking obsessively, keeping his mind closed against the invidious thought creeping closer and closer, the one that hasn't been mentioned, the elephant standing unmoving and unmovable. Dominic feels his mouth open and out come the words he has avoided saying aloud for almost two years.

"Why us, Ms. Turner? Can you tell us that? Why did we land up with a son like Noah? Why don't we talk about that, Ms. Turner? Why don't we go back to the scene of the accident?"

Kate's horrified, he can see, but there's no stopping him. He's on his way, siren wailing, lights flashing.

He's going to say things that can't be taken back, and once he does, once he sets foot on this path, there will be no turning back. He's going to pull them all along, and the only way will be down, with him.

He's letting it all out, and Kate finds herself wishing she could stop the flow, push his words back into that pent-up place where Dominic keeps all his emotions tightly bundled up and labelled "Do Not Open."

Return to the scene of the accident? Kate shudders. Is this what his marriage, their life together, their children are to him? One gigantic and ugly scene? And Dominic? He's not racing to save them. His family's standing at the side of the road, yelling for help, and he's screaming past them, his siren blaring defiance. He's cutting himself loose with every word that leaves his mouth, vanishing as fast as he can. Her husband won't be tethered to the crash site of their lives.

"Let's forget about guilt, Ms. Turner."

"I—" the young woman says, but Dominic interrupts.

"I'm not going to sit and wring my hands and feel sorry and guilt-ridden and ask what we could have done better and bemoan this decision we had to make and ask you to help us find some way of forgiving ourselves for putting Noah here."

Dominic feels a quick spurt of satisfaction. See how you deal with this one, Ms. Turner. Not exactly a textbook outburst, is it?

He's sitting so far forward on his seat that he's almost touching Ms. Turner's knees.

"Why don't we look at the facts, Ms. Turner, and forget about the feelings? Why don't we all take a deep breath and let the bullshit fly out the window? Here's the situation, plain and simple. Our son can't cope with life, and we can't cope with him. So why are you asking us to feel guilty about having him here?"

"I wouldn't say—" Ellen Turner tries to interject, but Dominic is ready for her.

"You wouldn't say? You don't have to. Just using the word presumes the feeling. My son is in the best place, Ms. Turner. Allow us to accept that."

Ms. Turner can't stop him, but Kate is going to try. It's her turn now. She's at the side of the road watching her life fall to pieces and her mouth is open and she's yelling at him to stop, calling him every name she can think of. He is smug, he's shallow, he's callous, he's an egotistical prick, he can't think of anyone but himself. He shuts himself away from her, she doesn't know who he is any more. Has she ever known who he is? But more than that, over and above all of that, just answer this question, she shouts: "Is this the way you've always felt, Dominic? Is this why you battle to look your son in the eye and call him by his name?"

Ms. Turner starts to speak, but this time Kate holds up a hand to silence her.

"Let him answer," she says.

He lifts his head, and looks her in the eye. "I don't know, Kate. I don't know how I feel. I'm glad Greenhills exists, that they're happy to look after him here. I know you want me to visit every Sunday, but I can't. I just can't."

Dominic turns his head to the window. He doesn't want to look at Kate, he wants to get it all out. "Life's easier without him."

Think of it as a new beginning, Mrs. Social-Worker says to Gabriel. She's holding his hand and Gabriel wishes he could pull away from her. In another room, somewhere in this building, with its long corridors and rooms with brown desks and shelves filled with folders, is his little sister. Gabriel knows this because he saw a car arrive at the same time as they did, and a lady got out holding Harry, but the lady wasn't Mum. He hasn't seen her since the night when Mr. George Fat found him hiding behind the hedge in his garden and said, Holy fuck, son, they're looking all over for you. He'd moved towards Gabriel, but Gabriel dodged him and sprinted from Mr. George Fat and Mrs. Gladys Thin's garden.

A mad dash, that's what Mum used to say.

Come on, Gabe, let's make a mad dash, and they're running across the sand and into the sea.

A mad dash and Dad's laughing and Mum's tummy is as round as the beach ball Dad blew up when they got to the beach. Mum touches Dad's shoulder and then she's saying, C'mon Gabe, come on, Gaby-Baby, what are we waiting for—let's make a mad dash for it—and the sea is cool and wet on Gabriel's ankles and then his waist and Mum is holding him and his legs are around her waist and the sea is rocking them and everything is calm. And Gabe and Mum are calm and enjoying the water.

So Gabriel makes a dash, he dashes along the road and Mrs. Cleans-Her-Windows yells, There he is! and Gabriel runs...straight into the arms of a man who smells of sweat. Long ago, when Dad was there and Mum was happy, Gabriel played with a big red fire engine, and there was a fireman with a yellow hat, and Mum said, One day, when you grow up, maybe you'll be a fireman, my Gaby-Baby.

The fireman's got him in his arms and he's swinging him up in the air, and he's saying, Easy now, easy. Come with me, son.

There's Mum, leaning against Mrs. Cleans-Her-Windows's wall, and she's not even looking at Gabriel. She's not looking anywhere except across the road to the burning house.

This is one of the things Gabriel will wonder, year after year after year: Did the old man wake up and smell the smoke and hear the fire crackling on the other side of his door? Did he take a deep breath to yell and did smoke rush in to fill his lungs, so all he could do was croak, Help me, please help me. But was his voice strangled so that no one could hear? Did he try to get out of bed, did he get tangled in the sheets, did a small flame lick its way under the door and find its way into the folds of his cotton pajamas (cheap polyester, they said later)? And then, did the fire have a field day, a picnic, a feast of old man's flesh, when it was too late for anyone to go in and save him? Did he know what was happening as the flames ate and ate and turned his pale white skin and strong body into a skinny black crisp?

Gabriel will think about this, year after year, as he leaves behind his past, and the burning house and Mum with her empty eyes, and his hands that smell of petrol, and his little sister in another lady's arms, and he hopes, oh, he really hopes, that the old man died screaming, choking in a smoke-filled room.

DAY 35 / 21:54

Noah switches off his bedside light, closes his eyes and listens. He has done this every night since his organizer was moved. He vows to stay awake, catch whoever it is in the act of disruption. But he can never keep his eyes open, stop himself entering the jumpy world of sleep. He'll never dream of blue again, he's sure of that. And he's glad—it was too cool, too relaxing. It moved him from high alert to deep calm, lowered his defenses. He'll never make himself that vulnerable again.

He's tried telling Ms. Turner about it, but when he opens his mouth the words don't come. Besides which, he knows the questions; he's asked them himself, over and over.

Are you sure, Noah?

Are you absolutely sure?

Were you just tired?

Is it possible you missed it when you did your final check?

And then of course, there's this:

You've been distracted. You're getting too comfortable here.

That's true. He's been slipping. He needs to double up his efforts. Check, check, check. Watch what he says.

He won't tell Ms. Turner anything about his blue dream, or his organizer. What he will do, however, is make very sure that everything is where it should be before he closes his eyes. There must be no doubt.

That's more like it. Keep your guard up.

DAY 36 / 12:36

Noah cannot, dare not, talk to Ms. Turner about the intruder in his room. But he needs to get it out, somehow. And if one thought leads to another—well, that's what he's getting used to when he writes things down.

Dear Ms. Turner

I'm writing this in my journal because I can't use words to talk. You say writing things down makes them easier to deal with, helps break down a large problem.

These are huge problems and I don't know how to cope with them.

Someone came into my room.

I'm pretty sure of it. But I can't be 100% positive, and that's what's worrying me. I have so much I need to be careful about and it feels as if I'm not being as vigilant as I should.

I always have this huge question in my head—what if?

It won't go away. It stops me from doing anything properly. I can't join in group properly, I can't make friends, I can't talk to you, I can't let my mother know I'm OK, I can't face up to my father and ask him what his problem is. Every time I do, the question's there. What if I do and something terrible happens to my family? It's my job, you see. I have to keep them from harm and if I break one of the rules...

When I sat down to write this, I thought, OK, here's one place where I can tell the truth. Really say it. Move it from inside my head. Even as I'm trying to write, I feel it building. It wants me to stop. It's going to start telling me what to do. It doesn't like it when I speak for myself.

I'm going to tell you about it, Ms. Turner.

I call it the Dark. It drowns me when I try to talk. It stops me moving. That's why I need my 5s, to push it away when it fills my head.

I can't talk about it. It's too risky. Too dangerous. I won't show this letter to you. But I'll write it. Anything to make it weaker.

It's there. The Dark. It's always there. That's what I find so hard to explain. There isn't a single moment when my mind is empty. I force it back, shut it down, but I can't make it disappear.

When it moves, every muscle in my back bunches and my fingers curl. I'm coiled and ready, waiting. It prowls, jabs at me.

Keeping you on your toes, Noah.

That's what it tells me, that sort of thing.

I have to tap, keep it contained, because if it explodes it will reach right down into me and destroy me. Leave me gutted, unable to crawl or call for help.

You know those scenes you see on the TV, after a hurricane has hit a town? The streets laid out, the grids, the pavements, the way the town was planned on paper, but now whole houses have been torn up, trees are upended, roots pointing to the sky. Everything's turned upside down, all the insides out.

That's what it's building towards when it gets really angry. I smell it, hot and ready to blow. I have to gather strength.

I have to stay on high alert.

The thing is, once a hurricane hits, you can't even *see* there used to be a town. And that's what the Dark is like. It's out to crush and destroy. Once it's done with me, it'll be off, unstoppable. My parents. Maddie. I won't be able to help them.

I've tried my best to describe it, but my words are too weak. The Dark is a hurricane, a tsunami, a raging forest fire, all swept into one. It hates to be controlled. And every time I close it down a bit, it resents me more.

It hates me.

I hate it.

I wish it would vanish, once and for all.

12:56

And should it vanish, "once and for all," do you think Fear will leave too?

It will still be out there. In the shadows, where your nightmares wander.

27 JULY 2011 / 02:56

The gate was closed. Securely locked, a new password keyed in to keep them safe. The front door fitted with a new lock.

His parents had gone to bed but Maddie's door was open. So was his. "Please, Noah," she'd said, "don't close your door."

"You can sleep in my room, we can bring in a mattress," he'd offered.

"No, it's fine. As long as I know you're right next door."

"I'll hear you, Mads," he said. "I'll hear you breathing."

And now he was at his window, awake in the dark, restive, on edge.

The sound of light breathing from the room next door signalled his sister was finally asleep.

Down at the end of the driveway, the gate was closed.

The smell of the men had gone with them, the meatiness of Gray-Eyes's breath, the acid tinge of fear on GapTooth's body, his cloying aftershave.

Noah pressed his hands against the windowpane. It was cold under his touch and as he watched two ghostly handprints formed. 5 fingers on each hand. He pulled his hands back and let each of them curl into a fist.

He ran his tongue over his teeth. It was still sore where he'd bitten it.

Outside the window, down the drive and beyond the gates, shadows shifted and shivered in the darkness and each was a shape, a man in black. They were still there and always would be; 3 bodies becoming 1 and then 3 and then 1 again, formless and forming, pushing hard against the wrought iron. Eyes flashed silver, orange. Strong fingers pulled at the iron bars and there was a grin, a quick baring of fangs. Then it all slid away, melted into nothing and the night folded back on itself. Still, Noah stood at the window, all 5 senses on high alert, ready to react at the smallest hint of danger. He would stand there all night if he had to.

Such a pathetically sad image. Noah Groome taking on the Dark.

WEEK 6: DAY 36 / 13:43

Juliet's hands are quick, excited. They punctuate her sentences, swooping and flying, diving and weaving with the narrative of her stories. Like her, they're seldom at rest. It's as if she's scared to pause, take a breath, take a break. Even when she's exhausted, there's always part of her moving. She listens to Noah, but her body wants to be up and gone. Especially her hands, knitting into and over each other, knotting into fists then stretching out into open palms. Her hands speak for her. When she's hiding behind words, her hands tell the truth.

Dominic is at his computer. It's two in the morning and he has slipped out of bed, leaving Kate undisturbed. Her light snoring is reassuring; if he wakes in the middle of the night he knows where he is, where he is meant to be. It was like that even when Noah was still at home, when life was far from normal.

Now, though, he's coming adrift. The cursor hovers over the file that says *Noah*. It's always been there, just like the one that says *Maddie*. If Kate came across it she'd think nothing of it, assume it was filled with reports and assessments, scans of documents, articles he hasn't read. But Noah's file is a loaded gun, safety off, cocked and ready to fire. It's the bullet his wife hears in her dreams that has her sitting upright clutching him, whimpering, "Dominic, Dominic," and has him holding her close, patting her back to sleep.

He doesn't open it. There's no need. He simply copies the latest email from his son into the file that carries his name and deletes it from his inbox. How much longer can he do this, though? Noah is too clever, too quick; he'll never stop asking questions, looking for answers that Dominic is unwilling to give.

DAY 38 / 20:23

Another good time...

Spit and Spot.

Spit is a rambunctious bundle of fur, but Spot is timid. He approaches everyone and anything with caution.

Noah's father was never that keen on them having an

animal, but shortly after the home invasion he agreed when his wife said, "It's another deterrent, Dominic. A black dog, everyone says. Maybe if we'd had one..."

His mom hadn't finished her sentence. She didn't need to. The next weekend, she took Maddie and Noah to TEARS to choose their dog.

It was early when they got there, a cold Saturday morning. Cage after cage of wagging tails, barks and whines.

"This one's called Spot," said Maddie, looking at a large black dog cowering in the corner of the cage he shared with two other rescue animals. He had a white patch over one eye, giving him the raffish air of a pirate. But there was nothing raffish about this boy.

"Well, he's certainly big," Noah's mom said, "but he's not exactly fearsome, is he? What could have happened to him to make him this scared of people?"

"Here boy, come. C'mon Spot." Noah crouched and waited.

Maddie bounced from cage to cage, wanting them all, loving them all, but their mother had been firm. "One only. I promised your father, kids."

Noah waited in the same place. "Here, boy."

"It says he's an African Sheprador," Maddie said, reading the description attached to the fence. "Africanis, German Shepherd and Labrador Retriever. That's a good mix, hey Mom? And he's four years old, like we agreed."

They'd decided to choose a full-grown dog rather than a puppy. "Puppies always go first, they always get homes," Maddie had said. She'd been researching rescue dogs ever since their dad had given permission for a pet. "Let's choose an older dog, okay Noe?"

When Spot finally sidled forward and pressed his muzzle against the mesh, Noah looked at Maddie. She nodded. Spot had chosen them.

On the way out they were ambushed by a quivering nose, a hopeful yip that begged, "Choose me too, choose me too!"

"Oh, Mom!" Maddie was close to tears. "I just love her."

Their mother bent and the small dog snuffled at her hand through the fence. "She's a real little spitfire," she said.

And that was it. The Groomes and their two dogs, bundled into the car.

Happy days. And they will never be here again.

Kate sits down to send an email, then stands and wanders outside into the heat. She can't settle. And for once, it's not because of Noah.

She forgets to collect Dominic's suits from the cleaner; she forgets to phone the Pool Guy to look at the pump again. They ran out of milk but she forgot to add it to her list and now Dom will have to collect some on his way home. If she were to say to him, "I'm sorry, I've been so distracted, thinking about Noah and how he's getting on..." her husband might sigh, but he'd understand.

Today, she nearly forgot to collect Maddie from gymnastics. She had to dash to the car, get to school as fast as she could. She, the mother who's always on time for her children, made her daughter wait in the schoolyard.

She finds herself apologizing all the way home, even though Maddie isn't upset.

"It's not a problem, Mom, I didn't have to wait that long."

But the thing is, she had to wait.

"I'm so sorry, Mads."

"Don't worry, Mom," Maddie says for the tenth time. And then she adds, "There's so much for you to think about, no wonder you got the time mixed up." Then she starts to tell her about how Miss Wilcox said that if she continues as well as she's doing, she'll definitely be selected for the school team.

"That's brilliant, Maddie, it really is! I'm proud of you, darling. Dad's going to be so happy. And Noah, we mustn't forget to tell him on Sunday."

What Kate can't quite admit to herself is that the thought of going to Greenhills this Sunday is making her more nervous than she's felt in ages. Giddy, almost. She wants to see Noah, of course she does, but she's also looking forward to talking to Mr. Bill, seeing his warm smile, sitting and chatting about her son.

Mr. Bill's face doesn't close against hers when she talks about Greenhills and how everything is going.

Juliet is at her desk. This is the time of day she hates the most, the half hour after lunch when they are expected to open their journals and write.

She looks at the line she's just written.

My mother doesn't really miss me and I don't blame her.

Her knees jiggle under the table.

There you go, Ellen. Plenty of meat there for you to chew on. But it's true. No smokescreen today for Juliet, no hiding behind her words and leaving it up to the therapist to snip away at them.

The thing is, Ellen's on to her. Juliet thought it would take so much longer, but she's underestimated her. She's no fool; she isn't taken in by Juliet's subterfuges.

So, maybe that's why Juliet has written that first line.

Or maybe it's Noah and his family, his mom and sister who've come to see him every Sunday without fail. You can tell just by looking at them that they miss Noah.

"Blues and black, my favorite colors," Juliet laughs as she looks around the circle. Oh God, how many times has she sat like this, leaning forward so that whoever sits next to her gets a good eyeful of her bra? Then smiling as she sees them looking. The trick is to sit like that for a while, let them relax, and then jerk your head to the side and catch them in the act. Then she'll smile at them sadly; a sorrowful lift of her lips.

"Black-and-blue, the color of bruises, you know? And then they turn yellow and a sort of purplish-green just before that." She looks around the circle and they shuffle their feet or shift in their seats and Ellen asks her if she wants to add anything. She ducks her head and says "No" in a tiny voice.

Ellen pauses, and then continues, but Juliet knows she's seen through her to the truth: No one has ever hit Juliet; she's never suffered the painful bruises she loves to describe. Ellen will bide her time and call her on it when she needs to. That's fine. It gives her time to spin a few more yarns, shake the others out of their stupor, and, quite honestly, do *anything* to stop Soppy Sadie boring them all to tears with another sad story about why she steals. It was only a chain for God's sake, Juliet wants to yell at her. Cheap jewelery. And for that they put you in here, to torture us with your endless whining?

"I know why they did," she says to Noah later, sitting in her usual place. "I'd do it too, if she was my daughter. Get her out of my house and into HappyHomes as fast as I possibly could, before she drove me insane."

He has his back to her and he's filling in yet another block on yet another chart, but Juliet doesn't mind. This has become their ritual. "Teatime with Noah," Juliet calls it, and as long as she uses her own mug, they're cool.

Day 40 / 20:16

"Why don't you just give up?" Juliet asks, looking at his lopsided Family Tree. "Why don't you believe him when he says he doesn't know, or, if he does, he doesn't want to talk about it?"

Noah can't give up, nor can he use his stash of words to tell her how it feels to be gripped by this need to find out. The answers *are* out there, and until they are found his Family Tree will bend even further to the right, crowded on his mother's side, underpopulated on the other. If only he had one name, one thread to pull at.

He's trying to allow himself the words to tell her, but can't force them past his clenched teeth.

Juliet steps up to him, pats him quickly on the back. "It's okay, Noah," she says. "Seriously, it's okay. I'll help you, I promise. Maybe we can ask Maddie, too. We'll both help you."

After she leaves he sits at his desk and looks at his journal. He picks up (down-up-down-up) his pen, blocks his ears. He has to get his thoughts sorted out on this one.

If he writes it down, it might make more sense. He's been kidding himself all along, he's given up too easily. It isn't his father's fault he can't finish this task. If Noah wants to find out more, it's up to him to do more digging. Go deeper, head in a new direction. See what can be unearthed. See what, or who, emerges from the shadows. That's his task, and Juliet's set the idea free.

Gabriel walks into the children's home, his feet dragging behind Mrs. Social-Worker who has bustled him out of the car, talked him through the doors and into a room with a large counter and two ladies sitting behind it. One of them looks up as they enter, the other's fingers rattle the keys of her typewriter. There's a ping! as she gets to the end of the line, and a wham! as she shoots the carriage back to the left.

Yes? Non-Typing Lady says, and Mrs. Social-Worker pushes Gabriel between the shoulder blades, and he's at the edge of the counter, looking up at her.

Gabriel Felix says Mrs. Social-Worker. His paperwork was delivered this morning.

Felix, Felix, Non-Typing Lady's shuffling through a pile of files so high it looks like they'll topple any second, but she lays a hand flat on them and the manila tower stops swaying. Her hand is broad, her nail varnish chipped, and Gabriel wonders if her fingers would be thinner if they were being exercised over typewriter keys.

Another ping! and another wham! And then Non-Typing Lady's looking down at him and saying, The admission's in order. Sit there. Mr. de Wet will see him soon.

Mrs. Social-Worker sits and the grip on his hand forces him to follow her lead. She has a name, but Gabriel can't remember what it is. He can't remember anything except the police station last night, Mum walking past him, staring straight ahead, not looking at him, not even when he calls out. And then, behind her, a lady holding Harry. She doesn't say anything either, just glares at him and shakes her head and Gabriel feels shame filling him, even though he has nothing to be ashamed about.

Come on, the policeman is saying, we'd better get you washed and out of these clothes. You stink. And then they're telling him to shower and wash properly, to get the smell of petrol off his hands, the smell of smoke out of his hair and off his skin. He doesn't like the clothes they gave him: the trousers are too long, the shirt is a funny color and the jersey is itchy at his neck.

And now, here he sits, waiting for someone called Mr. de Wet.

Maddie doesn't mind Sundays any more. She used to. Hanging around the house, homework still to be done. Heavy, unending Sunday afternoons. But now they're different. Now it's into the car, with her mom, off to see Noah. Her dad never goes to Greenhills, not even for meetings with Ms. T. Not since they came home that last time, looking like survivors of a bomb blast, faces white, eyes blank.

Since then, her dad hasn't been home much, leaving early and working late at the office. Her mom takes her to school most days, which is fine because Maddie likes being in the car with her—she doesn't have to fill the silence with music, the way she has to with her dad. And it's always his choice of music, "Either that or the news, Maddie," and sometimes, when she thinks she can't handle another plinking note of Chopin, she opts for the news, only that's often worse. She hates starting the day with soundbites about crime and murder and arguments between politicians.

Sometimes she thinks she'd like to live on a desert island. She'd happily be a Robinson Crusoe. She'd take Noah, of course. There'd be white beaches, blue waters, small fish scurrying in rock pools, coconuts galore. Maddie watches *Survivor*, so she knows how it's done, how to do it, how to survive.

But now that she can look forward to seeing Noah, Sundays are so much easier. Her mom's calling, "Maddie, are you ready?" She is. No going to see Noah unless her homework is done. And it always is. She's not going to risk missing a visit for the sake of algebra or social science.

That's another good thing about Sundays. She does homework the moment she gets it—no waiting till the last minute, no dilly-dallying, finding other things to do. Visits to Greenhills have cured Maddie of procrastination—something no one could have predicted.

So here they are, in the car, and her mom's saying something about Juliet. Her tone of voice makes Maddie sit up and pay attention.

"I hope we can see Noah on his own," she's saying.

"How do you mean?"

"Well, you know, Mads. Without Juliet. It's not that I don't like her..."

Maddie waits for the "but."

"...but I would like our visiting time to be spent with Noah. It's our only chance to see him."

So her mom's going to ignore the big "but' about Juliet—the one she really means.

"I like Juliet," Maddie says. And she does. She likes the way she always has time to talk to her, how she laughs at Noah and names his weirdness as if it's nothing to get all panicky about or go all silent around, like her dad does.

Maddie's been noticing the cracks more and more since her brother left. Bizarre, really. She'd have thought that with him gone, life would be a bit easier, especially as far as her dad was concerned. But the silences between her parents are getting longer, and they never do anything together any more. When Noah was around they had a common worry—without him, nothing seems to be holding them together.

Her mom's silent, probably thinking more about Juliet, reluctant to say any more, but Maddie knows. She looks at her, the frown deep between her eyes, and feels an aching pity.

"Don't worry, Mom," she says. "Juliet doesn't see Noah that way."

"That way?"

"I mean she's not interested in him in that way. You know. For sex."

"For sex?" Her mom's voice is faint.

"Sure. Mom, you know. That's why Juliet's in there. But you don't have to worry. She told me Noah's her friend. That's all."

"Oh." Her mom's voice is even fainter.

Kate imagines talking to her mother, telling her that her husband isn't interested in her any more, *not in that way*, but the thought fails her before she even gets to thinking about how her mother would respond.

Maddie touches her mom on the leg. "Noah's safe with Juliet. Plus, she's good for him."

"Good for him?" Kate's still digesting *"that way."*

"Yes. You know. She treats him like he's normal."

They're approaching Greenhills now and soon they'll be signing in and the high gates will swing open and then close behind them.

"Do you think you'll be speaking to Mr. Bill today?" Maddie asks.

"I'm not sure. Maybe. If he's there."

What Kate doesn't say is that she hopes he is. How easy it is to talk to him—share her fears and worries.

"So you won't mind then," her daughter asks, "if I talk to Juliet?" Her face is anxious.

Kate smiles. "I don't mind at all, Mads," she says, "as long as you and Noah are happy." As long as that girl keeps her claws out of my son. And, she allows herself the next thought, as long as I have Mr. Bill to talk to.

The guard's at the window and Kate's filling in the paper on the clipboard. Name, date, person to visit, time of entry, car registration number. Kate scribbles it down and the gates swing open. There are plenty of parking spaces to the left of the house and she chooses one in the shade. She and Maddie are always the first to arrive and among the last to leave. Nothing hurries their departure; their time with Noah is precious and Kate wants to see as much of him as possible. So why is she scanning the rolling lawn for signs of Mr. Bill? He isn't there, but her son is, sitting on their bench under the oak tree, looking at his watch.

"You run on ahead, Mads," Kate says. "I'll catch up."

Kate doesn't have the freedom to run like Maddie does, because today she is wearing slip-ons with a slight heel, the ones that make her ankles look even more delicate, her calves even longer. Before she left she'd looked at herself in the mirror, critically, appraisingly, but didn't allow herself to ask why she was choosing her outfit so carefully when she was going to see her son, who never really notices what she is wearing.

"We're going now," she'd said to Dominic. "Are you sure you don't want to come?"

He'd looked up briefly from his computer, said an equally brief no, then added that he'd be going for his run in a few minutes.

He didn't notice what she was wearing either. Kate can't remember the last time he commented on her appearance. Dominic isn't one for compliments—that's what he told her early in the relationship—but she used to be aware of him watching her. Days when the air between them was charged, when his eyes said what he was thinking and she couldn't wait for night to fall and the bedroom door to close. When was the last time she had felt that way?

Kate had lingered at the door. Should she go back, ask again, get him to look at her properly, but then Maddie was at her side, looking at the clock on the wall.

"Come on, Mom, we'll be late. Noah will be waiting."

Day 42 / 14:33

Maddie runs towards her brother, arms stretched wide, stopping short before she touches him. She always has so much to tell him: all the news she saves up from the week, school, gymnastics, Spit and Spot, and how it's nearly time to take them to the dog parlor. He's happy to sit and listen.

Juliet should be here soon. Noah looks at his watch. She's late by 2 minutes, 21 seconds—and she had promised to be on time. He's hoping Mr. Bill will stroll down and get his mother talking because Juliet and he need to get Maddie on her own.

But here she comes now, strolling along, hands in her pockets, her busy eyes shooting between them all, a wide grin on her face.

"Mrs. Groome," she's saying, "how nice to see you again," and she's being perfectly polite. She sits on the lawn and looks up at them.

"So how has your week been?" she asks. "We've had a blast here, haven't we, Noah? We've both done a bit of weaving. Cloth, mind you, not baskets. Noah's quite the weaving bomb. He's already produced more than enough material to make bedspreads for us all."

Kate's watching carefully and she sees her son's lips lift in a smile. A small one, but a reaction nonetheless. What does this girl have that she doesn't? How has she managed to transform the blank-faced boy who arrived here six weeks ago into someone who's relaxed anough to smile at the irony behind her words? She feels another irrational twinge of resentment. She's being cheated out of watching her son improve. She's had to deal with all the hard stuff for so long, and now here he is, responding to Juliet in a way that he never does to her, or even to his sister. Not that it seems to bother Maddie. She's looking at Juliet with star-struck admiration. All of a sudden Kate's angry. They don't belong to you, she wants to say. Get your own family. Leave mine alone.

Juliet laughs and Kate's mouth tightens. Even that laugh is enough to set her teeth on edge. Does she have to joke about everything? Noah's no laughing matter, Juliet, she wants to say. But she can't. The girl is bound to have summed her up in three quick words. Uptight, conservative, overprotective.

At least I'm here, Kate wants to say. At least I'm visiting my child, but she has to bite back on the thought. Juliet never gets visitors and if Maddie and Noah are happy to have her gate-crash their family time, Kate should be too.

If only—

And then, there he is. Mr. Bill. Kate smiles politely and hopes he hasn't noticed the flush rising in her fair skin.

Juliet jumps to her feet. "Tea anyone? Mrs. Groome? Mr. Bill? Come on you lot. Come and help me carry." Noah and Maddie stand up, leaving room on the bench for Mr. Bill to sit and chat and ask Kate about her week.

"Come *on*, Noah." Juliet nudges him.

"Mom, Mr. Bill? Tea?" he asks.

"Not for me, buddy."

Kate smiles. "Thanks, darling." Then, as he walks away, she says to Mr. Bill, "Did I just see what I thought I saw? Noah doing something spontaneous?"

He laughs. "Don't ask me. Juliet seems to have him taped. She tells him what to do and he does it."

Kate feels a deeper pang now. Fear. What if Maddie has got it wrong?

"But she doesn't...? I mean, she isn't...?"

"No, no," Mr. Bill says. "Don't worry about Juliet and Noah. She hasn't got him in her sights. In fact," he smiles as he says it and Kate's stomach does a loop, "Noah may well be the first man—or boy—that Juliet hasn't targeted in a long time. He could be the best thing that's happened to her."

"But what about *my* boy?" The words are out before Kate can stop herself, and she wishes she could take them back. They make her sound mean and churlish. Here's Noah, doing some good, even if he isn't aware of it, and there she is, begrudging Juliet the chance of a relationship that might help all of them in some way. And all the while, she's aware of Mr. Bill sitting close to her. Almost thigh to thigh. "I'm sorry," she says. "I am glad to see Noah coping a bit better, I really am."

"He's been out in the grounds quite a bit," Mr. Bill says. Kate can barely hide her astonishment. "I've given him a few small jobs. Trimming edges, raking leaves. It's good practice for him. Grass grows, leaves fall; he can't control that. He can only tidy up after nature, not force it into a box."

"That's clever. Is it something Ms. Turner asked you to do?"

"Ellen?" Mr. Bill laughs. "No, not at all. It's just what I think might work for these kids. There's no harm in letting them do everyday things, see how they manage them. And Noah likes being here. It's confined, with rigid boundaries'—Mr. Bill glances at the high walls—"but at least he's outside, in the fresh air."

"And he's coming out here for visiting hours happily enough," Kate adds. "The third Sunday, without too much stress about his routines."

Mr. Bill touches her arm lightly. "It's a big step," he says.

Kate's consumed by the need to press against him, feel his heat seep into her, warm her body in the way that a scorching sun can't.

"Well," he says easily, getting to his feet. "I need to talk to Simon's parents." He looks over to where a small woman is sitting silently next to a thin, bespectacled boy. "See you next week, Mrs. Groome."

Kate, she wants to say, call me Kate, but the words won't come. Her tongue is heavy, she can't make it move.

"You do take one sugar don't you, Mom?" Maddie's walking carefully, balancing two teacups, one for her and one for her mother, careful not to let the tea slop onto the shortbread perched on the saucer. "Only Noah says it's none and I told him you've started taking it again. That you need some sweetness in your life. I'm right, aren't I?"

"Thanks, Mads. You're quite right. One sugar for me." Kate wishes she had been there to hear their argument, to hear her son insisting that he knows his mother better than Maddie.

Juliet brings up the rear and flops down next to her children on the lawn.

What's going on here? Out in the grounds, off the bench, sitting on ground that might be damp. What's happening to her orderly son and his demanding need for structure?

Maddie chats to Noah while her mom sips her tea and gazes into space. Thinking about Noah probably. Maddie doesn't mind that. She's glad it isn't about her. She wouldn't be able to handle that. The intense scrutiny, every move she made, every breath she took...okay, so that's from one of her mom's CDs, but still. Maddie doesn't mind all the attention being focused on Noah. Her mom loves her and that's enough. Maddie stops. Rethinks. Her mom *and* dad. Her parents love her and that's enough.

"Maddie?" Juliet's voice is serious. "Noah's got something to ask you. He needs your help."

Then Noah's explaining and his words are flying out of his mouth, pulling strands of story together.

"It's the Family Tree. Look here, I've made a rough copy."

Maddie hasn't heard him speak so fast, or so easily, in ages.

"We have to be quick, Mads. Otherwise it will be time for you guys to go."

"Sure, Noah."

Relax, she wants to say. Easy does it, bro, but instead she looks at Noah's finger, jabbing at the sheet of paper.

"That's Dad's side, Maddie."

"There's nothing to see," she says.

A grin spreads across her brother's face. Mom! Mom! she wants to yell, Noah's *smiling*. But now Juliet's talking.

"Exactly!" says Juliet. "There's everything about your mom, about her family—"

"And there's nothing for Dad," says Maddie. "There never has been."

"There could be," Juliet's talking for Noah now and he's letting her. "Your dad says he can't help Noah. He says his parents are probably dead. In fact, he won't tell Noah anything. He says it's none of his business."

Maddie nods. "Yes, that's what he always says and Mom says, "Leave it, kids, Dad doesn't want to go there.""'

"So Noah's stuck," Juliet continues, "but I told him not to be such a wimp. Your dad must have an ID number. If we can find out what it is, we can get a lead, even if it's only where he was born."

"We're not sure if that would work," Noah's joining in now, "but it's worth trying. I wrote to him, Mads. I sent him an email...Well, actually, quite a few. I've been using all my Internet time on them."

Maddie can imagine. Noah's mega-persistent when he's obsessing about something.

"I told him it was really important. If I could leave it alone, I would. You know I would, don't you? But I can't." Noah's talking even faster now and his fingers are starting their pre-tap tremors. "If I could get Dad's ID number, I reckon I can at least make a start."

Maddie nods. It would be good to know if she has aunts and uncles, cousins, grandparents on Dad's side of the family. Interesting too. But if she never found out, would it bother her? Not much, she decides, and definitely not as much as it does Noah.

"He wrote back," Noah's filling Maddie in quickly, keeping an eye on their mother, "but he still says there's nothing to talk about. He doesn't want me 'raking over the coals of the past.' That's how he put it. He also said I had enough to cope with, trying to sort out my current problems, and adding this unhealthy obsession to the list of my complications wasn't going to help me get better."

"Pretty harsh, hey, Maddie," Juliet says. "So that's what we wanted to ask you. Can *you* find out your dad's ID number? Do you reckon you could do that?"

"Me? I don't know how—"

"Could you just try, Maddie?"

Maddie looks at her brother.

"Sure, Noah," she says, anything to take the worry off her brother's face. He smiles, just slightly, and when Juliet elbows him he says, "Thanks, Mads."

"That's cool, Maddie. Really cool. Okay then, I'll let you guys chat for a while." Juliet gets to her feet, "Bye Maddie, bye Mrs. Groome." And then she's gone and Maddie and Noah are left alone on the lawn.

"Noah," Maddie tries, "why is it *so* important to get all these details about Dad? Can't you just start another project?"

Even as she asks, she knows the answer. It's not the information that holds Noah in its grip, it's knowing that the information is out there, waiting to be accessed and organized and contained. And once he knows for sure (absolutely and categorically) that there are no further roads to go down, he'll be able to pack it all away. Their dad holds the key to Noah's peace of mind.

Her mom's standing now, but Maddie isn't ready to go. She wants to spend more time chatting to her brother, letting him know how strange it is without him at home, how distant her parents have become. Noah probably won't have any advice, but it would be good to share her fears with someone safe. Too much is happening too fast, and she's being swamped by it all. It's probably best for her to concentrate on one thing and worry about everything else later. And Noah is reminding her what that one thing is. "You won't forget?"

"No, of course I won't."

"Thanks," he says, as if Juliet's prodding him from a distance. "Thanks so much, Mads. See you next week." He looks up and says "Bye, Mom," and then he's walking away before his mother has a chance to pat his shoulder. They watch as he walks up to the steps where Juliet is sitting, waiting for him. As he approaches, she stands and smiles at him. Noah says something to her, opens the door, and the two of them walk inside.

WEEK 7: DAY 43 / 02:18

Noah dreams of a room.

It has 4 white walls, bright in the light of a 100-watt bulb, recessed in a white ceiling. There are no windows, just whiteness, immaculate, pristine. Nothing mars the walls. Not a jot, not a blot. Nothing, unless you look very, very closely. And there, just where wall meets wall (tap 5) meets floor, is a small, shadowy blot, ragged at the edges and about the size of a thumbnail.

Something happens in that room on a day when Noah does not complete his chores correctly. Millimeter by millimeter the Dark grows. It creeps along the floor and up the wall, barely discernible, but definitely there. The sort of thing Noah would bend down to look at, to check. There *is* something there, and now that he's noticed it, it starts to grow faster.

It's hard to tell what color it is. In some lights it's a crusty red, the color of a fresh scab, in others it's a deep purple. Almost black. Sometimes, when the light catches it at a certain angle, it's every color of a rainbow gone oily and dull. On bad days, when Noah hasn't completed his tasks correctly, when he hasn't had time to go back and start again, the Dark slinks almost to the center of the white room. And there it sits, grubby against the white.

On bad days, it takes on more of a shape. Sometimes it grows skinny arms and stalk-like legs, sometimes it's lumpy, a sulky mass of imperfection, sluggish and morose. It skitters, or it slumbers. It all depends on the nature of his offense.

In the middle of the room, gleaming and gold, stands a set of scales. On really bad days, the creature squirms up the shining leg of the scales and drops—with a light clink, or a squelching thud—into one of the brass cups.

The other cup is always empty, and the longer the Dark sits there, the larger it grows, until one cup sits alarmingly close to the floor, and the other is pulled upwards, to the very limit of its filigree chain. The scale teeters on its one shiny foot and threatens to topple over. If it does, the Dark will split—burst and splatter—and Noah will never be able to clean the room, no matter how hard he tries.

That's his job—to keep the room pure. Because what no one but Noah can see is what lurks behind and above the joins in the wall. Those long arms clamped hard to the outer walls, those long strong legs squeezing the white room between muscular thighs, a shaggy head on top of the white block, a hungry belly flat against the wall, pointed nails plucking.

No matter how high Noah builds the room, the Dark grows taller. No matter how thick he makes the walls, the Dark grows wider and broader, squeezing them until they threaten to crack.

Noah searches every day, but he can't find the small hole that allows it into his space.

It has Noah in a death grip, and one of these days it will become so heavy, squeeze so hard, that Noah's room will crack into useless chunks of brick and mortar and he will never be able to build it back up again.

In another corner, so far that Noah can hardly see it, there's a table with four seats around it. His family are sitting there. They're laughing and Noah can smell the supper his mother has made. They're far away from the creeping Dark, far from the teetering scales. Noah has managed to keep them safe. He pushes against the Dark, using his 5s. But in the hours after he closes his eyes at night and before he opens them fully in the morning, his powers are weak. That's when he needs to start counting and checking. First thing in the morning, the checks are essential.

Not much longer now, Noah. You can't keep this up for ever.

Her mother can't get it together to visit. She can't trust herself behind the wheel. Not with Lily in the car, not when she's started her day with a hefty slug of cane in her coffee. Juliet knows all this, and more, so why should she have to write about it? She could turn this into a story, a tall tale, another fantasy for Ellen, constructed from the scraps she has joined together to make her armor. It's not that well hammered together though, there are still holes where Ellen can slip in a question, a thought. She's one of the best Juliet has come across so far—she knows exactly what to ask, and when.

Juliet waits for her to probe, and then she dodges, parries, catches a glancing blow and prays her dented breastplate can withstand more. She's slowly losing the battle, though. She's got to play the game by their rules—just enough to make them think she's playing it because she wants to.

She picks up her pen.

I know Mom misses me, it's not fair to say she doesn't. It's just...she doesn't remember to call me, and when I call her she sounds surprised. But then again, she's surprised by anything that gets between her and what she drinks to make it from the end of one day to the beginning of the next.

Juliet hasn't told Ellen about waiting before she picks up the phone to call her mother. She never calls her Mom when she's in Ellen's rooms talking about her, it's always my mother, my father, my parents. Although, really, Juliet has to admit, she seldom needs to use the words "my parents." Her mother and father never present a unified front. She doesn't see them as a "together," a "couple." There's so little love there, Juliet can't imagine a time when they lay together in the same bed—

She can't think this, let alone spell it out.

She sits, strangely still for once, pen in hand, waiting to write it all down; her father's crumbling good looks, her mother's housebound sorrow.

Juliet hates Journal Time. She's tired of trying to spin a web of lies.

There are gaps in her story, the threads she has joined together over the years are wearing thin. Why not give up and let it out—the truth, the whole truth and nothing but the truth —and see what Ellen has to say about Juliet Ryan and her Shitty Little Life.

She pushes the thought away. She won't be defeated. Her father can't win; he can't be given the chance to say, "I told you so. I told you there's something wrong with her," and then look at her mother and add, as he so often does, that the gene pool on her side of the family runs weak and shallow and why did he ever marry her in the first place, and what a let-down she's been to him, they all have. "Even Lily is showing signs of—"

Juliet's back straightens at the thought of her father targeting her sister. If she can just keep Lily out of his sights for a few more years. She'll get her Matric and then a job. She'll get into UNISA and she'll qualify as a lawyer. She'll swoop in and get Lily out of there. Juliet and Lily taking on the world. She'll get there, one of these days. Until then, she'll play the game, follow the rules to the letter. She'll keep herself strong.

Gabriel is nine years old and he has been in this place for two weeks. They call it a children's home. They will not tell him where Mum is. They will not tell him what has happened to Harry.

Every day Gabriel asks, and every day he is told the same thing. Nothing.

No one says they'll try to find out, no one says don't worry Gabriel, your mum was a bit sick, but soon she'll get better and then she'll come and get you. But that doesn't stop Gabriel asking, every day. Where's Harry? When's Mum coming to get me? Because that's what mums are supposed to do. They're supposed to look after their kids, keep them safe, and deliver them from all evil, just like it says in the Our Father, the prayer they all say before they go to sleep, because then Our Heavenly Father will keep us safe. That's what the night warden says before he walks up and down between the two rows of beds, before he turns out the light and leaves them to whisper in the dark.

When it's dark, that's when Gabriel tries to remember everything he can about home and Mum and Harry. He tries to remember Dad too, his happy face and happy laugh and words of wisdom.

He tries to remember the smell of Mum's hair and the smell of Harry's skin, the special baby smell Mum says can only be found just there, Gaby-Baby, at the back of her head where her curls meet her neck.

Gabriel lies in his bed in the children's home and wills himself to remember everything about BEFORE. Before they went to live with the old man, before the jolly man came and took away all their furniture.

Before Mum ran to the window and saw the men leaping down the path and into their cars. Before the BAM!BAM! on the door when the men came looking for Dad.

He doesn't remember Mum saying, Not again Joe, what are we going to do now? but she must have, because that's what she says AFTER when she's sitting in the corner of their empty sitting room and says, I asked your father, Gabriel, I asked him over and over, but he couldn't stop. Wouldn't stop. And now where are we? What are we going to do now, Joe?

Gabriel tries not to remember that day when he sat right next to Mum in the empty house in the dark because the electricity had been cut off and Harry was crying and he was saying I'll change her Mum, don't worry, and Mum saying Thank you, Gaby-Baby. And then, Well Joe, there's nothing for it. I'm going to have to ask him for help.

Gabriel tries not to remember how she gathered herself up as if she was pulling all the pieces of herself together, bit by heavy bit, leaning against the wall, until she was on her feet and then they were all moving to the door, Mum and Gabriel and Harry heavy in Gabriel's arms. We need to pack, Mum said, and then she was laughing and crying and crying some more, saying, pack what? What are we supposed to pack?

Gabriel lies still in his bed, but his eyes are wide open.

The sheet is stiff, scratchy. Everything here scratches. Gabriel's shirt, the trousers at his waist, his underpants. Not like the clothes Mum used to wash and iron every week.

Hey, Felix? That's Gabriel's surname, and it's the first time his name has been spoken in the dark. It's Arendse, the boy in the bed across from him.

Yes? Gabriel's voice reaches cautiously into the dark.

You know she's not coming, don't you?

What? Who?

Your mother. She's never going to come for you.

Arendse is one of the boys who gets visitors from outside. A mother who says she loves him, who's coming to get him, he says, as soon as she can, as soon as she's got a proper job, as soon as they have a proper home. She comes to see him and she brings news from the outside. News of trouble and strife, of crime, stories about boys who set houses on fire and mothers who have been committed to institutions for long-term care.

She's going to be locked away, Felix. In the nuthouse. My ma says she's off her rocker.

Gabriel wants to push the words back across the cold polished floor, back to the iron-framed bed and the thin mattress and the scratchy blanket, to where Arendse's shaved head rests on a lumpy pillow.

That's not true, he wants to say. She is coming for me, and Harriet, and then we'll all go home together. But then, from further along, comes another voice, kinder this time, not filled with spite like Arendse's. Gabriel doesn't recognize it. He still doesn't know all the boys who share the room with him, who straggle onto the bus to go to the local school.

Felix?

Gabriel doesn't want to answer. This is not a night for good news.

Give up on your sister too. The babies always go.

Go? What do you mean?

What do you think he means, dummy?

Another voice and then another.

They always come for the babies.

All the moms and dads who want babies of their own, but they never want us.

We're too old for them.

We've been stuck here too long.

We've got too many bad habits.

We're just bad boys.

Gabriel pulls the blanket to his chin, burrows his head under his pillow to drown out the voices filled with knowing. Boys who have been here much, much longer than he has. Boys who know how the system works. Boys whose voices fade into darkness as the night warden patrols the dormitory, shining his torch into eyes closed tight against the light, boys pretending to be asleep.

Maddie walks through the gates, up the path, up the steps, up to the school's wide double doors.

Noah isn't at her side. So she doesn't have to worry about him, doesn't have to hear the rumble of his voice on a bad day when he's counting aloud or the regular sound of his breath on a good day when he's happy to keep the numbers inside his head.

She doesn't have to watch from the corner of her eye to make sure no one is messing with her brother. The only person she has to worry about now is herself. That's the way it's been for the last six weeks—forty-three days where it's just been her and her parents. Forty-three days, and in all that time they've only seen Noah five times, for a grand total of ten hours.

She stops in the corridor, letting the others flow around her, no pattern, no routine, no need to keep walking at a regular measured pace. She's on her own. How many times has she wished for this, allowed the guilty thought that life would be so much easier if it weren't for Noah. But now, now there's a gap at her side where her brother used to be and all Maddie wants—

A bump from behind and she stumbles forward.

"Sorry, hey." It's Kyle Blake and two of his friends. "Didn't see you there without your brother. So, what's new, Mad Dog?" He laughs and his friends do too.

Don't answer, that's what Maddie tells herself, they're not worth it, but anger wells fast and hot. The same anger that filled her when those bullies converged on Noah and mocked and prodded and tried to get a reaction from her gentle brother.

Kyle Blake hasn't moved on. He's standing in front of Maddie, eying her up and down, a slight smile on his thin face.

Maddie stares straight back at him. Don't. Don't answer him, she tells herself. But she can't help it.

"How are you doing, Kyle?" she asks sweetly. "How's your elbow?" She doesn't drop her gaze. "Are you going to be out of action for long?"

"Another six weeks," he says, his voice a snarl. "Thanks to your brother."

"Thanks to Noah?" Maddie says. "I reckon quite a few kids here are giving thanks to Noah."

"What d'you mean?" He has to ask the question.

"Well, it's obvious isn't it?" She takes a deep breath to keep her voice steady. "You won't be able to shove the little kids around half as well with only one arm."

There's a murmur of agreement from the students gathering around, eager to watch this peculiar standoff.

"It's easy, isn't it?" says Maddie. "Easy to pick on the little kids, or people who are different, like my brother."

"Your *brother*?" He's sneering now. "Your brother's a psycho. Everyone knows that."

"My brother wouldn't hurt a fly. He's O...C...D, Kyle." Maddie spells out the letters as patiently as a primary school teacher. "Do you even know what that means? Do you know the prison he lives in? His life is one big set of rules and regulations, one huge battle, from the time he wakes up to the time he goes to sleep. And even then, he never really relaxes. Can you imagine what that's like?" Maddie moves a step closer.

Kyle's cornered. The wall of people around them is growing deeper.

"I don't have to listen to this sh—" he tries to say

"Oh yes you do," says Maddie. "You have to hear this from someone. If your parents can't say it, I can. You're a *bully*."

"Yeah right, your brother—"

"Oh please. Give me a break. Your parents might buy that bullshit, and even Mr. Reynolds. But you and I know different."

Maddie stops, draws breath, looks at him quizzically. "So what's it like?" she asks.

"What's *what* like?" Kyle tries some swagger. "What's it like having to talk to a psycho-bitch like you?"

His friends snigger, but the rest of the students are quiet.

"No, what I meant was, what's it like being *you*? Do you actually *like* being mean to people? Do you *like* making them scared? Do you go to bed at the end of the day thinking, "Nice, Kyle, job well done"?"

Maddie's in full flow.

"You're cracked. I'm outta here." Kyle tries to shoulder his way through the crowd, but Maddie's next words stop him short.

"That figures."

"What?"

"When the going gets tough, guys like you can't handle it."

Kyle steps up close. "Listen—"

"Listen who?" She smiles at him sweetly. "Bitch, slut, slag, pyscho? How about Maddie Mad Dog? Is that who you're talking to? Go on, then." She smiles again. "I'm all ears, waiting for the great and brave Kyle Blake."

"You're as much of a freak as your brother. You should be locked up with him."

"Nice, Kyle. Very nice." Kyle is so close to her now that Maddie has to tilt her head up to look him full in the face. "I'd rather be with Noah than anywhere near you."

There's surprised laughter from the gathered crowd and Kyle's face darkens. He opens his mouth but Maddie's back in there before he can say a word.

"You *know* you bullied him. Noah could wipe the floor with you with one hand tied behind his back, but you *knew* he'd never retaliate. So you went for him. *Every* time you saw him. Day after day. Just like you go for anyone you think is weaker than you, or different, or smaller. People who can't fight back, especially when you've got your back-up buddies." Her lip curls as she looks at the boys standing behind

Kyle. "Don't you realize? Hanging around with people like Kyle doesn't make you better than anyone here. It just makes you..."—Maddie searches for a word—"*pathetic.*"

"Why don't you just shut up," Kyle says, and the boys behind him nod. "Shut up and get lost."

Maddie laughs. "You don't scare me. You and your mom and your dad, you think you've won. But all three of you are just *bullies.*"

She stops. She feels like she's going to be sick, but Kyle Blake and his henchmen can't see that. She wants to rush to the bathroom and puke her guts out, but they're not going to see that either. Instead, she turns away from Kyle Blake and leaves him yelling after her.

"Hey, Mad Dog. You're a whack job, you know that? Just like your brother."

Maddie walks through the students gathered three-deep around her. Someone touches her on the shoulder, another gives her a thumbs-up as she walks past. A small girl squeezes her hand.

Maddie keeps walking. It's only when she gets to the corner that she breaks into a run, heading straight for the girls' toilets.

Sunlight filters under the door of the small room where Gabriel sits on the floor, shut in to think about the wickedness of his ways.

Gabriel has been fighting. He leapt onto Arendse and punched him as hard as he could, over and over, until the boy's face was a bleeding, blubbering mess. Gabriel doesn't miss school, that would be against the law, but once he gets off the bus and finishes his home-work, the rules of the home apply. He's marched into this room for a month, left to eat his meals in the dark.

Gabriel is lighter than Arendse by at least twenty pounds, younger than him by two years, but on that afternoon in the dining room size and weight mean nothing.

It all starts when his name is called—Hey, Felix!—and Gabriel looks up and sees Arendse walking towards him. The boy is brutish, his shoulders pushing at the seams of his regulation shirt.

Gabriel takes another forkful of stew

You deaf?

Arendse's at the table now, his face close to Gabriel. Gabriel smells mutton on his breath, sees grease shining on his lips.

So Felix, my ma says your ma's off to the nuthouse today. You know what that means.

Gabriel has learned not to look Arendse in the eye.

You listening to me? Arendse flicks at the fork in Gabriel's hand and fatty meat spatters onto his jersey.

It means she's taken the rap for you, Felix. My ma says God knows when she'll get out, and all because of her son. Filthy little murderer, my ma says. That's all you are. A filthy little murderer.

Gabriel's going to be in trouble again, because his jersey is dirty, but still he keeps his eyes down.

I've got a present for you, Felix.

Arendse reaches into his pocket and drops something onto Gabriel's plate. It lands in the middle of his food, a small yellow box with a black border and a proud animal etched in red: Lion Safety Matches.

Gabriel stares at the lion on the small box, lying, waiting. He watches as the grease from the mutton stew seeps onto the label, stains it brown.

I'm sending your ma a box too, Felix. I'll get mine to drop it off on her way home from work. She's a lekker sexy little stukkie, your ma. Lots of mal ous waiting for her to light their fires, hey? The boys around them snicker as Arendse starts to sway on his feet, thrust his pelvis forward. Come on baby, light my fire. She'll drive them befokked, Felix, batshit crazy. Your hot little ma. He's licking his lips, running his hands up and down his body. Mmmm uhhh, light my fire.

More boys laugh as Arendse's movements become more crude. Oooh baby, baby, baby, Arendse's eyes are closed and he doesn't see Gabriel stand. He doesn't see him move closer. The laughter dies as Gabriel flies at him and Arendse's eyes open with the shock of the first punch. He falls backwards, hits his head on the wooden bench and then he's on the floor and Gabriel's on him.

Fight! Fight! Fight! A ring of boys surrounds them, but all Gabriel sees is Mum laughing up at Dad. Looking down at Gabriel and ruffling his hair. Hey Gaby-Baby, deep breath and blow. The candles flicker and then, under the gust of Gabriel's breath, they all die.

DAY 44 / 14:13

Ms. Turner's given them another sheet of paper and asked them to fill it in as fast as they can.

1.   If I could . . . .
2.   If I could . . . .
3.   If I could . . . .

Only 3 slots to fill in, but maybe, if Noah writes really fast, he can add a 4th and then a 5th.

When they've all finished they'll take turns to read one thing out. "You don't have to if you don't want to," says Ms. Turner, and Noah relaxes.

"If I could take a magic pill," Vuyokazi's saying, "just one a day. Enough to feed me and make me stronger. Just one swallow and then water for the rest of the day, I wouldn't care about the flavor. I'd even take it if it tasted like liver." She laughs. "The worst taste ever, but I'd line up for it every day, if it was one a day only."

"No. It's sour milk," Morné grimaces. "When you get to the fridge and take a swig."

"What about when you vomit in your mouth," Simon says. "That happens to me."

"Nah," Juliet's joining in now. "Eggplant. Slimy. Gross."

"What about you, Ms. Turner?"

Why do the people in this group have to talk so much?

Ms. Turner laughs. "This is going to sound very strange," she says, "but I've had a lifelong aversion to pears."

"Pears?" Even Wandile's talking now. "Pears are delicious!"

"Maybe to you, Wandile." She pulls a face. "Not me. I don't know. It's got something to do with the texture. That gritty feeling on your tongue. No thanks."

"Any of the above," says Vuyokazi. "Just one pill, once a day and my life would be a dream—"

"—sweetheart," Noah almost adds, one of his mother's songs humming in his head. Instead he raises his hand.

Do not volunteer.

He opens his mouth.

Careful. Don't give anything away.

But he does. Before he knows what's happening, he's reading from his slip of paper.

"If I could go back in time, I would. Back to before the day I broke Kyle Blake's arm."

As he finishes the last sentence, Juliet erupts.

"Oh, come on! Seriously? You'd go back to before, when jerks like him were bullying you? Pushing you, shoving you."

"I'm with J-J-Juliet," Wandile says.

At first Noah thought Wandile (Wordless Wandile, Juliet calls him) and he were alike, scared to use words in case something catastrophic happens, but that's not the case. He's heard him speak almost normally when they're in the dining room, or watching TV. Stuttered Speech Syndome. That's Wandile's label—sort out his Social Anxiety Disorder (SAD, something he and Simon share) and hopefully that will help with his stutter. Noah's watched him trying to talk to his parents out on the lawn. His mom and dad are always on the way from somewhere or to somewhere important. "Pots of money," Sadie says one day. "My dad says Wandile's father could buy and sell us all."

Wandile's their only child. Heir to all that fame and fortune. Quite something to have to take on.

"W-w-w-we h-h-h-h-have to st-st-stand-up-to bullies." The last words come out in a rush of air and Wandile hangs his head.

"Oh, wow." Juliet's eyes are wide. She leans over and punches him gently on the arm. "So many words, Wandile."

"What about you, Juliet?" says Ms. Turner. "Do you have a bully in your life?"

Juliet looks around the circle. Even Sloppy Sadie is paying attention.

"Yeah," she says, "I guess I have."

The attention has swung away from Noah, and that's a relief. It's one thing to write his lists of 5 or his answers to Ms. Turner's exercises, quite another to expose them to the group. But then again... those words: "The sooner you give them what they want, the sooner you'll get out of here."

You are stepping beyond the bounds. This has to—

Noah raises the shield of Juliet's words, dented and scorched, but still whole, and the Dark retreats with a hiss.

It's a 3-month program with 6 weeks, 2 days gone. If he wants to get out, he has to give them what they want. The more, the better.

Noah's hands are shaking, but his head is quiet.

"Do you have a bully in your life?"

Ms. Turner's question took her completely by surprise. Juliet knew she should always be on the alert, armored against intrusion. Instead, she's been drawn in by Noah's story, saddened by Wandile's stuttered outburst. She's doing what she promised herself she never would. She's becoming involved.

She looks out through her window, to the mountain in the distance. Maybe it's time to practice what she's been preaching to Noah, start telling the truth. That's all Ms. Turner wants for her. That's what she said the other day. "It's all you need, Juliet. To tell yourself the truth. It's hard, I know."

Thin clouds are crawling down the mountain now, joining heaven to earth in a gauzy band. They never last, never gather enough to let rain fall. All they do is waft, then fade away in the glare of the sun.

There's no one on the lawn, no one sitting on the benches. No one to smile and wave at and distract her by thinking about their sorry lives instead of her own.

Juliet's journal is open on the table and she thinks about filling the blank pages with thoughts about her father, her mother, her life. Writing down the truth of it. She closes her eyes and sees her father, his bald head sliding past her room, his ruined face looking in on her.

Never saying a word to her. Just looking.

Juliet picks up her pen.

"My name is Noah Groome and I have been a resident at Greenhills for 6 weeks and 4 days."

This is something he can say in group, then Ms. Turner can say, "How do you feel about that, Noah?" He can use a few words to tell her. "Fine," he can say. "I feel fine." He can even say he's getting *used* to being here. And if she asks him what that means, he can add, "I'm getting used to the routine and the sometimes-lack-of-routine, which is a challenge."

"A special challenge for you," Ms. Turner will probably say and then tell him he's doing well.

So yes, 6 weeks, 4 days, and counting—and a few things to say in group which show he's willing to participate, even willing to use some of his words.

But what he won't say in group is how he feels when he opens his eyes for the 46th time.

He still expects to hear Maddie's voice, Spot barking, and his mother calling, "Dominic, breakfast is ready." The walls should be pale blue, there should be cream curtains at the window and from his bed he should see the tangled green of his father's fynbos garden, the part where he says plants must be allowed to look after themselves.

When he gets out of bed, his feet should hit wide wooden floor-boards, warmish, even in winter.

Checking his room should be quick and easy because everything—
The door flies open and he's there again, the boy from last night.

Noah had seen him arrive, with his mother close behind, her hand floating forward, just about touching the boy's shoulder and then falling to her side. Behind them, almost the full length of the corridor, Noah had also seen a big man, burly in a dark suit, his face red, his mouth open to speak, but any words had been drowned out by the new arrival, who having reached his room, had shrieked, "Oh, Mumsie, I love it! I love what you've done with it."

The mother had glided forward on high heels and rested her hand on the boy's arm.

"Do you, Willa? Do you really? I'm so sorry, I would have done more. It's just we didn't have much time."

The boy had glanced down at her hand, and she'd removed it quickly.

"I do, Mums, I really do. You've done absolute wonders."

And now, here he is, the boy, in Noah's room, just inside the doorway. He's wearing the same clothes as last night, baggy pajamas in some sort of silky material, splashed in big circles of red, green and yellow. The sleeves are wide with a deep cuff, and they reach right to the tips of his fingers.

"Sorry," he says. "Sorry, sorry, sorry. Just been to the loo. Not my room. Sorry."

His voice is high, like it's waiting to break, but he's about Noah's age.

"No problem."

He's interrupted Noah's room check and now he's advanced to the desk. He's turning slowly like a skinny traffic light, his shiny pajamas flashing red, yellow, green.

"Very utilitarian," he's saying. "Minimalist. I have to say I like it."

Noah's sitting on the edge of his bed staring at him when he pivots and takes two long strides towards him.

"Oops," he says, "Manners. I'm so, so sorry. I'm Willa. I go by the pronoun 'they.'" He laughs lightly. "I'm in the room next door."

"They?" Noah says. "I'm sorry. I don't—"

"You don't understand?" said Willa. "Don't worry, quite a few people don't get it at first. But if you try, you'll get used to it. It's easy enough. Don't think of me as a him, or a he, or a her, or a she. Just as Willa."

"Hello. I'm Noah."

Willa holds out their hand. They brush their fingers across Noah's, then wipe them on a green circle. Their right-hand sleeve falls back slightly and Noah sees a thick white bandage. Willa smiles wryly, lifting their arms so that both wrists are exposed. "My badges of dishonor," they say. "Hence my rushed arrival. Poor Mumsie, she's been running around like crazy trying to get my room sorted out. Seems I'm going to be here a while."

DAY 47 / 14:06

"Man," says Morné, slouched in his chair. "Those boots."

Willa whips a cloth from their pocket, wipes the wooden seat of their chair, pulls a thin plastic bag from the same pocket, places the cloth in it and then puts it away. They sink gracefully to their seat, cross their legs and flash a broad high heel at them. "You mean these?" they say.

Morné nods.

"These boots," says Willa, "have walked with me through agony and pain."

"What's with this Willa thing?" Sadie interrupts. "Anyone with two eyes can see your name should be William."

"Sadie—" Ms. Turner's quick to respond, but Willa's already speaking.

"Thank you for asking. Sadie, is it?"

She nods.

"Well, Sadie, now's as good a time as any for introductions." Willa extends a hand to Sadie, much as they had done to Noah that morning. "Willa," they say. "Also known as William Forsythe when Daddy's around, but I'm working on that. But otherwise, please call me Willa. My PGPs are they, them, their, theirs and themself."

Sadie can't contain herself. "What's a PGP? Some sort of golf thing?" She catches Morné's eye and he grins.

Willa continues regardless. "My preferred gender pronouns," they say quietly. "Rather than he or—" they glance at Sadie and smile "—she."

"What sort of kak—" Morné sounds amazed, but Ms. Turner steps in before he can finish his sentence.

"Right everyone. Willa has told us how they would like to be addressed. It'll take a bit of time, but I'd like you all to try. Willa, would

216

you like to continue?"

"Thank you." Willa smiles at the group. "Okay, so you were asking about my boots, my little beauties."

Willa's not scared to use words; they fling them out extravagantly, as much of a challenge as their clothing—This is me, Noah can imagine them saying. Full-on, no-holds-barred, like-it-or-lump-it, me. He envies them; he wouldn't mind being given a few of Willa's words to see him through each day.

"They tilt me off balance you see, so I have to hold myself back to hold myself up." Willa pushes their legs out straight. "But they are *so* worth it," they say. "Daddy hates them, of course. He hates all my clothes. 'But Mumsie,' I say, 'Fuckit. If he can't love me for who I am, he's *never* going to love me, no matter what I wear.'"

They smile. "Guess how many sessions it took me with my therapist to be able to deliver *that* line so flawlessly?"

It looks like Willa has just walked off the set of a fantasy movie, their skinny legs in silver leather, their glossy black boots reaching just over their knees, their shirt white and frilled to death, the sleeves caught at the cuff, drooping over their hands, just touching the deep navy tips of their varnished nails.

"So now," they continue, "when we go shopping, Mums and I, the first question I ask, before I even take something off the rack is, "What would Daddy think?"" They pat a silver thigh for emphasis.

"He hates me calling him Daddy. He hates my wardrobe, and most of all, he hates these."

They look down at their boots fondly. "Maybe it's the platforms, or the height of the heels." They angle the platform heels towards the middle of the circle and Noah wonders what it must be like to walk 10 centimeters above the ground.

"You know what? These boots have walked past his door so many times. I practice, you see, I have to. How to walk without tripping, staircases, how to stay upright. Upright in front of my uptight dad.

"The best place is our passage at home, it's long and tiled. Slippery. If I can do the passage, I can do anywhere. And if I can pass by Daddy's door, over and over again, feel his hot eyes hating me, then I can walk anywhere, let anyone look at me. Daddy's useful that way." Willa swivels a leg, admiring the shiny length of their pointy-toed boot.

"I've had these a long time. They're one of my favorite pairs. It's so hard to find shoes to fit you know, when you're size ten heading for eleven. Whenever Mums and I go overseas, we hit all the specialist shoe shops. Here it's not so easy."

Sadie whispers something to Morné and he laughs. Ms. Turner frowns and Willa goes blithely on. There's no stopping them. Even Juliet looks stunned.

"They cost a fortune, but the moment I put them on, I just knew I had to have them. Daddy exploded at the dinner table. You can imagine. "If you want to spend thousands of rands on shoes, spend your own fucking money." Then all Mums does is raise an eyebrow because we all know who holds the purse strings in *our* house. Mums is the one with the real money. Daddy's the one who wears the suits and goes to work, but his salary doesn't even touch sides when it's tipped into the family coffers. "We're not supporting your lifestyle," Daddy says, and he looks at Mums as if he expects her to reply but he looks at me as if he wished I was dead."

They're all looking at the boots now—polished to a high gloss, catching the hot sun in the Rec Room and making it flare.

Sadie opens her mouth, but Willa isn't finished. She sits back and scowls.

"They got scuffed, though. See, just here." They turn their left foot, and there, at the back, just above the heel is a mark. "I like to think of it as *their* badge of honor."

Willa looks at Noah and smiles.

"What does he mean? I mean, they. What do *they* mean?" Juliet whispers, but Willa's still talking.

"The mark, that was from being thrown in the bin," they say. "Luckily, I found them just before the garbage truck arrived. Mumsie and I, we hunted high and low, every cupboard, under all the beds, and then, when I was looking under one of the sofas in the sitting room and Daddy was sitting reading his paper—I was in tears by then, floods of tears—I caught him glancing out the window.

"I flew. I literally flew down the path and there they were. In the bin. I *rescued* them. Though it took every last reserve of strength I had to even *touch* them. Daddy knew that. He knew how it killed me to pick them up after they had been lying there next to all sorts of God-knowswhat, but if it was the last thing I ever did, I was going to pull them out with my bare hands and walk past him, holding them and looking him straight in the eye. I rescued these little babies and I cleaned them. Mums wanted to help me, but I said, "No, Mums, I have to do this on my own." I polished them and polished them and then I put them straight back on. Killer heels." Willa laughs. "But I was so happy to see them. The pain was pure joy."

They smile. "So anyway, you're probably wondering why I'm telling you all this?"

They're all looking a bit dazed.

Juliet laughs. "Wow. TMI, Willa?"

"Well," they smile again, "with someone like me, you probably need quite a bit of info. Anyway, Ms. Turner said we had to fill in these sheets—these "5 Things About Me' thingies?"

They all groan.

"So last night I thought, "Willa, what can I tell them about you; how can I introduce myself? And then I saw my boots, standing tall and exquisite in the corner and I thought, *Well!* If nothing else is up to the task, my beauties certainly are.'"

They stand then and walk the length of the room.

Then they turn around, perfectly balanced, perfectly poised, and blow a kiss at Morné.

Kate and Monica never say, "See you tomorrow," but it actually happens quite often now. Kate drops Maddie at school and then heads to the same café where Monica and she bumped into each other. She knows that Monica can't get it together to ask after Juliet, let alone visit her, so she slips in a small comment now and then, about how Juliet's looking, or to share one of Juliet's quick comebacks. Monica soaks them up, grateful for the smallest drop of information about her daughter. And now, this morning, she has something to give Kate in return.

She's waiting when Kate gets there. Kate's never seen her looking this awake.

"Kate!" Monica's clutching her cell phone. "Have you seen it?"

Kate puts up both hands to stem the flow of questions. "Whoa, Mon. What is it?"

"Lily showed me this morning. "All the kids at school are talking about it, Mom." That's what she said, so I asked her to copy the link for me."

She's fumbling with her phone. "I'm no good with these things."

Kate catches a waitress's eye. "Two cappuccinos," she mouths.

As the young woman nods and turns away, a voice fills the space between Kate and Monica.

"Hang on. Is that—"

"Maddie? Yes, and she's *amazing*."

Monica turns the phone so that Kate can see the screen properly. And there's her daughter, arms waving, looking up at a tall skinny boy, saying, *It's easy isn't it? Easy to pick on the little kids, or people who are different, like my brother ...*

"Who— What—"

The video runs on. *My brother wouldn't hurt a fly. He's O...C...D, Kyle. Do you even know what that means?*

"I don't understand, Maddie never said—"

Monica couldn't grin any more widely if she tried. "It's on YouTube, Kate," she says. "Someone filmed Kyle Blake and Maddie. They put it up last night. And look." She points to a number. "Fifteen thousand views already. Your daughter's going viral, Kate."

"Oh, dear." Kate smiles properly for the first time in months. "Leonie won't like this."

"No," says Monica solemnly. "She most certainly won't."

Day 47 / 19:23

Viral.

A 5-letter word.

Everyone's saying Noah's little sister has gone "viral." The video filmed of her at school taking down a bully has spread. 21K views, Juliet tells him after Lily calls her. And counting. The comments are almost as good as the clip, Juliet says.

Noah reads as many of them as he can before going to group.

Comments from kids who've been bullied, from teachers who don't know how to put a stop to it, from parents who watch their children being diminished every day.

According to a guy called Kevin Nalty on YouTube, "viral' means getting 5 000 000 views in a 3- to 7-day period. He said that in 2011, so it's probably even more now. Mads isn't remotely close to that. But people have seen her confronting Kyle Blake. Most importantly, all the kids at school who Kyle has picked on. They'll have seen Maddie—tiny, bristling—challenging Kyle Blake. And all he had to fight back with were his tired insults.

"He's not very good with those," Juliet says. "Psycho-bitch seems to be the best he can come up with."

Not like Maddie.

Hearing her describe her brother—showing how deeply she understands him—fills Noah with wonder.

There was a time, not long ago, when he would have shrunk back into the wall if Maddie had told people like Kyle Blake to get lost. Now though, looking at the faces of the students surrounding them, seeing flashes of recognition as Maddie's words hit home, Noah realizes how many lives Kyle has made a misery.

But not Noah's, not any more.

He's going to phone his sister this evening. Tell her she's a star. In the meantime, though...

Noah waits to use the computer in the Rec Room, logs on, sees his YouTube user name flash up on the screen. NoahArkman.

What are you doing? You've been told, no contact with Kyle Blake.

But this isn't contact with him, or his parents.

This is Noah, talking to his sister, adding to the long stream of comments.

Noah Arkman
Thanks, Mads. You're the best. See you Sunday.
Noah (Maddie's brother—Greenhills Clinic)

DAY 48 / 10:39

"So, like I was saying, my sister called last night."

"What?"

It's Saturday morning and Juliet's there, putting the kettle on.

"Yeah. I was surprised, too." Her tone is mildly sarcastic, but she grins at Noah.

"Sorry." He's learning, slowly, that it's worth paying full attention from the moment she starts talking, otherwise he lands up lost and confused, wandering in Julietland. One of these days he's going to tell her what it's like being on the receiving end of her constant stream of information.

"Yep, Noah. Lily called with some interesting news."

"Shouldn't you tell Ms. Turner?"

She laughs. "Why should I tell her when I have you to talk to, Noah? So ready to listen, so full of good advice."

"That's me," he says. "Pearls of wisdom."

Her eyes widen. "My God, Noah. A joke. Maybe that's something you should share with Ellen?"

"So," he says, "Lily? She phoned?"

"Yeah." Juliet looks down. "It was quite something, actually."

Juliet, silver-tongued Juliet, goes quiet.

"And then?" He moans about Juliet talking non-stop, but seeing her like this is worrying. "Are you sure you don't want to talk to Ms. Turner?"

"I will," she says. "I think I will, but I need to tell you first, Noah. Get my head around it all."

One of the most frustrating things about being here is your chatty little friend, Noah.

The Dark is trying to squeeze its way in, but he's listening to Juliet, trying to figure out why her face is happy and sad and almost tearful at the same time.

She swipes at her fringe and looks at him, her smile looking like she's hauled it up from the depths and stuck it on her face. "Bart's left."

Juliet's father. Bart Ryan. Noah's father is his boss.

"Yep. Finally packed his bags and gone. Not too sure how it's going to work out, but one thing I can tell you, Noah," her voice is fierce, "I'm *so* glad he won't be there when I get home. I won't have to feel him looking at me as if I'm never going to be quite good enough. So, that's the one thing. But there's more."

The anger's gone, replaced by confusion. "Really don't know what to make of this one. Lily says Mom drove her to school this morning."

"So?"

"So? *So*? Shit, Noah. My mom hasn't driven for almost two years. Not since she got pulled over and nearly lost her license. If it hadn't been for Dad, she would have. But, "Never get behind the wheel again." That's what he said to her. "I don't work my arse off so that you can prang my car. Do you know how much it cost me?" We were in the car once when she hit this huge tree, almost head on, but he wasn't worried about Mom, or me, or even Lily. No, all he was worried about was his precious Lexus."

Noah has no idea what to say.

"Well, not even *that* stopped Mom drinking. She tries, you know, Noah. Sometimes she gets all the booze in the house into the kitchen and then she pours it all down the sink. Only he says, 'Why bother? The only thing that does is make the place smell like a distillery. And then you go straight out and buy some more. Do me a favor, Monica. Just drink the bloody stuff, instead of wasting it. You're cheaper that way.'"

Noah passes Juliet a cup of tea in her mug (the one she leaves here now) and she smiles, properly this time.

"Thanks, Noah. So anyway, the thing is, my mom never drives. I do. I take her car and drive places—like the supermarket to buy us food, or taking Lily to extra math classes."

"But you don't—"

"Well *obviously* I don't, Noah. How can I have my license when I'm only fifteen? But someone has to do it. Most of the time Mom doesn't know if we're there or not. And Dad? He never asks how come there's food in the pantry when he's forbidden Mom to use a car." Juliet pauses for breath. "Only, yesterday, she did. And Lily said she was fine. She didn't smell, she had a shower, her hair was clean. She told Lily she's going to stop. "I mean it, Lil." That's what she said."

Juliet takes a sip of tea and looks up at him, her eyes full of tears. "I want to believe it, Noah. I really do. Maybe now she'll come visit me. And bring Lily."

"Just close your eyes and listen," Ms. Turner says. It's time to relax, calm down, think—feel, even. This time to music, the theme from *Schindler's List*.

Juliet's eyes half-close and she looks around the group. Sadie's face is vacant, as if the music has washed everything out of her. The new arrival, Willa, is sitting very straight, eyes closed, hands loose in his lap. *Their* lap, Juliet reminds herself. Noah's trying hard to keep his eyes closed, but he's clearly not comfortable, his shoulders are high and tense.

The music is gentle, very gentle. Eventually, Juliet's eyes close.

When the music stops she comes to and looks around the circle. They all look dazed, even Noah, as if by switching off the sound, Ms. Turner has woken them from a deep, dream-filled sleep.

Juliet feels something warm and wet land on her knee. A tear? She hasn't cried in years. How can a piece of music have the power to make her cry? It's not as if she's opened up more than she has before, not like she's stopped trotting out the same lines she's been feeding to people like Ms. Turner for years.

But something has changed. Something is shifting. Whatever it is, though, Juliet isn't sure if she's ready to examine it all that closely.

WEEK 8: DAY 50 / 08:54

Juliet is walking next to him and, as usual, she's talking. Would she ever try to hold her words in, contain their power, so that they make her stronger? Noah can't imagine her doing that. Everything about her is light and quick and momentary, as thoughts land she says them aloud, flicking from idea to idea, filling empty spaces. Even on a day as hot as this, Juliet hasn't stopped talking, moving, gesticulating.

He doesn't mind it all that much. She's fast and funny, and besides, when she's around, he doesn't have to worry about the words inside his head, or the ones he struggles to say. She's useful that way.

"One of the things I miss about home is my cat," Juliet's saying now. "You'd love her, Noah."

Spit and Spot flash through Noah's mind and he's filled with a sudden longing to be home, to see his dogs running to meet him, tails wagging like crazy.

"Smudge," Juliet's saying now. "Her name is Smudge. Dumb, I know, but Lily chose it." Her voice softens as she mentions her sister. "She's got a mark on her nose. Smudge, I mean, not Lily. A little gray smudge. Otherwise she's black. A sleek, black, beautiful cat called Smudge. I would have called her Midnight. But I like her name now, can't imagine calling her anything else. What about you, Noah? Do you have pets? What are their names?"

He doesn't answer, but she doesn't mind. He's there to listen as she goes on (and on). He knows what she's doing; the more she talks, the less she has to think.

They're at his room now, and he pushes the handle (down-up-down-up-down). The door swings open.

"Bye, Noah, see you at—"

But he's not listening. He's standing in the doorway, stock still.

"What is it, Noah? What's the matter?"

He moves into his room and looks around slowly. He turns carefully, checking everything as he moves.

Juliet's looking around, too. "Noah," she says. "Why are you so freaked out?"

He can't answer her, can't pay her any attention. He's still moving in a slow circle, but his eyes are darting all over his room.

He stops.

He's facing the small table where he keeps his kettle, mugs, biscuits.

"Noah? What's wrong?"

He moves to the table, picks up a mug—his indigo one—and holds it for a moment. Then he carefully closes the gap between it and the navy and royal blue ones on either side. He puts the indigo mug at the end of the row. Very carefully, as if it might fall and break if he does not exercise extreme care.

"Noah?" Juliet's really worried now.

Do you see? Things fall apart if you give away too much, and now—

He can't listen. All he can do is stare at the shelf.

"My mug," he finally manages to say. "Someone moved my mug."

Someone has been inside Noah's room. They've touched things. His mugs—"Definitely, no doubt about it"—Noah says again and again, when Juliet asks him if he's sure.

He is adamant. "This one is my Sunday mug. It's always at the end."

Juliet can't say (she'd really like to, but she can't, never would), So what, Noah? Does it really matter? Because it does, it matters a lot, and she knows that now.

She thinks of the easy mess and clutter in her room: jeans slung over a chair, her book lying open on her bed, trainers at an odd angle near the door. It drives Noah mad, he can never come into her room and sit there with her. The one time he did, his fingers twitched and his feet tapped and Juliet could almost see the number five dancing around his head, making his eyes bug, turning his mouth into a straight line that wouldn't let any words out.

What must it be like to live a day in Noah's skin?

And now he's jittery again. He can't sit still, keeps getting up and turning slowly, even though he's checked his room four times since he last spoke. Juliet feels a slow heat rising. Anger, different to the sort that fills her whenever she thinks about her father. Juliet's not angry *about* someone, she's angry *for* someone. She's angry because someone has messed with her friend.

Kind, gentle Noah, who doesn't have it in him to hurt anyone.

Gabriel is eleven years old, lying in a hospital bed in a ward filled with people in pain. He hears them moaning and wailing and swearing and calling, Nurse, nurse. There are people dressed in white with stethoscopes around their necks hurrying from bed to bed. Gabriel knows what a stethoscope is because, before he was admitted to the children's home, the doctor checked him out, Looking for complications, Gabriel heard him saying, from the smoke inhalation, and then he was pressing a small cold metallic circle onto Gabriel's chest and saying, Breathe deeply, son. Big deep breaths.

That's what Gabriel is telling himself to do now as he lies on the hard bed, staring at the pockmarked ceiling. Take deep breaths, Gabriel, he whispers. But he can't because it hurts so badly when he does. He cries out, a sharp high sound that makes the doctor standing at the bed next to him turn quickly and say, Nearly finished. I'll be with you soon.

Gabriel can't even nod his head. If he moves, pain slices through him with a hot knife, cutting him into pieces.

Bloody hell, that's the night warden, when Gabriel cries out, when he can't keep the pain inside him any more. Bloody hell, Felix. Let's have a look at you. Touching Gabriel's forehead, saying, Shit, and then running, yelling for help, yelling for an ambulance, Get a move on, come on, come on, come on. The dormitory light snapping on and Gabriel moving his head, squeezing his eyes shut, And one, two, three, lift, and Gabriel's on a gurney, being wheeled through the double doors of the children's home, into the waiting ambulance, lights flashing, sirens screaming. That's what Gabriel remembers, sirens screaming louder than his pain.

He's doing his best to hold the pain in, to be a Little Man, but he can't. It's escaping in bursts. Tears are running down his face, a steady stream that he can't stop, and now the doctor's here and he's leaning over Gabriel's bed, lifting his T-shirt, touching him, gently, but not gently enough, because when he reaches Gabriel's belly and presses lightly, Gabriel shrieks.

Appendix, the doctor says. We'll be lucky if it hasn't burst. Who let it get this bad? Gabriel can't talk, and even if he could, he wouldn't say anything about going to sick bay and how the matron told him there was nothing wrong with him.

Gabriel hears them talking around him, above him and they're fading in and out, talking about surgery and speed and the sooner the better. His eyelids flutter, he tries to keep the doctor with the gentle hands and the stethoscope in focus, but nothing stays clear, nothing feels real. The room begins to circle, slowly, slowly, then faster and faster and Gabriel is whirling with it. His bed is a spinning top.

The colors of the ward melt into a shimmering blur, and there, at the edge of the blur, are Mum and Dad. He's hugging her, holding the tight swell of her belly. Harry is in there and Gabriel smiles because he knows she's safe. Mum is safe too, and she's saying, There you are Gaby-Baby. We've been looking for you for so long. She's holding out her hand and Gabriel feels the bed beneath him still, the shimmering blur steadies and becomes pure light. Mum is holding out her hand and Gabriel's getting out of bed, one leg, two legs over the side. Dad is laughing and Mum is too.

There they are, waiting for him, and all Gabriel has to do is walk over to them. He moves his feet, but pain cuts him in two.

Easy now, easy.

Gabriel doesn't recognize the voice. He opens his eyes and sees a masked face hanging over him.

He's coming to, Doctor, the voice says, and a man in a coat appears next to Gabriel's bed.

Gabriel closes his eyes. A phone rings, a machine bleeps, a voice calls. Too many noises, and beneath it all the pull of pain. All keeping him awake, keeping him from going back to where Dad and Mum are waiting for him.

DAY 50 / 08:58

He has to tell Ms. Turner about his mugs, how it felt to see them out

228

of order.

Out of order. The worst phrase Noah can think of. Once Juliet leaves and he's alone in his room, he stands there, tapping, not caring that the door's open and anyone passing can see him. He has to gather all his strength, draw on his 5s as fast as possible.

Then there's the violation. His space at home, it's his, no one ever enters without asking. Not Maddie, not his mother, not even his father. The few times he's come to Noah's door, he's always made sure to knock.

The indigo mug means he wasn't mistaken about his desk organizer. Someone has invaded his space, and not once, but twice. And now he has a witness: Juliet.

Maybe more than twice, Noah. Have you thought about that?

He'll have to do another check, and another, to make sure that's not true. He's going to be late for Ms. Turner, but that can't be helped. He has to inspect every corner, look under his bed, inside his cupboard. He wastes minute after minute. Tries to calm down, sits at his desk and looks around again.

He's trying to call on his senses, follow Ms. Turner's advice. Move from 5 to 4 and down to 1, but he can't. Everything around him is a possible area of attack and he can't narrow his focus and pull himself back into the Here and Now.

What if they'd stood at his wall, laughing at his charts, his Family Tree? Even if they didn't move anything else (and he's still not sure they haven't), they've stood in *his* space, looked where they shouldn't. He will have to check at least 4 more times to make sure he hasn't missed another cruel trick. He looks at his desk. The organizer is in the correct place, they haven't messed with that again. His desk drawers—

His journal! What if they've been inside his mind, too, reading about things he can't even tell Ms. Turner? He slides open the top drawer—slowly, carefully—and his heartbeat slows a fraction. It's still there, in its correct place, and as far as he can tell it hasn't been moved.

But who's to say it hasn't been? If they could get in and move your mugs—

There's a terrible banging in his head and it's getting worse.

He reaches into his drawer and takes out his journal.

What's that for? What are you doing?

Noah pushes against the Dark as hard as he can, he starts counting his way down the corridor, 1 2 3 4 5, and he doesn't care who hears him. Not Simon on his way to the bathroom, nor Morné or Sadie standing in the doorway of Morné's room. Not even Mr. Bill, who passes him on the stairs. "Everything all right, Noah? Off to see Ms. Turner?"

He nods, walks faster, keeps counting.

He's going to Ms. Turner and he's taking his journal with him.

09:22

"The thing is," he says, after he's told her about the organizer and mug, "I have to tell you everything, but I can't. But if I don't, I won't know how—"

What are you doing, *Noah?*

His hand is in his pocket, fingering his pebbles. His journal is on his knees.

"Take your time, Noah," Ms. Turner says. "Remember, Here and Now."

"I need to explain something. But..." He opens his journal. "Can I read it out loud?"

"Of course."

He looks at Ms. Turner's kind face, sees her kind eyes. Then he opens his journal to the page he thought he would never reveal.

Stop this.

The Dark is swirling closer and closer. A furious roar fills Noah's ears, but he has the words...all he has to do is read. Noah is still in control, and this time he's not going to be defeated.

"Dear Ms. Turner, I'm writing this in my journal because I can't use words to talk. You say writing things down makes them easier to deal with..."

09:47

"So, Noah. Who, or what, can keep the Dark from growing?"

He wants to answer her, but he's exhausted. Reading from his journal was hard enough. He leans his head back, closes his eyes, and breathes, slow and regular, each inhalation steadying him. He feels for his pulse, counts the beats there. His feet are quiet on the floor.

Ms. Turner allows the silence to linger for a few moments after he opens his eyes. Then she says, "We've come a long way, you and I, Noah."

Noah agrees. Ms. Turner knows what's lurking, how hard Noah has to work to keep calm.

Does this woman know what she's dealing with?

"Look at me, Noah," Ms. Turner's saying. "Pay attention to me, don't listen to anything else." Her voice is firm and the Dark pulls back, sulking.

"You've got a phenomenal imagination, Noah," she's saying now. "You've created the Dark, and you've given it power."

He tries hard to listen, give her words space to land and make sense, but—

Imagination? Imagination? You're the creator? She has it all wrong.

Noah's shaking so hard he doesn't think his body will ever be still again. His feet start tapping furiously, his fingers are blocking his ears, but still Ms. Turner's words get through.

"Every beast has its nemesis, Noah," she says.

"Shut up," he's saying. "Please, please just shut up."

Ms. Turner carries on talking.

Get her out of here. Get her out—

"What does the Dark fear, Noah? What is it afraid of?" Her voice is insistent.

What does it fear? You're the one who's petrified. What does she think? That anything's afraid of her?

And then all goes quiet.

Noah lowers his hands, looks around cautiously. Listens.

Nothing, not a sound.

"What's it afraid of Noah?"

"You," he says. "It's afraid of you."

She smiles. "I'm so glad."

She looks at him intently. "Now all we have to do is make it scared of you too."

He listens. Still nothing. She's got it well and truly whipped. He'll pay for it later, but for now he soaks up the silence.

No one comes to see Gabriel during visiting hours. No parents bring him a book to read or sweets to suck or Barley Water to add to the flat water in the jug on the pedestal next to his bed. He's in the children's ward, a row of beds down each side. Every hour, it seems, a nurse comes to take his temperature, just as he's starting to doze off.

He's lucky to be alive is what the doctor says when he does his rounds. We nearly lost you, young man.

The shimmering blur returns as the doctor speaks and Gabriel wishes he could go back to that pure and radiant light, but he's here and he's half-awake and half-asleep and once he's on the mend he'll be going back to the home.

He's half-awake and half-asleep one afternoon when he hears voices from the bed next door. The boy in the bed next to him is never short of visitors.

Felix? Isn't that the name of the family who—

Shush, he'll hear you.

But Gabriel's eyes are shut tight and after a few seconds, the first voice continues.

Burnt alive in his bed.

I know, awful. But the article I read said they found his body near the door. Scratching to get out, probably.

An old man. Left to die like that.

Behind Gabriel's eyelids, the shimmer flares into orange.

They say she started it, but I'm not so sure. I reckon it was the kid. Little pyromaniac. She was probably covering up for him.

Look where that landed her.

And he gets away scot free. Kids and matches, never a good combo.

Especially when there's petrol to add to the mix.

A laugh, and then, Shame. We shouldn't jump to conclusions.

Maybe he's a different Felix.

Not a common surname, though.

A rustle of sheets being pulled straight, the soft pummelling of a pillow, the sound of a kiss landing on a cheek. Comfy, darling? Daddy will be here to see you tonight, on his way home from work.

DAY 51 / 09:35

"What words does it hate to hear?" That's what Ms. Turner asks Noah the next time he sees her. It's a terrible question, because if he tries to answer, the Dark will return. He doesn't like the idea of rousing it on purpose. The whole idea is to keep it at a distance, cage it if he can, fasten the latch so that it can't slip out.

Noah hears the snap of a whip. Today, the Dark is like a ringmaster, calling in its horned furies, muscles shifting under sleek coats, lowering their heads, charging straight at him.

They come from all sides, carrying the names of all his fears: helplessness, disorder, incoherence, instability, chaos...death.

"You can do this, Noah." Ms. Turner's voice breaks into his heaving mass of panic.

"I can." Noah's speaking out loud, and he says it again. "I can. But I *have* to count."

Ms. Turner doesn't bat an eyelid. "That's fine."

He makes his way to the center of the circle of fear and starts up with his 5s. He makes them cower, 1x1x1, and as they retreat the air around them moves from black to red, to orange to misty gray. It will never be blue, he thinks, the color of utter safety. Noah is ever alert, waiting, always aware of the signs, feeling the Dark pushing at him, desperate to pitch him over the steep edge into a bleak hole of fear.

"What makes it retreat, Noah?" Ms. Turner's voice breaks through and he looks at her, dazed.

What stops that slender, vicious whip? My 5s. That's what Noah wants to say. I gather them around me. There's more to add, though.

1. Top of the list are his 5s.
2. And there's his journal. Writing in it quiets the monster

in his head.

3. Juliet and her incessant chatter also keeps the Dark at bay.

4. Even group, he now realizes. Even during group, the noise lessens.

5. And of course, the more he talks to Ms. Turner, the quieter the Dark grows.

One after the other, realizations come barreling in and fall into place.

"Noah?"

He blinks, shakes his head. "I'm not sure. I think—"

He stops. That's enough for today.

It certainly is.

Noah gets to his feet. He needs to think everything through.

Ms. Turner isn't ready to let him go, though. She has a weirdly brilliant idea.

20:17

What is it?

It's filmy, tired, paler somehow. Noah pauses, Ms. Turner's words from the morning loud in his mind.

"I don't know exactly what it is, Noah," she'd said, "but you have a sense of it in your mind, right?"

He'd nodded. He'd already said too much, daren't let any more words escape.

She'd taken his hands in hers. "Okay if I do this?"

He'd lifted his head and nodded.

Her eyes had been serious. "I'd like you to try something. Take that image—"

"It changes, though," he'd managed to say. "Sometimes it's a shape, sometimes it's sort of foggy and dark, sometimes it's nothing but pitch black."

"Try this, Noah. Choose one aspect, the worst one."

The Dark had twisted into being immediately. It was at its most fearsome, curling into and onto itself, ballooning out, filling every corner of her room. Noah had tried to pull back, but Ms. Turner was right there, her hands still firm on his.

"Ready?"

He'd nodded, his feet jiggling 5s.

"Look at it, Noah."

He hadn't wanted to, he was scared of looking at it directly.

Good. Scared is good. Nothing *vanishes just like that.*

"Now, this is the easy bit. The Dark is there, right?"

A fraction of a nod.

"So what can you do to make it into something ridiculous? Something to laugh at? Or even something you might actually like?"

What?

Noah had stared at Freud and Jung. Behind them the Dark had tried to surge forward, carrying all that was awful with it, but he'd held onto Ms. Turner's hand, feeling her anchoring him. As he stared, he remembered lying on the lawn next to his little sister, looking up at puffy clouds floating against a bright blue sky.

"Look, Mads, there's an elephant."

The Dark, backlit, began to fade.

"And there, Noah, that one looks just like Spit with his mouth wide open."

The memory of Maddie's laugh had made him smile.

Ms. Turner had squeezed his hand gently. "That's it, Noah, you're getting there."

He'd swallowed, trying as hard as he possibly could to keep that elephant intact, afloat. But he couldn't. A dark mouth yawned from behind and devoured it in one go. Spit vanished into the murk. A roll of thunder became a raging storm, one louder than Noah had ever heard, and he'd pulled his hands away, buried his head between his legs in an attempt to block out the Dark and its all-consuming rage.

Ms. Turner had stood, and placed her hands on his shoulders. "You're free from harm here, Noah. Everything's all right."

Noah had been alive with tapping, every part of his body vibrating, and she hadn't tried to stop him. He had 1 2 3 and 4 and 5 and he'd rattled them out like crazy. Ears, cheeks, mouth.

Noah fought back and the chaos in his head had reduced to a slow simmer.

🕐

DAY 52 / 07:47

As a little boy, Noah was blessed and protected by the power of 5.

It saw him through those first days of school, helped him navigate strange new buildings, the playground, the distance to the gates where he waited anxiously for his mother.

Gradually, the worry that was school faded away. The days became stable and predictable and 5 could slip away. But other, smaller, less obvious compulsions took its place. His parents bought him a watch for his 8th birthday and he learned to tell the time. From then on, he would glance at his watch and fret, waiting for the bell to ring, exasperated if it was late. He hated days that fell outside of the normal Monday-to-Friday pattern of the school week. What was the point of sports day, for example, or going to see another school's play? School celebrations, competitions and excursions threw him off balance and left him out of sorts, but never so much that he did anything specific to set things right. Back then, he knew nothing terrible would happen if school was disrupted by an outing or a class visit from the school nurse.

He'd hug his mother and say to her that he loved her. He'd tell Maddie long and complicated stories, spend hours playing with her, help her to organize her toys or make mud pies in the garden.

He liked things to be neat and orderly—he was, as his mother often said, a real creature of habit—but his quirks and need for order didn't paralyze or control him. The sky didn't fall on his head when the school term ended and he had to face endless, unstructured days.

Then it all changed. Noah turned from a creature of habit into a habit-obsessed, frightened, panicked, compulsive teenager.

This is what Ms. Turner needs to know more about, and he's going to have to tell her how it happened, and soon. What brought the Dark hurtling into his life. Could it ever be persuaded to leave?

Noah ticks all the boxes that label him and slide him into a file tagged

"Noah Groome, OCD." He knows the date his fussy habits started to change from annoying tics into a full-blown and frightening disorder. He knows when his behavior escalated and his obsessions began to take control. He knows when it started in earnest, the exact time that awful visitor entered his life.

He knows this, and so does his family, and therapists 1 through 4. Ms. Turner too, after speaking to his mother, reading all the notes on him.

He's getting the words out, some words, but there are piles more still locked inside him. It's Week 8 at Greenhills for Noah, and some days do feel lighter now, less ominous. But the others? Noah can't think about the *really* bad days, let alone write about them. He sighs and puts his pen in (out-in-out-in) his pocket.

DAY 52 / 09:51

"Do you think I'll ever be ready to leave?" Noah's asking Ms. Turner a proper question. "I want to, but..."

He wants his head empty, its dark tenant gone, bags packed, running fast. Let it go and live inside some other sucker's head.

Thoughts like this are dangerous. His feet and hands begin to tap, the 5s working hard for him. Slowly, the fury in his head subsides.

"I'm so screwed," he says.

She tries to tell him that he's not, but he doesn't believe her. He's stuck. There is no safe place waiting for him.

The sooner you learn that, the better. The better for everyone.

DAY 52 / 18:27

Everyone is quiet. It's too hot to think, never mind take part in one of the spats that flare up regularly.

"I hate it." Juliet's voice cuts through the stupor. "Hate it. Every other day we sit in this stupid circle and all they want us to do is to talk about the past, yadda, yadda, yadda. About who we were, what we did, why we did it. Moaning and groaning about my mother doing X, my sister doing Y. Whining about the fact that my father smacked me when I was three and my brother hates girls. Oh, and that my dad says I'm...a whore."

She stops and glares at them, defiance written all over her face. "All the talking in the world isn't going to help us. All the writing in our stupid journals, getting touchy-feely with our true selves. Nothing's going to work. We all know it, so why even bother? Who wants us cluttering their perfect little lives? *They* certainly don't. Oh no, it's much better to sweep us under the Greenhills carpet, or whatever other exclusive dump they can shunt us off to. That way their friends and colleagues know we're getting the best care possible. We're embarrassments and they've found a place to hide us. Now they can snuggle into their perfect little beds and get a good night's sleep, because—don't you know—they've done everything they possibly could."

Juliet's on a roll, words flying, but her eyes remind Noah of the terrified dogs at TEARS. Newly rescued and ready to snap if anyone comes too close.

"Aaaand now," she draws out the word like a professional showman, "ladies and gentlemen, boys and girls, here we all are!"

She looks over at Noah. "Mr. Don't-disturb-me-I'm-counting-every-single-thing-I-can-find." Then she glares at Sadie. "And you, Miss Oh-so-needy, look-at-me, hear me whinge and whine, make sure we all hear every detail of every miserable part of your pathetic little nobody-loves-me life." Sadie shrinks back in her chair.

She turns her attention to Morné. "And then we've got you. My God, Morné. Why don't you just give up now, put yourself into a corner and eat until you burst?"

Sadie's recovering, and she's looking at Juliet, her eyes vicious. "But what about you?" Sadie says. "I know why you're here. We all do. You're hardly Miss Perfect. No, you're more like Miss, Miss—"

"Go on. Find an adjective, why don't you? Rummage through that tiny pea-brain of yours and see what you can come up with."

"You're *sly*!" Sadie shouts. "You are sly *and* you're slippery. My dad says you're a slippery little minx."

Morné smirks. Sadie looks triumphant.

"Oh, he does, does he?" says Juliet. "And when did your father come up with that description?"

"During visiting," Sadie shouts. "He says you're clever, sneaky. A right little minx."

There's a smile on Juliet's face as she says quietly, "And was that before or after he said he'd like to have his wicked way with me?"

Maddie wants to be part of Noah and Juliet's adventure, she wants to do as they've asked, as if it's the easiest thing in the world.

But it's not. She has to get into the study without her dad seeing, or her mom. And her mom is always around. Except when she goes shopping or to help at one of her charities, which she does in the mornings, when Maddie's at school. The only solution is to pretend to have a crushing headache on the same day that her mother volunteers at a shelter for abused women. It's always short-staffed, so her mom won't want to let them down.

"I'll be fine, Mom. I promise. I just want to go back to sleep."

"I'll get back as soon as I can."

Her mom's standing over her bed now, and Maddie feels bad for deceiving her. Why couldn't she just ask her dad for his ID? She'd asked Juliet and Noah that, but Noah had been insistent. "I've tried that, Mads," he'd said. "I've asked him all sorts of questions. Besides, he'd want to know why."

"It's true, Mads," Juliet said. "Noah showed me his emails." Maddie had looked at her in admiration. How had Juliet got Noah to drop his defenses so quickly? He doesn't let people in that easily. "But if we get his ID number, we can start somewhere. It's really important to Noah, you know that. And if that's a dead end, at least we've tried."

So now Mom's gone and the house is quiet. Maddie's in the study, a forbidden space. She's never been in here on her own.

It's just an ordinary room, she tells herself, and no one's home but her. Maddie walks to the desk and pulls at a drawer. Locked. She tries all of them, three on one side, three on the other. Each one is locked.

Right. His desktop. She sits in his chair and hits the keyboard. A password screen pops up and Maddie looks at it in dismay. That's it then, there's nothing in the study that she can explore. Nowhere to snoop, sneak into. Nothing to lift and look under. No loose papers. Not even a plant that might have a key under it.

There's nothing on the walls either. No photos of Mom, or of her and Noah. Just his desk, an angle-poise lamp and the chair she's sitting in. Maddie sighs. Juliet and Noah are going to be disappointed. She's no super-sleuth, that's for sure.

She knows what they asked her to do isn't that difficult, so why does she feel so worried? She's not really scared of her dad catching her, she tries to reassure herself. Noah has it so wrong. He's exaggerating. It's not like an ID is such a big secret, is it? *Everyone* has one, after all.

But they'd been adamant.

"Try to get into the study when he's at work, Mads. We don't know why he won't tell Noah."

Even though she can see how much better he's getting, she really misses her brother. Noah may be weird, but he's her weird, and she just wishes she could sit on the rug near his desk and talk to him, about everything and anything. At Greenhills, Noah's truly beginning to seem at ease—he's more content, lighter somehow. No one taunts or bullies him, and he doesn't have to deal with the deepening rift between her parents.

Her mom doesn't much like Juliet, but Maddie's glad Noah finally has a friend. She's happy that he's becoming happier. But that doesn't stop her from wanting him to come home.

DAY 53 / 09:00

Down the passage, 30 steps, and Noah's outside Ms. Turner's room.

Down-up-down-up-down and he opens the door.

She's not sitting behind her desk. He knows why. Of course he does. They've been talking about this for the last 2 sessions. She's not in her sugarbird chair, which is where she belongs, or even on the sofa, where she often sits. She's waiting right next to the door. He takes 1 deep breath and steps into the room. Another deep breath and

Noah fills himself with as much power as he can.

The air around her is growing thicker, darker. He watches her mouth. It opens, wide and wider. Noah's anger answers from way down deep. Fine then, Ellen Turner, fine, they've talked and talked about this, but does she really have any idea of what she's asking him to do? Does she know there are days when the Dark refuses to vanish? Today is one of those days. It took Noah ages just to be ready to leave his room.

But no. Here Ms. Turner is. She's clueless. Trying something different, something new, is the very last thing Noah wants to do today. But he promised. He committed to this, like a dumb-ass.

He's bathed in sweat and fear. Then it comes, the feral stink. Dread is rising, clawing at his throat. He can't breathe. He can't see.

"...new...different...try. Just try, Noah. Give it a go." Ms. Turner's words make their way through.

Her words are buoyant, they're holding him up. Shadows shift and stir, but they don't disperse. There's a glint in the Dark, a silver gleam.

Noah breathes. In, out.

He taps. It doesn't help.

He hears it, a rasping breath. He tastes blood. He feels it, squeezing his windpipe.

Ms. Turner touches his arm. A feather of a touch, but—
Get her away! Who does she think she is?

She's speaking and Noah has to listen because he promised he would.

"It's difficult, isn't it?" she's saying, "I know."
What could this bitch possibly know?

He nods.

And then it roars.

What are you? Some dumb animal that can't speak? Use your words. Tell her—We do not want this.

Noah finds his 5s, finds his breath. In, out. 1 2 3 and pulling close, 4 and 5.

"Ready, Noah? Take a minute and then we can start."

Start? He'd laugh, but he's too busy counting.

This all "started" when you opened her door.

That's so true. Noah wishes he'd never pushed that handle down (up-down-up-down). He wishes he'd gone back on his contract with her. He wishes he'd never said, All right. I'll try.

Now, all he wants is for this to finish.

The only way that's going to happen is if he really does try. He puts his fingers to his wrist, feels his blood pulsating. He knows what's coming next.

Exposure to fear. Preventing response.

No!

Spitting in Noah's head now.

She has no *right to ask you to do this.*

Noah can't shut it out, he can't shut it up. The Dark bellows, trying to drown out Ms. Turner, but her quiet words are more potent. "Remember, Noah, you're going to try to respond differently to the demands your fears make on you."

They've talked about this step. It's a big one.

This is not a big step. This is an unacceptable *step. Do you hear?*

"Noah," Ms. Turner's voice is cool, like cool water, and she touches his arm again. Today, she wants him to try not to react like he normally does. Doing so is up to him, and only him. He'll give it his best shot. "That's all anyone can ask of you, Noah." Ms. Turner's been saying this for the last 2 days.

That's all he asks of himself. His best effort yet, on his 53rd day in Greenhills.

He breathes in, 2—

The numbers are there, but Noah bites down on them. He will not call on 3, 4 and 5.

The Dark pulls back, scalded. Noah has seared it and it's hurt. But not for long. Soon it will gather strength.

Okay, okay. We can discuss this.

It's paler than usual, conciliatory. Noah almost wants to say anxious, but he's not sure if he's reading its mood correctly.

Perhaps we can amend the rules.

The sound is a wheedling whisper and Noah's inclined to listen, but...Ms Turner's voice reminds him she is there, outside. "I know it's hard. But you're doing so well."

Noah's white shirt sticks to his back, his hands are clammy. The Dark is lifting, heat boiling out of it.

He clenches his teeth, remembers what Ms. Turner said: "Make it into something absolutely ridiculous." A feather-shaped cloud, misty and light. Noah places it on his palm and blows the Dark away.

Is that the best you've got?

He breathes in again, resists his 5s. Steadies himself. Watches the Dark gathering.

Ms. Turner's hands are on his. He feels their calm pressure. His feet twitch but he will not let them tap.

It's crawling back now, and this time it's a little old lady, escaped from her bed. A blistering glint in her squinty eyes. Furry neck straining against a lacy collar. Big ears, big eyes, big teeth—"All the better..." Noah hears his mom's voice, the mock growl that used to make him squirm, half delighted, half in fear, and a laugh rises, from deep, deep down. Way deeper than the place where anger lives. Not a child's giggle, but a wild laugh, a maniac's laugh. Noah daren't let it explode.

Stop! Stop this at once. This is no laughing matter. You stupid, stupid—

Ms. Turner reaches across to her desk and holds up her phone. "Let's keep on going, Noah, and afterwards, I promise, we'll phone your mom."

Your mother? She can't help you.

Ms. Turner's voice breaks in before it has a chance to say anything else. "She's waiting for us to call, Noah. She'll be able to tell you everyone at home is safe."

Liar! Liar! This woman lies!

Eyes flare gold under a lace-frilled cap. The wolf leaps up, and the nightgown tears across its brawny shoulders. It bounds towards him, baring its long claws. Sharp-fanged, drooling, growling, *What about your parents? Your sweet, little sister? You're going to put all of them—*

Ms. Turner's voice is firm. "Noah," she's saying, "Noah. Don't think about anything else." Her voice engulfs the Dark; it's not strong enough to drown it completely, but it fades, and now he can *see* Ms. Turner's hand. It's moving to the handle of the door. It doesn't stop.

A deep breath in, and out, 2 3 4 5. Noah *has* to call upon his 5s, call on them as his number for being human, his symbol of balance. He fills himself with power.

Ms. Turner's hand pushes down and the door opens a crack.

It's there and it's bloated—

Invincible. Try that *for size and power.*

It balloons forward, but before Noah can scream, "Watch out!" Ms. Turner pushes the door to.

Click.

Such a quiet click. The door shuts and there's a frenzied fuming on the other side.

"See, Noah?" Ms. Turner says. "Let's do it again." And there her hand is and the door opens a fraction.

Through the gap comes a shrunken whisper.

Who does she think she is? And who exactly do you think you *are?*

But Noah can't listen because Ms. Turner lets go of the handle. "Noah? You try this time."

Noah is frozen in place. Only her words are moving, landing on his ear, crawling into his head to where all that is frightful and fearful and terrifying lives.

"Put your hand here. Open the door."

Noah uses his 5s.

He grabs hold of the handle and he pushes down—once. The door opens.

He opens the door 4 times more, and each time he pushes the handle down only once.

09:49

Noah stops.

He collapses onto the sofa, too tired to fight the screeching that fills his head, no words, no power left. Nothing to hold off the black and terrible fury.

"Breathe, Noah." Her voice filters in. "Slowly. In, 2 3 4—" She's leading him, and he breathes with her, in 5 and out. He lets his fingers find his pulse, breathes and breathes again until he feels it slow.

"It's angry," he manages to say. "With me. You."

"That's *great!*" Her voice is jubilant. "It didn't stop you, though! You did it. The most difficult thing so far. I'm so proud of you."

Let her have her little moment. It takes more than opening a door, you know.

The voice is sullen and Noah raises his tired head. "5 times," he says, his voice a croak.

Ms. Turner smiles broadly. "Five times, Noah."

DAY 54 / 13:14

"So Ellen's got me talking about my dad again and my mom, and how she's stopped drinking: 'And would you like to talk more about that, Juliet?'"

Juliet's wandering around his room, inspecting his shelf with its kettle and mugs and packets of biscuits. She's bored, looking for something to do, something to talk about. But she knows the rules. Walk, but don't talk; look, but don't touch. If you do move something, make sure you put it back *exactly* where you found it.

There's a rustling behind him.

"I wonder," she's saying, "if these...? Yes, they do." She laughs. "Hey, Noah! Did you know, these biscuits may contain nuts?"

He swivels his chair and looks at her.

"Get it? Nuts. Even a packet of *biscuits* contains a warning. Whereas here—"

He smiles. "Yeah. Greenhills could also do with a health warning."

Juliet laughs. "Exactly."

"Greenhills Clinic," he says. "May contain nuts."

She laughs again, and suddenly he's smiling too. Laughter's rising and—

Stop this now.

The Dark is steaming with frustration, but it can't surpress the gurgle in his stomach, laughter, bubbling and irrepressible, his throat vibrating, lips twitching and his mouth open and—

STOP!

But it's too late.

Mr. Bill glances in and sees them, tears streaming down Juliet's face, Noah laughing uncontrollably.

"What's the joke, guys?" he asks, and Juliet holds up the biscuits.

"May—" she splutters.

"May contain—" Noah manages and they're off again, riding waves of glee.

"You wouldn't get it," Juliet says. "Sorry, Mr. Bill."

He shakes his head and continues down the corridor, their happiness trailing behind him.

DAY 52 / 07:47

"Today," says Ms. Turner, "I want to try something different."

Everyone groans.

Noah lets a sigh escape. Not 1 session follows any sort of structure. They've all been different; that's the only consistent thing about group so far.

Ms. Turner's handing out sheets of paper. There's his name in the middle of the circle in the very center of the page. Radiating from it are spokes, each with a new circle at their end. Inside each circle are words: hobbies, food, music, holidays, time of day, relaxation, clothing.

What does she want now?

"This is an extension of your '5 Things' sheets," says Ms. Turner. "I'd like you to create a mindmap about yourself."

She's standing at the whiteboard at the end of the room, drawing a circle around her own name. *Ellen Turner.* Inside another circle at the end of a spoke, she writes *Clothing*, then *comfortable, casual.* Another circle, another line and then the words *hates high heels.* Now she's writing *Food*, and then, in a series of circles and lines, some of the things she likes or hates to eat (including pears).

"List them as you think about them," says Ms. Turner. "The things you like to eat, or the things you hate to wear. You can move on to what you like to do for fun, your favorite places." She's handing out pencils and clipboards for them to lean on. "This shouldn't take more than ten minutes or so," she says. "And then we can compare notes."

18:34

Noah didn't find it easy to fill in Ms. Turner's mindmap.

There's plenty he *needs* (clothes of the same make and color, an accurate clock); lots he *has* to do (checking, counting and so on), but there's not all that much he *likes*. If anything. By the end of the 10 minutes his sheet of paper was still largely blank. So when Ms. Turner said, "Noah, anything you want to share?" he'd said no, because all he had were 5 names: Mom, Maddie, Spit, Spot, Juliet, and then, further down the page, Dad, with a question mark.

Noah's trying to write it down now, figure out what it is that rises up every time he thinks about his father and, for that matter, every time his father sees him.

He does like his father, but he's not sure if his father likes him back. If someone doesn't like you can you add them to a list? Ms. Turner wants him to lead some of their conversations, find useful ideas to discuss with her, and that's one. The question mark next to his father's name.

Things he *doesn't* like are easier. He could have filled those circles in no time. His non-favorite colors for example. Just thinking about them he needs to breathe a few times, feel the security of 5 gathering.

But Ms. Turner had said something else the other day. "Try to write out the tough stuff if you can, Noah. If you do, it will lose some of its power and then you might be ready to talk it through with me."

She's patient, Ms. Turner. She doesn't rush him, but he's going to have to rush himself, pick up his pen (definitely down-up-down-up it) and scribble the tough stuff as fast as he can. It feels like the words he writes will burn the paper.

Here goes.

He never wears red or black. (Just writing the words is hard.

Danger colors. They scream. Red yells warning, black booms danger.

Danger is coming, danger is upon us.

Red is a spark in the Dark. Red is darkness flashing.

Black is a yawning hole with nothing to hold on to, everything to be terrified of.

Normally Maddie's full of bounce when they're on their way to meet her brother, but today she hardly answers when Kate talks to her.

"What is it, Mads?" Kate asks, and is alarmed to see her daughter's eyes fill with tears. "What's the matter, darling?"

"I miss him so much, Mom. I love seeing him every Sunday, but I hate him being there. I hate Kyle Blake and his stupid parents. Why can't he just be at home with us? We could look after him. You and me, Mom. We could help him if Ms. Turner told us what to do."

She doesn't mention her father and neither does Kate. Staring out the window, tears streaming, Maddy says, "When I'm older, I'm going to buy a house, with a separate flat, and I'm going to live there with Noah. Not with all those other people. Maybe not even with Juliet." She sounds like a little girl again, not her adolescent self. "I wish I could do that right now."

"Noah might be lonely if you took him away from Greenhills," her mom says. "He's settling in there. Making friends."

As she says the words, Kate feels as if part of her is breaking off. Until now, she hasn't thought of Noah being away from her permanently, but it will happen, one of these days. Even now, in Greenhills, Noah's happier than he's been at home for a very long time.

"I don't care," Maddie says. "I don't care if he gets lonely. I want him back."

WEEK 9: DAY 58 / 12:11

Noah's life is full of dangerous edges. A step too far this way and he'll tumble into the Dark, a step too far that way and he'll fall, like Alice, down a deep, deep hole. Only for him, there will be no bumpy landing. He will fall and keep falling, further and further from the people he loves, the family he has sworn to protect.

He's boxed in by demands. Never mind what Ms. Turner says, Noah can't afford to mock the Dark, he can't ignore the words that thump into him whenever he tries to banish it entirely.

What if he stops trying, and gives up on his 5s? What if his rational mind is wrong when it says he cannot possibly be responsible for shielding his family from harm? Because, if he's *not* wrong, by stopping his protection of them, he's inviting the Dark to step right in, he's giving it the power to destroy them. What if...?

He can't risk it. He just can't.

He has no choice but to obey, to do as the Dark instructs.

DAY 59 / 02:33

Dreams of running, balancing, keeping time, those are getting easier to talk to Ms. Turner about—but ever since conjuring up fantastical clouds, since opening the door, he's been having a new dream.

I told you. Danger is lurking everywhere.

A thick, sludgy coil edges forward.

Noah's standing in the middle of his white room. The scales are in place and his family are at the table, everything as it should be, and then—faster than ever before—in comes the Dark. It's around his ankles, at his knees, pressing onto his chest, around his neck and into his mouth, nose, eyes, ears.

He can't see, smell, hear, taste. He can't feel anything between his fingers. The senses Ms. Turner tells him to rely on are gone; the Dark, deeper than any night, has stolen them.

There's no hope of light returning unless...Unless he can make it to the wall.

But his hands are tied. He can't reach out. He's brought to his knees, lower, until he's crouched in the middle of his room. He cannot tap out for help. He's panting through his nose, shallow, fast, irregular. If he opens his mouth, the Dark will take all his breath. It's seeping in through his pores. It's drowning him.

A glint of gray, a blink of an eye, and Noah's sight returns. Rancid breath close to his face and he can smell again. The pressure at his throat eases, claws no longer dig so deep. With a laugh the Dark dissolves and takes with it his white and shining room. No scales waiting to hold his life in balance. No table. No mother, no father, no sister.

He's floating in bleak nothingness, asleep, dreaming, battling to wake up.

The more Ms. Turner smiles, tells him they're gaining ground, slowly but surely, the deeper the dream-time Dark grows. Noah will have to tell her this soon. But now, as his alarm shrills, he wakes, gasping for air, frantic to beat out 5s on every part of his body.

He fumbles for his senses.

1. The sheets are soft.
2. He needs to brush his teeth.
3. He hears himself gasping.
4. He forces his eyes open to see his Family Tree, lopsided on the white wall.
5. He lifts his arm and breathes in the bitter smell of fear.

One by one he lets his senses fall away until the Family Tree fills his vision. He stares at it and remembers Juliet saying, "I'll help you, Noah, I promise." Something to hold on to in the Here and Now.

That's all very well, but what about your plan? You've enrolled your sister now. Hardly sensible.

Here and Now, Noah reminds himself. It's taken him 16 minutes but he's managed to use Ms. Turner's technique and it's holding him calm. That's something, at least.

Mum never protected him. Dad didn't either: Dad died. Gabriel's pretty sure that's what happened to him. Dad's dead and Mum's gone and Gabriel can't join them. They thought he was going to die too, but he didn't. He's here and he's alive; thirteen years old, stuck in a children's home.

Little Man, he remembers Mum calling him. My Little Man. He didn't want to be her Little Man, and now *all* he wants is to be a normal boy. He wants to play with his little sister in a normal house, with a mum and a dad and a room of his own and no chores and no punishments and no one watching his every move. That's all Gabriel wants.

Juliet's at the breakfast table before Noah. Usually he's there well before the others, giving him time to make sure his knife and spoon and fork are in place, getting to the front of the queue before the eggs are all messed up and the butter is smeared with marmalade and toast crumbs. She watches him as he walks, measuring his steps.

There's something slow about him this morning, as if he's swimming on the surface of a dream. He joins the short line of people in front of him, slotting into place behind Wandile. Juliet catches his eye and mouths a concerned "All right?" at him. He nods and blinks, almost yawns, still trying to shake himself awake.

When he finally makes it to the table, Juliet leans across and whispers. "I've got something to tell you, Noah. It's important."

"Okay." He nods.

"Now," she says, "before group."

She shuts up then, which is unusual at the best of times. She's looking at Morné and Sadie, her face serious.

Day 60 / 08:15

Noah should pay Juliet more attention, but he's more concerned about catching up on the minutes he's lost oversleeping. He's promised Ms. Turner he'll try to stop doing this, and it does work, quite a bit of the time. He's managing to stress less about the odd minute here and there, even (occasionally) the odd 5, but this is a big chunk of time. He's thrown his timetable out by 18, if not 19, minutes. That's a lot of recalculating and readjusting to work in if the rest of the day is going to run smoothly.

As he stands up from the table, Juliet's at his side. "Walk with me, Noah?"

He looks at his watch. "I can't. Sorry. I'm late."

No time for talking, no time to dawdle. Minutes to make up, chores to hurry through before it's time for exercises. He'll talk to her at their usual time.

Things are slipping. You need to put some real time in. Make an effort. Show you really care.

Noah stops. He should walk with Juliet, he should do what Ms. Turner urges—practice a nonchalance he can't feel as he disregards the jibes and the hectoring. But he can't. 20 minutes now, 21 if he doesn't hurry. Too many seconds to ignore.

🕐

Kate's in bed, the sheet pulled over her T-shirt and baggy shorts. Cool, easy to sleep in. It's not like she needs sexy nighties. Their bed has become a place for sleeping, reading, relaxing after the hard day is done.

Dominic's next to her, staring up at the ceiling.

"Dom? Are you okay?" He's not, she knows, and nor are they, but it's something to ask, to try to get a little closer to him.

He pats her thigh absently. "I'm fine. Let's go to sleep."

She wishes suddenly, fiercely, that he would leave his palm there, warm on her leg.

Warm and wanting, yet her mind is wandering, moving closer and closer to thoughts of tomorrow and going to see Noah. And Mr. Bill.

Will he be there? Kate doesn't know whether to hope that he will be or pray that he won't. Thoughts of Dominic's hand, of Mr. Bill and his strong body, melt into one. Kate closes her eyes.

Mr. Bill has no place in her life. Noah is the only one who matters. That's what Kate tells herself as her breathing deepens.

🕐

It's three in the morning and Dominic is in his study. Alone for two precious, silent, undisturbed hours.

The pressure from Noah is growing. An email every other day from his son now, all asking questions. He's a bright boy. His brain might have been strangely wired in some ways, but the parts of it that function, function well—too well, in fact. The questions his son asks are accurate, pointed, shooting straight to the heart of things.

"There must be records of your birth, at least," he wrote in his last email. "Like I said, Dad, your ID would be a good starting point."

Anger rises in Dominic as he reads. Why can't the boy take no for an answer? Instead, he has to deal with this persistent, relentless nagging, picking away at his past, determined to uncover...

He leans back in his chair and closes his eyes.

What? What could his son uncover? And if he did, would it matter now? The past is past. Long gone. Buried. Nobody cares any more. For some people, though, the past is as alive and meaningful as the present. It carries unhealed wounds, as raw and sore as if they had been inflicted yesterday.

DAY 61 / 18:22

"My dad says these people, you know, the lesbians and gays, the BLTS—"

"LBGT," says Willa quietly, putting down their fork. "Lesbian, Bisexual, Gay, Transgender. LBGTQ, if you want to be more specific. There are other terms too. I can direct you to a good website to explain—"

"BLT, LGB—whatever. He says we need to legislate against them, not for them. Stop them infiltrating our society. He says they're sick and if we don't do something, the sickness will spread."

Noah can't believe Sadie just said that. Nor can Willa. They're looking at her in amazement, like she's a strange creature who should be caged before she bites and the poison spreads.

She's slouched forward, her eyes glinting. Sadie isn't as dumb as she makes herself out to be. Her whining, her "poor-me, pity-me" is deliberate, aimed at making everyone hear, see and reassure her.

Now, though, she's taken her attention-seeking to a whole new level.

Willa's face is white. "Does your father often talk like that?" they ask.

Juliet's furious. "Do you have to share all this crap with us, Sadie? I can't tell you how tired I am of your "My father says" bullshit." She picks up her knife. She's eaten her chicken, and now she uses her knife to separate the bones.

"First your father says that the present government should never have come to power. Then he says that abortion is a crime. But Sadie, when you think about it, is it? Is it really?" One small bone parts company from another. "Imagine how much better this world would be if you hadn't made it to the nine-month mark."

Sadie squawks in protest but Juliet holds up her knife-wielding hand. "Let me finish. Ms. Turner isn't here to bitch at, so you can just listen to me."

Willa looks over at Juliet. "Don't," they say. "Please, Juliet, don't." They've put a lot of effort into getting ready for supper, their hair styled, a faint blush to their cheeks, their eyes ringed with dark eyeliner. "You'll just make it worse."

"And if she d-d-d-doesn't?" Wandile asks. Juliet's hand drops of its own accord.

Wandile who never talks, hasn't said a word in group since he talked about bullying, looks at Sadie. "I f-f-f-eel so s-s-s-s-sorry for you, S-S-Sadie," he says.

"Sorry?" Sadie yelps. "Why should *you* feel sorry for me?" Then she goes for it. "My dad says *you* shouldn't even *be* here. Not in a facility like this. Especially with me. I'm his only daughter, after all."

"Yes," says Wandile. "It's a sh-sh-sh-shame you have him as a f-f-f-father. A great shame."

Suddenly Willa laughs. "You're right," they say. "You're so right, Wandile. Sadie's cursed with her father, I'm cursed with mine." They pick up their napkin between thumb and forefinger and use the corner to wipe the tip of each finger. "I suppose quite a few of us are?"

Noah nods. It's not like his father's loving every little thing about him right now.

"My father left when I was seven," Simon says. "It's just me and

Mom-and-Gran at home now."

"You mean Mrs. Regular-Bowel-Syndrome?" Juliet asks.

"That's her," Simon says. "The one and only." He's smiling. "Loosening up" is what Juliet's been saying and Noah can see what she means.

Wandile's nodding too. His father's one of those guys who wants his son to be a copy of himself, a perfect mini-me.

"If only your father was a little kinder, Sadie," Vuyokazi says. She picks up a crust from her side plate and nibbles, small mouse-sized bites.

"My dad *is* kind," Sadie says. Her voice has lost its little-girl whine. "My dad is *very* kind. He loves me. I'm his precious girl. Just because you don't have nice fathers, don't take it out on me. I've got the best dad, hey Morné, haven't I?"

"Have you had enough of your chicken, Vuyokazi?" Morné asks.

She nods and slides it onto his plate. Then she looks at Sadie. "I don't think your father is kind," she says. "Why don't you ever talk about him in group?"

"I do!" Sadie yells. "I tell you about him all the time. What he thinks, what he says, what he says about me."

"Yes," Vuyokazi nods. "But you never tell us what he does."

These people. Seriously, how much longer do you have stay here?

Noah's head fills with noise for the first time that day. He can't listen, though he's trying to hear what Willa's saying.

Willa's being kind, kinder than Sadie deserves. "Shame, Sadie—"

Sadie spits at them, her mouth loose and ugly. "What do you mean, 'shame'? I don't want your pity. I don't want any pity from a screaming faggot. That's what my dad calls people like you: 'screaming faggots.'"

Willa doesn't say a word, nor do they drop their head. Sadie's staring at them and they stare right back, until she looks away. "That's what my dad will say when he comes to see me on Sunday," she mutters. 'What's that screaming faggot doing here, Sadie? What's this place coming to?'"

"That's what I'd like to know, Sadie," Juliet says, "because they sure as shit dropped the bar when they let you in."

Do what you need to get out of here. Tell that Turner woman anything *you have to. And whatever you do, get away from this table.*

Maddie worries. She's tried every way she can to find another clue for Noah to solve the mystery that is Dad, but nothing's worked. She'll have to report back to him and Juliet and say she's failed. Noah will understand, of course he will, but still. She can't help but mope around the house on a Saturday afternoon, wishing she could be the one to find the Big Clue.

At first, when she hears the noise, she thinks it's the radio or the TV, but no, there it is again—her dad's phone.

"Mom," she calls, but of course Mom's not there. She's taken the dogs for a walk. Dad's not home either. He's at work, had to rush to the office to sort a few things out.

It's louder now, more demanding, but Maddie turns away from its persistent "Answer-me! Answer-me!"

Invasion of privacy, that's what answering the phone will be. You don't go digging into your mom's bag, your dad's space is his (and Maddie has already invaded that). Answering his phone...

But what if it's an emergency? What if he needs something urgently? If only Mom was here, but she's not, and now it's ringing again and it sounds frantic...

Beep = Danger

Beep = Worry

Beep = Alarm

Beep-Beep-Beep = Alarm-alarm-alarm.

Maddie turns and runs into the office. Her dad's jacket is hanging off the back of his chair, the light linen vibrating with frustration.

"Answer me! Answer me!"

So, Maddie does. She reaches into the inside pocket, takes out the phone, slides the green icon across and puts it to her ear.

"Hello," she says.

Maddie doesn't know what to do with this information. Who should she tell? If she tells her dad, what will he do? Will he find a way of ducking it? Carry on not telling the truth, not explaining?

Noah is the one who needs to know. If she tells him, though, what will happen? She could tell her mom, but what then? The air between her parents is as good as ice. They say things like "Please pass the butter' and "Don't forget to call the dentist," but that's about it. So how could she possibly tell them that a woman phoned yesterday afternoon and asked to speak to her dad and said his mother—Dad's *mother*?— was asking for him and would he be able to get there during the week to see her because she (Dad's *mother*!) had been very agitated and seeing him always calmed her down.

When Maddie had answered the phone and heard a voice talking about her dad and his mother, she'd stumbled and stuttered and said yes, yes, she'd pass on the message, adding sorry, sorry, because the woman sounded so stern, like Dad had behaved really badly in class and only Maddie was there to apologize.

Her dad, who always said he had no parents, that his parents were dead. Her dad, whose ID number Noah wanted her to try and access, so that he had a starting point for filling in his family tree—the side with no names, no family stories, no ancestry.

But that wasn't all. As one relative sprang up on her dad's side of the tree, another branch sprouted. The stern voice at the end of the phone had asked if Mr. Groome could please come to see his mother again, and then added, "Her daughter says she'll be here, as usual."

"Her daughter?" Maddie had said. The old lady's daughter...Dad has a *sister*?

"Yes," said the voice. "Mrs. Davenport. She'll be here tomorrow, so if Mr. Groome can make it too, that would be most satisfactory. Now be sure to pass on the message, dear."

"I will," said Maddie.

So, yes. Two new relatives. Not new buds settling gently into place, but—wham!—solid, fully grown branches, leaving Maddie standing in the office, phone in her hand, wondering what to do, and who to tell.

She's confused, and then she's angry. Incredibly angry. All those years of feeling sorry for her dad because he had no one. All the times

Noah asked for his help, for details for his family tree. Noah's frustration at not being able to complete his project. And her father, knowing what that is like for Noah. Like a tooth with a cavity that's become infected, which your tongue can't stop worrying at until you get to dentist and he cleans it out, fixes it up. That's what their father has done. Left Noah with a jagged, aching hole.

Who else might be waiting, peering out from behind the leaves? In Maddie's mind, her father starts to grow roots in the soil, branches above his head. And, above him and next to him a mother and sister she can tell Noah about.

Maddie and Noah have a second grandmother. They have another aunt. The problem now is working out how to meet them. Maddie knows that they will though, and soon. Noah will think of something, she tells herself.

She stares at the phone, at the digits glowing on the screen. And then she realizes...the answer is, quite literally, staring her in the face: The number of the place where Dad's supposed to be going...to visit his mother.

Maddie quickly types it into her phone and, before she loses courage, calls the new contact.

"Silver Oaks Retirement Village."

It's a different voice. Maddie must be through to reception.

"May I speak to Mrs. Groome, please?" She uses her father's surname, and as she does so realizes that it's probably wrong, but today the gods are smiling on her. She's back on track in seconds.

"I'm sorry," she says, laughing. "So sorry. I keep forgetting. I mean Mr. Groome's mother of course. I'm her niece, just out from England."

"You mean Mrs. Felix? She's in frail care, dear. I'm afraid she isn't really up to taking calls."

"Oh." Maddie is disappointed. "Would I be able to visit her?"

"But of course you can. As long as you check in at reception. I'm sure Mrs. Felix will be delighted to have more visitors. Frail care visiting hours are every day, from 2.30 to 4."

"More visitors?" Maddie keeps her voice light, interested, niece-like.

"Yes, well, her son, Mr. Groome, he visits regularly and his sister too, Mrs. Harriet Davenport. Perhaps you could come with them?"

"Yes, yes. Thank you. That's a very good idea," Maddie hangs up quickly. Silver Oaks. She scribbles down the name of the retirement village where her grandmother, Mrs. Felix, is in frail care, where her father and her aunt, a Mrs. Harriet Davenport, visit their mother.

Maddie waits until her mom's in the kitchen before she phones her brother.

"Noah! Call for you," she hears someone bellow. There's a rush of footsteps and then her brother's on the line. It's just before he goes in to supper, and Maddie hears the hurry in his voice.

"What is it, Mads?" She knows he's looking at his watch.

"I'm sorry, Noe, I wouldn't have called, but it's important."

And then she tells him what she's discovered, words tumbling out. "Frail care visiting hours, Noah. Every day from 2.30 to 4 p.m."

"Hold on, Mads, let me get this down. What did you say the place was called?"

She repeats herself, keeping her voice low. "Silver Oaks. She's in frail care. Her name's Mrs. Felix, Noah. And the visiting hours—"

"14:30 to 16:00," Noah interrupts. "This could be it, Mads. You're brilliant. And you even got the phone number?"

"Yes." She reads it back to him.

"I'm going to talk to Juliet about this. She's really good at making plans."

"There's one thing." Maddie's worried.

"What is it?"

"What if Dad sees a call from Silver Oaks? He'll know someone answered his phone. I can't tell him I did."

"No," says Noah quickly. "You can't do that, Maddie."

"His phone rang a lot after I spoke to the lady at Silver Oaks," Maddie says. "It didn't stop, all afternoon, until he got back."

"Well, that's something," says Noah. "Unless he scrolls down quite far you mean?"

"Yes," says Maddie. "And also, I checked, he's answered all his calls from the Silver Oaks number, so hopefully he won't look too closely at the dates. He's so busy at the moment."

"Good work, Maddie," says Noah. His voice is filled with admiration and Maddie glows.

"Do you think we'll get to see her, Noah?"

"I don't know," her brother says. "I don't know. But at least we know she exists."

"And her daughter—Dad's sister—don't forget," Maddie says. "This will help, won't it?"

His voice is quick. "It's a real breakthrough, Mads. Look, I have to go. I'll talk to Juliet and then we can decide what to do next. See you tomorrow afternoon."

Day 62 / 20:22

Each entry in his journal gives Noah an increased sense of release. But that's often tempered by intense fear. He's scared of digging too deep, finding himself so far underground he'll never find his way back up again. He's in Greenhills to find ways of understanding himself, to recognize patterns and habits, to uncover stuff, layer by layer. Uncovering, discovering, recovering. These are words that scare him. Especially when he thinks about that night.

He can't discuss it. The moment he tries, the Dark envelops him. The moment he opens his mouth to speak, he sees that gun, gleaming in the dull night light, pointing at his mother.

Will he ever be able to talk about it, from beginning to end, in his own words? Will he be able to force the words out, expose himself to suffocating fear? Talk about it without tapping, without counting, without feeling horror surge inside him? Just writing this, his breathing's speeding up and the Dark is hovering, ready to consume him.

No, Noah can't afford to lose control. And if that means that he has to sacrifice closeness to the people he loves, there's nothing he can do about that.

Such lofty aims, such agonizing. *But do you not realize—*

He snaps his notebook shut, imagines for one blissful moment that he's trapped all fear inside it, squashed flat like a bug.

It's time to put the kettle on. Juliet will be here any minute now, and they have to finalize their plans for getting to see an old lady in frail care.

Day 63 / 14:36

Noah starts talking before they've even sat in their usual place on the lawn. "Mads," he says, "I told you Juliet was the right person to talk to. Will you and Mom be coming to visiting next week?"

"Of course we will!" She's indignant. How could he possibly think they wouldn't?

"Okay. okay. Keep your hair on." Noah sounds amused, as if he's smiling inside. "I just had to check."

"So, what do I have to do?" Maddie's whispering excitedly. It feels like she's stepped into one of the adventure stories she loves reading.

"It's so easy, Mads. You know where Mom and Dad keep the keys? Next to the front door? The spares are there too. Right?"

"Yes. But, Noah?" Maddie can't believe where the conversation's going. "You're not going to—"

"Don't worry, Maddie. We've got it all worked out. Here's the plan."

Week 10: Day 64 / 09:09

Noah is back in Ms. Turner's office, staring at the corner of her desk.

"What happens is up to you, Noah," she says.

Ah, but she doesn't know what is going to happen, does she?

Shadows shift and the rasping purr of its breathing deepens. Noah's fingers clench.

"Don't worry, Noah," Ms. Turner says. "I'm here. Right here. I won't leave you alone."

There's a stirring and the room darkens around him.

"Look outside," she says. "Turn your face away. Look at the oak trees, Noah. Some days when I sit here and look out of the window, it's as if they're glowing from deep within...and then, with the sun glinting off those leaves, they glisten. They throw off so much light, it's like looking at green fire."

Noah follows her gaze, tries to see what she's described, but all he can focus on is the bench where he'll meet Maddie and his mother on Sunday...

Ah yes, Noah. So...have you told her about the plan you've made with your little friend? Now might be a good time.

"Noah, are you sure nothing's the matter?"

He's counting now, clocking every second, wishing he could just get out of her office before she asks him any more questions.

This hour with Ms. Turner has been wasted.

DAY 64 / 12:31

On the night of the home invasion, Noah studied the ghostly outlines of his handprints on the windowpane in his bedroom. His arms hung by his sides and he remembered how small he had felt, how insignificant, how helpless against the combined power of 3 men with guns. His fingers curled into fists and he punched the air, wishing he could feel flesh turn to pulp, hear whimpering cries.

He watched as the shadowy images faded from the windowpane, then pressed his hands there once more. As he leaned into glass, supporting his weight with his hands, it felt as if all that was evil and cruel and chaotic was being kept well away. He stood sentinel, warding off danger, keeping his family safe.

In the days that followed, Noah remembered how he'd felt as a small boy, counting in 5s, finding 5s, calling on them to get him from one end of the school day to the next. Now they seemed to be gathering with a different sort of force—one that kept darkness and fear at bay. It was up to him to exploit their capacities to the full. He combed the Internet looking for information to add to their strength. He found page upon page of facts, all waiting to be organized into categories and subcategories.

First came the words like "pentacle" and "pentagon," "pentathlete" and "pentasyllabic" (which, as luck would have it, was a 5-syllable word). He arranged them in blocks of 5, sorting them according to the ability he felt each held, shuffling them to make space as he discovered newer, more effective words. Noah was well-armed when the Dark first started to appear; all he had to do was chant his most potent words and it left his head.

But that wasn't enough. It kept returning, and each time it was harder to dislodge. The more he gleaned, the more he seemed to need. There was always another fact, and that led to another and yet another. The stronger the 5s became, the longer Noah could keep the Dark from encroaching. The more powerful they grew, the more he could rely on them to hold things steady and in balance. He needed his 5s desperately, because the Dark was always there, always ready to wreak havoc, waiting to take over completely.

One of his best discoveries was Sir Gawain, a Knight of the Round Table. His shield bore a Pentacle, and each of its 5 points represented 5 knightly virtues.

Gawain had also used 5s to protect himself.

On the evening of 26 July 2011, at 19:22, 3 men invaded the lives of Noah's family. And every day since then, Noah has gone into battle. Every day, he raises his shield and its 5-pointed star.

Noah fights back with 5s.

Maybe one day he'll tell Ms. Turner about how the 5s arrived and how they grew, about how he prepares himself to repel the darkest of shadows.

Even so, Noah Groome, your so-called power is never quite *strong enough, is it?*

It's back. Mocking him. Picking away at his defenses. This time, however, it bothers him less. For the 24 minutes and 19 seconds he's been writing in his journal, he hasn't heard its voice. Even he has to admit that's progress.

DAY 65 / 09:10

Noah has to stop fretting about Silver Oaks and Juliet and his father and the intricacies of a plan that is becoming more and more outrageous. They have fewer and fewer days to put it all into action and he has to do what he can to bolster his defenses. He wishes he could stop the clocks, put everything on hold while he wraps his head around the problem, works out every detail, down to the last minute. Time really is his enemy now. And on top of that, he has to do The Work, and do it properly.

This is why he finds himself telling Ms. Turner about his scales. It was her first question today: how he manages to balance it all.

...tell her anything you have to.

Those were the words the Dark spoke, just the other day. And that's exactly what he's doing now.

That's not what was meant, and you know it.

But Noah has begun, and he's not going to let anything stop him.

He tells her how his scales are made of beaten brass, how they gleam when everything is in order: "I don't know when they arrived; it feels like they've always been there, helping me to keep everything stable. I have to be ready all the time."

"That sounds like really hard work, Noah."

"It is." As he admits it, his fingers start to tap. He hurries through the rest, speaking quickly to keep the Dark from breaking through. "They're Scales of Justice, and they've been entrusted to me. It's my duty to keep them balanced at all times."

"That's almost an impossible task, wouldn't you say?"

He'd like to answer her, say more, but he can feel the scales starting to tilt, listing, threatening to topple.

No! She's going to try to take them away from you. And then what?

He's tapping like crazy, his head is shaking, from left to right.

He can't say any more.

Ms. Turner starts talking quietly, telling him to breathe.

5 deep breaths, and the weight in the scales slowly shifts, reapproaching equilibrium.

If your precious scales go, don't think they'll go alone.

Noah feels her hand on his shoulder, her fingers pressing down gently. She waits as he takes another 5 breaths. "Easy, Noah. Easy. We can leave it at that for now."

Leave it? After what you've told her? Any more, and all strength will go and what about your precious family then?

"I can't lose them," he manages, and for the first time he's telling Ms. Turner something he wants to say, rather than something she wants to hear. "I can't lose my scales, my 5s, I can't. They're all I've got."

"Don't worry, Noah. We'll find other ways to keep things in check."

DAY 65 / 14:19

"I don't want to talk about my mom or my dad, not even about Lily. Is that all right?" Noah's surprised to hear Juliet ask permission, and so politely. She must really want to say what's on her mind.

"One of the things I wonder about is the history of this place. The smells here are heavy, like they've been cooked into the walls. Each person who's stayed in one of these rooms left something of themselves behind, and it's not always Eau de Happiness. If these walls could speak. Such a cliché, but..."

She looks around and they all nod. It's true, the rooms at Greenhills do carry a strange weight, and it's mainly sadness.

"Who was in my room before me? And before them, and before them? Who unpacked their bags, stood at the same window as me, staring at lawns and trees and high walls? The benches, who was sitting on them? And how did they arrive? What fears came in with them? Did they have hope? Did they imagine themselves getting better, pray they'd walk out all fixed and new? Three months to a new and better you."

For once, Juliet is not joking, nor is she being flippant or cynical. Her voice is quiet, serious. "That's what I hope for sometimes," says Juliet. "A new and better me." She laughs. "Sorry." She ducks her head.

"Don't be sorry, Juliet." Ms. Turner is quick off the mark. "I'm sure everyone here has felt the same at some time. Right?"

"I'd like that." Sadie's voice is small. "I *want* that. To be new and better, because then, if I was...I'd be strong."

"Are you sure you want to say this now, Sadie?" Ms. Turner asks.

"I'm sure," she says, tossing back her hair. "They've all probably guessed there's something seriously wrong in my house. Might as well tell them what it is." Her words aren't defensive or whiney as they usually are. She simply sounds weary.

"I'm so tired." She looks up at all of them. "You all think I do nothing but complain. I can understand that, I really can. But that's what I do. Complain and whinge and moan. Try to get you all into trouble. Anything to stop people asking me questions."

There's silence in the Rec Room.

Sadie's staring down. "I'm his perfect little girl," she says. "He'd do anything for me. As long as I'm prepared to do anything for him." She pauses, takes a deep breath, doesn't lift her head. "And his friends. It's dirty. So dirty, and yet he still calls me his perfect girl. That's when my mother isn't around."

A tear runs down her cheek and Ms. Turner leans forward and passes her a tissue.

"So I whine," says Sadie, "and I bitch and I steal and this is my fourth time in Greenhills. Three short-term stays and now the full residential program. I'd do anything to come back here for ever. I do everything I can to get them to say I need help and care.

"You know that feeling you were talking about? From the ones who have been here before?" She looks up and Juliet nods. "Well, one of them is me. I'm one of those people who wants to leave here strong and new, because otherwise," her hands bunch on her lap, "I'm scared. I'm so scared I'm going to take a knife and slit him wide open." She laughs, but it's one of the saddest sounds Noah has ever heard. "Then I'd definitely get to staying shut up. Forever."

"Sadie," Juliet says. She leans over Morné and grabs Sadie's hand.

"Don't worry, Juliet," Sadie says. "How could you know? I'm pretty good at hiding it. Even my Mom...even she doesn't know."

Her mouth's saying the words, but her eyelids flicker, like she's blinking the truth away.

Ms. Turner looks at her watch. "We've still got 15 minutes," she says, "but I'm going to cut this short. What I'd like you all to do is go to your rooms and write in your journals about today's session. How it made you feel. Can you do that?"

They nod as one.

She turns to Sadie. "Would you like to talk more, Sadie?"

"Sure." Sadie's voice is quiet. She stands to follow Ms. Turner out of the Rec Room. As she passes Noah's chair she stops. "Hey, Noah?"

"Yes?"

"It was me who moved your mugs and that desk thingie. Me and Morné."

Noah stares at her open-mouthed. "You?"

"I'm sorry. You're just so, so *perfect*, you know. Always neat, nothing ever out of place. Morné and me...We were going to do more, mess with you a bit. Disorganize you. You know."

"That's what I wanted to tell you," Juliet says. "But then Mad—" She breaks off and recovers quickly. "But then I forgot. I saw them, Noah. Standing near your room. Looking back into it. Not actually doing anything, but..."

Now Morné's looking at Noah, sneering. "It was a fokken mug, man. And that stupid plastic thing. It's not like we broke anything."

Sadie touches Noah lightly on the arm. "Sorry, hey. It was just for fun."

Fun? Are you prepared to put up with this?

Morné is still staring at Noah, unblinking.

Noah looks away, and back at Sadie. Ms. Turner's right there, her arm around Sadie's shoulder, but Sadie's waiting.

He takes a deep breath, and allows himself a silent out, 2 3 4 5. "Don't worry, Sadie. Morné's right. They're only mugs."

Sadie smiles sadly and walks away, leaning into Ms. Turner.

"...what evil lurks in the hearts of men."

The Shadow knows the answer to this, and so does Juliet. She can't forget the sound of Sadie's voice, or the sight of her face.

Ellen's just been here, to her room, and that's a first. Normally Mr. Bill's the one who does the rounds, but Ellen also wants to check in. "You know you can always schedule another meeting with me if you need to talk."

She does. Need to talk, that is. But even as she thinks it, her mouth opens and she says an automatic, "No thanks. I'm fine," when clearly she's not. Ellen knows it, but she nods and tells Juliet she's always there, she only has to say the word. She moves away and Juliet hears her at Vuyo's door. "Everything all right, Vuyokazi?" and then again at Morné's, her voice firm, "I'd like to see you later, Morné."

She's glad Ellen's looking in on them, glad when Mr. Bill does the same later.

Sadie's secret. Shit. What a thing to carry around with you, day after day. All the things she couldn't say, all the things she did to try to make people notice there was something seriously wrong. Did her mom know? How could she *not* know something like that? Then again, when Juliet thinks of her mother, and how out of it she is most of the time...

Juliet hopes that her mom's drinking is something she can put into the past tense. How out of it she *used* to be.

She hopes that her mother and Lily will visit soon. The three of them, her mother and Lily, sitting on a bench, under a tree. That's all she needs for now. If only she could hope the same for Sadie. But she can't. Her wish for Sadie is that her father never comes to see her here, or anywhere, ever again.

Day 66 / 09:28

Noah has 2½ weeks left at Greenhills; 18 days to tame the Dark, make it vanish for good.

That's never going to happen. Not even worth considering.

He's sitting in Ms. Turner's room and she's saying, "I know you read it to me, from your journal, after your mug was moved, Noah. That was so brave. Can you do it again today? Say its name out loud?"

He knows what she's talking about. He also knows he has to face into her questions, no matter how badly he wants to block her, not say anything that might disturb the silence.

They've been talking about facing fear, how naming it detracts from the power it holds. When Sadie and Morné moved his mug, they forced him into a corner; he had no option but to tell Ms. Turner. But this is the first time she has asked him to name it voluntarily.

"When you're ready, Noah. But I think it's time, don't you?"

Time to name the biggest fear of all.

Noah's in the Here and Now. Naming will take away from its strength. Noah is the one with the power. He tells himself all of this, willing himself to speak. Ms. Turner's beside him on the couch, offering her hand.

"No," he says. "I can do this." He places his hands flat on his thighs, pushes down to keep his legs and feet from moving. Fear is nothing but a 4-letter word. So is—

"Dark," he says in a whisper. "I call it the Dark." His lips hardly move, but he might as well have yelled so loudly everyone in Greenhills could hear him. He sandwiches his lips together, waiting for the sky to fall on his head, but there's nothing, only a shocked, echoing silence.

Then Ms. Turner asks something more. "Noah," she says carefully, "what else can you tell me about it?"

"Nothing," he says. "That's all."

"Not even a tiny detail?" she asks.

She's concerned, and Noah wishes he could say something, but the heavy mass is starting to move.

"Well," says Ms. Turner. "It's good that you've said its name, Noah."

No it's not. How could that possibly be a good thing?

The Dark has regained its voice, but Noah manages to talk over it. "Yes, that's something."

"Here's an idea, Noah. Where does it come from? Maybe it would help if we could figure that out?"

"I can't," he says, "I just can't."

"Well, how old is it?"

"Old," he says. His fingers fly to his mouth but there's more pushing its way out. "As old as forever, but sometimes it feels young." The words are falling out of him.

Careful.

The Dark is steaming in, alert to the sounds of danger.

Ms. Turner's gaze is fixed on Noah, and this time he doesn't look away.

"And before that?" she asks. "Was there something before that, Noah? Before the Dark."

"I don't know," he says, even though he does. He knows.

He sees shapes, moving, dissolving, misting, merging into a larger whole.

Stop!

The word snaps out and the parts shift back into place.

But the idea has arrived. Noah prods at it with a thought and the Dark reacts immediately.

Stop. Do not even think about going there.

But he finds himself wanting to. Suddenly he knows, more clearly than ever, that he has to explore the idea that this thing that has taken up residence wasn't always complete and fully formed.

A huff and a puff.

Any minute now, Noah, and your house will be blown to smithereens.

"Some of it comes from my childhood," Noah says, "from when I was little. But the rest arrived much later."

"Arrived? Baggage and all?"

She has no idea.

Ms. Turner smiles. "You do know that most guests only stay a while before moving on?"

Guests? What exactly is she getting at?

Noah has a guest who's become a sitting tenant, paying no rent and occupying his mind without permission.

Occupying, that's the word. Let me remind you of a small detail. Possession is nine-tenths of one of your precious laws.

It's true. Just as Noah thinks he's scored a point, it's lobbed straight back, like a grenade with the pin pulled out, about to explode at his feet.

Noah is breathing in, and blowing out, fighting for every breath.

His body has turned to jelly. His feet tap and his fingers splay on his left thigh, and then on his right. His ritual goes full circle and starts all over again. Noah is doing whatever he can to keep his words where they belong.

His mind and body are all but consumed by the Dark and what's left of Noah has no idea what to do.

Gabriel remembers lying in hospital, the right side of his abdomen sore, the stitches pulling when he moved too quickly. He remembers the word spoken in a hushed voice from the bedside near him. *Pyromaniac.* It wasn't the first time he'd heard the word, and it wouldn't be the last. For as long as people remember the fire where an old man burnt alive, the word will follow him. Gabriel has been branded, and when people learn his name and ask him about his family, someone will remember that night and that there was a boy and petrol and matches. It wasn't me, Gabriel remembers saying, over and over. And then he gave up. Because no matter how hard he tries to explain, he'll always be able to read their thoughts: No smoke without a fire.

It's group time, and everyone is waiting for Ms. Turner, wondering what she's got up her sleeve for today.

"Who was that I saw you talking to during visiting?" Juliet asks Morné.

"My brother," he says abruptly.

"Nice," Juliet says, "very nice."

She'd seen the two of them standing deep in the shade and wished she could snap a quick shot of them, Morné's hands waving in the air, his brother listening, nodding, reaching out. She'd watched Morné jerking away and stomping back inside.

Morné's brother is as tall and broad as Morné. Same coloring, same sandy hair, same pale skin.

But that's where the resemblance ends. Morné is round-shouldered, lumpen and morose. His brother's good-looking, open-faced.

Juliet can imagine him in a sports blazer, striding onto a stage, accepting a trophy for the best sportsman—rowing, tennis, rugby, cricket, you name it, it looks like he could easily sweep the boards.

After Morné had stormed off, he'd stood there for a while. When he walked back to the car park, Juliet got a better look at him. His face was deeply troubled, and she wondered what he'd said that made Morné so angry.

"So, is he older than you," she asks, "or are you the big brother?"

She doesn't mean to sound cruel, bites her lip, says a hurried "Sorry, man."

"No," says Morné. "He's the oldest. And then there's my little boet."

"Three boys," Juliet says. "What's your little brother like?"

Just then Ms. Turner walks in and takes her seat. She waits till they're quiet, then says, "Sadie's not coming to group today."

"Is she okay?" Morné's voice is urgent and he half rises from his chair.

"She's managing," Ms. Turner says.

Morné's standing now. "I have to go see her," he says. "She shouldn't be alone. How could you leave her—"

His voice is rising.

"Mr. Bill is with her," Ms. Turner says. "She's not in group because her mother's visiting this afternoon."

"It'll all work out, Morné." Juliet's voice is kind and he looks at her in surprise.

Si shifts in his seat, Vuyo's hunched forward, her shoulder blades sharp wings beneath her cotton sweater. Everyone's restless today; Sadie's story has untethered them.

"She never told me," Morné's saying now. "Her father...She never told me. I thought I was her friend. I told her everything, but she kept that all to herself."

"Just as well," Juliet says. "I reckon you would have klapped him one if you'd known."

"Taken his head off his fokken shoulders." Morné's hands curl into fists.

"So anyway, Ellen," Juliet looks at Ms. Turner. "Morné was telling us about his brother. The good-looking older one who was here on Saturday. He has a younger brother, too."

"That's wonderful." Ms. Turner is trying not to sound surprised.

Willa chips in. "Stuck in the middle, hey Morné?"

"Piggy in the middle," Morné mutters. He sits back in his chair and stares at the mound of his stomach. *"Varkie in die fokken middel."*

The first thing Gabriel does, when he leaves the home, is to go to Home Affairs. He's written his Matric, he's left school. He's an adult now, old enough to be in control and do what he wants with his life. He can recreate himself, become the man he has imagined all these years. He will be rich, he will be successful. He will drive a good car, wear the right clothes, speak correctly, behave correctly, live well inside the lines. He will not be like his father, his feckless father, who ran out the back door and left Gabriel and his mother and Harry all on their own. Nor will he be like his mother, who turned to a cruel old man for support because she couldn't think of what else to do. No, Gabriel resolves, as he walks through the doors of the children's home, he is going to be his own man. He is going to reinvent himself. Become someone perfect, someone to whom only good things happen.

DAY 67 / 20:22

"I dream in words," says Juliet.

"Words?"

She's caught Noah's attention immediately. Juliet, who can never stop talking, who has to fill every gap in every conversation, every gap in her day (and quite a few in Noah's) with words, dreams in them as well.

"No images? No colors?"

He's using up words. He can't afford to waste them, but he wants to know more.

"That's right," says Juliet. "No pictures. I have dreams, and they feel really vivid, but I can never *see* anything, so the words, say for instance, "green eyes" and "dark hair" are meaningless..." She flicks her gaze up to meet his and grins. "Just joking, Noah, don't have a heart attack. Yes, so if, say, it's green eyes and dark hair, I *know* what's there, but it's not like a green-eyed, dark-haired person appears on some sort of screen."

"What about clothes?"

"No," says Juliet, then blushes. "I mean, yes, he's *wearing* clothes, I know that, but I don't *see* them. I have to wait for the words to describe them."

"And the words themselves?" He can't help asking, he has to know how Juliet's dreamwords work. "Do you *see* the words, as you dream?"

"You mean like subtitles? On a big screen?"

He nods, imagining Juliet's words floating. If he dreamt like she does, he'd watch words clump, catch them in batches, swallow them and send them down deep.

She stops to think. "Not really. It's more like someone's reading me a story, you know? Like the ones my Mom never read me when I was little. But then, when I was old enough, I'd sit on Lily's bed and read her all her favorites. So it's like that. Words from stories in my head."

She sighs. "Sometimes it's one I've heard over and over and I know it's going to end badly, but I can't ever rush to the end, even when the words are really terrible."

And then she stops. There's a gap in her never-ending tide of words and that's all that's needed.

How much longer are we going to have to listen to this? Get her out.

Out?

Of your room.

No.

Noah wants Juliet to keep talking, but she's still quiet.

"It figures," he says.

"What? What figures?"

"You use so many words every day, every minute even. It makes sense that it doesn't stop when you dream."

It's only much later, when he's reviewing his day, that he realizes something profound.

The Dark had complained about Juliet—*Get her out*—and for the first time ever, he'd challenged it. And then, even more amazing, he'd been able to shut it out completely so that he could find out more about the words in Juliet's dream world.

Not a wise move. Not wise at all.

Who's afraid of the big bad wolf, the big bad wolf, the big bad wolf? Who's afraid of the big bad wolf, nananananaah.

It's Saturday. Juliet is singing to Lily and her little sister is staring up at her from the crib. Lily laughs when Juliet moves her head close to her sister's face. Her tiny fingers grab at Juliet's hair and Juliet laughs too.

Juliet, Mom calls from downstairs, and Juliet says, Lunchtime Lily.

She wants more than anything to pick Lily up and take her downstairs but she's too little, she might drop her. Only Mom and Florence, the lady who cleans the house, and sometimes Daddy, are allowed to pick Lily up. Juliet thinks this is wrong, because Mom doesn't always walk straight and when that happens Florence says, Here, Monica, let me take her. Lily is safe on Florence's back, but when Dad carries her, he says, For Chrissakes, Monica, this baby stinks. Juliet doesn't think he should talk about Lily like that, even if she is too little to understand. Juliet understands, but she will never ever tell Lily that Daddy says she's a smelly little girl.

Sometimes Mom's dress smells of vomit from Lily and the perfume she keeps spraying on, even when Dad says, I don't know why you bother, Monica, I can smell the booze a mile away, everyone can.

Then Juliet and Daddy and Mom are sitting around the dining-room table. Lily is in her pushchair and Mom rocks it now and then and Lily falls asleep. Cold meats and fucking salad again, says Dad and Mom says, Sorry, Bart. It's so hot I thought—and Dad says, Don't. Don't think, Monica, thinking isn't your strong suit.

Daddy goes into the kitchen and comes back with a long green bottle. He pours some of it into his glass and drinks.

Mom watches him while he drinks and he smiles at her. Have

some water, Monica, he says, and Mom reaches over and picks up the jug and pours the water into a glass, only her hands are a little shaky, so she spills some on the tablecloth. Dad smiles again and sips some more. His drink is the same color as Juliet's wee when she sits on the toilet. If Juliet was Mom, she wouldn't drink that yellowy stuff, but Dad likes it because he sips and smiles and sips and smiles.

Please may I leave the table, Juliet asks, because Dad has told Mom the child needs to learn some manners, but Dad says, No, not yet. Wait here. He goes out of the dining room and then comes back holding a little square box with a shiny black eye. He points it at a corner in the room and says, This will do fine.

What, Bart? says Mom, and Dad says, What do you fucking think, Monica? I promised your parents a family photograph.

Family. Juliet knows that word. Photograph is a new one.

This is one of Juliet's earliest memories. She remembers it often, examines each detail. She asks herself if it really happened that way. She thinks it did. She remembers looking at the photograph of the family on the piano and seeing a father, a mother, two children.

The father has gathered the small girl, the mother, and the baby for a family photograph. The mother is holding the baby in her arms. The father wants the mother to show the baby's face, the mother says the baby is asleep. The father shouts. The baby begins to cry. The baby is now awake. The father says, Ready, smile! He puts the camera on the table and runs to the empty seat next to the mother. The little girl stands between the two chairs, one for the mother, one for the father.

The father says, Smile. The mother is smiling. The little girl is looking at the camera, the camera is blinking. It makes a beep-beep-beep noise. The father says, Smile, again.

The little girl looks at her father and says, I am smiling, Daddy.

There's a long beeeeep and then a bright flash.

The father says, Fucksakes I said smile, not talk. The father says he doesn't know why he bothers. He gets up from his seat.

The little girl stays standing, staring forward. The little girl is smiling.

The photograph looks like this: Back row: Two adults seated, with a baby in the woman's arms. Front row: A little girl standing on her own, looking up at the man behind her. The man's right hand is on the little girl's shoulder. The little girl's shoulder tilts down on one side.

Daddy says he's going to attach the photograph to an email and send it to the grandparents all the way across the sea in Australia. Juliet doesn't understand what that means, but when Granny speaks to her on the phone she says Juliet's a beaut and how she loves the way she was looking up at her dad. Grandpa says, Isn't she a cute little thing, blonde, just like her pretty mom.

Such a happy snap, Granny says and Grandpa says mmmhmmm because he's listening in on the other line.

Dad brings home a copy of the photo. He slips it into a silver frame and puts it on the top of the piano.

There Juliet is, dressed in her tutu and pink T-shirt. Mom is holding Lily and Dad is grinning with all his teeth. Juliet is looking up at Daddy, her mouth half open. Mom's mouth is smiling, but her eyes aren't squinched up like they are when she laughs.

The piano gathers pictures year after year. Happy snaps for the grandparents. Juliet growing taller, Lily standing on her own feet, Mom's lipstick red on her still pretty face, Dad growing a little less handsome with a little less hair.

Cameras are magic, Juliet thinks. She still does. They keep secrets. They make things different to how they really are.

DAY 68 / 13:51

"Hey, Noah. Can I tell you something?"

He turns his head cautiously. "That depends—" he starts, but not quite quickly enough.

Juliet's off. "You know how much I talk, how I can't keep still?"

"Yes." Yes, of course he does; it's one of the things that makes her who she is. Non-stop, on the go.

"Well, I have to do it," she says. "It's my armor. I wake up every morning and I put that armor on."

Noah nods. He knows all about that.

"So, anyway, the thing is, if I keep talking, laughing, putting people down even, I don't give them a chance to get *under* the armor. Inside my skin. Does that make sense?"

He nods again. It does.

"So, there's that, and I can also use my words against my father and even my mom."

Juliet pauses and takes a deep breath.

"But the thing is, I also use my words to lie. Ellen knows it, of course." She laughs. "It's getting so we have a routine. I lie. She catches me out. I lie again, she calls me on it, and so on. Finally, though, by the end of the session I've managed to tell her one thing that's true."

Noah's interested. Juliet uses words like weapons; he's scared of letting his out.

"The only thing is, Noah. I can't lie to you. It's like nothing I say or do can shock you...So what's the point?" Another laugh, a shrug of her shoulders. "You're my truth serum. So everything I tell *you* about—mermaids, Smudge, dreamwords—it's all true. I can't bullshit you. Telling you stuff makes it easier to talk to Ellen. You know what I mean?"

He shakes his head. He's not entirely sure. And then, he opens his mouth. "I mean, I do believe you. It's just I don't know what you mean about using words."

Juliet nods, understanding. "Sure. I get that."

There's a peaceful silence in the room for the first time since Juliet arrived.

"There's something I really want to say to you, Noah. Only thing is, it's hard. You know all the shit you've heard, about me and, you know, the sex thing?"

He nods.

Juliet looks down, and even her hands are still. This time, when she starts talking, her words rattle out at speed.

"It's not true, Noah. I just make stuff like that up. To piss my father off, try to make my mom see me. I don't know why I do it. Actually, *that's* a lie. And I promised myself I'd tell you this straight. I do know. It's because I'm so mad, Noah. At everyone. My father, my mother, all the stupid people who can't see I'm lying. Who never say, 'Juliet, why do you do this?'"

"I'm not talking about Ellen—she's *paid* to try and understand me. It's my mom, Noah. Why didn't she ever lift her head out of it for just five minutes and ask me what was going on. My father...Especially him. He can't be *bothered* to care."

She's still staring at her knees and her bright hair is hiding her face. "I'm good at that, making him see me in the worst way. But I want you to know, Noah. A lot of what I say and do? It isn't me at all."

2001

Something else happened when Noah was 5 years old, right at the end of the year when they were all getting ready to leave Ms. Jonas and go into Pre-school 2. It was something really bad. No one told him what was going on, but a big voice reached right inside him and said, Look, Noah. Mom's crying and Dad's face is like someone hurt him.

Dad came home in the middle of the afternoon. He never did that, not unless they were having a Special Family Day. Mom loved Special Days. She'd *spring* them on Dad, and he'd say, Really, Kate. Tomorrow? and Mom would say, Yes really, Dom, otherwise when will the kids and I ever get to see you? Then he'd laugh and say, Fair enough, you win. He'd kiss Mom and she'd smile at him and he'd pick up the phone and say, Cancel all my appointments for tomorrow, please, Ms. Jonkers, I have a personal engagement.

Then they'd all do things like go to the beach, or out to the farm to see Ouma and Oupa, Mom's mom and dad. They'd sit under a big tree there and eat bread and cheese and Oupa would let Noah sip his wine but first he'd have to sniff it and say what it smelled like, even if it was like when Ms. Jonas sharpened all the crayons, ready for drawing.

But not that day.

When Dad walked through the front door, Mom rushed up to him and he held her really tight.

She said, Oh Dom, Dom, and he hugged her and she said, There's another one. Another one's been hit.

Go and play, Noah, Dad said. Off you go. Play with Maddie.

And ask Sibongile to make you a sandwich, said Mom.

They went into the sitting room and closed the door, but not before Noah heard a lady saying, This is an attack on the American way of life. Behind her, on the TV, there was a tall tower, taller than any building Spiderman ever crawled up, but this one had smoke and fire coming out of it on the side near the top.

Sibongile looked after them all afternoon and when Noah asked her if they were going out for a Special Day, she said no.

That afternoon, instead of vacuuming and dusting and cleaning the showers, she played games with Maddie and him, and she even allowed them to go into the kitchen and help with the washing up. They were very careful, but it was quite safe, Sibongile said, because the water was warm and the plates were plastic.

Sibongile told them about her brother who used to be a postman, riding up and down streets like theirs, delivering letters, only one day he fell off his bike and broke his knee. It was a very bad break, and now he can't ride his bicycle or walk very far, said Sibongile. She told them he couldn't find a job and that she was helping him to look after his family and now they all lived together in her small house.

Noah and Maddie had so much fun that afternoon, it was almost as good as a Special Family Day.

And then it was time for Sibongile to catch a taxi and then a train and then another taxi, which was how she got home.

Mom said, Thank you so much, Sibongile. I couldn't have...and then she looked like she was going to cry again. She stood at the door and her face was white and sad, and Dad was standing inside the sitting room. The TV was switched off, but its big green eye looked straight at Noah.

Juliet has only told Noah some of it. It's not that she doesn't trust him—he's the safest person she knows right now. The best friend she has, really. Girls at school defintely don't trust her; she's sharp-tongued and flirty, their boyfriends are vulnerable and if they let Juliet too close, who knows what she's capable of.

Boys at school?

As if, Juliet wants to say to the ones like Kyle Blake and his grubby little band of alpha-male losers. As if I'd want anything to do with you. She sends the disdainful message out, loud and clear, and they hate her for it. They let the stories about her grow unchecked, adding to them when they can.

Juliet's trained herself not to care. She's counting down the days until she finshes Matric, and until then she's going to hold it together for Lily, and for herself.

She goes to her cupboard and opens her suitcase. There, tucked into the elasticized compartment in the lid, is her folder. It's the most precious thing in her life. No one knows about it, and there's no way she's going to show it to Ellen. Not even to Noah, for that matter.

A sheaf of photographs slides out and she gathers them back together carefully.

Some were taken during the day, but the majority are night shots.

The camera can lie—Juliet learned that early in life—but not always. It can also reveal truths that would otherwise remain unseen. If people don't know you're there, hidden behind a parked car, angling a lens from a street corner, that's when it happens. Catch a man leaning from a car window, negotiating with a prostitute; a bag lady trundling her shopping cart festooned with the portable essentials of her life; a mother pulling a toddler along by the arm; a boy leaning in for a sweet kiss; girls at a cosmetic counter pouting into mirrors. The mayhem of a city nightclub; a rendezvous on the common on a Sunday afternoon, a balding, middle-aged man meeting a girl young enough to be his daughter.

Outside of Greenhills, Juliet carries her camera whenever she can. Here, it's on the list of restricted items, along with any electronic device that can take photos. So no phone, either. She misses being able to slip her mobile out of her pocket for the odd quick pic. But way more than that, she longs for the precison and complexity of her SLR.

She's taught herself everything she knows, from books, from the Internet, through trial and error. She could have signed up for the photography club at school, taken advantage of all the programs on offer, but Juliet's a loner, roaming the streets, capturing life as it happens, not as it's been arranged. She steals moments from other people's lives, gets as close to the truth as she can, as far from the manufactured lies that adorn the piano top in the living room at home.

Dominic has no family. That's what he told Kate in one of their first getting-to-know-you conversations. "I don't know anything about my parents," he'd said.

"That's terrible."

Kate can't begin to imagine what his childhood must have been like. No one to call his own. Her large family included aunts and uncles, brothers, sisters, cousins, grandparents, in-laws, step-cousins, nieces, nephews—relatives by the dozen.

Dominic has no one, not one single relative he can claim, no way of looking back into the past, no one to take after, or wish he could discard.

He was abandoned by his mother, he tells Kate, and he knows nothing about his father.

"But don't you want to look for them? Find out who she was, where he is. They might still be alive, Dominic." Kate's seen the the TV programs about lost siblings, lost children, lost parents. "You could go to the—"

"No," he'd said. "I made up my mind long ago. If she doesn't want to find me, then I won't look for her. I'd just be asking for a world of trouble."

"So you were adopted, then?" Kate had asked.

Dominic shook his head. "Care." His mouth twisted on the word. "I was in care."

Kate reached for his hand, but Dominic slid his away. "That's about it," he said. "A children's home until I was eighteen. And from there, out into the world and on my own."

Dominic's life is a tower of lies, and it's crumbling around him. Brick by brick, the tower is falling, but he can't escape. He's trapped, locked in his turret. He threw away the key long ago, when he didn't tell Kate about his past. And now, when she begs him to, he daren't tell her a thing.

Kate doesn't give up though, not when it's something that might benefit her son. *Their* son, he reminds himself.

"Dom," she says, "we can find her. We can get a history from her. Even if you don't want to know, what if we can help Noah?"

Dominic refuses to take it any further. "Leave it, Kate. She abandoned me."

"But if we knew more, we might be able to—"

He cuts her short. "What good would it do, Kate? Noah is what he is, who he is. Don't we have enough to deal with without bringing my mother into the picture? Besides, who's to say she's even alive?"

2012

Gabriel's getting feedback from Sebastian Crown, the man hired to track down his sister. He's given him all the information from the brown envelope they handed him when he left the home. Gabriel keeps it locked away, hidden from prying eyes, this past he cannot throw away. The past he hates to remember but cannot forget. Lately, over the last year or so, when he's had a drink, he'll open the envelope. Mainly to hold a small photo in his hands. If he's had two drinks, or sometimes three, he'll murmur, "Where are you, Mum? Where are you, Harry?" Then he'll phone Sebastian Crown and ask if there's any news.

DAY 69 / 05:12

Noah wakes up early.

He stretches. Checks. Everything's fine. The still-rising sun throws dappled light onto the chair by the window, turning it from midnight black to blue.

Nobody else is up. The corridor outside his room is silent.

He throws back his cotton sheet, gets out of bed and checks his timetable. 6.30 a.m. is when it all begins—the list of things he has to do. He looks back at his bed. According to his timetable, he should still be sleeping. And, when he does wake up, he should check his pulse immediately, then flex each of his muscles in order. But he's awake *now*.

He stops. Closes his eyes, checks again. No, he's not tired. If he goes back to bed, he'll just lie there. He'll waste a full hour.

The lawn at Greenhills, this home of no hills, glows in the early light. Noah moves over to the window, puts his hand on the latch. If he pushes the latch down (up-down-up-down), the window will open and all the sounds of the early morning will enter his room. He hopes there might also be a breath of cool early morning air. Soon the temperature will rise; last night the EWN weather forecast promised another steamy day, with temperatures in the high 20s. Rain's been forecast, but so far it hasn't arrived.

As he stands there, he sees a flick of light. And then another and another. The Greenhills sprinklers activating, one by one, in the cool of the morning. Noah watches them spurt, throwing water into the air, letting it fall onto thirsty warm ground. His toes curl into the roughness of his sisal rug. And then, with a quick look at the clock on his wall, a quick check of his timetable, a quick listen to the regular, so-no-need-to-worry-about-that beat of his heart, he walks to the door. Down goes the handle, only down, and then he's hurrying along the corridor, past the Rec Room and the Visitors' Lounge, through the lobby to the doors of the main entrance.

They won't open. Noah stands, looking to where the spray is playing with rainbows in the early morning sun. He moves, faster now, to behind the desk. How does she let people in, Sally-Anne, who sits here all day, every day, controlling the flow of people in and out of Greenhills?

He runs his hand along the underside of the desk, finds a button and presses. With a click, the large glass doors open slightly. He hurries, his feet making no sound on the warm tiles of the lobby floor. He slips through the gap in the door, then stops, strips off the T-shirt he sleeps in, folds it into a very neat square and wedges it between the two doors.

And then he's on the move.

On the lawn, regular arcs of water mist the air. The grass under his feet is prickly—and cool.

Noah stops and listens. No one is awake. No one is moving. Only the birds in the trees make a sound, and as he waits, silent, they begin to fly in and out of the spray, ducking and diving close to where Noah is standing, his face turned to the sky. His dark hair is plastered to his skull, water is falling onto his bare chest, his cotton pajama pants are wet, clinging to his legs.

Everyone's forever talking about the heat and how it's never cool, not even at night. His duvet doesn't quite fit into a bag under his bed. The thought of it makes his skin tight. But right now he's wet, from top to toe, dripping with water, and wonderfully cool. Around him the birds fly, catching water on their wings, swooping to the lawn to sip in small drops.

Then, over the sounds of the birds and the soft murmur of sprinklers, he hears another sound—the crunch of tires on gravel. He stands there, unmoving, his toes digging into the wet grass.

"My God." Noah hears a voice, but he ignores it.

"Noah, is that you?"

He doesn't turn his head. He needs this air that allows him to breathe deeply, without once feeling he has to count in and out.

Noah closes his eyes and turns in a slow circle. Water runs down his stomach, it courses down his back. Mr. Bill's calling his name again, telling him to go inside. He smiles. He has absolutely no intention of moving.

DAY 69 / 13:10

It feels like the hottest afternoon on record, one of those clammy, muggy days when everything feels sticky to the touch. Noah and Juliet have been over their plan again, making sure that they haven't overlooked a single detail. Or rather, Noah has, while Juliet calms him down.

"Relax, Noah," she's said, over and over. "It'll work like a charm." She's in her usual place, and now she's talking about the sea and swimming and how once she's out and home the first thing she's going to do is go to the beach with Lily and her mom, and this time it'll be her mother doing the driving. Then she jumps to what they had for lunch and how the menu at Greenhills is so boring. From there she launches into her sessions with Ms. Turner and how they're getting easier. "She's not so bad after all," Juliet concedes.

Her mind is all over the place and she's more fidgety than normal. She keeps looking down the corridor, then back up at Noah.

Noah stands up from his desk. He takes Juliet's mug from its place, just to the left of his row of seven blue ones and switches on the kettle.

"Tea, coffee?"

As he asks, Sadie and Willa appear, each holding a mug. Each looking like they expect him to say something, but Juliet gets there first.

"I asked them to come, Noah. Is that okay?"

He waits for a ripple of discomfort, for a waking moan, but there's nothing. He waits, just to make sure, but all is quiet.

Sadie looks anxious. "We don't have to stay." She looks at the navy blue mug in Noah's hand and a flush colors her cheeks. "I mean, we don't want to disturb you, or mess with any routine. Only Juliet said—"

The kettle's boiling now and Noah switches it off. "Sure," he says.

"I asked Morné too," Juliet says casually, as if his room has suddenly become the Mount Nelson, "but he didn't want to come."

"We brought our mugs," Willa says, raising theirs in the air. It's purple with a gold rim. "I've even made my own tea. And, if you're worried about these: Ta dah!" They wave a packet of biscuits in the air. "Plenty to go around."

Juliet slips into his room. "Can I lean against your bed, Noah?"

"Umm...sure."

"You guys sit down here with me."

Willa looks at the floor in distaste and stays in the doorway. "I'll stand, if you don't mind."

"Pass your mug, Sadie." Juliet looks up at him. "Are you cool with this, Noah? I thought we could all, you know, hang for a while." She flashes a smile at Sadie. "No need to talk about anything heavy."

Sadie's still anxious. "We can go if you want?"

Noah waits. No reaction. Maybe having so many people in his narrow space has blocked the sound waves.

He lifts the kettle. Easily enough for four cups without adding more.

Once upon a time there was a very large house called Green Hills. No one is entirely sure who built such an expansive home, but the pediment over the door is dated 1853. When the owners moved in, bringing with them their fine furniture, paintings, carpets and hiring a multitude of servants to cook and clean, the lady of the house looked beyond the tall stone walls, designed to keep all the danger out, to the wild untamed countryside where, far in the distance, she could just make out the ocean.

She pined for the misty hills of home, with their soft and constantly changing hues. So when her husband asked what name they should give their new estate, she smiled sadly and said, "Green Hills, my sweet. Green Hills."

Over the years, the layout changed. Wings were closed off, rooms were built on and, eventually, a smaller dwelling was constructed to accommodate the lady and her husband when their offspring took over the big house.

Slowly, Green Hills became Greenhills and then, the family moved on. Perhaps the great-grandmother who could never quite settle in a foreign land eventually went back "home." Who knows?

For several years Greenhills, a place of towering stone walls but no hills, stood silent and empty, dismissed as a ruin.

One day, though, its luck changed. A doctor happened to peer through its unlocked gates, push them open and see a house that could be rescued, restored, reinvented as a tranquil refuge for souls in need of a safe haven. For souls who found it too hard to inhabit the world outside its walls.

He spoke to some more doctors and, working together, they took the old house and carved large rooms into smaller ones: rooms for sleeping, meeting and eating, rooms where people said nothing at all, or spoke about everything they had been guarding for years.

Eventually the doctors decided that they needed more space and they turned their attention to the smaller house. It too became a refuge, a home, for young people, made up of rooms for sleeping, meeting, eating, rooms where nothing was said, or where everything that had lain hidden could come to light.

Typically, tales that start with 'Once upon a time' end with the words 'And they all lived happily ever after.' This will never be entirely true of Greenhills. Many of its stories will never end. Yet in these never-endings there can be new beginnings, new ways of living and new ways of seeing life.

III

Day 70 / 14:27

"Way to go, Noah." Juliet was impressed when she heard about Noah and the sprinklers. After a moment's thought, she added, "So if you can break away from your timetable like that, you *can* do anything."

She'd looked so hopeful, filled with hope for him, that he couldn't remind her that that those cool, soaked moments on the lawn had taken nothing away from his timetable. It was free time, early-waking bonus time put to good use.

There was something else he couldn't tell her: The truth. Noah was scared. The more he thought about what they were planning, the more words filled his head.

This is madness. You say you want out of this place, and now you're embarking on this...this...lunacy?

The last word was an angry scream and from then on it felt like the Dark would never let go.

"You can do anything, Noah." He'd held tight to Juliet's words and tapped like crazy, counted like crazy, breathed like crazy, so much so that Ms. Turner was worried. "What's happening, Noah? Is there anything you want to tell me?"

But he couldn't. All he could do was pull the 5s close, raise his shield and get through the two days until Sunday visiting hours as best he could, telling himself it was okay to be scared. He marked off every hour on a new chart, and then, sooner than he wanted, it was minutes, then seconds before his mother and sister arrived.

14:29

Noah sits outside on the bench, looking at his watch, not ready for it to begin, but knowing it has to.

Rags to riches. This is the story Dominic never tells, but there are plenty of people at Goodson, Stander & Groome who remember the arrival of a young man in a shiny, ill-fitting suit. Later, after he's been working there long enough to save some money, he goes to a factory clothing outlet and buys a suit that doesn't sag at the knees, with trousers and sleeves long enough for his tall body.

Those first months, all Dominic Groome, junior clerk, does is sit at the desk he shares in an open-plan room. He sits there and eats there and frequently sleeps there. The moment he finishes one task, he's knocking on the manager's door and asking for another. He ignores his colleagues' snubs, can't be bothered to listen when they talk about him being overly ambitious, heading for a fall.

He listens and he learns, and when he gets the opportunity, he remarks on the behavior of certain stocks. He reads the newspapers from cover to cover and broadens his knowledge of world affairs. He studies what happened during the 1973 oil crisis and the '73–'74 market crash, one of the worst stockmarket downturns in modern history. He looks further back to the sixties, to Nixon and what it cost to fund the war in Vietnam, how much the President had needed to spend to expand Social Security with elections approaching.

He comes to understand how politics affect business in South Africa and the response of the South African stock market to different exchange rate regimes. He learns the words of the financial world. Before long, Dominic starts to predict how certain stocks will behave and can make informed comments about how the fluctuating price of gold is affecting the rand and the price of exports sold overseas.

One day—one fateful day—he stops a partner in the corridor and speaks to him about investing in non-gold mineral exports, putting clients' money into harbor facilities, railway lines and mines. His suggestion is later discussed in the boardroom, where it is taken seriously, especially as revenues have been increasing at a noteworthy rate.

Whenever his peers talk about his rapid ascent, how his superiors often call on him to take figures and analyze and compute them, there's more than a touch of peevish envy in their voices. And on the day when Dominic arrives in the office wearing a suit that comes from one of the better department stores, designed by one of the better fashion houses, teamed with a striped shirt, a dark tie, and highly polished shoes, he hears one of them mutter, "Check, it's rags-to-riches guy."

Dominic shows no sign of having heard. He simply takes off his jacket, hangs it over his chair and gets on with his job.

Kate notices everything about Mr. Bill.

She is aware of him sitting next to her on the bench, his size, his strength, his quiet gentleness. There's a faint sheen of perspiration on his face and forearms. Kate's sweating too, she can feel the moisture under her arms, the dampness on her thighs.

She blushes as she thinks about how often he's been in her mind, how glad she is that Dominic isn't here this afternoon, and that he didn't come last week either.

This heat. Searingly hot days, stifling nights when she and Dominic lie on opposite sides of the bed. The moment skin meets skin, the heat in their bed seems to double. Dominic somehow manages to sleep, his breathing deep and regular, while Kate lies awake, her hair damp, her thin cotton T-shirt sticking to her. All she wants is to sleep, to close her eyes and fade out all thoughts of Mr. Bill.

It's the heat that makes her get out of bed and go to the window and stare out at the garden, walk to the kitchen, get a glass of water and sit there in the dark, thinking about her life: her husband, and why she can't talk to him any more, what to do about Noah, worrying about Maddie and how she's coping...These are the thoughts keeping her awake, she tells herself. These are good, wifely worries. These are legitimate concerns. And then, she tells herself, she should think about making a shopping list for tomorrow. Maybe give Monica a call and see if she wants to meet for coffee.

That's what I'll do, Kate tells herself as she sits in her dark kitchen fanning herself with the newspaper Dominic left on the counter, sipping her water, ice cold from the fridge. Dominic's wife sitting in the house that her husband has paid for with his high-powered job and his long hours at the office. Dominic's wife, sitting alone in the dark, keeping her mind busy with thoughts of anything and everything—anything but Mr. Bill.

Once, when Kate was small, Pa took her out on a lake in a rowing boat. Or maybe it was the sea, on a calm day. All Kate really remembers is Ma saying, "Etienne, be careful," and Pa replying, "We'll be fine, won't we Katjie-Kat, we're not going far."

And there she was, sitting in a boat on a wooden plank, her pa opposite her, sliding the oars into the rowlocks and pulling away from the bank—it was a lake—where Ma stood waving, waving and getting smaller and smaller. And there they were, out in the middle of the calm green and Pa was saying, "This is the life, nè, Katjie-Kat?"

Kate looked at the water on all sides of her and her pa in his shorts with his strong tanned legs and his strong tanned arms. She closed her eyes and felt the boat rocking her very gently.

And then, Pa leaned forward and pulled back, and leaned forward and pulled back, until the side of the lake came closer and closer. Ma was still standing there, trying to put a smile on her worried face, and holding out her arms for her Katjie.

Then her feet were on the ground and nothing was moving underneath her and Pa took one hand, and Ma took the other, and "Ein, twee, drie, oopse daisy' they went, all the way back to the car.

That's what Kate remembers now, how safe she felt with Pa in the boat, how glad Ma was to have her in her arms, how cherished she felt swinging between her parents, one small daisy on a chain of love. How happy she was. The same way she feels now, sitting on a wooden bench, next to Mr. Bill and wondering if it's her imagination telling her that he's also glad to be there. She looks at him, a quick sideways glance of a look, at the line of his nose, the corner of his mouth. That's all she dare risk. She can't turn her face to look straight at him and let him see her longing. Her guilt. How can she be thinking of looking at the full curve of his lips, the slope of his cheekbones, his deep brown eyes? How can she be thinking of Mr. Bill when she should be focusing on her son? Noah's the reason she's here.

Noah, sitting on the lawn, barely ten feet away from her, arms locked around his knees, looking at Juliet, his new friend. Listening as she talks, her arms waving, his face breaking into a genuine smile and Juliet smiling back at him. He's happy here, more so than he ever was at home, and Kate feels the joy of this, and the sorrow.

There he is, barely ten feet away, but it might as well be ten miles.

14:39

Maddie passes him the keys.

"Thanks, Mads." Noah slips them into his pocket.

Madness. Absolute madness.

Crazy, madness, insane, lunacy, mental...

These are its words of the week, but at least Maddie's here now. Things can start to move.

"What's the plan?" she asks.

"You know the guy on the gate, the one who lifts the boom?" Juliet asks.

"Yes?"

"I've been watching him. He has a pretty regular routine. He's a smoker, but he's not allowed to smoke in the guardhouse. So he sneaks off for a cigarette. Usually two an hour. So all we have to do..."

Noah's breathing quickens as she speaks and he forces himself to slow it down.

"...is wait for him to leave the guardhouse. We'll have enough time to get away before he's back on duty. He stands where he can watch for visitors, so we'll have to be really quick."

"Speed is so important, Noah." Juliet's told him this over and over. "We can't afford to spend any time calculating, or timing, or starting over. Do you reckon you can do that? And no counting? At all?"

"I wish I could come," Maddie says. "Please, Noah?"

"You have to stay, Mads," he says. "You have to look after Mom. Tell her not to worry, we'll be back soon."

He puts his fingers to his lips, lets them stay there for a moment, then looks at Juliet.

"Ready?" she asks.

He nods.

"All right then. Let's do this."

"I'll go first," he says, "then you, after 2 minutes. Okay?"

"Sure." Juliet smiles. "Two minutes on the dot."

Noah walks up to his mother. She's laughing at something Mr. Bill has said. It's a good sound, one he hasn't heard much in the last few years. He hopes this afternoon's plan won't change that, won't stop her laughing.

"Mom?"

She looks up, then glances at her watch. "Yes, sweetheart?"

"I'm just going to get something from my room for Maddie. I promised I'd work through some math problems for her. Show her all the steps. Can I have a pass, Mr. Bill?

Mr. Bill rummages in his pocket and pulls out a laminated yellow card.

"Good for you, Noah," Mom says. "Is Maddie going with you?"

"Yes." He's just made a decision, faster than he ever has before. "Yes. I need to make sure she understands. Ready, Mads?"

She leaps to her feet. "We won't be long, Mom. See you in a few minutes."

Juliet lies back on the grass, her eyes closed.

Kate watches her. "I can't fathom that girl," she says quietly. "Are you sure it's appropriate that she and Noah spend so much time together?"

"It's the best thing that could have happened to either of them," says Mr. Bill. "Noah demands nothing of Juliet and she wants nothing from him. Not often you get a relationship built on such unconditional terms."

A sudden burst of adrenaline buzzes through her. What do *you* want, Mr. Bill? she wonders. And what would you give in return?

By the time Dominic is twenty-three years old, he's made his mark. That's what one of the senior partners of Goodson & Stander says when he calls him in to his office. He wants to talk about Dominic's future.

"Potential, my boy," he booms and his white moustache quivers as if it will never get used to the shock of his loud voice. "Potential. I see myself in you. Rags to riches, that's my story."

"But sir—"

"No buts, son. No buts. Just one question. Where do you see yourself in five years' time?"

Dominic looks at the smooth jowls, the silk tie, the well-cut suit of the older man. He knows that the shoes under the desk cost more than his month's salary. Before he can clamp his mouth shut, he replies, "Sitting where you are, sir."

The words are out and Dominic can't take them back. He sits and waits for the axe to fall.

Instead, there's another boom, this one of laughter, and the moustache quivers again.

"Quite right, my boy. Quite right." He looks at Dominic, his blue eyes shrewd. "We can make something of you, Groome. And in return, you can make us money. Lots of it."

And so Dominic goes to night school, he enrolls at UNISA, he translates his shabby matric into one degree and then another. And all the while, slowly and surely, he makes his way up the corporate ladder, first into a corner office in a large open-plan office with a second-floor view of Cape Town harbor, only the tips of the cranes showing and a small sliver of sea. Higher he climbs and higher, until people start greeting him in the corridors, "Hello, Mr. Groome," "How are you, Mr. Groome?" "Yes sir, Mr. Groome." Yes sir and no sir and eventually, three years later than his original five-year plan, his former mentor is ready to retire and Dominic Groome is sitting behind his desk. He organizes the farewell party, tells his secretary exactly what gift to buy, and takes over the reins.

He sits in the swivel chair and spins round until he's looking down on the harbor, the blocky reds, grays and blues of the cargo on the container ships, the sea a dark sheen in the afternoon sun.

The youngest man to ever hold such a senior position at Goodson

& Stander, and soon the youngest man to be made full partner. Goodson, Stander & Groome. Dominic climbs and climbs, and on the way he meets Kate Cilliers. Beautiful Kate, with her blonde hair and her long limbs and her quick smile.

She's several years younger than him, but Dominic, who'd long thought of himself as a permanent bachelor, turns his back on the single life. He'd never bargained on children either, but soon they form part of the picture too. Dominic Groome, top-flight executive, husband, father, all-round family man. The sort of man people want to photograph in his home, interview in lifestyle magazines. "What's the secret of your success?" they always ask, and Dominic always gives the same answer: "Hard work and tenacity." He never says anything about the rags, and he's reticent about the riches.

Kate hears Mr. Bill's rolling laugh as he tells her about Noah's escapade in the garden. "He was just standing there, in the spray, drenched. Surrounded by birds. It was like a scene in a movie. He looked happy, Mrs. Groome, so cool."

Kate smiles. Would your skin feel cool too, she wonders. Would it be chilled by sweat, or warm, alive, ready to burst into flame?

Her thoughts are smashing against each other. Kate has to get a grip. She has to return to the main topic and ask about Noah, what his foray into the garden means, is it a good thing that her son acted so impetuously, and so very out of character? Instead, she finds herself asking, "Five thirty in the morning? You must have to leave home at sparrows to get here so early."

"It's not too bad," Mr. Bill says. "I live just around the corner."

Kate is embarassed by her presumption that he'd be living somewhere further away, like Khayelitsha, or Langa, and have to get up at four in the morning and catch a taxi and then a train and then another taxi.

"That's convenient," she manages to say.

"Yes," says Mr. Bill. "My wife and I moved here last year. It makes everything so much easier."

Kate looks down at her fingers, interlaced on her lap. Her hands are swollen from the heat and her wedding ring bites into her flesh. She is suddenly lightheaded, thrown by the words he has just spoken. She can't speak, can't give herself away by asking about Mrs. Bill.

Juliet's standing now, sauntering over to them. "Mr. Bill," she's saying. "May I have a bathroom pass?"

"Sure, Juliet." Mr. Bill digs into his pocket and pulls out a sheaf of the laminated cards. His wallet falls out and lies open on the grass. Kate's hands tighten, her wedding ring bites deeper as she sees a photo of a young woman, a small baby and a tall, dark man behind them.

In the envelope Gabriel's holding there's a photograph of a woman holding a baby, a small bundle of blanket. Gabriel can't see eyes or a nose or a mouth but he knows it's Harry. The tall, dark-haired woman holding Harry is his mother, Martha. Gabriel runs the name over his lips, letting the "M' hum and sting a little before he releases it. He does it again, this time allowing it to form the word "Mum."

My mum, Martha, he says as he strokes the small square of paper, as if he might get the sleeping child to wake at his gentle touch and turn her face to him. My sister, he says and the letter "s" hisses in his mouth.

My mum, Martha, and my sister, Harry, and who knows what became of Joe?

It's taken Gabriel Felix months to find his sister. He's on the doorstep of a house in Kenilworth and his hand is raised, ready to lift the knocker.

14:47

Maddie and Noah are hurrying; no time to count steps, no time to stop at corners.

Maddie skips at Noah's side to keep up. "Does that mean I can come, Noah?" she asks breathlessly. "Can I?"

"No, Mads." He looks at her seriously. "Saying you were coming to my room just means we can get away more easily. It gives us more of a head start." He slips his hand into his pocket. A slide of metal, the slick of plastic casing, his mother's car keys, and in between, his pebbles.

His sister's face begins to crumple, but he has to stand firm. Valuable seconds are ticking away. Noah doesn't look at his watch—he promised Juliet he wouldn't.

"I'm sorry Mads, I told you. And besides..."

"What?"

"Well Juliet *says* she can drive, but I'm not so sure. I don't want to put you in danger." He touches her arm, but Maddie's too upset to notice.

"Mom won't expect you back immediately, so take your time," he tells her. "And then, when you get back to her, just say I had to go to the toilet."

"Sure." Maddie lunges forward and hugs him. "I love you, Noah."

"Love you too, Mads. See you when it's over. Now go." He watches her run off, then he turns and walks to the car park. Juliet's there, leaning against the car.

"Ready?" she says.

Ready? *Of course you're not ready. Turn around right now.*

Noah doesn't have time to listen; there's no time for anything except sticking to their plan.

He hands her the keys. "Are you sure you know how to drive?"

Juliet grins. "Sure as I'll ever be. C'mon, Noah, let's do this."

A single bleep of the remote and they're in and on their way.

Broekie lace and a deep stoep, a door painted red with a gleaming brass knocker. Cheerful flowers in a deep planter.

Gabriel lifts the knocker and lets it fall.

He hears footsteps approaching. The door opens. Gabriel finds himself staring into eyes the same color as his—a deep, deep green. This woman's hair is blonde though, and she's far shorter than he was expecting.

May I help you? she says, and Gabriel's stammering. He's rehearsed this often, in front of the mirror, putting out his hand and saying, Hello, Harriet. My name is Gabriel Felix.

Those are the words that finally come out. Then Gabriel remembers his hand. He puts it out and it stays there, awkward, waiting for the woman standing in the doorway to shake it and say—

Excuse me?

Gabriel hasn't rehearsed this part, what does he do when she doesn't shake his hand or recognize his name? And why should she? She lost hold of the name Felix a long time ago.

I'm sorry, he says, and his hand falls to his side, I shouldn't have bothered you.

This is a terrible, terrible mistake. Months of searching, of paying Sebastian Crown to move from province to province, and putting him on a healthy retainer...only for it to end on the doorstep of a woman who is looking at him with suspicion.

Walking down the passage towards her is a pleasant-faced man.

Harriet, who's this?

She didn't lose her birthname, or ever feel the need to change it. She's still Harriet, even if this man doesn't call her Harry, like Mum and he used to when she was a baby and Gabe would feed her and change her and make her laugh, because he was Mum's Little Man, and he was in charge of making sure his sister was happy. He did the best he could, but he wasn't able to hold his family together.

The woman who is definitely Gabriel's sister is saying, Gavin, this is...

She looks at Gabriel enquiringly but his tongue is in a knot.

Can we help you? asks Gavin. He looks from Harriet to Gabriel, frowning.

I...Yes. Yes, please. You see, the thing is...I'm Gabriel Felix. Your brother.

Gabriel looks directly at Harriet. He wants to smile, but instead his eyes fill with tears. I'm your brother, he says again.

Harriet steps back and her husband puts his arms around her, holds her safe from the stranger making this ridiculous claim. But then Gavin looks at him carefully. Yes, Gabriel hears him saying. Yes.

I can see that you might be.

Gabriel's legs are struggling to hold him up. He'd like to sink to the ground, let the tension of months of looking and hoping drain away, down into the small patch of grass in front of the house.

You'd better come inside, says Harry.

14:49

Noah opens the passenger door. He should be sitting in the back, behind his mother, like he always does, but this is a day of sudden and unexpected changes. Like asking Maddie to come with him to his room, for math. "Stroke of genius, Noah," Juliet says when he tells her about it. "Now keep quiet for a while, I need to reverse this baby without hitting anything."

He looks back nervously and she laughs. "Relax. I won't damage your mom's car." She swings the wheel deftly and maneuvers the car out of the parking space. "Like I said, I've been doing this since I was twelve. Good thing you hooked up with a delinquent, Noah. We're a regular Bonnie and Clyde."

Her voice is reckless, excited and Noah wants to tell her to calm down. He knows who Bonnie and Clyde were. Juliet and he are hardly on their way to a heist. No shotguns in the trunk, no small-time grocers to rob, just an old lady in a retirement village to spring a surprise on—a happy one.

He sits next to her, his shoulders stiff. Soon Maddie will be finished in his room, on her way over to...

But no, clearly not. There's his little sister, stepping out into the driveway, standing in front of the car, hands on her hips.

"I'm coming," she says loudly. "And if you don't let me in, I'm going to scream. Really loudly, Noah. So you better—"

Juliet laughs and turns off the central locking. "Come along then, Mads."

Maddie grabs the handle and bounces onto the back seat before he can say a word.

"I told him," Juliet says. "I said it wasn't fair to leave you behind, not when you're the reason we've even got this far, but he was adamant."

Looks like little Maddie's putting a spoke in the works. Why you even thought this would work—

"Quiet!" Noah's voice is loud, almost a shout and the Dark's squawking turns into silence.

Juliet shoots a sideways glance at him. "Nobody's talking, Noah."

"I know," he mutters.

"Are you okay?"

"I'm *fine*. It's just..." His fingers start their nervous rattle "We can't waste any more time."

"Don't worry, Noah. We're still on schedule."

He clamps his jaw shut. Soon the man on duty at the gate will be back at his post. Soon someone will see them and it will all be over before it's even started. His fingers reach for his pebbles.

Juliet said be quiet and that's what he'll do, give her peace and quiet while she drives the car to the boom. He stares straight ahead. The driveway out of Greenhills is long and straight and visible from the lawn. Soon his mother will look up and see her car vanishing.

They're at the guardhouse. "Quick as a flash, Noah," Juliet reminds him and he jerks the car door open. Quick as a flash to the boom, to push down on the heavy end, hold it while Juliet drives through to the magic spot marked X that will make the gates swing open.

There's the guard, walking up the drive...and now he's lumbering, and shouting, but Noah can't hear his words. He's back at the passenger door.

The man is closer now. "Hey! Hey, you! Hey!"

"Go," Noah pants, flinging himself into his seat. "Go!"

"High five, Noe," says Maddie from the back seat and a triumphant grin spreads across his face.

"Good work, dude," Juliet says, and then she's pulling away and the gates are opening. They've got less than a minute, 30 seconds if that, before the man gets to the guardhouse, comes up with a feasible excuse for letting 2 of Greenhills' residents escape, lifts the phone and raises the alarm. But they might have a little more time, while the staff figure out who's gone (unless Noah's mother realizes it's her car that is missing). A little more time before everyone realizes that Noah Groome's done the impossible: deliberately smashed every single one of his rules. He looks over his shoulder. No one there. He glances at Juliet and she grins.

"Ready?" she asks.

Noah pushes back the urge that says Stop and Check. Stop and Plan and Stop and Time Each Part. STOP. He feels for his notebook, and there it is, tucked into his top pocket. Later, he'll find time to break down the events of today into hours, minutes and seconds...He allows himself a wry smile. He doesn't have a clue where to start, how he'll possibly be able to make sense of it all, let alone impose any sort of order onto a day like this.

Right now, though, he has other things to focus on. Juliet has the indicator on and they're waiting at the intersection. There's a gap and she turns left and joins the steady stream of traffic.

Kate sits on the green bench, the slats hard against her back, looking up at the leathery green leaves of the oak tree. Her gaze is caught by a bank of solar panels on the red brick tiles of the roof.

"Greenhills is going green, I see," she says to Mr. Bill, breaking the easy silence between them.

Kate doesn't normally feel comfortable with silence. It's her duty, her need, to fill the gaps. Just like she fills the gaps in her day with busy work. But with Mr. Bill beside her she can let her mind rest; while Noah is under his wing, she can relax.

She glances over to the car park. She and Maddie need to go soon.

Only they won't be able to. Because her car isn't there.

Gabriel's inside Gavin and Harriet Davenport's house now and she's asking him, But how? and he tells her of all the time and money he has spent tracking her down.

I've been looking for you for nearly two years. I tried through the adoption agency, but they told me you didn't want any contact with your family.

They didn't tell me I had a brother, or that you were looking, Harriet says. They said family member and I just assumed they meant—

Mum? asks Gabriel.

Yes. I didn't want to have anything to do with her. And then there's *my* mom, the one who's loved me since I was a baby. I didn't want to hurt her. If I'd known it was you. If I'd known I had a brother...I'm sorry, Gabriel.

I found her, Gabriel says. I found Mum. She's not well, Harry. Harriet.

Harriet's face hardens and Gabriel wonders how he's going to explain it all to her. How he found their mother, how she tried to find them but wasn't allowed to have any contact with them, how he discovered what had happened to their father.

Harriet's face is white and Gavin's massaging her hands, as if that will bring some color back into her cheeks.

I'm sorry, Gabriel says. It's a lot to take in. I should have phoned, but I didn't want to take the chance...

That I wouldn't want to see you? But I do, Harriet says. I do. It's a shock, that's all.

Maybe if you come back another time, Gavin says. Gabriel likes the way he holds his wife, the love in his eyes when he looks at her. He's glad she has a good man, that she's living in a comfortable house, sitting on a comfortable couch with bright cushions behind her and a warm carpet under her feet.

The fireplace is bricked up, a huge vase of daffodils filling the alcove. There are a number of framed photographs on the mantelpiece. Harriet and Gavin on their wedding day, pictures of babies and those same babies growing up. All safe, all smiling into the camera. Harriet has a family. Two children. A boy, he's the older one in the pictures, and a younger sister. Not such a big gap between them though. Not like nine-year-old Gabe looking after his little sister.

Gabriel looks around, spots a tell-tale plug. You have an electric heater? he asks.

Harriet looks at him curiously. Yes. I hate real fires. They scare me. I don't know why.

Me too, Gabriel says.

She still looks puzzled.

It might be a good place to start, Gabriel says, when you're ready to listen to my story.

"My car," Kate says stupidly. "My car. It's gone."

But it hasn't quite gone, not yet. There it is, her zippy little Polo, almost at the end of the long driveway. It all seems to happen in slow motion: the gates slowly opening, the guard puffing up the drive, his hands waving. She can't hear what he's saying, but she knows he's in trouble. He left his post, he wasn't at the checkpoint with his clipboard. And on top of that, someone has just stolen her car and driven away. But who?

Kate slips her hand into her bag. Her keys are there. Then she realizes how this has happened. She strains for a last glimpse of the car. Of course. It has to be. Maddie looking back, Juliet in the driver's seat and Noah next to her. The three of them have just driven out of Greenhills and there's no way to find out where they're going.

But there is. Of course there is.

Kate thanks God for Dominic, for his absolute insistence on security at every level, the house with electric fencing, its alarm systems, the cars, each armed with a tracker. Ever since the home invasion, safety has been an imperative for him. For all of them, really. There must be a way to log in to that tracker, work out where Noah and Maddie are going, and catch up with them. Moments later she's on the phone, gabbling to her husband, telling him what's happened and asking him to find their children.

When Gabriel phones Harriet to set up another meeting, her voice is polite but edgy. Yes, she says, she would like to see him again and Gavin would like to be there too. Would that be in order and what time and date would suit Gabriel.

Gabriel puts down the phone. Relieved, glad of the chance of seeing his sister, but worried. He hadn't expected her to sound so formal. Maybe it's because it's all so new and Harriet isn't quite ready to start a relationship with her long-lost, newly found brother.

He's back at their home the next Saturday afternoon, only this time Gavin answers the door and says he wants to speak to Gabriel on his own. He leads Gabriel through to the sitting room.

He's done some digging, Gavin says, and the thing is, Gabriel, I'm not so sure...

Gabriel's stomach tightens then drops.

Some digging? he says slowly.

Yes. It wasn't difficult. Your surname, you see. Your name. Gabriel. Harriet's. Your mother's.

Martha.

Yes, says Gavin. Martha Felix.

And the fire, says Gabriel.

Yes. Gavin's face is sympathetic. Look, Gabriel. The thing is, in the papers it says that the fire was set, but it never says by whom. Well, of course, they would say that. The records would have been sealed. You were only nine at the time, right?

Gabriel thinks of the frail care unit where they are taking such good care of his mother. He imagines guiding Harriet into her room and saying, Look, Mum, here's Harry come to see you, and maybe, in a flash of lucidity, his mother will recognize her and say her name.

Yes, he answers. I was only nine at the time.

Kids, hey? says Gavin and Gabriel manages a smile.

The only thing though, says Gavin, is the aftershock. You know. When they discovered—

Yes, says Gabriel. The old man.

Edward Felix, says Gavin. Dead before anyone could get to him. That's a bit much to cope with, Gabriel.

It is. Gabriel feels like his mouth has been stuffed with cotton wool, blurring his words.

And then, there's your mother.

Our mother, says Gabriel. Harriet's and mine.

Yes, well. From what you've said, and from what I've learned, it sounds like she's pretty unstable.

Gabriel nods. His mother is unstable. No getting away from that.

And your father.

I know. Gabriel nods. A small-time cardsharp, got into debt, over his head.

Large debt, from what I can gather, Gavin says. Look, I'm not trying...He spreads his hands. But, you know...

It's all stacked up against him. Gabriel gets to his feet.

Thank you, Gavin. I'm still glad I had the chance to meet Harriet.

You understand where I'm coming from, don't you, Gabriel?

Yes, yes of course. You want to protect your family. I completely understand.

But what if I don't want protection? Harriet's standing in the doorway and her eyes are pools of green fire.

Harriet. Darling, we spoke about this.

You spoke, Harriet says. You spoke and I listened.

I thought we'd agreed.

Gabriel sees the worry on Gavin's face. All this man wants, and he's a good man, is to keep his family safe.

Really, says Gabriel, it's fine.

Really, says Harriet, it's not. She turns to her husband. Don't you see, Gavin? He's my brother. The only one I've got.

There's also Mum, Gabriel says quietly. He's not going to give up that fight easily.

Harriet frowns. That's true, she says. There's her, too. You'll have to give me some time on that one, Gabriel.

She'll come around, he hopes, once she's heard the full story, but now it's time to reveal the next part of his life. Get it out in the open before it all becomes more complicated.

Actually, he says, I'm not called Gabriel, not any more. I changed my name years ago. I decided to use my old one in case you recognized it. I'm Dominic now, Dominic Groome.

Gavin's mouth falls open. Dominic Groome? You wouldn't by any

chance be—

Probably, Dominic says. That's if you're talking about Goodson, Stander & Groome. That's me.

14:54

Juliet turns on the radio and Bon Jovi rocks through the car. Noah winces, leans forward and switches it off.

"No noise," he says. They have to listen to Mrs. G. That's what Dad calls her, the bossy lady who tells you when to turn and how far to drive down certain streets. Who says "recalculate" every time you make a mistake, who pings if you turn into the wrong road. He's keyed in the address for Silver Oaks, and now it's up to Mrs. Garmin to do the work.

When Dad first got the GPS, Noah was fascinated. Mrs. Garmin knew so much about where to go and how to get there. Nothing made her excited, nothing upset her. Once, when they passed a 4-car pile-up on the freeway, he was sure she would react, but no. Mrs. G simply said, "Ping-ping-ping' as his father changed lanes and took the next off-ramp. Ping-ping-ping, and suddenly there they were again, their purple car beetling along the blue roads that appeared in front of it. "We'll have to head back a bit," his father said, but Mrs. Garmin was way ahead of him. She knew how to get them to their destination safe and sound and in the shortest time possible. That's what Noah wants now, a safe and sound arrival in the shortest time possible.

"Remember, they can track this car," he says. "Mom will alert the security company and tell them her car's missing."

"She'll tell them we're missing, too," Maddie says, "but don't worry Noah, I'll say I wanted to come, that wild horses couldn't stop me."

They're on the freeway now and Juliet's shifting gears, moving carefully between lanes. Noah glances at the speedometer: "100 km an hour here." Mrs. G agrees with his caution and chimes sympathetically. As he speaks, a raindrop lands on the windscreen and then another. Noah opens his window and the air rushes in. He leans back against the headrest. The air's fresh, cooling his face and he can feel his pulse steadying. He calls on his senses to feel the rain, smell it, taste it. Soon it will bucket down and he'll hear it and see it. He'll drink it in, with all 5 of his senses.

Gabriel walks up the shallow flight of steps and into the offices of Home Affairs. He joins the queue at the information counter and when it is his turn, he asks the woman sitting there, bored and bloated in a shapeless yellow dress, what he has to do to change his name. He thinks it will be easy, but he soon learns that it is not. He cannot take on a completely new name, she tells him. The best she can do for him is give him the forms that allow him to change his forename, and the ones that allow him to take his mother's surname.

Gabriel stands there and thinks. That will have to do. He has all the necessary papers. They gave them to him when he left the home, the registry details of his birth, his parents' marriage certificate. You may not want them now, his caseworker said, pressing the envelope into Gabriel's hands. But don't be rash. You might need them down the line. She was right. He doesn't have a single detail about Harry, though. All he has of her is a small black and white photograph of a little boy and a pretty woman holding a bundle in her arms. Mum and Harry and Gabriel, before. Before.

Gabriel opens the envelope and hands the lady his birth certificate. She shows him what to fill in, and where, doesn't notice Gabriel adding an e to the end of his mother's maiden name. She simply tells him how long it will take, and when he can come back to collect his new papers.

Nine weeks later, Dominic Groome walks down the steps of the Home Affairs offices, leaving the boy who was once Gabriel Felix in a folder in a metal filing cabinet.

14:59

There are six cars ahead of them, all slowing because the rain is falling faster now, but Juliet still hasn't turned on the windscreen wipers. Maybe she should. Noah doesn't want to tell her to, because for all her nonchalance in the driveway, she's gripping the steering wheel really tight and he doesn't know what will happen if she lets go—with one hand (5 digits) and only has one hand left (the other 5 digits) to control the car.

His mother likes her new(-ish) car. It's not fancy, nothing like her Audi, but it's nippy, not like his father's 4x4, which she says is a monster to drive. But right now, even her small car feels really, really lethal.

What was Dominic hiding from? Ancient history covered layers deep in lies, that's what. The lies that have made him into who he is now. Looking back to the boy he was then is like falling down the rabbit hole, into a place where nothing is familiar.

Once he breathed, slept and ate in a different life, he followed different rules, he answered to different masters.

When he looks in the mirror now, he can't see any trace of the person he was then. That boy has been dead for years and Dominic's finding it difficult to resurrect him. Gabriel Felix, spliced from his old roots, transplanted, watered, allowed to grow and to build a new history.

That's what he tells Harriet and Gavin: the story of his life after they were separated that night. A muscle works in his jaw. This is who he has been for so many years, he says to Harriet. Dominic Groome. Father deceased and, until recently, no mother, no siblings. Just him, making his way through the world, holding in his secrets, holding back the truth.

Harriet is so angry, she can barely speak. How could she do that to you? she wants to know. Why didn't she come for you? I mean, I know, or at least I can understand, why she might have decided not to look for me. I was adopted. I landed luckily and happily, they found me a good family. But you? All those years in that place?

I couldn't understand that either, Dominic (who is Gabriel when he talks to his sister) says. I was angry with her too, for a long time. And then, Harry, I found her. Or Sebastian Crown did. A tall, skinny lady in a bed in a state psychiatric hospital.

They were kind to her, in their fashion, Dominic tells her. They called her "The Great Escaper' in her early days there. Each time she tried to get away, it was because she was looking for her son and daughter. They'd find her on the streets, talking to strangers.

Do you know my son, she'd be asking. Have you seen my daughter? I'm looking for Gabriel. He's got Harry. He's looking after Harry. He's my Little Man.

The nurses would approach her quietly, but she'd always spot them and start running, her long legs pumping in baggy tracksuit pants, bare feet hitting city pavements.

She never got away though, Dominic tells Harry.

As she grew older, she gave up trying. Instead, each time a new patient was admitted she'd make a beeline for them. Have you seen my son? Do you know my daughter?

Harry's crying now. Gabriel puts his arm around her shoulder and hugs her tightly.

She did care about us, Harry.

When he got to her, he continues, she had a small box under her bed, filled with her precious bits. A photograph, similar to the one Gabriel had found in his envelope, the edge of a baby's blanket, and letters. So many letters, scrawled on scraps of paper. Their contents were heartbreaking: *My darlings, Mum's coming. Dearest Gaby-Baby, Where are you, my little man? Look after Harriet for Mummy and Daddy.*

They kept her quite heavily medicated, Gabriel tells Harriet, and most of the time she was placid enough. You don't remember her, Harry, but our mum was gentle. And kind. When I spoke to the doctors and the ward staff, they said the only times she became agitated, aggressive even, were when someone tried to take her box away. She took to carrying it around with her. She'd show the other patients the photo of three of us, but I was so little and you, Harry, well, you were just a baby wrapped in a blanket. Nobody would have recognized us, but she never stopped trying.

One of the nurses, Nurse Daniels, did her best to help. She had retired by the time I found Mum, but the hospital gave me her address.

She was living in a place called Silver Oaks and she was delighted to meet me. She remembered Mum so fondly, Harry. She found out what had happened to me, went to the children's home, asked to see me, to tell me that Mum was trying her best to get me back. She wanted to let me know that Mum cared, that she hadn't given up on us. They never let her see me, though. She wasn't a family member, they said. Mum wasn't of sound mind, she'd never be well enough to look after me. Why make things worse than they were? They had to be cruel to be kind, that's what they told her. Nurse Daniels gave in; she never told Mum that she'd tracked me down. Instead, the day after she found me, she picked her a small posy. Lavender and rosemary and some bright red poppies. Oh, she gave me the sweetest smile, Nurse Daniels said, and as she spoke, I remembered Mum smiling, laughing even. I wish you'd known her, Harry. Before.

Gabriel's holding Harry's hand now, pressing it gently.

Most days she knows who I am, Harry. She gets tired and confused, can't hang on to what happened a few hours ago very well, but she knows me. And if you come with me, and they tell her who you are...It's not too late. I've been visiting her every Sunday for the last few months, and I go to see Nurse Daniels, too. She's convinced it would do Mum the world of good to see you. And it might be good for you, too.

15:10

"Oh...My...God...this place."

They're at Silver Oaks and Juliet's looking at row after row of houses as they approach. Small, neat blocks of pale pink trimmed in white, like God's been playing with a little girl's Lego. All exactly the same size, all with exactly the same path, leading to identical doors.

Noah likes it. He likes the way the houses are joined by a common wall, 2 + 2 + 2 = 6, and then a break, and then 2 + 2 + 2 = 6. Further along, the houses become bigger, 2 + 2 = 4, and then a break, and 2 + 2 = 4.

They come to a long, low building. It's the same color as all the houses and faces a large parking lot. "This must be it," says Juliet. "This is where the guy at the gate said to go." She looks at the dashboard. "It's three twenty," she says. "We made really good time."

She gets out of the car, stretches and looks around, but quickly, because the rain's coming down hard and they're getting wet.

Juliet looks at Noah: "Okay?"

He nods. He's okay to be here, doing what has to be done, 1 000 000 miles outside his comfort zone.

It'll take even more than that to get back there.

It's the first time Noah's heard anything since he shouted at it in the car, and it sounds peeved.

It's going to take some serious work for you and your 5s.

"Cozy...Very cozy." Juliet interrupts the whinging and the Dark draws back, huddles petulantly out of sight.

Maddie's run ahead and is talking to the lady at reception. Skinny, with a long narrow face, she looks like she'd welcome a lump of sugar or a carrot offered in an open palm. She smiles as Maddie says, "My name's Maddie Groome. This is my brother Noah and our friend, Juliet. We're here to see Mrs. Felix but we can't remember which room she's in."

"Lovely, my dear, lovely. She's in Room 24, down that corridor and to your right."

The carpet under their feet is thick and soft. All along the corridor are framed prints, fields and cows, and more fields and more cows. And barns, all in gentle colors. Nothing to leap out and demand your attention.

"Why don't they just call this place Happy Pastures," says Juliet and Maddie giggles.

5 paintings on one wall, and 5 on the other, so that's good. Noah runs his left hand along the wall, no corners to stop at, but he can count each step he takes. In the right-hand pocket of his jeans are his pebbles, 1 2 3 4 5 of them, there to keep him calm.

Room after room, the doors open onto neatly made beds, little rectangular containers holding little old people, all clean and ready for visitors.

"Okay, Noah?" Juliet knows to check. Maddie looks back at him and smiles encouragingly. The door of Room 24 is open and Maddie steps back to let him in first.

The soft carpet gives way to tiles, shining under a long fluorescent light. The curtains are blue, so are the cushions on the chair in the corner, and the blanket folded at the foot of the bed, all the colors melting into the pale blue walls and the misty gray-blue of the sky outside the window.

There's a body in the bed.

1. Long, thin limbs.
2. A small head, thin wisps of hair.
3. Skin tight over nose and cheeks.
4. A sunken mouth.
5. Eyes hiding in a bag of wrinkles.

Noah steps closer. The body doesn't move.

All this way. And for what?

Juliet moves in behind him. "Shit," she says. Her voice blocks out the Dark's shrill glee. "Is she alive, Noah?"

They're next to the bed now, and still the body hasn't moved. The arms are outside the blankets, the hands folded together.

There's no smell in the room. Nothing to say there's an old body in here and it's not moving.

On the bedside table there's a battered cardboard box, held together with with parcel tape. Close to that a jug and 2 glasses, 1 with teeth grinning inside. That's probably why the mouth has collapsed, no lips showing, just a folded-in hole.

Maddie notices them too. "She must be alive," she says in a whisper. "Her teeth. And look here."

Under the bed, is a pair of slippers, and hanging on the back of the door, a blue dressing gown.

Noah doesn't know what to do next. Should he lean closer and try to hear breathing? Should he touch 1 of those hands? If he does, will the skin move under his fingers? Will a skinny claw grab his wrist and never let him go?

On top of all this, there's the gloating.

Oh, my, my, what have we here? What big ears she has...

And she does. Her ears are large flaps, scarcely covered by curly wisps of silver hair.

All the better to hear you with...

The Dark is a cartoon wolf peering up at him from under a lacy cap, a slurping red tongue in its wide-open mouth.

Maddie leans forward, listening. "She's breathing," she says, and strokes a thin shoulder under the nightgown. Then she gently strokes it again.

The old woman's eyes snap open.

Dominic settles into a wicker chair in the small café in Silver Oaks. The rain is sheeting down and the tarmac is steaming. He remembers the rain of his childhood, falling on a tin roof, spattering a dirty window pane, creating rivulets in the dust, making the soil heavy and dark. The sky, gray in the morning, gray at bedtime. The sun struggling through the clouds, like a headlamp in the fog. Day after day of winter rain, everything cold, his trousers permanently damp from the knees down.

Dominic's waiting for Harry. The café has become their regular meeting place since he first took her to meet their mother a few months ago. A cup of coffee, and then they'll make their way to her room, spend some time with her before Dominic gets back in his car, hits the paths he likes to run and then heads back home and into the shower before Kate and Maddie get back from Greenhills.

The doctors don't advise spending too long with Martha. It's good for her to see them, they say, and now she knows who they are, their visits brighten her week. But she's frail, easily tired and twenty minutes—fifteen even—is as much as she can cope with. Dominic and Harriet spend half an hour or so chatting. Catching up on the week that has passed, catching up on the years they were separated. Harriet wishes the two families could meet—let in-laws, nephews and nieces, cousins, get to know each other. Dominic has promised this will happen. Soon, he tells her. "I just need a little more time, Harry.

Especially now, with Noah..."

Harry understands, of course she does. *I'm holding you to that promise, Gabe.* He's Gabe to her, and she's Harry to him, and every Sunday afternoon, their Mum is just a few meters away.

But today, as he waits for Harriet to arrive, his phone rings. Kate's on the other side, frantic, and Gabe becomes Dominic. "Oh, Dom, I thought you'd be running, thank God you took your phone with you. Dom, you have to phone the tracking company, you know the one, for the car—"

"Kate," he cuts across her. "Kate, what is it?"

"The children, Dom. Noah and Maddie, they've gone."

"They've *what*? How?"

Harriet's walking in now, sees her brother and waves. Dominic holds up a hand, mouths a "Sorry" at her as he listens to Kate and tries to make sense out of her panic.

"They were here, with me at Greenhills and then Maddie—well never mind about that—the thing is, they were here, Noah and Maddie, and then they were leaving."

"And you couldn't just go after them? Pick them up?"

"No, no, Dom. I couldn't. The thing is, they were in my car."

"What? Noah was driving? Kate, that's impossible, he doesn't know—"

"No, not, Noah. Juliet—Bart Ryan's daughter. She was driving and—"

"The Ryan girl? Driving our children? Why—"

"I don't *know*, Dom! If I knew..." Kate's voice is breaking. "It's not important for now. What I need you to do right now is get on to the tracking company and tell them I need to know where they're going. Where they've gone. Mr. Bill will take me to them."

"I still don't understand—"

"It doesn't matter, Dominic! Can you just do that and we can sort everything out later? I'm so worried. What if Juliet has an accident? She's got *our children* with her."

"Yes, yes, of course." Kate's words are making sense now, her panic and fear spreading to him. "I'll do it now."

Dominic cuts the connection and scrolls through the names in his phone, searching for the number of the security company.

"What's the matter, Gabriel?" Harry can see just how worried her brother is.

"It's Noah and Maddie. They've taken Kate's car and we've no idea where they've gone."

15:22

The mouth mumbles and Maddie leans closer.

Hands spasm on the white sheet.

"Mmmmuh. Mmmmuh tuhhh." Her head turns and looks at the bedside table.

"Tuhhh."

A hand waves at the glass.

"Her teeth," Juliet whispers. "She wants her teeth."

Careful now. All the better to eat you with.

Maddie picks up the glass, takes it to the sink in the corner of the room and pours out the water.

As she does this, a pair of green eyes fix themselves on Noah. He tries to look away, but a hand reaches out and plucks at his arm.

"Gahh," the mouth says. "Gahhh bahhh."

"Don't worry," Maddie's voice croons, "don't worry. We'll have you sorted out in no time." She comes back to the bed and holds out the lower plate. The mouth opens and gulps it in. Then Maddie does the same with the upper plate and it's sucked in too. The teeth close with a click and a soft voice wavers into the room.

"Gabriel?" She's staring at Noah. "Gabriel, Sunday? Sunday after-noon?"

Noah doesn't know what to do. He nods and she smiles. "Gabriel." The plucking stops and her hand lies quiet.

Kate sits in a car next to Mr. Bill, driving along slick, shiny roads, on her way to find her son and daughter. The security company is feeding her directions over the phone.

Rain is falling, sluicing away the heat, sending it swirling down gutters. Thunder claps its mighty hands and lightning jags through the sky. The road is barely visible and the windscreen wipers are squealing, struggling to do their job.

Mr. Bill's hands are steady on the wheel. "Don't worry, Mrs. Groome," he's saying. "We'll find them."

Kate tries to smile, to say thank you to this kind man. She remembers (as if it happened in a long-ago dream, and not just this afternoon) how she thought she'd ignite if he so much as touched her, recalls the warmth that had risen in her every time she thought of seeing him walk across the lawns at Greenhills to greet her. Now her mind feels washed clear; the only thoughts in her head are of Noah and Maddie.

Where on earth could her children be going? Is this just a joyride, a way of thumbing their noses at all of the rules and regulations of Greenhills? Surely not an idea Noah is even remotely capable of entertaining, never mind executing.

The security company breaks into her thoughts, telling her to turn left into Maple, keep on for 500 meters and then first right in Elm and second left into Oak. "That's where your car has stopped, Mrs. Groome. It's in the parking lot of a retirement complex. One of our vehicles will meet you there and make sure everything is in order."

"Thank you." Kate gives the directions to Mr. Bill. "I must call my husband," she tells him.

Dominic answers on the first ring. "Kate?"

"It's all good, Dom. They've found the car, we're just arriving there now. It's a place on Oak Street."

"Oak?"

He stops abruptly and Kate says, "Don't worry, I can see it. I can see my car. But...this is really bizarre, Dom. What in God's name are the children doing *here*? It's a place called Silver Oaks.

"Kate—" Dominic pauses, and then Kate sees a familiar maroon 4x4 parked under the trees. *Dominic's* car? In the same car park?

"Kate? Kate!" Dominic's voice, tinny and frantic.

Are Noah and Maddie really here? And Juliet?

Kate needs answers. She cuts Dominic off and turns to Mr. Bill. "I'm sorry. I have to..." She's fumbling with the seatbelt and he leans over her and unsnaps it. "I don't know what's going on," Kate babbles. His hand covers hers, warm and comforting, and Kate feels stupid, so stupid to ever have thought—but there's no time for that now, no time to think about anything except getting out of the car.

She's standing in the parking lot, hardly feeling the rain, staring at her husband's car.

"Are you sure you're all right, Mrs. Groome?"

"I'm fine," Kate says. "Fine. Thank you, Mr. Bill. You've been so kind."

"I'll come with you. Check up on Noah and Juliet."

Together they hurry into the building and up to the front desk to ask for help.

15:29

The old face lights up as she looks over Noah's shoulder.

"Gabriel," she says again. "Gabriel, you're here." This time it's not Noah she's looking at.

His father's in the doorway, out of breath, blinking.

"Hi, Dad," says Maddie, as if she's been a visitor in this room every day of her life.

"Maddie, Noah..."

Juliet steps forward. ("Into the breach," she says to Noah, later. "I hope you appreciated my heroism, dude.") "Hello, Mr. Groome. We haven't met. I'm Juliet, Noah's friend."

Dominic shakes her hand, but doesn't say a word.

"Gabriel. Gabriel, who are these people?" The old woman's eyes flicker and her voice rises on the question. "Where's Harry? Is Harry here?" She's lifting herself off the pillows, pushing back the blanket, her thin legs reaching for the floor.

Noah's father is next to her in seconds. He's holding her down, firmly, gently.

"Harry's coming, Mum. She'll be here soon."

But she isn't listening. Her eyes are back on Noah. "Is everything all right, Gaby-Baby? My Little Man?"

Puzzled, Noah looks at his father. He's sitting on the edge of the bed and the shape of his body has changed. Before, it was all squares and rectangles. High squared shoulders, tight rectangular jaw. Now, he has no edges. His shoulders have relaxed and his face is softer.

"Dad?"

"Noah." Dominic stands up and walks towards his son. For the first time in ages, they are so close they are almost touching.

"Felix?" Noah says, "Gabriel?"

That's right. You ask him. Ask Dominic-Gabriel-Dad. Looks like he's got some explaining to do.

"Yes," his father replies without hesitating. "Gabriel Felix. Father, Joseph Felix. Mother, Martha. Martha Felix, née Groom, aged 82."

It all happened when Dominic was so young. When Dominic was Gabriel.

"Just a boy," they said, "and who could blame him?" That was the official line. But blame him they did, of course they did. He saw it in their eyes as they watched him coming down the corridor. The corridor, with door after door leading into room after room, lined with metal framed beds, each with someone like Gabriel, like Dominic, sleeping in it.

That was when he hadn't been separated from the other boys. For yelling too loudly, screaming that it wasn't him, it wasn't him, it wasn't him.

It was all terrible. Terrible, terrible, terrible.

15:37

Noah looks out at the rain. It's hard, steady. The lightning has ended and the thunder has gone. It's still windy, though. There's still an edge to the air.

It's raining, it's pouring, the old man is snoring. Only, there's no old man here. Just an old lady, looking mighty confused.

Noah's fingers tap on the windowsill. They tap, tap, tap-tap-tap, keeping him company. The rain beats down and the wind swirls through the trees and his fingers tap tap, tap-tap-tap, left hand. Tap tap, tap-tap-tap, right hand.

If he angles his hand slightly his nails catch and click on the wooden windowsill and the sound becomes more of a tip-tip-tap. More click than clack. Tapping, tipping, clicking.

An old man shuffles past the open door, nodding as he goes. "Good afternoon, Mrs. Felix. I'm afraid rain has stopped play. Indefinitely."

There's the slow whine of the wheels of a tea trolley.

The wheels on the bus go round and round. And round and around and around.

Noah's thoughts circle, his eyes flick around the room. From his father to his sister, to Juliet. She smiles at him and mouths a word. He can't figure out what she's saying and then he sees her breathing in deeply. And out. And in and out. He does the same. There's so much to take in, so much to work out.

He breathes in and out. His thoughts slow and he's able to look around the room. Now there's a woman in the doorway. She looks almost as nervous as he feels.

"Harry?" the old woman squeals in excitement. "Harry, you came!"

"Yes, Mum," the woman with green eyes says gently. "I always do."

She's going to take up a whole page in Noah's notebook, maybe even more. And then she's going to find her place on his family tree, just below her mother. Mrs. Martha Felix née Groom; Mrs. Harriet Davenport.

"Name?" asks the woman briskly.

Kate says, "Groome, but I don't know—"

Before she can finish, the lady is beaming and saying, "My word, more visitors for Mrs. Felix. Is it a special day, dear? Normally it's just her son, and her daughter."

Kate looks at her, wide-eyed, but the lady is too busy telling them where to go to notice. "Down to the end of the corridor, and turn left—that will take you down to frail care. She's in Room 24."

15:41

More voices outside, except this time they are far from calm. "This is it. Room 24." Noah's mother appears, with Mr. Bill just behind her.

"Noah!" She sees him first. "Maddie! Juliet..." Her breath comes out in a rush. "Thank God. Oh, thank God."

Only then does she take in the other people in the room: his father, Harriet Davenport, Martha Felix tucked into bed.

"Dominic?" she asks. "What on earth is going on? Why are you all here?"

"Kate, I can explain." He reaches out to take her hand but she steps back.

"Explain? Explain what, exactly?"

He waves an arm, taking in the whole room. "This," he says. "All of this."

His father's sister—Noah's new aunt—manages a smile. "Hello," she says. "My name's Harriet Davenport. And this is my mother, Martha Felix. I'm...We're..."

Mr. Bill breaks the awkward silence. "Come along, Noah," he says. "We'd better get you back. And you too, Juliet. It's getting late."

Juliet's face is tight. "I suppose we can say goodbye to all our privileges. No phone time, TV, Internet? Not to mention how my father's going to take this one."

"Oh, I don't know about that," says Mr. Bill. "There are bound to be consequences, but I'll put in a good word for you. About how you were trying to help a friend. Ms. Turner will be pleased to hear that."

He turns to Noah's mother. "Will you be all right getting home, Mrs. Groome?"

"Me?" She looks at him blankly and then the question registers. "I'll be fine," she says. "Thank you. But before these two go back to Greenhills, before *anyone* goes anywhere...I want Dominic to tell us why he is here."

"Dominic?" Noah's grandmother turns her head from side to side. "Who is Dominic?" Her voice is low and whispery.

Noah's father's face is etched with sadness. "I'm so sorry, Kate. I've wanted to tell you, I can't tell you how many times I wanted to let you know."

"Gabriel? Gabriel?" The old woman plucks at her blanket."Is that you, My Little Man?"

Noah's father bends down and kisses her cheek. "It's me, Mum," he says. "It's Sunday afternoon and I'm here to see you."

She smiles up at him, and Noah wonders if there are dimples hiding in her lined cheeks.

Mum?

Her husband—the man who has called himself an orphan these many, many years—has a mother who is very much alive?

Kate studies the woman in the bed. Green eyes. The legs under the covers are long, the sleeves of her nightgown too short for her arms.

"Who *is* she, Gabriel?"

Who are you? is what Kate wants to ask, but she stops herself when she sees how agitated the old woman is becoming. "Before we go *any*where, Dominic," she says again.

"Of course," her husband says. "There's a little coffee shop near the entrance. Why don't we all go and sit there for a while." He looks over to the woman who called herself Harriet Davenport. "Harry? Would you mind staying down here with Mum, until..."

"Of course I will," Harriet says quickly, her voice full of understanding. "Take your time, Gabe."

There it is again. *Mum. Gabe. Gabriel.* Kate's head is spinning. Nothing's sticking. Nothing's falling into place.

Dominic looks at Mr. Bill. "Will you wait a while?"

"Sure. I'll just let Greenhills know that there's nothing to worry about. Panic over."

Noah looks at his watch for the first time since arriving at Silver Oaks with Juliet at the wheel.

Ms. Turner will be delighted. That's what she says whenever they make progress. "I'm delighted, Noah. Delighted for you." And then she'll make a note in his file at the end of the session, confirm the exact time that she'll be seeing him next. Well, Ms. Turner's certainly going to be more than delighted by these 4—no, 5—facts:

1. Noah Groome has not looked at his watch for nearly an hour now.
2. Noah Groome abandoned his Sunday-afternoon routine.
3. Noah Groome found out all sorts of things about his family—all waiting to be filled in on his Family Tree.
4. Considering what he has done and where he is, Noah Groome's anxiety levels feel remarkably low.

He stops, listens carefully, then adds the last item to his list of 5 Things About Noah That Will Delight Ms. Turner.

5. Noah Groome cannot hear one peep. Not a snigger, a rumble, a growl. All is silent.

Maddie's at his elbow, and Juliet's next to her and they're following his parents.

Kate knows she should be incandescent with fury. She should be screaming, shouting, but the more she reaches for feelings of anger, disbelief and total and utter bewilderment, the further they retreat.

Is this what betrayal feels like? A dark and emotionless void? Everything solid now vanished. Everything she once stood on, whipped away from under her. It must do. Because here she is, floating without feeling. Trying to find something to grab on to. But how can she steady herself in a world where all that was once trusted and true is false? Where she's the fool, the dupe, the sucker who swallowed it all—the hook, the sinker and the long line of lies trailing behind?

She's walking behind Dominic, concentrating on putting one foot in front of the other. He turns, waits for her to join him, but she shakes her head. They're walking to the "little coffee shop" that Dominic knows all about. Dominic sits in a coffee shop in a retirement village, every Sunday, with his sister, Harriet. Harriet Davenport. Kate's sister-in-law. The thought lands with a dull thud and then rolls away.

Left foot, right foot, one foot in front of the other until they reach the place where everything will be explained.

Kate's mind is clearing, it's trying to force an idea to the surface.

Reason. The word fights free.

There must be a *reason*, but what? What could be so awful that a man could keep a secret like this, and for so long?

But Harriet knew. Dominic shared something with his sister that he couldn't tell his wife.

Other thoughts are pounding through now, crashing so hard she staggers, lurches sideways and leans against the wall.

Her husband is an imposter. Imposter. Fraud. Cheat. He's a trickster, a con artist. Her husband is all of these things and like everything this man turns his hand to, he has done it all so very well.

And now comes the hurt, so sharp and so deep, she wonders why her heart is still beating.

15:51

They're sitting in a circle around a small table: Kate, Dominic, Maddie, Juliet and Noah. Mr. Bill's there too, waiting to take Juliet and Noah back to Greenhills.

Noah's mother examines the menu: "Well, I don't see G&T here, so a strong coffee will have to do." Her voice is light, like she's making a joke, but there's no hint of a smile on her face. She's sitting opposite her husband, but when he leans forward and says, "Kate, I—" she pushes her chair back so hard that it scrapes into the wall behind her.

"Maybe we should discuss this at home," his father says, and she flinches and pushes her body back even more.

"Home, Dominic?"

Maddie looks over at Noah, scared. Juliet's also looking worried and Noah must be too, because his mother tries to smile and says, "Sorry, Noah. Mads. Sorry, Juliet. I'm sorry for being rude."

"Would you like me to leave, Mrs. Groome?" Juliet asks, her voice small. "I can wait in the car."

Noah grabs her arm before his mother can reply. "Stay, Juliet. You're the one who—"

"Yes," Maddie's determined, nodding her head. "Juliet's the one who came up with the plan, Mom, Dad. She's *brilliant*. She knew exactly what we should do. And it worked, didn't it, Juliet?"

"I'm not sure it did, actually," Juliet says and Noah's never seen her look so unsure of herself. "Look, I—"

"Oh, I think it did, Juliet. Thank you." Noah's mom tries to smile at her, and waits until Juliet gives a small smile back. Then Mr. Bill takes charge.

"Why don't Juliet and I wait over at that table." Mr. Bill gestures to a small, round table in the corner of the café. "We can get a coffee, can't we, Juliet? Give you folks a bit of time to yourselves."

Juliet gives Noah a quick, encouraging smile as Mr. Bill ushers her away.

There's a small silence, then Noah's mother looks at her husband for the first time since they walked out of Martha Felix's room.

You mean your long-lost grandmother's room?

The Dark is growing, ready to consume Noah, but—

Quiet! he yells inside his head. He doesn't have time to be messed around. His mother's talking and he needs to hear what she's saying.

"Dominic? Gabriel? Who am I talking to?"

How could she have slept next to him for all these years and not suspected? She's lain beside him, night after night, hearing him breathe. She knows the sounds he makes when he dreams. It's dawning on her now. All this time, and she knew absolutely nothing about him.

"Well? What should I call you?"

"The bruises showed and she couldn't hide them from me."

Dominic steps away from the memory of his mother's face. "I couldn't understand why anyone would want to hurt my mother. She was kind, gentle. She never harmed anyone." He looks down at his hands, strong fingers, square tips. "All I wanted, when I was nine years old, was to hurt him back, but I couldn't. I was too weak. I couldn't do anything to help her."

Maddie moves closer to him, puts a hand on his leg.

"You were young, Dad," she says. "Not too weak."

"Sometimes..." Dominic's voice is quiet, "sometimes I was so angry with *her*. Why didn't she grab that cane and hit him back? Or go to the police and show them her bruises? I didn't know why we were there. Why we couldn't just leave.

"Now, of course, I know why, why we were there—money. My father left her destitute. One day the Sheriff of the Court arrived and took practically everything. We were evicted because my father hadn't kept up the bond payments. He left her penniless, floundering in debt. And then we had to move to his house..."

"So this is why you didn't want to come and see Noah?" Kate says slowly. It's the first time she's spoken since he started his story.

Dominic rubs his eyes hard. "That and a lot more," he says, his voice tired. "Oh, Kate, there's so much more I should have told you, but somehow I couldn't. When we met it was like I was these two people: the boy I was, the man I've become. I don't know if you can understand, but that's what happened."

Kate's eyes close. "Two lives," she says. "And where do we fit?"

"I was determined to bury Gabriel, not let any part of him make his way into Dominic Groome's life. That's how it was when I met you. Honestly. And I managed to keep him buried until..." Dominic looks at his son and smiles wryly, "Noah and his family tree. I was scared when you came home with that project, Noah. You just wouldn't let it go. All your questions...Nothing I did or said deflected you from needing to know where you come from. You were the catalyst."

"Me?"

"You." Dominic leans forward, touches his son's hand.

There've been lots of firsts today, the first time in ages he's looked Noah in the eye, the first time in a long time since he's shown him any affection.

"The more you wanted to know who you were, Noah, the more I wanted to hide who I was. I kept thinking, What happens if they find out? What will happen to this life I've built from nothing? This perfect life...I..." He falters for a moment, shrugs and spreads his hands.

"But you wanted answers, Noah, and suddenly everything was under threat. I was on the defensive, ready to fight to preserve..." Dominic stops and looks at Kate, but she's resting her head against the wall and her eyes are still closed. "It hit me then. Fight to preserve *what*? A lie? Fight to bury a kid who had nothing to apologize for?"

He will always remember the terror. It was the sound of the fire, the smell of it. Orange dancing in the wet night air, sparks flying, water gushing from the hoses in the firemen's hands.

Dominic lifts his hands to his face and smells them.

"I had to wash my hands over and over," he tells his family. "Again and again, until the smell of soap was stronger than the smell of petrol."

So many things to remember about that night. Heat following him along the passage, fire rushing forward, his sister's thin cry and dry cough as she inhaled the smoky air. Smashing the window, letting Harry go and praying that the earth outside would be soft enough to break her fall. Scrambling through after her, scraping the backs of his legs on the broken pane.

Maddie leans forward when Dominic gets to this part. "Oh, Dad. That must have been terrible."

"It was, Mads," he says. "It really was."

"But you got out. And you rescued your sister, too. Everybody must have thought that was brave. Didn't they say that? That you were really brave?"

Dominic strokes his daughter's hair, but his eyes are still on Kate. His wife isn't looking at him, but her face is more open. "Not really," he says. "It was my mum, you see. She was still standing just outside the kitchen door, holding a can of petrol."

"And you had to get rid of it?"

"Exactly. I had to make sure no one knew the fire was her fault. I didn't think about the smell, not then. All I wanted was to hide that can. Keep her safe."

"So, you didn't even think they would blame you?"

"Not then," Dominic says.

"But later?"

"Later?" Dominic says, and shrugs. "Later they blamed me for everything. The fire, the old man. It was all my fault."

"But it wasn't." Maddie is close to tears. "None of it was."

"I began to think it was, though. I told myself I should have done something. If I'd shouted loudly, told them what he was like, how he'd treated Mum...Maybe someone would have listened. Instead, I was labelled: a pyromaniac, the boy who let his grandfather die, the boy whose mother couldn't help him, the boy whose mother was mad. All I wanted was to leave that boy behind. Leave it all behind. Start anew... And that's what I did. It was all going so well, or so I stupidly thought. Then, along came Noah and his family tree."

"I'm sorry, Dad."

"No, Noah. Don't be. I started allowing myself to wonder, just like you were: Who *was* Gabriel Felix? What happened to that boy? That led me to other questions. Big ones. What about my sister? What happened to her? And Mum. Was she still alive? Once the thoughts were there, they wouldn't go away. So, eventually, I hired a PI—Sebastian Crown. He's the one who found Mum. That's when I started my Sunday-afternoon runs."

"And that's why you didn't want to come to see me at Greenhills," says Noah.

"I couldn't. Mum...Well, she expects me here now. Every Sunday afternoon. If I'm not here, she gets upset."

Noah can see his father is exhausted. His head suddenly sinks forward, like the weight of all he's telling them is too heavy for his neck to hold. His mother, though, looks like she's just starting to wake up.

"And your sister?" she asks. "Harriet?"

"It was harder to track Harry down, but eventually Sebastian found her too. Harry and I made this our regular meeting place. Once a week, on a Sunday. We're getting to know each other. Taking it slow. She's been encouraging me to tell you the whole story, Kate. And you as well, Maddie, Noah. I told her I would, and I was nearly ready." Dominic looks at them in despair.

"And then Kyle Blake and Greenhills happened and suddenly it was even more important that I tell you. But when it came to doing it, opening my mouth and saying the words...I was terrified. What if you walked out, Kate? What if I never saw my children again? What if I made their lives as difficult as mine when my father, my mother..."

His face is wretched, and Noah wishes his mother would reach for his father's hand, say something to take the pain out of his eyes.

But then the waiter arrives with more coffee and Noah's mother pulls the sugar towards her, opens two sachets and pours them into her husband's cup. "Here, Dom."

Something sweet, my pretties? For the shock?

The voice is high and fluting as a little old lady's, tucked up in bed, welcoming Noah into a cottage in the woods.

Such a confusion of lies and secrets.

That's right. It's certainly confusing. And yet, it doesn't feel chaotic. If anything, the more Noah's father talks, the more it feels like things are slotting into place, making sense.

Noah waits though, just to be sure, to see if he needs to use his 5s. His right foot feels like tapping, but then his father starts talking again.

"I wanted to pull both halves of my life together." His dad brings his palms together with a small clap. "Gabriel, meet Dominic. Dominic meet Gabriel, but then, with Noah in Greenhills and Ms. Turner asking all sorts of questions—wanting me to tell her my deepest, darkest secrets—I panicked. I couldn't do it. Not that quickly, that suddenly and not there, in her rooms. I swung between wanting to put it all out there, and wanting to bury it even deeper than before. I felt cornered, scared. And I was so cruel, Kate."

Noah's mother nods, but says nothing. She's looking at his father now, her gaze unwavering. It's not an accusing look, more a questioning one that asks, "And now? What more do you have to add?" She wants the truth, the whole truth and nothing but the truth, Noah thinks, and that's what his father is ready to give.

"I'd hear the words coming out of my mouth and wonder who this man was, why he was behaving so abominably to the woman he loved. I didn't know myself, Kate. And I didn't expect you'd ever forgive me for behaving the way I did...And then, when you told me Noah and Maddie were missing...It was one of the worst moments of my life."

"Mine too," says Noah's mother.

"I felt like it was all my fault. If I'd been there with you. If I'd kept a better eye on all of us..."

"...a better eye on all of us..."

Kate ducks her head. If she hadn't been so involved in thoughts of Mr. Bill...She looks over now to where he's seated, talking to Juliet, and sees a tall, compassionate man. Someone who always has a smile for everyone, an encouraging word, a joke to relieve the pressure. A young man with a wife and a baby.

"When you told me the car was here," Dominic's saying now, "all I could think was, they're safe, my kids are safe. And that was all that mattered. And then I realized, of course, you were here too. And I'd have to tell you...everything."

Kate nods again.

"I knew it meant I couldn't hide my past any longer. And you know what? I didn't care. As long as Maddie and Noah were all right, it didn't matter. I spent so long worrying about hiding, I lost sight of the most important thing: the four of us."

Kate's face has softened, but she still feels disoriented. "It's so much to take in. Everything I thought I knew—it's all gone. I need—"

"Time?" Her husband's face is sad. "I understand that. Whatever it is you need. I can move out for a while if you think that will help..."

Maddie gasps, and Kate closes her eyes again. This isn't Maddie's mess, nor is it Noah's. They both have enough to cope with, they shouldn't have to deal with this too.

She waits for fury to come raging through her. That's what she wants. Rage that will allow her to explode, throw something at Dominic, her coffee mug, perhaps. Throw it and watch him duck. She draws breath as deep as she can into her aching lungs.

"No," she says finally. "I don't want you to move out."

Maddie slumps against Dominic, and his arm tightens around her shoulders.

"Thank you," he says.

"What I do want," Kate says slowly, as if it's becoming too much effort to form whole sentences, "is to talk. Really talk. With someone like Ellen Turner."

16:28

More talking? More digging into the past? Enough, already.

Its voice is thin and depleted and Noah feels a flash of sympathy. It must be hard, fuelling all that malice, day after day.

Keep your sympathy. Who needs a little nobody feeling sorry—

Fine. Just keep quiet for now.

Noah has answered again, in his head, without thinking. Without even worrying.

He's been listening to his father intently, taking notes, questions for later.

1. Joseph (Joe) Felix, criminal records?
2. Gabriel Felix/Martha Felix/Martha Groom(e).
3. Newspaper reports. Fire.
4. Police reports.
5. Dominic Groom(e).

Noah closes his notebook. His father will tell him now, everything he wants to know. He'll get birth dates from him, and the name of the place where Martha was born. She doesn't have much of a hold on reality, but maybe Noah will get a chance to talk to her about her family, and her husband's. Already the left-hand branches of his tree are growing stronger, getting ready to carry all the members of his father's family.

He turns his notebook over and looks at the back cover.

Noah Groome
5 Things About Me

There are lists and lists about him inside it. Some contain information he's shared in group. Others are things he's finally been able to tell Ms. Turner. And now there's more to write down, to talk about, but only when the time is right.

He has 2 weeks left at Greenhills.

The Dark hasn't vanished, but ever since his father started talking, Noah has been in control. That's definitely something else to tell Ms. Turner.

Mr. Bill is hovering. "Sorry, but it's time for Noah to get going," he says. His phone beeps and he pulls it from his pocket, types something quickly.

"Thank you." Noah's mom smiles at him and her cheeks are pink. Thank you for everything. I don't know what I would have done if—"

"No need," says Mr. Bill. "Glad to help. Especially when it's these two." He looks at Juliet beside him, and then at Noah. "We'll talk about all this in the morning."

"That'll be fun," Juliet says.

Noah just nods. Yes, he wants to say, but it was worth it. Worth breaking all my rules. Worth it to have an old lady, his *grandmother*, look at him and say, "Is that you my Little Man?"

"Right then," Mr. Bill says, "let's get going, before they send out a search party."

"Oh, Mom. Can't Noah come home?" Maddie's tone is beseeching. "Just for a night? We can take him back in the morning. I mean he's already going to be in so much trouble. Him and Juliet. They could both sleep at our house."

"I'm sorry—" Mr. Bill starts to say, but Noah interrupts him.

"It's okay, Mads. Really it is. Not much longer and I'll be home. Back with you, and Mom." He looks over to where his father is sitting, quiet and wrung out. "And Dad, too. Things are getting better, Mads."

Now is as good a time to ask as any and he gets his words out quickly. "Mr. Bill, can I keep seeing Ms. Turner, even when I've left?"

"Of course you can, Noah. You can keep coming to group if you want."

Mr. Bill looks at Juliet.

"I'll come too," she says. Her voice is resigned, full of "whatever."

"I hope you will, Juliet," Kate says quietly, kindly. "I'll phone your mom, meet her for coffee, tell her what a good friend you've been."

Juliet blushes, disconcerted. "Yeah, well...Noah here, he's a pretty good friend too."

His father gets to his feet. "Noah. I—"

"Don't worry, Dad. We've got time. Lots of time. See you on Sunday?"

"Sure," Dominic says. "I'll go to Greenhills first and then I'll come on here. Maybe Mom, or Maddie, will come with me?"

Noah hopes his mother will say yes, that she will get used to the idea of Dominic being Gabriel, a man who has a mother and a sister.

That's quite a stunt your father pulled.

Noah shakes his head hard. There are more important things to worry about than the Dark right now.

His father has told them so much, he's laid himself bare, hoping they won't reject him. He's also had a demon to fight, only his was a mean old man who lived and breathed in the real world. Noah's demon lives in his head. He thinks of all the steps he's taken to get rid of it. His mother, Maddie, Ms. Turner, Juliet, Mr. Bill—they've all helped him. All 5 of them.

His notebook is filled with facts, all things he'll tell Ms. Turner...

one of these days. Today though, instead of putting it in his pocket, he stands and holds it out. "Mom, Dad. You can read this if you want. You too, Mads."

There's a startled silence. Still he holds the notebook out.

"Noah?" His mother is concerned, but that's nothing compared to the state the Dark is in. It's charging up, breathing hard and heavily.

Noah closes his eyes. He thinks of the pile of notebooks in his desk drawer, sees himself labeling a new one to see him through till next Sunday, when his family come to visit him. He sees himself walking up to Ms. Turner's door, knocking and maybe pushing down the handle—just that, 1 movement.

Maybe the voice will be silent, subdued. Maybe it will be frothing at the mouth.

If only you knew, Ms. Turner. If only you knew. Our Noah has quite the surprise for you.

The thing is, Ms. Turner does. She does know 5 things about Noah—and 5 and 5 and 5 things more, with more to come.

Noah's hand wavers as his father reaches for the notebook, but he doesn't change his mind. He lets his father take it.

Maybe the Dark will never fully let go, or leave him alone. For now, though, it doesn't matter. He will tell Ms. Turner more about it, all the parts it's made up of. It's shadowy, he'll say. A shape-shifter. Impossible to hold in one place.

Noah's dad is holding the notebook, turning it over and over in his hands.

"Are you sure about this, Noah?"

"Yes." Noah says. "I'm sure." Then he adds, "You can give it back to me next week. At visiting hours, Dad."

Acknowledgements galore (Again!)

First person, third person, past tense, present tense...poor Noah has been through so many incarnations. And now there's another! I was thrilled when Jessica Powers of Catalyst Press said she'd like to publish *The Enumerations*. Thanks to her good offices, ably assisted by publicist, SarahBelle Selig and cover designer Karen Vermeulen, Noah's story is going to travel further and wider than it did before!

The Enumerations now has a new cover, with Noah looking as I imagine him to be, vulnerable, reserved, resisting contact. He's wearing blue, a color that is intrinsically linked to his wellbeing.

Something else that's different is that the Catalyst team has been able to create a great package, with comments and feedback from reviews and readers' reactions to the South African publication. It's very reassuring to know that Noah is launching into new and different spaces from a well-established base.

One thing that hasn't changed, though, from the first iteration of *The Enumerations* is my long list of thanks. I am as grateful now as I ever was to the many, many people who provided advice, support and countless warm beverages as *The Enumerations* was written.

The Enumerations was first published by Umuzi (Penguin Random House) and my gratitude to the folks there knows no bounds. Some of the people I mention now have moved into other beautiful spaces in publishing, editing and book design, but at that time Beth Lindop, Fahiema Hallam, Frances Marks, Anna Hug, Rhonda Crouse, and Jacques Kaiser, all helped to make the first edition of *The Enumerations* a thing of beauty!

Writing a character with OCD is a challenge. It's not one I intended to take on, but Noah appeared in the early pages of another story and wouldn't leave, even when I told him it wasn't about him. So, there he was, protected by the number 5. Once I knew he was going to be the main character, I started reading and researching. OCD manifests in so many ways, but once again, Noah showed me his own obsessions and compulsions. Many thanks to Professor Dan Stein, the Head of the Department of Psychiatry and Mental Health at the University of Cape Town (who was glad I hadn't written an ending where love solves all problems); Dr. Ulli Meys, an eminent child and adolescent psychiatrist; and Richard Vergunst, a post-doctoral fellow in the Department of Psychology at Stellenbosch University with expertise in neuropsychology, abnormal psychology and clinical psychology, for their professional views on OCD. I discussed a range of issues with them, including their views of the symptoms of OCD, medication treatments for OCD, and whether touch can be appropriate in a psychotherapy session.

I also happened to mention to my friend, Colleen, when she was in South Africa on holiday, that I was writing a book about a young boy with OCD. She told me that when her daughter, Hannah, was seventeen, she was in one of the best residential clinics in Germany for adolescents with OCD. Hannah is in her thirties now. Colleen and Hannah, thank you for sharing how the novel worked for you both, a mother–daughter team. Our two-hour Skype session was wonderful on so many levels: to watch as you looked back on tough times and described how they became happier, to hear how you both coped, and, sometimes, to hear one or the other of you say, "I didn't know that." Hannah, thank you especially for your drawing of the hectoring, bullying monsters who took hours away from your day, telling you how to do things, telling you off when you didn't get it all absolutely right. Hannah learnt how to overpower her OCD and fear and now leads a fully normal life. When the monsters do start their rumbling (as sometimes they do) she is able to turn her back on them and carry on.

As an editor, whenever someone asks me to provide feedback on their writing, I always suggest that they ask friendly readers first; people who love reading, who belong to book clubs, who are also writers. If you ask friends like these to read your work and respond to specific questions, you receive a wealth of truly precious feedback, from toning down on the horror, to dialling back on the slapstick, to building up characters, or, indeed, slimming them down. It's also a really great way of finding out what worked well for readers, an important question that we often forget to ask. So dear friendly readers, young and old, from the bottom of my heart, thank you all! Dan Fisher, Ashleigh Butcher, Lara Featherstone, Anne Bennett, Christine Coates, Frank Doolan, Joan Adams, Tracey Farren, Daisy Jones, Anna Hug and Chantal Stewart. Your insights helped to shape Noah and his families both at home and at Greenhills. (I only wish that Joan Adams could be here to watch Noah leave South African shores and venture abroad. She would be so excited for him!)

Bits and pieces of this story grew from workshops and at writing retreats facilitated by Chantal Stewart. Thank you for carrying the flame passed on to you by Anne Schuster, our dear writing teacher and friend, and for inviting me to share facilitation with you. The next best thing to writing in a workshop is watching other writers scribble at speed.

Willa, one of my most beloved characters in *The Enumerations*, appeared in a magic barn during a Stanford Barn Writing weekend. Many thanks to Rahla Xenopoulos for creating such a fine place for writers. (I know for a fact that Rahla is now creating equally wonderful spaces in the US.)

Talking of Willa—such a welcome arrival, quite late in the novel— I wanted to make sure that everything about them was appropriate. My subsequent research led me to Priscilla's Services (danitgirl1@ gmail.com), a South African company based in Gauteng that caters to the needs of the transgender (in its broadest sense) community, whether crossdresser, transgender or genderfluid. Dani was kind enough to talk to me for an hour. They also took the trouble to confirm that a seventeen-year-old, non-binary South African in 2013 would definitely be using they/them/their/themself as personal gender pronouns. It was wonderful to see Dani at my launch in Johannesburg, and to receive permission, once again, to mention Priscilla's Services in this new edition.

I wrote so much of *The Enumerations* in cafés in along the shoreline of the Southern Peninsula. It's seldom you find a place where writers aren't made welcome, even when they take up a whole table for a morning. (A maxim worth repeating from novel to novel: always tip well!)

One of the cafés I visit regularly is Cinnamon and Sage, part of a beautiful nursery in the Deep South. The breakfasts there are legendary, and it's here that Book Befok* my writing group meet every Tuesday morning. We share our joys and sorrows, update each other on what's happened in our writing lives, and we write! Many, many thanks to you all, darling Befokkers, but especially to Cathy Kelly Park who has kept our wonderful group connected for so many years.

So yes...acknowledgements galore, with the last and most important to come. Dan and Kieran, who will always own the hashtag #bestsonsever, and, of course, my husband Rob, who encourages his writing wife, even though she is yet to make any sort of fortune from her novels. Thank you, my darling. Maybe this one will hit a small, sensibly-sized jackpot!

*An Afrikaans word, not, as the Dictionary of South African English warns, "...in polite use. Messed up, 'screwed up'; 'not right in the head'. https://dsae.co.za/ (Because, after all, what writer *is* right in the head!?)

www.ingramcontent.com/pod-product-compliance
Lightning Source LLC
Jackson TN
JSHW082301261224
76058JS00001B/1

* 9 7 8 1 9 6 0 8 0 3 0 8 5 *